ASK
ME
ANYTHING

a novel by

Molly E. Lee

Entangled Publishing, LLC
2614 South Timberline Road
Suite 105
Fort Collins, CO 80525
rights@entangledpublishing.com

Entangled Teen is an imprint of Entangled Publishing, LLC.

Visit our website at www.entangledpublishing.com.

Edited by Stacy Abrams
Cover design by Molly E. Lee and Heather Howland
Cover images by
Getty Images/maciek905
Getty Images/CoffeeAndMilk
Interior images by Molly E. Lee and iStock/art-sonik
Interior design by Heather Howland

Print ISBN 978-1-64063-658-3
Ebook ISBN 978-1-64063-659-0

Manufactured in the United States of America

First Edition May 2019

10 9 8 7 6 5 4 3 2 1

ASK
ME
ANYTHING

ALSO BY MOLLY E. LEE

THE GRAD NIGHT SERIES

INDEPENDENT TITLES

For n0decaf

PROLOGUE

AMBER

NightLocker: Please talk to me
NightLocker: Let me explain
NightLocker: Pixie...I'm sorry
NightLocker: There are things you don't understand

I tucked my fingers under my arms, ignoring the tingle to respond immediately.

Damn straight I don't understand.

Betrayal stung like a paper cut while opening a package of lemonade mix.

My heart *hurt*. Like, I'd been burned before...but this? This physically turned my stomach and seared my chest.

This...

This was true heartbreak.

This was can't sleep, can't eat unless it's chocolate, can't breathe without sharp spikes rattling my lungs, *relentless* heartbreak.

NightLocker: Give me a chance
NightLocker: I can make this right
NightLocker: I want to...
NightLocker: I need you...DC remember? Doesn't that mean anything to you anymore?

Tears stung my eyes as I read his pleas. His use of our secret word, a code that had become something so much more than a warning. Something as vital as breathing and as true as the ache in my heart.

Some deep part of me, the one he'd branded his name on, wanted to forgive him. Needed to.

Because who was I to judge...after what I'd done?

I *should* forgive him. I should tell him the truth about what I knew.

But what was the point? Once he uncovered it...once he learned what I'd *really* done...

He'd hate me.

I reached for the keyboard, the motion almost painful.

NightLocker: I need you...DC remember? Doesn't that mean anything anymore?
PixieBurn: everything & nothing
NightLocker: Amber
NightLocker: Please
NightLocker: What does that even mean?

I paused my response, choking back a sob.

It didn't matter. He'd find out soon enough.

Might as well endure the break now.

I just wished like hell it didn't have to hurt so damn much.

PixieBurn: It means
PixieBurn: Hack my gear like this again
PixieBurn: for a chat
PixieBurn: for help
PixieBurn: for anything
PixieBurn: and I'll crash your entire system

I hated myself a fraction more with each message sent.

NightLocker: No!
NightLocker: Amber
NightLocker: Listen to me

God, did I want to. I wanted him to not be breaking into my system, showing up on my screen...I wanted him *here*. Telling me we could find our way back to common ground or, hell, hit the reset button and start fresh. Erase every dark piece of our past.

But this was real life.

And it was heavy and hard and harsh.

PixieBurn: goodbye, Dean

I logged off and shut my gear down. He couldn't find me if I wasn't online.

Unless he shows up at my door...again.

My heart skipped at the thought—it was betraying me as much as he had.

I'd barely survived his friendship, his light.

I certainly wouldn't survive his hate, his disappointment, the way he'd judge me when he knew...

CHAPTER ONE

AMBER

Six months earlier...

"And then I actually got the condom *out* of the wrapper," Hannah whispered as we walked toward the largest seminar room in Wilmont Academy. "But I wasn't expecting it to be...*slimy*"—a shudder rippled her long blond hair—"so I freaked. And that freak-out resulted in me kneeing his junk." She clenched her eyes shut, rubbing her palms over her face. "It was a disaster. Jake is probably going to dump me."

"No, he isn't," I said, resting my hand on her shoulder. We stopped outside the lecture room doors as the rest of the school filed in. "You've been together, what? Eight years?" I asked, totally blanking on the actual mileage of their relationship.

"Ten," she said, sighing. "It was the second grade when he asked to trade sandwiches—"

"And you've been in love ever since," I finished for her.

I'd heard the classic tale of love at first sight over a hundred times. Hannah and Jake were the perfect couple—they challenged each other, supported each other, and, well, they *loved* each other.

"In all that time," I said, lowering my voice to ensure we weren't overheard, "you never once put it on for him?"

I wished I could ask the question without blushing, but no matter how hard I tried, it was useless. Hannah was my best friend. I knew all about her sex life with Jake, but I had little experience myself. Whenever we talked about it, I felt like *zero* help.

She shook her head. "He always does it."

"Why try to switch it up?"

"Because," she said, shrugging, "I was, like, trying to be adventurous. I don't know. It was a total, horrid fail." She glanced toward the seminar room and lowered her voice to barely a whisper. "You think Ms. Conner will cover the art of rolling a condom onto your boyfriend's dick in the 'sexual awareness' assembly today?" Hannah put the words in perfectly timed air quotes.

A laugh ripped from my lips, and soon she giggled with me. The tension broke for a moment before reality crashed it hard. "No," I said. "She won't."

Every year on the first week of school, the students of Wilmont Academy were ushered into seminar room #3 for an education on the dangers of being sexually active. Wilmont might be the last non-religious school on the planet still operating under the *abstinence only* policy.

Ms. Conner and Principal Tanner *had* to know more than half the juniors and seniors, and, hell, some underclassmen, were having sex. They couldn't be *that* blind. But they treated the topic like a plague warning—if you have sex while in high school you will either suffer from diseases or get pregnant. Not once had they ever talked about where to get birth control or how to handle a pregnancy scare. It was ridiculous and totally not helpful to those seeking advice on how to be safe and healthy. Like Hannah.

"This is such a waste of time," I whispered. "If they're not actually going to teach us anything about healthy sex, then they could at least use this time to talk about more important things."

"Like what?" Hannah asked, looking happy to delay entering the room for as long as possible.

I shrugged. "Maybe a lecture on sexual harassment? Or voting awareness—some of us are actually old enough to vote now. Or the double standards between boys and girls in this school?"

"Whoa," Hannah said, her eyebrows climbing high on her forehead. "Someone ate her feminist Wheaties this morning."

I chuckled, waving her off. "I'm just saying *those* things would—might—have more of an impact than this." I jerked my head toward the door. "Everyone tunes this out because barely anyone in school actually believes in abstinence."

"Ugh," she groaned, pushing off the wall and turning into the room.

Our chat had forced us to the back of the long line of students piling in, and that meant the only available seats were front row and, miserably, center. We both swallowed our groans as we sank into the practically spotlighted chairs.

Hannah leaned close to me while Ms. Conner shuffled her note cards behind the podium on the stage not three feet from us. "*Cosmo* makes me feel like I'm in way over my head," she whispered into my ear. "My mom would have a legit aneurism if I tried to broach the subject with her. You're the only sister I have..." She winked at me. "And I tried typing it into Google—"

"Omigod, you *didn't*." I clamped my hands over my mouth.

"Totally did. Totally regret it." Another shudder shook her body. "Blech," she said, sticking out her tongue. "Don't ever Google anything with..." She huffed. "Just don't Google. It's dangerous."

We laughed until the sound of the doors sealing shut rang out like a prison sentence. The lights dimmed enough to illuminate the giant screen behind Ms. Conner, who clung to the note cards like a lifeline.

Principal Tanner stood at attention in the front right corner of the room, just to the side of the screen. His arms were crossed tightly over his chest, but the navy suit he wore wouldn't dare wrinkle. Not only was he the stiffest, *strictest* human being I'd ever met, but so was his wardrobe. It was no wonder he'd forced me and my fellow classmates into a suffocating uniform that sucked creativity and individuality from everyone who wore it. No use trying to be yourself at Wilmont—not when Principal Tanner was dead set on pumping out legions of worker drones.

I shifted in my seat, itching to pull out my laptop and play with a tricky set of code that had been giving me a headache since this morning. The security measures around the site were a real jerk, but I'd crack it eventually. Though, I'd be just as willing to start Googling, as Hannah had warned me *not* to do, if it meant I wouldn't have to pay attention to this.

One more look at Principal Tanner shot down that blissful idea. I didn't need to give him another reason to hate me. He barely tolerated my presence with my pixie-cut dark hair—the left side streaked with a few strands of light pink.

Also, my mom was an erotica author.

I got away with the hair because it was *technically* within the school's guidelines of not being distracting enough to draw away from academics. The erotica author mom was easier to get away with because she donated boatloads of cash to extracurricular activities in need. Tanner would be selfish to question her motives because her profession "disgusts me"—as he'd once boldly told me when I'd been caught chatting with my ex over Messenger instead of working on actual class work during computer science last year.

I crossed one leg over the other, satisfied that underneath the horribly thick black pants I wore as required by "school policy," I could feel the warmth of my purple-and-pink-striped socks. They were enough to earn me detention, but he'd never see them.

Ms. Conner paced around the podium situated on the stage, the massive white projector screen behind her. She had to be the sweetest, gentlest, and clearly the most uncomfortable one in the room. Her pale pink sweater hugged her tiny shoulders, the light blue blouse she wore underneath tightly tucked into a floor-length black skirt. Tanner hand-selected our school nurse to run this assembly every year, even though she fumbled over her words whenever the discussion even came close to sex. Which it rarely did at Wilmont.

"What about someone else?" I finally whispered back at Hannah.

"What, like a teacher?" she scoffed, her blue eyes narrowing on Ms. Conner.

"Or, I don't know," I said, glancing to the right, where the most popular seniors sat. Girls like Sabrina and Morgan. The ones with shiny hair and perfectly polished nails. The ones who always looked like they walked off the pages of *Teen Vogue*. "Them?" It wasn't a secret that Sabrina and Morgan's clique knew their way around guys...and girls... or sometimes both at the same time, if the rumors were to be believed.

Brandon included. Not that I cared where my ex-boyfriend had wound up.

"You're joking, right?"

"I'm trying to help."

"I know," she said. "But seriously? If I approached them it would be all over school in, like, two seconds."

"So?" I said. "Everyone knows you and Jake have been together forever. Who cares?"

"I know that," she answered. "But I would rather the entire school *not* know I'm a complete loser when it comes to this kind of stuff. Just because we've done it multiple times doesn't mean I'm confident I know what I'm doing."

My cheeks heated again. "If you're a loser, that makes me a social reject."

"You know I didn't mean it like that." She wrapped her arm around my shoulders.

"It's fine." I shrugged. "Look, I'm not dying to hand out my V-card, but I hate that I'm totally useless to you right now. You should be able to talk to someone about this stuff and not feel like you're breaking the damn law."

She giggled. "It *always* feels like that."

"It shouldn't."

"Well," she said, lowering her voice even more despite the chatter in the room. "It may not be that way anymore."

"What do you mean?"

Hannah glanced around to make sure no one was listening. "You know my mom's on the review board, right? The one Tanner answers to?"

"Yeah."

"I overheard her talking to Dad last night. More like venting. She was going on and on about the start-of-year meeting. How Tanner had dug his heels in when some other board members suggested a more progressive change to the school rules."

"You're kidding."

"Nope. Looks like a lot of people think this approach is

outdated. But he swore up and down that this has been the way Wilmont has done things for decades. Brought up his grandfather and his father who were principals before him." She rolled her eyes. "Claimed that his approach equated to better standard test scores and more Ivy League college acceptances."

"Wow." I was stunned that anyone would try to go up against Tanner. Stunned and awed. It was about time someone pushed for change at this school.

Sure, Wilmont had the best academics program in the state—the sole reason my parents, and many others, tolerated the school's more archaic rules—but I thought it was more detrimental than helpful. Trying to keep my friends and me ignorant on sexual health was ridiculous.

"I know," Hannah said, drawing me to the present. "Mom said they gave him a year to prove it—she didn't mention how—but if we thought he was strict before, I can't imagine what he'll be like now that his job is on the line."

I chewed on my lip, gazing behind Ms. Conner.

Dean Winters sat at the desk to her left, clicking away on the keyboard, his blue-gray eyes flitting over the monitor screen. *He* was dubbed Wilmont's resident genius hacker—mostly because his older brother, Sean, had made a name for himself here before graduating two years ago—but I wasn't far behind Dean's skill level.

We'd made a game of topping each other in our coding class, but he had this laid-back calm about him that always combated my can't-sit-still-for-one-second persona that drove me nuts. I was certain Dean didn't need any advice on the stuff Hannah and I were talking about. He was wicked gorgeous, and though he likely could have his pick of any girl at Wilmont, he flew solo on the reg.

I understood that. The hacker lifestyle—late nights lost

between codes and crossing boundaries that begged for it—was hard to understand if you weren't also into it.

Brandon had complained on a daily basis about the amount of time I spent with my gear.

Dean pushed some stray sandy-blond hair off his forehead, his eyes sharp on the computer screen. No doubt booting up the presentation that Principal Tanner created himself every year—slides and videos with facts on how sex was as dangerous as drinking and driving. I don't know why he had to enlist Dean to get the presentation up; it wasn't any more technical than pressing play, but then again, Tanner loved a power trip.

"I still think you should give it to him." Hannah nudged me, and I tore my gaze from Dean.

"What?" I blinked at her, and she laughed again.

"Your V-card."

I gaped at her, my mouth opening and closing several times. "Stop it," I finally managed. She'd brought it up more than once since Brandon and I broke up. "If I didn't give it to Brandon—"

"Come on," she said. "Brandon was an absolute dick. And you broke up two months ago. Dean would be perfect for you."

"I have no idea what you're talking about."

"Really?" she asked. "I think it's time you admitted it. It makes total sense. He's a hacker, you're a hacker—"

"That is horrible logic," I cut her off. "That's like saying *you* play basketball, *he* plays basketball…"

"Ugh," she said. "That is *so* not the same thing. And you know I meant more—"

"I'm happy with the way things are."

And I was. I'd dated Brandon for a year too long. I wasn't ready to dive into a relationship again.

"You've been friends with Dean almost as long as you have with me," she said, like that explained everything.

"Right, but it's not like we're *out of school* friends. We only hang in the coding room or random times at lunch." I sighed.

"He gave you his cell number a year ago."

"Yeah, to swap tech or stories." I rolled my eyes. "It's not like he told me to call him for *fun*."

And why would he? He was Dean effin' Winters. A hot hacker-boy-after-my-own-heart genius. In a snap, he could have Sabrina, the most beautiful, popular, and hard-to-get girl in school, turn to putty in his hands. Besides, we may have been friends in class, but my dating Brandon had always made me see Dean as a non-datable entity.

"Right," she said. "And he just happens to bring you venti iced green teas to coding class…for what? Professional hacker courtesy?"

"Exactly," I said. He'd brought me my favorite late-night fuel on four different occasions, but I tried not to read into it. He was a decent guy. A good friend. A gorgeous, mysterious, funny, perceptive, way-out-of-my-league friend.

My eyes drifted back to him. His fingers flew fast and confident over the keys. What *would* it be like to cross that line with him? To feel those fantastic fingers in my hair as we kissed…

I bet he tastes like that spearmint gum he's always popping. I bet his lips are warm and—

"You can have herpes without even knowing you have it." Ms. Conner's voice was higher than a mouse's, but it soared easily enough through the domed lecture hall, dousing my thoughts with a giant bucket of ice water.

The room instantly fell silent, and she pointed behind her without bothering to look. Dean ducked his head and clicked a few keys. The projector lit up with the first slide.

HERPES: DO YOU HAVE IT? ONE IN FOUR
SEXUALLY ACTIVE TEENS DOES.

I cringed at the picture that accompanied the headline. I understood her need to shock the room into attention—especially with the school year just starting, none of us actually *wanted* to be here—but the pictures were a little much. I glanced around the room, and it was clear she'd scarred half the audience while the other was ignoring her scare tactics by discreetly checking their cells.

Sinking back into the chair, I demanded the blueberry scone I'd had for breakfast to sit tight. A hard feat as slide after slide of the diseases that can occur with unprotected sex flashed across the screen. Not that Ms. Conner or Principal Tanner's presentation taught us about *protected* sex.

"It's not just intercourse, either," Ms. Conner continued after the fifth slide on HPV popped up. "Most of these diseases can be contracted from oral sex as well." She let out a deep breath, her arms behind her back. "The safest way to protect against this stuff?" she asked, scanning the faces that still paid her any attention.

Prophylactics.

Safe sex.

Communication.

I thought about raising my hand, but I didn't want to steal her thunder. Especially if she was about to *finally* show a slide worth something—like how to get and properly use birth control.

"Condoms," Chase, from the JV soccer team, mumbled from the center of the room. His buddies chuckled around him.

"No." Ms. Conner fiddled with her note cards, her cheeks flushing. "The only surefire way to keep yourself healthy is to *not have sex*. That's why here at Wilmont Academy we practice and preach abstinence."

A few students groaned, and I rolled my eyes.

Sure, I wasn't having sex, but almost all my friends were. And it didn't mean that I *wouldn't* do it someday if the perfect opportunity presented itself. Ms. Conner and the principal telling us not to have sex was about as helpful as saying don't speed, don't drink, don't smoke, don't swear, don't, don't, don't.

It didn't matter that not everyone chose to do every item on the *don't* list. There were people who *did*.

"Whoa," Hannah said, gripping my elbow. "Are you all right?"

"What?" I whispered.

"You're all red and glaring."

I relaxed my tense muscles as Ms. Conner motioned for the next slide. Another wave of Dean's magic fingers, and it came up.

"It's just so dumb, you know? Acting like this will make everyone stop having sex."

"Totally."

"Here are some proven ways to enjoy your partner while maintaining an abstinent lifestyle," Ms. Conner said. She pointed at the slide behind her that had a picture of a couple holding hands. "Hand-holding can be a *very* emotionally connecting and satisfying experience."

A few more barely contained laughs and groans came from the mass of students in the rows behind us, and Ms. Conner cleared her throat. I almost felt bad for her. This ridiculous presentation wasn't *hers*; it was Tanner's. She was simply the one forced to present it.

"This"—she glanced at Dean—"is a video Principal Tanner has put together to show more examples of safe ways to enjoy your partner. Like hugging and high-fiving."

Dean clicked another button, and a video popped up on the screen.

ABSTINENCE: THE WILMONT WAY AND HOW TO UPHOLD IT displayed in thick white letters, and a classic Bach song played in the background. Then the video faded to black, and the music instantly transitioned to a *bow-chica-wow-wow* tune straight out of every cheesy romantic movie ever.

A couple appeared on the screen—two vampires from a popular show. My jaw practically came unhinged as I watched the sexy af male vamp throw the blond against a wall. She hooked her legs around his hips while he kissed the breath out of her.

A startled gasp rolled through the audience like a tidal wave—myself included—as we watched a compilation of the hottest make-out scenes from every hit show currently on television.

One blink and the scene transitioned to a new couple kissing and sighing while a steamy shower soaked the little clothes they had on.

Another flash—sighs and kisses and moans.

Over. And. Over.

Ms. Conner dropped her note cards. Principal Tanner nearly slipped on them as he hurried over to Dean, the purple vein in his forehead damn near ready to pop. The fury rolling off him was enough to shake Dean out of his shock, and he quickly axed the video, the screen returning to white.

Dean held up his hands like Tanner had come at him with a loaded gun. "All I did was hit play on the video you had on here," he said, his voice barely audible over the laughter and chatter rippling through the crowd.

And that much *had* to be true. Principal Tanner would've already had the video on his personal computer he'd given Dean to hook up to the projector. Dean was good, one of the best, but there was no way he could've switched out the videos that fast. Someone must have broken into the principal's computer before the assembly. Which technically *could've* been Dean, but I highly doubted it. He was smarter than that. If he wanted to prank the principal, he'd do it without a trace.

Principal Tanner smoothed down his unwrinkled suit and faced us. The look was enough to suck all the sound from the room. "That was unacceptable." He shook his head. "Be certain the responsible party *will* be punished."

My stomach sank. With Tanner on his new personal warpath, I pitied whoever had decided to pull the prank.

CHAPTER TWO

DEAN

"Choked pretty hard in there, didn't you, Dean?" Tessa's voice was two parts smug and just this side of nervous.

I stopped my hustle down the hall toward coding class and turned to find my little sister leaning against her locker. Her bright red lipstick wasn't exactly in regulation with the Wilmont uniform and presentation rules, but I'd never be the one to point that out.

"Whoa," she said, popping off the locker when I reached her. "Did he expel you?"

I rubbed my palms over my face, forcing back the adrenaline that had shaken my muscles since the epic fail of a sexual awareness presentation a few hours ago.

"Course not." I hiked my bag onto my shoulder, flashing her my *everything's fine* smile—one we'd shared more times than I could count over the years any time she thought Mom was about to ground me.

She was the only girl in our family, and so I had this unavoidable instinct to protect her.

"I didn't do it," I continued, shaking my head. I studied her not-at-all-surprised face for a few seconds before the proper shock registered in her eyes.

"You didn't?" she said, but I could see straight through her.

"Tessa," I groaned. "What do you know?" I'd never peg my sister for tampering with Principal Tanner's precious presentation, but one of her rebellious friends? Maybe. The boyfriend she'd had since she was six? Maybe times two.

"Nothing!" She gaped at me before rolling her eyes. "You worry a helluva lot for someone who's ready to buck the system any chance he gets."

"One," I said, holding up a finger, "don't ever say *buck the system*. Two" — I held up another finger — "just because I like to test weaknesses in any given security system doesn't mean I'm not going to worry about my baby sister when she *clearly* is in way over her head."

She scoffed and pulled out her cell, fingers flying across the screen. She pocketed it after a good fifty-six seconds of ignoring me. "I've got to meet Colt," she said and flashed me a perfectly innocent smile. "I'm glad he didn't expel you." She punched me on the shoulder. "I'd hate not having my over-worrying brother here to protect me."

I snorted. "Tanner knew I didn't do it. Whoever jacked with his video had to break into his office last night or early this morning before the assembly, and I was with him setting up the system." I watched every line of her face, wondering if she would give anything away. Her features were smooth as she stared right back at me.

"Sounds like a hassle for just a few laughs."

I arched a brow at her. "A *few*?"

The entire school had found the updated presentation hilarious. Hell, it had shocked me — the fact that someone had the balls to pull that on Tanner — so much that I hadn't gotten the vid down quick enough.

That had earned me a half-hour lecture in his office — an endless stream of negative criticism against my "computer skills." Please, he would shit his pants if he knew half the things I could do with a cell phone, let alone my own perfectly configured laptop.

Still, he'd been pissed enough to punish—more like embarrassed enough. It wasn't every day he was thrown off his crisp, pristine routine of perfection. He needed someone to blame and for now he only had me. Not for the vid, because I'd been at home last night—as he'd called and confirmed with my mother—but because I hadn't checked the video before I'd hooked up his computer to the projector. Then again, neither had he.

Could've been worse, I suppose. He could've expelled me or refused to recommend me when MIT called to gather my stats closer to the spring—he had that much power. Instead he decided to "teach me a lesson" and ensure that my "skills" would improve at the same time.

"*Code Club*," he'd called it. Said it with the same bravado as a frat-dude would say *Fight Club*. I was to hold an extracurricular club after school, three times a week, educating any student who wanted to learn more about anything involving computers. "*No better way to improve your skills than teach. And after the horrid fiasco you let me walk into today, Mr. Winters, you clearly need more practice in all matters electronic. In addition, you'll maintain, update, and streamline the academy's website.*"

His words echoed through my head as I glanced at my cell. "Tell Colt he's a douche," I said, glancing down at Tessa, who waited patiently as if I'd say more about Tanner. Almost like she *wanted* me to say more. I sighed, lowering my voice. "Tess."

"What?" she snapped. "I'm not going to tell him that. He already knows you hate him."

I rolled my eyes. I didn't hate Colt. He actually treated my baby sister better than I'd ever seen any of my friends treat their girlfriends. *But*, he was dating my sister. I had to give him shit on principle. "Tess," I said again, guiding her back toward her locker. "This is your one shot."

She swallowed hard before a muscle in her jaw ticked. That same anger trigger I'd seen in Sean too many times—like the one time I'd cracked his password on the desktop in his room and reconfigured all his specs.

"Talk to me."

"I have nothing to talk about. You're being weird." She avoided looking me in the eye.

"Damn it, Tess," I said, pinching the bridge of my nose. I was going to be late to coding. "If you know who pulled that crap this morning—" I glanced around, making sure Tanner wasn't going to rappel from the ceiling or something. "You could catch a lot of heat." Whenever Tanner found out who did it—and he *would* because he always did—then he'd likely punish the culprit's circle of friends, too.

That was his style. Probably one of the main reasons I'd never pulled a stunt on his system even though I'd been dying to since the sixth grade, when he'd forced me to peel off every sticker on my laptop that I'd collected from my summer computer science boot camp. I'd *earned* those tiny, sticky badges of honor, and he'd claimed they were a distraction and forced me to toss them in the garbage.

"Whatever," she said. "You're delusional. And now *I'm* late." She brushed past me, hurrying down the hallway that was now almost empty of students.

Maybe I was. Maybe none of her friends would be dumb enough to pull a prank like that, but when it came to Tessa, I was on high alert. We were only two years apart. She'd been my best friend since my parents brought her home—not that I'd ever tell her that—and I couldn't stop the instinct to protect her. It was in my blood. Probably why Sean—my older brother—was always riding me about shit, too. He likely felt the same way, but whenever he came home to visit and started hovering over me, I told him to eff off.

Kind of like how Tess just did to me.

Huh.

Perspective.

I blinked a few times, crawled out of my head, and rushed down the hall.

Thirteen strides later, I dashed into Mr. Griffin's room.

His full, quiet room.

I swallowed hard, ducking my head under the light of the projector as I found my seat in the back.

"Mr. Winters," he said, drawing more attention to my entrance as I settled in my desk. I dug my laptop out of my bag, firing up the screen in seconds.

"Sorry," I said before he could continue. "Principal Tanner had a technical issue." May have been with "my skills" and not a computer, but close enough for the excuse.

Mr. Griffin waved me off. His black polo was untucked, one hand loosely hanging in his khaki pocket. Fresh out of college, he had to be one of the youngest teachers at Wilmont, but no one could deny his enthusiasm for teaching code. "No worries," he said. "I wanted to ask you what *your* favorite coding language is." He glanced around the room at the other students who had been taking notes before I dropped in. "I know you've been at this for longer than some of the class."

I scanned the room. The only other true hacker in the room was a swirl of light pink in a sea of blind curiosity.

Amber Henderson.

The girl had *skills*. She also happened to be funny as hell, sharp, and wicked hot. The fact that she'd had a boyfriend for the past year had kept us merely acquaintance-like friends. Her fingers currently clicked her keyboard—she was locked in—the rest of the room vapor. Griffin could've easily called on her for the question, but he was ribbing me for my late arrival.

Touché.

"Python," I finally answered, returning my focus to the front of the room. The words *Programming Language* were in black letters on the screen behind Griffin.

He nodded rapidly, clicking to the next slide where five bullet points listed the most effective coding languages. "You probably like that because you're a pen tester, yeah?"

I held my hand out and did the universal *so-so* shake. I loved breaching walls and locks and codes meant to keep me out, but I hadn't chosen cybersecurity as my only flavor of hack. Not yet. Not when there were so many more avenues to take.

"Well," he said, mimicking my *so-so* shake, "Python is a great language. So is C or C++." He pointed to the slide behind him. "Coding languages are not only important if you want to break into something or build something. They're vital to *understanding* what you're working on. If you can't read the language, you're not going to get far with the given task." He smiled, an easy grin that was rarely seen on the staff here at Wilmont. "Which," he continued, "is why we'll be spending the next few weeks on languages…" Griffin launched into his lesson, and I lost myself in a project I'd meant to wrap up last night but had crashed before I could.

I already knew my preferred language. I already knew almost everything Griffin would cover this semester, but this was an advanced computer course—one of many offered, the only perk of sticking it out at Wilmont. I couldn't *not* take it. Plus, the hour block gave me extra time to code on my own.

Fifty minutes and a blink later, I dragged myself out of the zone and bounded up to the front of the room before

Griffin could excuse everyone.

"Winters?" he asked while he powered down his gear.

"I've been appointed head of"—I cringed as I tried not to puke over the words—"Code Club."

Griffin's eyes widened, and he choked on a laugh. "Principal Tanner sent me an informative text before you stumbled in here." He gave me a pitying look before he gestured to the students dying to get out of their seats. "Feel free."

"Okay," I said, turning to face the room.

I focused on Amber, the few streaks of pink in her dark hair that fell just short of her eyes and tightened around her ears. She was beyond easy to look at and took some of the sweat out of my palms. "If anyone is looking to get in some extra coding time or needs help with other programming stuff..." I lost my train of thought when Amber's green eyes popped up to mine as if she just realized I'd been speaking. "Um." I cleared my throat. Today had been too long already, and now I'd have to stay after school three hours longer for this damn *club*.

I needed to reboot.

I cleared my throat. "I'll be here right after school. Today, Wednesday, and Friday."

Amber tilted her head.

Another student, Holly, one of the sole six girls in the class, shot her hand into the air. "Is it an extra credit thing?"

I shook my head, my palms smacking against my thighs. "Nope. Just a...club." I refused to call it Code Club. It was bad enough on its own. Anything truly worthwhile would be strictly underground; putting a spotlight on what we were doing kind of took the point out of hacking.

"It's just for knowledge," I continued. "Practice. That sort of thing." Now that the words left my mouth, I could practically feel Tanner laughing his ass off in his office. He knew as well as I did that Griffin was lucky to have a full eighteen-student class. Coding was tricky, hard, and really only enjoyable to those who actually wanted to learn the skill. Doing it for an extra three hours a day without any other incentives? Forget about it.

"Thanks, Winters," Griffin said, patting me on the back. "I encourage anyone who wants to up their game to spend the extra time given." He joined me in staring at a bunch of blank faces. All except one. A pixie with pink in her hair who couldn't help but smirk. "Okay then," Griffin continued. "You're free to go." The room instantly transformed into a flurry of motion with his magic words—a scene I was usually happy to be a part of, except for when they were all running away from me *and* what I loved to do in my spare time. It was almost comical.

Almost.

I supposed if no one showed up, I could at least use the time to maintain the website like Tanner had demanded and then prep for the TOC coming up in March. I'd just have to make sure I did a damn good job on the website so Tanner didn't find a worse way to punish me for not being able to stop something I hadn't seen coming.

Something worse than a Code Club.

Something like shining his shoes or catering one of his social dinners.

I was so fucked.

CHAPTER THREE

AMBER

"You're good to ride home with Jake, right?" I asked Hannah while we dropped books off in our lockers.

She wore a cheesy grin as she closed her locker door. "Oh, you know I am."

I laughed. "Why are you looking at me like that?"

"I'm just excited for you," she said. "A cool after-hours computer club? With *Dean*? Sounds pretty...romantic."

I rolled my eyes. "Please stop. You're killing me with all the gushy stuff." I sighed. "Besides, the idea of Code Club is actually pretty sad. The true grit of what we do is underground, not...you know, in a school club approved by Tanner himself."

And I suddenly wondered why the principal would approve something like this. Especially after the fiasco this morning. Add to it that Dean had been front row and center to the train wreck? Something didn't add up.

Maybe the club would look good for whatever information he compiled over the year to keep his job? Did he think having a coding club would make him look more progressive? If that was the case, he should've asked me—a *girl*—to do it. Not that Dean wouldn't nail it...but girls—to my utter disappointment—made a small percentage of coders across the nation. There were only five others in Griffin's class. And I wanted to see those numbers soar. I'd tried and failed miserably to recruit Hannah into coding, but she didn't have the patience or the interest.

Either way, it didn't stop me from jumping at any chance to test my skills against Dean's.

"Whatever, hacker. Act like you're not bouncing up and down inside at the idea of clicking Dean's keys late into the night."

I scoffed, gently nudging her shoulder. "You're impossible."

She stepped closer to me, lowering her voice. "I think it would be good for you. To..." She chewed on her bottom lip. "Spend some time with a boy who isn't Brandon."

The memories of my last relationship twisted my stomach. "I hang with Jake all the time," I said, my tone missing the joking beat I'd intended. I glanced behind her, motioning to Jake walking toward us.

"That is *so* not the same." She spun around, instantly melting into his open arms.

Damn, these two were so sweet it was almost disgusting. If I didn't love them both I would be totally, absolutely... jealous of them.

Jake brushed some of Hannah's hair off her shoulder and then planted a quick kiss on her lips. The motions were so natural, so effortless. Hannah didn't hesitate when Jake reached for her, she didn't flinch when he outwardly showed affection. There was a hard-earned trust between them, gleaned from years of friendship and compassion. And they had a sixth sense when it came to sneaking the intimate moments during school—like they had a teacher radar that alerted them whenever one was close. Practice makes perfect ftw.

I didn't need to spend time with any other guys to know that not every male was a dick like Brandon—who thought of women as a game. Something made for him to enjoy.

Not that he'd always been like that, or shown me that side of him right away. In the beginning, he was nice. Funny. Smart. Attentive. We'd been friends before we'd dated. We had fun. I'd never seen him treat another girl like he'd treated me in the end…and maybe that was the game he played. Prince Charming until he didn't get his way.

A cold chill raced down my spine.

Not all boys were like him.

All I had to do was watch how Jake treated Hannah to know that maybe someday I'd find someone who wouldn't push me where I didn't want to go or shame me for not wanting to go there.

But, then again, what Hannah and Jake had was clearly true love. And not everyone was guaranteed their happily ever after.

"You riding with me or Amber today, babe?" Jake asked, one arm draped over her shoulder.

"You," she said without glancing up at him. Her eyes were on mine, perceptive and too knowing. There was a flash of pity mixed with anger. She knew my thoughts had turned to Brandon and everything that had happened between us. "He's a dick," she said again, no need to explain who she was calling out. "You want me to stay? I can sit with you while you hack."

The gesture was enough to warm the ice crystallizing over my heart.

"Who's a dick?" Jake asked.

Hannah gave him a quick *duh* glare.

"Ohhh," he said, nodding. His brow knitted in the middle. "Did something happen again? I'll fuck him up. Just say the word."

"No," I said, mustering a genuine smile. "Thank you." I shrugged. "I'm going to have fun giving Winters hell over this new club."

Hannah clapped her hands together. "Yay! Okay," she said, wrapping me in a fast hug. "Text me later with all the details. I'll want to know *everything.*"

"It'll be coding talk. That's *all* that will happen."

"Sure, sure." She waggled her eyebrows and interlocked her fingers with Jake's. "And we're going to go *study.*"

"You two are disgusting."

"Love you!" she called over her shoulder as they walked down the hallway toward the school's exit.

"Love!" I hollered back, already turning toward the coding room.

My heart sped as I neared the entryway, the door wide open but the interior quiet. Such a contrast from the normal school day. Nearly everyone on campus was already in or headed toward the parking lot, ready to put this day behind them.

I turned the corner, pausing a few steps in, my breath catching.

Dean had picked a desk in the far corner of the room, his custom laptop out, his headphones on and over his ears. They made his shaggy hair ruffle even more, and his sharp eyes were locked on the screen.

I wetted my lips, stepping farther into the room.

He continued to click away, fast and sure and steady.

Locked in.

Not about to interrupt, I sank into a desk a few away from him, and set up my own gear. Before I opened a capture the flag pwn challenge, I scanned the empty room. It wasn't a total shock that no one from coding class had shown up, but I assumed Mr. Griffin at least would be here.

They don't know what they're missing.

I slipped on my custom Loki emblem headphones, cranking my electronic list on Spotify, and set my fingers on the keys. The sweet repetitive beats pulsed and thrummed in my ears, each thump taking me further away from the room and deeper into the task.

An hour later, I'd captured the flag by exploiting the program to gain remote coding execution. I rolled my neck, sighing with the release of a completed challenge. The angle locked me onto a pair of blue-gray eyes and I jolted.

Hi. Dean mouthed the word despite sitting in a chair an arm's length away.

I furrowed my brow. "Hi!" The second the loud word left my lips, I realized my playlist still blared in my head. I yanked off my headphones, laying them on the desk next to my laptop. "Sorry," I said much quieter.

"How long have you been here?"

I glanced at my cell. "A little over an hour?"

"Why didn't you tell me?"

I leaned back in my chair, stretching out of my stiff position. "I'd never break your rhythm."

He pursed his lips, nodding. "Nice." He glanced back at his gear. "I didn't expect anyone to show up. After fixing some things on the school site, I launched right into a password cracking algorithm I've been working on."

"Tanner has you maintaining the site?" I chuckled. "That sounds thrilling."

"*Riveting* stuff," he said.

"I just owned in capture the flag. A pwn challenge. I had to locally exploit the server and then use it against itself. Found the flag after switching up the language."

Dean whistled, sitting in the chair right next to mine. He placed his elbows on his knees, putting him eye level with me. "Clever."

I shrugged. "It happens sometimes."

"Which site? CTFtime?"

"Pwnable. You know it?"

"I haven't done one in a few months, but yeah. They've got some good challenges."

The earbuds buzzed on my desk as my playlist switched to a new song, and I shifted to end it on my cell.

"Is that deadmau5?"

"Yeah," I said, watching him. "You know him?"

"Hell yes," he said. "'Animal Rights' is on almost every one of my lists."

"Are you messing with me?" I asked, suddenly wary he'd snuck into my system and snagged all my info. That wasn't his style, but still. How was it possible we loved the same DJ and he'd just named my favorite song?

"If I was going to mess with you," he said, smirking like he could read my mind, "it would be infinitely more involved than stealing a playlist."

A warm shiver danced down my spine as he licked his lips, that damn smirk both inviting and a warning sign.

"True," I said, hating the crack in my voice. It was hard to focus with him so close, his eyes on mine. He smelled like Red Bull and cedar and I was hard pressed to remember what exactly we were talking about. "You do WebWars?" I asked, noticing a patch on his messenger bag.

"I did last year," he said, rubbing his palms together where they hung between his knees. "And I've just earned my ticket to the Tournament of Champions this year."

My eyebrows rose. Damn, he was even better than I thought. The TOC, or Tournament of Champions, was a prestigious cyber intelligence competition held every year. The winner not only received major bragging rights, but a trophy, a ticket to next year's tourney, and an all-expenses-paid boot camp of their choice. Add to that all the connections to VIPs employed by top corporations, it was *the* competition to enter.

"Damn it," I said, crossing one leg over the other. "That settles it then. You *are* a better hacker than me." My shoulders sank a little at the thought. There was something about being better than the infamous Dean Winters that totally would've boosted my confidence.

"What?" He chuckled, shaking his head. "That is impossible to tell."

I scoffed. "I tried and failed to get into the TOC." Though, in all fairness, I hadn't configured my equipment to the optimum performance standards that I knew about now, and a few seconds had cost me a ticket, but *still*. He was going. I wasn't. And the competition was beyond insane—all ages could compete, meaning there were veteran hackers who had started movements all the way to pre-teens wanting to be the next Google intern.

"Which day did you compete on?" he asked.

"Two. You?"

"Three."

"Well," I said, sucking in a sharp breath. "I'll come watch you. If you want support."

"I'd love to have you there," he said, and it actually sounded like he meant it. "But…"

Oh shoot me now.

"It's in Boston this year, second week of March. Wouldn't want to rob you of pre-spring-break parties."

Sure, Boston was over two hours away, but it would be worth the haul to watch him win.

"Parties? Have you spotted me at many this summer?" Ice splintered in my stomach—I hadn't been to a party since Brandon. Since…

"No," he admitted. "Not that I've been hitting many, either, though." He glanced back at his gear. "I lose time."

"Me, too." I nodded. "Brandon always gave me shit about wanting to spend time with my computer over doing keg stands or Jell-O shots." The words were out of my mouth before I could stop them and I shifted in my seat.

Damn Hannah for making me think about my ex too many times today. Not that I could totally blame her. I constantly saw the guy in the halls. Usually that's when I sprinted in the opposite direction with acid building in my throat threatening to spew *Exorcist* style. I totally needed to get a handle on that reaction, but I was lost on how to do so.

"Brandon is a dick." A muscle ticked in his jaw as he leaned back in his seat.

I pressed my lips together, trying to contain my shock. They weren't friends, but most of the school adored Brandon. The star football player who won Wilmont championships, maintained a 4.0 GPA, and threw all-expenses-paid ragers.

Not many people knew what he turned into when he drank said Jell-O shots.

My skin prickled and I folded my arms over my chest.

"Sorry," Dean said. "I know he's your boyfriend—"

"He *so* isn't my boyfriend," I cut him off.

"What?" Dean cleared his throat. "I mean…when did that happen?" He leaned on his knees again, the warmth from his shift in movement soothing the cold in my veins.

"A couple months ago."

"I didn't know."

I chuckled again. "I didn't post it on a blog or anything."

He laughed, too, and damn if it didn't unwind my clenched muscles. "Noted."

I waved my hand like I could shoo the subject away. "So…*Code Club*." I said the words with a shit-eating grin.

"I know." Dean cringed, rubbing his palms over his face.

"I mean, you could've at least come up with a better name."

"Wouldn't have helped, would it?" He smirked.

"Nope."

"Tanner made me do this."

I narrowed my eyes. "Because of the presentation?"

He nodded, smacking his hands on his jeans. "Like I could've stopped it."

"Of course you couldn't," I said, and he arched a brow at me.

"You're not going to ask if I did it?"

"No." I shook my head. "One, if you wanted to pull something on Tanner, it would've been a hell of a lot more stealth than whatever that was this morning." My heart stuttered when he smiled. "And two," I pushed on, "there would be no trace of you there. No reason for you to get punished."

He inched closer to me, studying. The breath in my lungs stalled, heat raking across my skin like flames.

"You're one to watch, *PixieBurn*." He leaned back again.

I jolted at the use of my alias but quickly adjusted. "Whatever you say, *NightLocker*."

He chuckled, crossing his arms over his chest.

I sucked my teeth. "Now, what are we supposed to do in this club?"

"I'm supposed to tutor all our interested classmates." He dramatically looked around the empty room. "That and maintain the school's website. Which will take me all of two seconds each club. So…whatever we want, I guess," he said, shrugging. "I mean, as long as Tanner forces me to hold it. I'll be here. Three times a week…"

"For the rest of your life," I joked.

"Tanner would like it that way."

I groaned. "I wasn't totally unhappy to see him humiliated today." The man cared about two things: his awards from the district and state boards and the grants/bonuses he received because of *his* outstanding student performances. And after what Hannah said about his job...God, he'd likely get worse.

"Whoever did it sure fucked me over," he said, and I softened my features.

"Totally. Sucks." The conversation with Hannah this morning, the presentation, and the crazy prank all swirled in my head, an idea taking shape in my mind. "You know," I said, "someone *should* really put him in his place. Someone with more tact."

Dean arched a brow at me. "Careful," he warned. "You sound dangerously close to posing a challenge."

I hadn't been...but the boy was always one step ahead of me.

"Maybe I am."

"Terms?"

Heat flooded my cheeks at the spark in his eyes, the excitement mirrored in my own. He loved the rush of a challenge as much as I did. I had never felt that kind of camaraderie before.

"Rile up Principal Tanner, of course. Call it our epic senior year hack."

"And the winner gets?"

"*Besides* bragging rights?" I bit my bottom lip. Most challenges between hackers were kept low-key, the bragging rights being the sole focus of the challenge—in the end, topping another skilled hacker was the ultimate prize. *But* a little added incentive never hurt. "A deadmau5 T-shirt."

Dean smiled, tipping his chin up. "Rules?"

I sighed, nodding.

Rules. There always had to be rules.

While we liked to work beyond normal limits, it was unwise to work without a net.

"It has to be white hat," I said. "No one can get hurt, livelihood or otherwise."

"Naturally."

"And it has to be a secret between us. No one can know. *Siblings* included." I eyed him, knowing how close he was with his sister.

"Then friends can't, either," he countered.

"Of course." Hannah wouldn't want to know anyway. Not about a stunt this big. Not that I had a clue what I'd do yet.

"Time frame?"

"Spring break? So, that gives us a little over six months?" I smirked. "Maybe I'll win and it'll soften the blow of not competing against you at the TOC."

Dean continued to look down at me with those blue-gray eyes. I tried not to budge. Tried to present a strong, independent front. Inside I was trembling. The rush of a bet, of a challenge with a more than formidable opponent, was a high I didn't want to end.

"Deal," he said, sticking out his hand.

I took it, chills ghosting my skin as he wrapped his fingers over mine. We shook hands, and his was *so* warm. Electric shocks buzzed where we connected, and I kept shaking his hand until he finally arched a brow at me.

Quickly I dropped it, brushing back some hair that had fallen over my eyes.

"Did we just turn a principal-appointed club into command central for the ultimate prank *against* him?" Dean asked.

I stood, gathering my gear. "Too much for day one?"

"Nah," he said, grabbing his stuff and walking me toward the door. "Just the right amount."

We walked silently to the parking lot, our cars not far from each other in the near-vacant lot.

"You have an idea what you'll do?" he called to me from his car.

"No." I tilted my head. "Do you?"

He smirked. "Oh yeah."

I narrowed my eyes. He might be totally gorgeous and smell like a dream, but I was never one to back down from a competition. "Mine will be better."

"We'll see, Pixie."

"Whatever, Locker." I glared at him, but there was a full-on smile over my lips.

"I'm really glad you showed up," he said. "This is going to be fun." He winked at me before getting in his car and driving away.

I sat behind the wheel of my car, cranking my music as I tried to get my heart to stop racing.

Dean was right.

Code Club just got a whole lot more interesting.

CHAPTER FOUR

"Whoa," Sean said the instant I rounded the corner into the kitchen. "What did you do?"

I furrowed my brow, sneaking a taste of the sauce Mom had simmering on the stove. "What are you talking about? And what are you doing home?"

Sean was a sophomore at MIT and the current cybersecurity lead at Inkheart Corporations. We rarely saw him unless it was a holiday or he was overdue on his laundry. It was a hole that had stopped being so hollow over the years, but I still missed him. Not that I'd ever admit that out loud.

"I have the next two days off," he said, closing his laptop he'd had open on the kitchen table. "And don't dodge the question."

I sucked the marinara off my finger, my eyes rolling back in my head. One perk of Sean showing up was that Mom made his favorite dish, which happened to be mine, too. "What was it again?"

Sean rose from the table, dipping a clean spoon into the pot and taking a lick. We were the same height despite our age difference, though he was more jacked than I was. I was fit, but he *loved* the gym on campus. Most of my spare time was spent locked in and prepping for the Tournament of Champions, but I made a point to do a quick workout before school almost every morning. Helped me focus my mind for the day.

"You're grinning like the Cheshire Cat," he said, taking another lick. "Which either means you cracked something huge, or—" His eyes lit up. "You met a chick hot enough to take your mind off your computer for once."

Was I grinning?

My lips dropped the second I felt it and I waved him off.

"Holy hell," Sean said. "You *have* met a chick."

Amber's pink-streaked hair and perfect lips popped into my head. The way she'd looked, locked onto her screen, her villain headphones blaring my favorite artist to tune out the world.

Good God, she was gorgeous and tempting and all things I didn't need to think about. We were friends. Cordial friends at that. She'd *just* broken up with that d-bag Brandon. I couldn't begin to think of her as anything more than a fellow hacker.

Sure, we had fun trying to top one another in class, and yes, maybe sometimes I bought her favorite drink just to see that over-the-top smile of hers, but there was nothing beyond that. She'd always been with golden-boy Brandon—someone who talked shit when no one was looking and thought he ruled over everyone else. I never understood why they'd been together—she was a fierce girl with a rebellious streak when she locked in. Maybe that's why the relationship had ended. The two didn't compute.

"I had a good day." I walked away from the sauce before I put it in a bowl and drank it *Beast* style.

"Wait, what?" Tessa's voice snapped as she rounded the corner, plucking the spoon out of Sean's hand and taking a taste for herself. Mom was going to kill us. "You were hauled into the principal's office and forced to run some stupid club, eating hours of your personal time. How is that a *good* day?"

I groaned, taking a seat at the table. "Thanks, Tessa."

Sean smirked as he sat across from me. "So, not only

were you deflecting, you were lying, too. I'm your brother!"

"Like I could forget." I glared at him, but I was only half serious. He knew I loved him, just like Tessa knew, but that didn't mean I wanted to divulge every single detail of my life to them.

"Why did Tanner haul you in?" Sean asked, more serious.

Tessa snorted. "Someone pulled a *brilliant* prank on Tanner during his abstinence only presentation."

"No shit?" Sean gaped at her.

"Dead serious," she said. "Awesome clips of sexy make-out sessions and all."

"It wasn't that awesome," I said. "Or brilliant."

"Just because you're immune to romance doesn't mean the rest of us are," Tessa quipped.

"That's not it," I said, rolling my eyes. "Whoever did it will get caught. Tanner is too smart and paranoid to let it slide. He knew it wasn't me. Which means he has at least an idea of who it might be, and that person and all their friends will suffer when he nails them."

"He was always strict, but is he getting worse?" Sean ran his fingers through his hair, and I nodded in answer. "If he knew it wasn't you then why did he bother bringing you in?"

"Because I was behind the computer when it happened. I'd only pushed play on the vid, someone else had tampered with it before I got there."

Sean hissed.

"Tessa!" Mom chided as she came into the kitchen and snatched the spoon out of her hand. Tessa blinked, then glared at the two of us at the table.

"They did it first!"

Sean and I gave Mom our most innocent faces possible. One I mastered by watching him. Tessa growled and rolled her eyes.

"You're all in trouble," Mom teased. "Do it again and I'll burn the bread."

A collective gasp damn near shook the room. Mom's homemade garlic bread was just about as close to heaven as one could get.

"Never again," I said.

"Promise," Tessa added.

Sean laughed, and the rest of us followed. When Dad came in and instantly stuck his finger in the pot, it only made us laugh harder. The sounds filled the kitchen, and the ache in my chest that always missed my brother soothed a fraction. Normally I'd already be up in my room, headphones on, sneaking in two hours of coding before dinner, but not tonight. Family nights like this were rare, and after the day I'd had, it was beyond welcome.

The thought made me return to Sean's first words to me, and I sat there wondering why I'd been a grinning fool when I'd walked in. It wasn't Code Club, because kill me now. No, it had to be the rush of the challenge Amber had set up. This ultimate bet with someone who would put up a proper fight. The idea of crushing her in this competition had fueled that ridiculous smile on my face earlier, that's all.

I set the table and then Mom dished the plates. Sean launched into stories from MIT and Inkheart, and I soaked it in. His tales were enough to make me drool—his future so solid and close to the dreams of my own. Sean was eons ahead of me, but I'd catch up to him one day. As long as I earned my acceptance letter from MIT, but that wouldn't happen until March. Months away. Then the battlefield would be even and never ending.

"Anyone want to shed light on what went down today?" Mom asked, glancing at Dad.

He nodded. "We received an interesting email from

Principal Tanner earlier."

"What did it say?" Tessa blurted, her mouth half full.

I tilted my head, slowly finishing the last bites on my plate.

"Something about someone…" He cleared his throat. "*Porn-bombing* his presentation?"

Mom choked on her bite, she laughed so hard.

Sean snorted.

"It wasn't porn." I rolled my eyes. God, if Tanner thought a few CW make-outs were porn… "Someone just put a few kissing clips over his *sex is the road to death* video."

Dad arched a brow at me.

"I'm not that stupid," I said.

"Oh, honey, we know that," Mom said, reaching over the table to touch my wrist. "And I said as much when Principal Tanner called to confirm you were home last night."

Dad grumbled as he stabbed a meatball on his plate. "Sometimes I wonder if Wilmont's stellar academics are worth the ancient approach they have to certain forms of education."

"It's fine," I said.

"But Tessa mentioned he got on to you about the video?" Mom asked, eyeing us both.

I glared at Tessa across the table. Not that I was trying to hide anything from my parents, but because it wasn't even relevant. I shrugged. "It's not a big deal. He's pissed I didn't see it coming and stop it." I set my fork down. "I have to host an after-school thing now, three days a week. And maintain Wilmont's website. So I'll be late on those days."

"That's an odd form of punishment," Dad said.

I glanced at Sean, knowing the hell I was about to catch.

"It's called Code Club." Tessa took my silence and filled it with the cringeworthy words.

Sean burst out laughing. "Oh, damn, brother. That is horrible."

"What?" Mom's eyes darted between the two of us. "You love hacking."

I clenched my eyes shut. "Mom," I groaned. "Yeah. It's just that it's an underground thing. *Private*, for the most part."

"What about all those boot camps and competitions you enter?" she countered.

A small smile softened my embarrassment. Had to give it to Mom, and Dad, too—they were fully committed to our choices in life in terms of what we were passionate about. "Those are the exceptions. And tournaments are about challenges and topping other hackers and earning bragging rights. This *club* isn't like that. Tan—Principal Tanner wants to cut into my personal time by forcing me to host it and do whatever he requires for his site."

Mom glanced at Dad and shrugged, the point clearly lost on her.

"Did anyone show up?" Sean asked, the pity clear in his tone.

My heart did a hiccup. "Yeah," I said.

He raised his brows, waiting for me to elaborate.

"Just one person," I said.

"Who?"

"It's not like you'd know her."

Sean clanked his fork down. "Why are you dead set on hiding things from me?"

"Oh, I don't know, maybe because you're constantly cracking my stuff and messing with me." Last month he'd replaced my entire music collection with Taylor Swift songs. I mean, "Blank Space" was catchy but *damn*. Those lyrics got in your head and *never* let you go.

"Sean!" Mom chided while Dad chuckled. She cut a glare to him.

"What?" Dad asked innocently. "It keeps him sharp."

Tessa rolled her eyes, content to finish her food out of the spotlight.

"Exactly," Sean said, motioning his full fork to Dad. "What he said. I make you a better hacker."

"Spare me," I said, trying not to laugh.

"Stop dodging," he said. "Who showed up?"

A pixie-hacker who was suddenly single. I wetted my lips, unable to shake the sweet scent of whatever concoction she'd had on her skin earlier—something like vanilla and mint and lavender all in one.

I forced out a laugh. "No one," I said, pushing from the table and carrying my empty plate to the sink. I returned only to kiss Mom on the top of her head. "Great dinner, as always, Mom." I bounded up the stairs and to the seclusion of my room.

I needed away from the conversation—hell, I needed away from my own thoughts. Now that this club was forced onto my plate, I had to focus up. All extra time had to be spent hacking. Practicing. Prepping. Winning the TOC was my sole goal—it would go a hell of a long way in an MIT interview as well as almost guarantee me a job at a major corporation. That's where true improvement would happen, in the field, and I was beyond ready to start that chapter in my life.

One more school year.

My headphones were halfway to my ears when a knock sounded on my door. I sighed, not bothering to spin my computer chair around. "It's open, Sean."

"Hey," he said, closing the door behind him. He sank onto my unmade bed across from my desk. "Did I do something?"

"You mean besides rearrange all the letters on my keyboard?" I smirked.

He gaped at me. "That was two years ago, bro."

"I don't forget."

"Yeah, but you do forgive. And get even. You totally crashed my server with the spam-bomb you sent in retaliation. It took me a day to get it back to normal speed again."

"Learned from the best." I smiled at him. "It gets boring here without you, man."

"I bet," he said, leaning his elbows on his knees. "But it sounds like you've got plenty to keep you occupied." He glanced at my computer, then back to me. "Nice job on scoring that entry to the TOC."

My chest puffed out a bit. "It wasn't easy."

"No doubt," he said, shaking his head. "I've never made it in."

"You've only tried once. And you were a baby."

"Sixteen is hardly a baby." He laughed. "And once was by far enough. Too much pressure. No thanks."

"I like it."

"You thrive off that rush. I like the slow-burn hacks. The hunt."

The room fell silent for a few moments, Sean's mind working out a problem somewhere else. I could see it in his eyes, recognize the same faraway look I wore when a challenge nagged me.

Speaking of.

"Hey, you set up the security system for the academy, right?"

"Yeah. Why?" He cocked a brow at me. "Dean," he chided.

"What?"

He sighed. "I get it's your senior year. You want to do something epic to sign off with…but stay away from Tanner."

"He's such an—"

"Asshole. I know. I spent a decade under his reign, too."

"Yeah," I said. "Well, I think he's gotten worse."

"How so?"

"You hear things." I shrugged.

"High school has a way of embellishing."

I shrugged. "I don't need rumors to know he's had a stick up his ass for the past ten years. Or more."

Sean nodded, a smile on his face. "You remember when the fire system malfunctioned and soaked the teachers' lounge?"

I sat up straighter, thinking back to the epic day in history. I was a sophomore. Half the teachers had been doused, including Tanner. "Yeah?"

"That was funny." Sean stood up from the bed.

I furrowed my brow. "That wasn't you, was it?"

The teachers, Tanner, too, had all claimed it was a legit tech malfunction. No one had gotten in trouble for it. In fact, Tanner had brought Sean in to help fix the problem.

"Of course not." He shoved his hands in his pockets. "It was a common hiccup in the system."

His gaze didn't match the explanation his lips gave.

Holy hell.

"No trace," I said, nodding with understanding. He might be telling me not to go after Tanner, but underneath the advice was the even bigger order: don't get caught. Leave no trace. Be so good they don't even have the chance to think a human was behind it.

And wasn't that half of what I killed myself practicing for anyway?

This would take some thought. Careful plotting, planning,

and painstakingly double-checking everything.

But it had to be big.

Nothing less would beat Amber.

"Dean?" Sean asked like he'd said my name more than once. He was standing by the door. I hadn't even realized he'd moved, lost in the swirls of my plans.

"Yeah?"

"Who showed up to your club?"

"Amber Henderson." I relented, knowing he wouldn't stop asking.

His mouth dropped. "The girl with the pink in her hair?"

"How do you remember her?" It'd been two years since he went to our school, and he'd been a senior then. We were barely on his radar.

He chuckled, tapping the side of the door with his knuckles. "She cornered me one time."

A muscle in my jaw ticked out of instinct.

Sean quickly raised his hands. "She just wanted configuration advice. A new piece of equipment was giving her trouble. I helped her, but she'd already been halfway there."

I released a tight breath, telling myself to get a damn grip. "That sounds like Amber."

"Look, I promise I'm not trying to lecture you about the sign-off stuff," Sean said. "I know all about locking up for competitions and jobs and side projects. Fucking kills me to say it, but I'm proud of you. Okay? You're on track. Further along than I was at your age. Just…" He rolled his eyes. "Don't waste your last year as a *kid*. Have some fun. Get reckless, but be smart about it. Safe. Because once you hit the real world? Shit changes. For the better, mostly. But it *changes*."

"You regretting something, brother?"

"Nah," he said, but I didn't quite believe him. "I just don't want to see you get so good that you miss out on living."

I swallowed hard, wondering what was going on with him that would make him take this serious turn. I pushed out of my chair, crossing the room. "You okay, Sean?"

He blinked a few times, forcing a smile. "I'm golden." He punched me in the shoulder, and I flinched from the sting.

I hit him in the gut, hating that it hurt my knuckles to take the punch. Asshole gym rat.

"Be smart," he said again. "If I find out you haven't been?" He glanced behind me, eyes landing on my computer, a vicious smile shaping his lips.

"What?" I asked, panicked. "What will you do?"

He laughed. "You'll never know until I want you to."

With that, he spun out of my room and down the hallway to his old one.

I shut the door, the threat ringing clear in my head.

Have fun. Be smart. No traces.

I could handle that and win the TOC, too.

Now all I had to do was figure out something epic enough to beat Amber.

But with the way she somehow managed to be sharp, stealthy, and sexy as hell all at the same time? I couldn't help but think this might be the one challenge I would have fun losing.

CHAPTER FIVE

AMBER

I dropped my bag on the wooden bench in the entryway and beelined it straight to the kitchen after we'd wrapped up Code Club. I flung open the silverware drawer, grabbed a spoon, and snatched the Nutella jar from the snack cabinet. After unscrewing the lid, I flung it to the side, dipped the spoon into the hazelnut gold, and shoved it in my mouth.

"Bad day?" I jolted at Mom's voice from behind me.

I spun around to face the bar that connected the kitchen and living room, watching as she eyed me from the other side.

I licked the heaven off the spoon.

"Yes. No, not really," I said.

"Well, now that that's all cleared up," she said, laughing.

I chuckled, too. "You know, some days I just…" I huffed. "It was sexual awareness day today." Mom rolled her eyes. "Right? And Hannah! I mean, I can never help her. And the school isn't helping *anyone* in that department. *Pretend like it'll kill you, that'll teach 'em!*" I did my best principal impression and tossed my spoon in the sink, grabbed a clean one, and dipped it into the jar again.

Mom raised an eyebrow, her gaze following the spoonful into my mouth. "You need a bowl?"

"No," I mumbled around the spoon. "And then someone totally up and pranked the video at the assembly today."

"No way. How?"

"Crazy sexy clips blasted over Principal Tanner's usual one."

Mom cleared her throat, hiding a laugh. "Can't wait to read *that* email," she said.

"It was funny, but Tanner was super pissed."

"Naturally."

"And, I don't know. I just...hate it."

"Oh yeah, sure," she said, nodding, though I knew I wasn't being coherent. I was fuming, but that was the great thing about Mom; she could always keep up regardless of if I made sense or not.

"I swear if Wilmont wasn't the only academy to offer those extensive computer science courses you love, I would've yanked you out of there years ago."

I gasped. "I'd never want to be away from Hannah."

"Of course," she said.

I cleaned the spoon, tossed it into the sink to be with its sister, and took a deep breath. "I joined an after-school club today."

"That's a twist! Which one?" she asked, leaning her elbows on the bar, giving me her full attention. Her long auburn hair hung in waves around her shoulders, half covering the loose, flowery top she wore.

I closed my eyes. "Code Club."

"Oh?" she asked, standing up straight. "Won't that be fun?"

"Yes. Well, sort of," I said. "It's just me and one other person right now." I wished my heart wouldn't race so hard when thinking of the challenge... Damn, I needed to come up with something good. Something epic.

"Not a ton of people joining where coding is concerned?" she asked.

"Not so much," I said, laughing.

"Good for you." Pride beamed from her eyes, but I shook my head.

"For what?"

"Being you and owning it 100 percent no matter what anyone else is doing."

I shrugged. "We'll see how long the club lasts without any other members." My mind calculated all the ways in which I could make Principal Tanner's life difficult—without hurting him, of course. I wasn't into black hat.

I wanted to do something epic, beat Dean, *and* maybe be helpful at the same time. I chewed on that for a minute before focusing on Mom again. "I'm sorry," I said, the conflicting emotions from today finally settling. Mom had that effect. Just venting to her always made things better. "Did I break your stride?" I glanced to where her office door was opened.

"No, honey." She waved me off. "I've already hit my word count for the day." She grinned. "I was just online, researching this new toy called the Smile Maker." She pointed her fingers about a foot apart. "It's supposed to—"

"Oh God, Mom, *no.*" I clenched my eyes shut as if that would make me temporarily deaf.

"What?" She laughed, and I peeked my eyes open. "I thought maybe you could run a blog on it. I bet Principal Tanner would think the video prank was tame compared to a full write-up about the Smile Maker!"

I burst out laughing. "Truth," I said between gasps of breath. I could just picture Tanner's face if I did a public blog about that. "But anything looks tame when you put it next to your work, Mom." Having an erotica author for a mom had that tendency.

She chuckled and walked behind the bar to wrap her arms around me. I hugged her back, shaking my head. "I do wish I could help Hannah," I said, my thoughts returning to our conversation this morning.

"Oh, honey, I don't think she needs a Smile Maker. She seems pretty content with Jake."

"Ew, gross, Mom. *No*." I shuddered. "I meant with all the other stuff. The advice and...I don't know."

"I know, Amber," she said, patting my back before she let me go. She looked me in the eye. Waiting.

"It's not just birth control info they hide," I said. "It's everything. *Anything* to do with sex." I chewed on my bottom lip, thinking about that ridiculous presentation today. "It's archaic. Hulk Smash. Sex bad."

Mom brushed back the feathered ends of my hair. "I'm sorry. I don't know what to do about that..." A light clicked behind her eyes. "Should I write the school? Tell them their education on the subject is outdated? I could send a few signed books as a bribe? Or maybe to show them that what you all want to know is...what was the word you used? *Tame?*"

"No, Mom," I said, laughing. "I heard a rumor that the board is already trying to move the school in a different direction."

"Oh really?" She grinned. "Seems I need to give Hannah's mom a call and get the scoop." She sighed. "But you know you can always ask me if you're ever curious about something."

I nodded. We'd always had an open-door policy. I was free to ask questions without judgment. Dad was a youth psychologist, so he was beyond chill whenever I came to them with anything. Not that I usually hit them with anything too crazy.

Like what happened with Brandon. Mom knew most of the details. She'd been there to help me through it, help me understand that I wasn't in the wrong.

"Hannah, too," Mom said, thankfully yanking me away from the past. She reached for the Nutella, grabbed her own spoon, and took a bite. "I know Connie can be a little...I don't want to say uptight, since I like her so much but..." She chuckled. "My knowledge is Hannah's knowledge."

I pressed my lips together. That wasn't a half-bad idea. Hannah loved my mom, but then again, it might be embarrassing. And not everyone had a mom like mine—willing and able to offer healthy advice on sex. And, sure, Google had information, but there was a huge difference between reading an article or watching a video created by a total stranger and gathering advice from someone you trusted. Someone who could understand you more than any clinical website or school lecture ever could.

Mom set the Nutella down. "Anything," she said again. "The pill. Flavored condoms vs. regular—"

"Mom!" I groaned, raising my hands in defense. I chuckled. "Let *me* come to *you*." I walked past her, heading toward my room.

"Amber," she said through her laughter.

I stopped halfway to my room. "Yeah?" I asked timidly, terrified of another mention of the Smile Maker or flavored condoms.

She stopped before me, her hands on my shoulders. "Jokes aside," she said. "You know you can always ask me anything, right?"

"I know, Mom. And I love you for it." I patted the hand that held my shoulder.

She was the best mom ever, but she wasn't *in* high school. And that's who people like Hannah needed.

Someone in the same situation.

Someone she could trust who wasn't an adult.

Someone who wouldn't judge...who would *get* it.

An idea burst in my mind like a bright flash of lightning.

"Uh-oh," Mom said. "What's happening up there?" She pointed to my forehead, and I blinked a few times, her earlier words echoing in my head.

"I've got to make a call," I said, still more in my head than with her. I reached into my back pocket for my cell and headed to my room. "Thanks, Mom!" I called over my shoulder as I shut the door.

I leaned my back against it, staring down at the number I'd never used for anything other than tech support.

A slow smile shaped my lips.

It's crazy.

But it just might work.

I pushed call, my fingers shaking as I held the cell to my ear.

"You know we've only been apart a couple of hours, Pixie," Dean answered, his smooth voice heating my skin. "You can't be ready to forfeit the challenge already."

"Hell no," I said, praying I didn't sound as nervous as I was. "I need to pose a hypothetical question."

"Intrigued. What's up?"

"If I was searching for a site but couldn't trace it, where would you think it was?" I asked, hoping he wouldn't connect the dots on my plan.

"Are you asking me for *advice* on how you plan to beat me?"

"Maybe," I said, grinning. "You never said that was against the rules."

"Clever, Pixie."

"Sometimes," I said, mimicking our earlier conversation. "Now, thoughts?"

"Okay..." He dragged out the word as if he were calculating it in his head. "If it were me," he said, "and I was searching for something but struggling...I'd probably hit up Tor or a similar place. That's where things are usually buried."

"Perfect!" I'd thought about using Tor—one of the dark webs—to carry out my plan, too, but I needed to be absolutely certain. I'd never messed around there much, so I had to make sure there weren't other options. Normally I'd avoid it, but this wasn't a normal challenge.

"But," he added, "nothing is completely dark. If someone digs deep and hard enough, there is always a trace."

A risk, but I doubted my idea would stir up enough interest to result in someone *actually* hunting for the source. No, it'd be just enough to act like a thorn in Tanner's side. A piece of reality to counter his fantasyland perfect-boasting website. And, hopefully, a safe space for my classmates at Wilmont.

"Amber?" Dean said my name, and I snapped out of my thoughts.

"Sorry," I said.

"It's okay. I get it. Just don't think too hard on it, okay?"

"Why?"

"Because," he said, a laugh in his tone. "I'm not prepared to lose to you."

I grinned, biting on my lower lip. "Well, you better *get* prepared because you're going down."

"Not a chance."

"Thanks for the advice," I said. "See you tomorrow."

"Can't wait."

The response made my stomach flip, and I quickly hung up the phone. What was wrong with me? I'd sworn off boys after Brandon. Not that Dean was Brandon, but what did I really know? I thought I'd known the type of guy Brandon was, and that all changed in the course of one night.

The butterflies in my stomach took a nosedive into a

crashing wave of acid, and I huffed out a breath.

Damn him. I wished I could delete him from my mind. Erase every date, every hour I spent with him. It didn't matter that we'd had fun in most of those memories—the worst one was enough to taint them all.

Hands everywhere, greedy lips, demands.

No.

I wasn't going there again.

I had work to do.

Work was always the best distraction, and this would be the biggest challenge to date for my hacker career. I needed 100 percent focus.

I rolled my neck, grabbed my headphones, and sank in front of my computer.

First, I had to write up a rough draft.

Second, I had to take a swim in the deep end of the dark web and make sure an average person—i.e., Principal Tanner—couldn't find it. No cracks. No way to trace this back to me.

And third?

I had to stop thinking about how good Dean would look in a deadmau5 shirt if he beat me.

F our hours, two Red Bulls, a few pieces of code, and three drafts later, the site I'd built from scratch was one button push away from going live on Tor. All I'd need to do was make sure the right person at Wilmont found the secret link and hope they deemed it interesting enough to spread the word. That, plus the giveaway I'd listed, should help gain some traffic.

I leaned back in my seat, rubbing my ears where my

headphones had made them overly hot.

"Well, here goes nothing," I said, staring at the grueling work I'd just done.

If it worked, I'd win.

If it didn't, but I could at least help *one* person, then every risk would be worth it.

Because I knew what it was like to have something happen...something out of your control, and feel completely alone afterward. Yes, I'd been lucky enough to have my mom and Hannah to help me through it, but they didn't understand the nightmares. The flashbacks. The fear that jolted me every single time I saw Brandon in the halls. That was something only another person who'd experienced something similar could truly relate to. And I never wanted anyone to feel that alone. Not if I could help it.

And if I got caught?

Ice froze the adrenaline in my veins.

I'd probably be expelled, which would then result in a rejection letter from MIT in March instead of an acceptance letter.

I won't get caught.

I'd taken too many precautions.

I was too smart to get caught.

Repeating that internally about a dozen times, I reached for my keyboard...

And clicked.

ASK ME ANYTHING

ABOUT   USEFUL LINKS   FAQ   CHAT WITH ME

Who else is totally sick of the school's so-called *sexual education*?

Who here hates that Google is a one-way trip to *I'll-never-unsee-that-ville*?

Who here is over the school's blog pushing an outdated agenda?

Who here wants a place to vent and discuss topics that we're constantly told to stay away from?

I'm here to help. I'm here to say:

Ask Me Anything.

Want to know where to get birth control without your parents knowing? I'm here.

Want to know the pros and cons of flavored condoms vs. regular? I'm here.

Want to know if that after-sex burn is normal or something to worry about? I'm here.

Want to vent about something in general? I'm here!

Now, I know what you're thinking. That I'm probably some adult in disguise, luring you to this blog to trap you. I get why you'd think that...because if I stumbled onto this, I would, too.

But I assure you, I'm one of you. That's right. I'm a female student of Wilmont Academy. I likely see you in the halls. I may even have classes with you.

Don't believe me? If I wasn't, how would I know about the top-secret elevator that is underneath the gym? You know, the one only upperclassmen know about?

How would I know that the softball captain sang the best rendition of Bohemian Rhapsody while standing on the diving board above a certain party hoster's pool this summer? How would I know that a JV soccer player nearly broke his leg zooming down a hill on a minibike on an icy night last winter?

Have I proven myself yet?

Look, everything on this site will be 100 percent anonymous. Use a code name when you post your question, or simply leave it blank. I will approve each question before posting publicly, and if you feel the need for extra privacy, you can email me at the address listed.

So, I'm here. I'm ready to listen. I'm ready to answer.

Ask Me Anything.

Oh, and that birth control I was talking about? Check out the useful links tab to find the best locations to score some safely.

In the meantime,
Stay Sexy. Stay Healthy.

CHAPTER SIX

DEAN

NightLocker: Crash before 2am?
PixieBurn: Does it look like it?
NightLocker: Didn't mean it like that
PixieBurn: Sure
NightLocker: I didn't stop coding until 4
PixieBurn: Overachiever
NightLocker: Have to be to beat you
PixieBurn: Flattery won't help you win
NightLocker: DC!

I frantically typed our standard code word for killing an illegal chat—DC, aka *don't chat, don't code*—when a teacher was too close to walking by one of our screens.

Amber quickly clicked off-screen, allowing the Spanish assignment to fill the space. Mrs. Francesca wasn't the strictest teacher at Wilmont, but she'd be pissed if we were caught.

After she'd taken an unexpected walk around our quiet classroom, I flashed Amber a smile. She was six rows away from me, and we'd adapted this way of chatting a couple years ago when we'd gotten bored during Computer Science class. It was a good, solid class. It simply was teaching us things we'd known for years—it wasn't until we'd accelerated to the more exclusive coding courses that we were actually challenged. The one saving grace of this school were those higher-level computer classes. And though Amber and I had always been in competition with each other, we'd come up with the code word to let each other know when push came to shove, we hackers had each other's backs.

Or, at least, Amber and I did.

The word had saved me plenty of times—even when I hadn't been actively chatting with her. A few times she'd thrown it in a chat box on my screen when I'd been coding or locked into another hack.

Amber yawned as she tried to return my gesture.

I chuckled under my breath, giving her a too-knowing look.

She'd been up as late as I was last night. Working on our challenge. Not that she looked like she was tired, like she'd implied, but I could see it in her eyes. The heavy way they gazed at the assignment on the screen—seeing it but not computing. The same way I was, because I'd stayed up entirely too late and gotten up way too damn early.

A tremor of nerves rolled through me. I didn't have a clue what she was preparing, but I was sure it'd be incredible. The girl knew her shit. Born with a gift. And I'd have to up my game in order to fully beat her.

Once Mrs. Francesca returned to her position behind her desk, I opened another chat box, completely unable to resist.

NightLocker: Will I see you tomorrow?
PixieBurn: Why wouldn't you?
NightLocker: Didn't know if you were going to come again
PixieBurn: Wouldn't leave you to host an empty room
NightLocker: Ha. Ha.

PixieBurn: Think you can beat me in a round of CTF?
NightLocker: Name the time
PixieBurn: Code Club. Tomorrow
NightLocker: God, we have to come up with a better name

She snorted quietly and shook her head.

PixieBurn: You do. I'm just a dutiful member
NightLocker: Not fair
NightLocker: I thought we were in this together?
PixieBurn: I thought we were always competing to see who would wind up on top?

The last line made a deep ache wrench in my stomach. Flashes of her on top of me, smiling with those perfect lips, her short hair falling gently across her forehead as I held her.

Barely able to escape the involuntary fantasy, I was typing a response before I could get the feel of her phantom-self out of my head.

NightLocker: I think it would be fun with either of us on top

The sentence repeated in my mind the second I hit enter, and I jolted. Fuck, that sounded *so* wrong.

Or completely right.

I hushed my inner voice and risked a glance at her.

She stared at the screen, her once-tired eyes wide and alert, a beautiful rosy color flooding her cheeks.

NightLocker: Calm down, Pixie
NightLocker: You're blushing
PixieBurn: It's hot in here
PixieBurn: Don't flatter yourself
NightLocker: I rarely do. You're the one clearly dreaming of me in all sorts of naughty ways
NightLocker: Cause you know I didn't mean it like that.

I tried to make light of my blunder, but I was equally surprised that was where her mind went first.

Did that mean she was thinking about me, too?

Damn.

Why did that make my heart race?

A sweet smirk shaped her lips as she reached for the keyboard.

Well, as long as we were playing.

NightLocker: Or did I?

She paused her typing, hitting the backspace button over and over again as she read my message. Her shoulders dropped but didn't make a move to respond. The smirk had left her face, the joking gone from her eyes.

Shit. I crossed a line.

I clicked the keys in a hurry.

NightLocker: Hey
NightLocker: Pixie
NightLocker: I was only joking. I promise
PixieBurn: It's moot either way
NightLocker: Reasoning?
PixieBurn: I've sworn off boys.

PixieBurn: Scratch that. Love. I've sworn off all forms of it.

I glanced at her, swallowing a lump in my throat.
What happened to make you say that?
It was written all over her face. The pain. The regret. And...fear?
Brandon. He must've torn her heart to pieces.
Dick.
I cleared my throat, straightening in my chair with my fingers on the keys.

NightLocker: That's a shame...

I hit the backspace.

NightLocker: Too bad...

I deleted that one, too. Because even if I hated seeing those words—that she'd shut down her heart for good—it was for the best. I could joke around all I wanted, tease her to get her a little out of her head, but in reality? I'd never want to cross a line she'd drawn. Especially when the relationship she'd just gotten out of was so clearly hard.
So I typed the words I didn't want to say but knew I needed to.

NightLocker: I understand. Who has time for that anyway, right?
PixieBurn: Not me.
NightLocker: Not people like us
PixieBurn: Truth

She closed the chat box, slowly turning her head to glance back at me.

The breath knocked from my lungs at the direct look in her eyes. So much brewing there — laughter and understanding and fear and…something else I couldn't quite figure out. I sure as hell wanted to. I *wanted* to know her story. Wanted to know what had turned the once-outgoing pixie I watched from a friendly distance into a timid, internal being.

I wanted more than the passing convos we had during class, mostly revolving around coding or hacks or techniques.

I wanted to be a *real* friend.

I gave her my most understanding smile. I could be there for her without actually being *hers*. I could spend time with her without losing sight of my goals. I could have fun with her without falling for her.

Friends.

Finally…maybe we were ready to cross over that gap.

CHAPTER SEVEN

AMBER

The cheers of more than half of Wilmont saturated the stadium as our football team stormed the field. I forced my way through the flailing arms and foam fingers, weaving in and out of the crowd as I climbed the bleachers.

"Amber!" Hannah shouted from three rows up, her golden hair held back by a black headband. She practically swam in Jake's practice jersey, the bottom of the number thirteen hitting her knees. "Up here!" She waved, a wide smile on her face. "You're late," she said once I took my spot by her side.

I shifted my bag over my shoulders, the gray T-shirt I wore ruffling under the weight. "Not even," I said, pointing to the field as everyone took their seats. "They haven't started yet."

Hannah rolled her eyes but gave my shoulders a squeeze. "Are those new jeans?"

I nodded, glancing down at the ripped black skinnies I'd treated myself to last weekend on a fun shopping trip with Mom. "You like?" I asked, shifting so she could see where they tucked into my silver Chucks.

"Love," she said.

That was the one good thing about sporting events for Wilmont—we were allowed to wear our own clothes.

Setting my bag between my feet, I gazed out at the field as the game started, my eyes finding number nineteen out of sheer muscle memory.

Even with the helmet and the bulky jersey, anyone could tell Brandon was in good shape. Muscles for days upon days, biceps thick, thighs thicker. Something I used to admire, used to compliment on the discipline he had when it came to training.

I rolled my eyes.

I used to love coming to watch the games, too, but he'd ruined it for me.

Not that I'd ever mention it to Hannah. She attended every game, rain or shine or sleep deprived. She'd never miss an opportunity to cheer for Jake.

Her sharp whistle jolted my senses, as did the loud crowd. All I'd wanted was to go home and crash for a couple hours—catch up on what I'd lost last night building the blog—but I'd promised Hannah I'd be here.

She followed my line of sight, huffing. "Wish they'd bench him."

A laugh ripped from my chest. "The only way coach would bench Brandon is if he broke something." I shook my head. "Seriously, it's fine, Hannah. I'm here for you. And Jake."

"Thanks," she said. "It's always so much more fun when you're here."

I tore my eyes off Brandon, trying like hell not to remember how I used to clap and cheer and scream his name just like Hannah. I'd even gone so far as to paint his number on my cheeks last year.

Stupid, stupid girl.

"No Code Club today?"

"Tomorrow. And Friday."

"That's exciting." She waggled her brows at me, and the look took me straight back to Spanish class this morning.

Dean's and my chat had been fun, borderline flirty compared to our normal recaps of codes or techniques. But I'd choked when his words had sent my heart flying. Made me picture things. Want things I knew I shouldn't. Because the relationship road only led to pain or humiliation or both.

I'd learned that in a harsh way.

"Totally," I finally said, swallowing hard. It wasn't a lie. I was looking forward to spending the extra time in the coding room—with Dean or without.

Okay, with.

But mainly I was happy because it'd be uninterrupted time spent on the challenge between us. I'd need every minute of it to top him.

Color flooded my cheeks at the thought, my mind circling right back to the joke he'd made. The way I'd been ready to respond with my own innuendo, rile him at his own game.

The memories—*they* stopped me.

Because I didn't want to give the wrong vibe. Didn't want to invite unwanted advances, not that Dean was advancing…

I sighed, rubbing my palms over my face. I needed sleep. Every time I crossed that line of deprived, I became delusional. I was an over-analyzer by nature—something that helped my natural ability to read code, exploit systems, and more. But pair *that* with little sleep and a wave of emotions that wouldn't stop crashing? I was downright loopy in my thought process.

"Omigod!" Hannah gasped beside me, and I snapped the eff out of it.

My eyes darted from her to the field and back, worried Jacksonville had scored on us. It was a time-out. "What?" I asked, noticing she held her cell.

"Check out what Sabrina just Snapped." She handed me

her cell, and when I saw the screen, I damn near dropped it.

Plan worked.

It actually freaking worked.

Clinging to it with weak fingers, I forced my breath to slow. It wasn't Sabrina's model-worthy selfie that had me fearing I'd pass out right then and there. It was her comment splayed over a screenshot of the bio page of the website I'd launched last night—at *two a.m.*

> *Whoever is behind this is a flippin'*
> *goddess! I don't know about y'all, but I*
> *could use the $250 gift card. Here's the*
> *code to find the page. Everyone follow it.*
> *Now. Party at my place if I win!*

"This is her messing around, right?" Hannah asked, taking the phone back, and I pressed my lips closed.

I had posted the giveaway as an incentive for web traffic—sacrificing half my regular check from the coffee shop—hoping someone found it and spread the word, but *holy Loki's helmet*, I didn't think the most popular girl at school would get a hold of it so quickly. Sabrina was connected to *everyone* on social media—Wilmont and plenty of other schools surrounding us. And she'd just shared my midnight creation to all of them.

"Maybe?" I said, my voice coming out a whisper.

This is what I'd wanted, right? A following from Wilmont. That way I could potentially help someone who needed it. And it would get back to Principal Tanner and throw his tight-gripped rule off kilter.

"No," Hannah said, completely ignoring the game to swipe on her cell. "Check it out. The site is legit."

I glanced at the screen again, already knowing what

she'd pulled up.

My site.

My stomach rolled as I pretended to read what I'd spent countless hours crafting. I hadn't expected it to reach my best friend so fast...

"Huh," I said, instead of a proper response.

"Huh?" She scoffed, taking the cell and pocketing it. "That's it? This is exactly what we were talking about yesterday! Do you think someone heard us?"

I chuckled. "Nah," I said, shrugging. "You saw the prank. We're not the only ones totally over the way Tanner runs this school. Someone just decided to take the rebellion a step further." I motioned to the cell I could no longer see, unable to meet her eyes.

"True," she said. "This is crazy, though." An excited smile shaped her lips. "I can't wait to see who actually writes in."

Me, too.

I cleared my throat, ignoring the urge to dig in my bag for my laptop and check if Sabrina's post had resulted in any questions.

A cold sweat broke out on the back of my neck. How the hell would I find the answers? What if I couldn't? What if I failed someone who needed me?

This is really happening.

"Amber, you okay?"

I snapped my eyes to hers, taking a deep breath to calm the nausea rolling my stomach.

"Yeah. Why?"

She arched a brow at me. "You look..."

"Tired," I filled in for her. "I was up late."

"And that's different from any other day?" she teased.

I forced a laugh. "Right. Later than usual."

"Did Dean have anything to do with that?" She nudged

me, and I was grateful that the topic had shifted from the website calling for my attention.

I wanted to tell her about it. Wanted her to be there to go through this massive project with me. But I couldn't risk her involvement. I'd locked up the site's origin so well I didn't think anyone would be able to trace it, but still. I was taking a big enough risk pulling something like this at Wilmont, over Principal Tanner. Plus, I'd promised Dean I wouldn't tell anyone, and I expected him to do the same. Fewer people involved to get burned if we got caught.

Which I had no intention of doing.

Ever.

Besides, no one could even write in.

"Yes," I finally admitted. "We have a bet between us. I was working on my end of it." I sighed. It felt good to at least tell her a half truth.

"Ohh," she said over the roaring crowd. Wilmont had just scored. "I love this so much! What are the terms?"

I pressed my lips into a line, shaking my head. "I'm sworn to secrecy."

She stomped her foot. "That is so unfair!"

"It's techie stuff." I laughed, the tension breaking within me. "It would bore you."

"Anything with you and Dean working together or against each other or whatever is *so* not boring."

"Why are you so obsessed with the time I spend with him?"

"Because," she said. "He's a good guy. And you deserve to be around a good guy who gets all that intricate wiring you have tangled in your pretty little head."

I grinned, rolling my eyes.

We'd thought Brandon was a good guy, too.

A cold chill raced down my spine. The same deep iciness

that built a wall around my heart, forbidding me from even thinking of Dean that way.

"You really can't tell me?" she asked.

"No. It's no big deal. Just something between us."

A massive grin slid over her face. "Sounds romantic."

"Platonic. Promise. He's a friend. That's all."

A gorgeous, delicious-smelling friend. And this challenge was bringing us closer, despite being in opposition. Maybe it *would* be good for me. To get to know him beyond the halls of Wilmont, beyond our normal exchange of hacker-only info. It could be nice…having him as a friend.

Something I'd never really entertained before, because Brandon dominated all my free time, ensuring I barely had time to hack, let alone get closer with someone else.

"Fine," she said, her tone completely understanding. "That's a start, anyway." She winked at me, her focus returning to Jake on the field.

I didn't see the plays or touchdowns. I didn't hear the cheers of the crowd around me. I was in my head, contemplating my next step with the website, wondering how many hits Sabrina's post had gotten me, wishing I could ditch the game and check but at the same time grateful that I couldn't.

Because once I did, it would be real. More real than it lighting up my best friend's cell phone. More real than Sabrina telling thousands about it.

I wasn't ready.

But I had to be.

"Yay!" Hannah clapped and cheered as the game ended, Wilmont winning. "Come on!" She clutched my wrist and propelled me down the steps. She shoved her way through the bodies doing the same thing, pushing us through the pack and to the fence that lined the field.

I sucked in a breath when we cleared the crowd, the pressure easing on my lungs at being pinned among so many people. The fence was less packed, the mass of students heading toward the exit in drones.

"Great game, Jake!" Hannah called as he walked to the other side of the fence, his helmet tucked underneath his arm.

"Thanks, babe," he said.

Sweat dripped down his golden-brown skin, a clear line of dirt showing exactly where his helmet had been. He leaned down, planting a deep, long kiss onto Hannah's lips, and the girl didn't flinch at the ick of the game all over him. No, she snaked her fingers around his neck, soaking her nails in the dripping black hair at the base of his neck, *tugging* him closer. If the fence hadn't been between them...

I shuddered and turned my head the opposite direction. I'd seen them embrace like this plenty of times—my house was one of the only places they could be fully relaxed and themselves. Hannah's parents weren't the strictest, but there was one issue they'd never budge on and that was sex before marriage. But it didn't mean I enjoyed being the third wheel to their true-love show.

It hadn't always been like this. For a while I'd been a *fourth*. Smiling and congratulating just like Hannah—

"Amber."

My spine turned into a steel rod while my legs felt like Jell-O.

I swallowed a mouthful of acid, turning to set eyes on Brandon. He brushed past Jake, who was still completely tangled up in Hannah, their PDA totally concealed by the bustling crowd still leaving the stadium.

"Brandon." His name passed my lips quietly, timidly, where I'd intended it to be sharper than a razor. I was stronger than this, damn it. Why did one look at his dark eyes, muscles, and shiny, buzzed-black hair turn me into a weak...*victim*?

He shifted his helmet under his arm, stopping at the fence right in front of me. His eyes roamed up and down my body. I was suddenly conscious of the rips in my new jeans and the tiny strips of skin they exposed.

I took one step back, clutching the strap of my bag.

"Didn't think you'd show," he said, his tone smooth, casual, like our breakup never happened. Like I wasn't glaring at him as if I could mentally throw him across the football field.

"I'm here for Jake."

Brandon cut his eyes to my best friend before returning to me. "See they appreciate it."

I rolled my eyes—anger helped loosen the tight air in my lungs. "What do you want?" Why was he here? Why wasn't he having a post-game celebration with his new girl? I'd heard it was Sabrina, but that could just be a rumor. It was hard to tell anymore, especially since I'd stopped paying attention.

"Why does it have to be like that?" he asked, and he had the audacity to genuinely look confused. Like I should be pumped about him talking to me again.

You know why.

I furrowed my brow.

He sighed, shifting his weight. "Just thought I'd say hi," he said, shrugging. "You coming to Sabrina's party after?" He motioned toward the exit.

"That'd be a no," I said, a dark laugh on the end of it.

"We used to have fun." He narrowed his eyes. "You used to *be* fun." He shook his head. "Now you're just..."

I swallowed the rock in my throat.

Whatever I am, it's because of you.

"Brandon?" Jake snapped, looking like he only now realized he was next to him.

Hannah was at my side in an instant, dagger-glares and claws bared.

Brandon chuckled, holding up his hands—one with his helmet—as he backed away from the fence. "Yeah, man," he said, eyeing Jake. "I get it." He planted his dark eyes on mine. "Was just saying hi to a friend."

"Don't," Jake said, his tone sharp and everything I'd wished mine could be.

Brandon huffed, spun on his heels, and jogged toward the exit.

"Sorry," Hannah said. "You could've said something."

"No use. He doesn't merit the energy." I wished my heart would believe that, be as strong as that thought. "But," I said, glancing between them, "thanks."

Jake flashed those white teeth. "I've always got your back."

Hannah nodded her agreement, rubbing her hand up and down my back.

I sighed, the internal shaking subsiding with my tribe surrounding me. "That's more comforting than you know," I said, grinning softly. After a silent shared look between Jake and Hannah—their own brand of communicating that was perfected over years of being together—I stepped out of Hannah's touch. "I've really got to crash," I said. "My brain is going fuzzy."

"Oh no," Hannah said. "We all know that leads to binging on Oreos and fail-YouTube-videos." She laughed, jerking her head toward the exit. "Let's get out of here."

"You don't know me."

She scoffed. "Yeah, right." She glanced at Jake. "I'll text

you later." She blew him a kiss and we fell in with the last stragglers of the crowd leaving.

I hugged her outside my car, silently siphoning her happiness and support to wash away the bad taste that talking to Brandon had left in my mouth.

"See you tomorrow," I said, sinking behind the wheel.

As I watched her walk to her car parked a few spaces down, I sucked in a sharp breath. I didn't have time to dwell on my past or Brandon's need to seek me out tonight. I had a challenge to cultivate and hopefully, classmates to help.

I pulled out of the parking lot, wondering just how I'd go about doing that, and hoping like hell I'd be enough.

For once.

I knew I needed sleep, that I needed to unplug and recharge. But after seeing Sabrina's post, I knew I wouldn't be able to resist checking the site when I got home. A few more hours awake wouldn't kill me.

So, instead of heading straight home, I drove toward my favorite taco shop to grab some much-needed fuel.

CHAPTER EIGHT

DEAN

"What brings you out here?" Tessa asked from behind the counter, her bright yellow shirt clashing with her dark hair.

"I brought you a treat," I said, handing her the grande iced mocha I'd picked up on my way over.

She eyed the drink, then me. "Why?"

I tilted my head. "Act like I don't do this on the reg."

"Thanks!" She chuckled, her suspicions clearing as she took the drink. "I *so* needed it. We just finished a major rush."

I scanned the quaint taco shop, noting the packed tables. It was a laid-back place, its regular customers that of the Wilmont variety. Tessa had worked here for a year now, and I made sure to stop by randomly sometimes when she had a shift—check up on my baby sister *and* free tacos. Win, win.

She slurped the drink, her eyes rolling back in her head for a moment before she set it behind the counter. "So. Good." She glanced behind me, her customer-service smile dominating her face. "What can I get you?"

I stepped to the side, not wanting to be in the customer's way.

"Number four. To go, please."

Amber's voice had me whirling around like I was hooked on a magnet she controlled. "Pixie," I said, eyeing her. "Shouldn't you be in bed?"

That beautiful blush I'd seen earlier flushed her cheeks,

but she sharpened her features.

I smirked, loving the way she could be soft and fierce at the same time. Remembering our earlier chat, I cleared my throat and dropped the flirt that came automatically. "I mean," I said, stepping closer to her, "haven't you been running full-speed all day on only a few hours?"

"Haven't you?" she challenged.

"Yes," I said.

"And yet you're allowed to be here and I'm not?" There was a tease in her tone, but I held my hands up.

"Not what I meant."

She popped her hip to the side, which only drew my attention to the sexy black jeans she wore tucked into a pair of silver Converse. I hadn't seen her outside of school that much, but when I did? Damn, I couldn't get enough of those glimpses of the real her—the pixie not buried underneath the school's uniform.

"You seem to do that a lot," she said, and I snapped my eyes back up to hers.

"What?"

"Say one thing and mean another."

I shook my head. "Now you're just twisting things."

She shrugged. "I call it how I see it."

"That's not—"

"Dean," Tessa cut me off. "Can you let the girl get her food on?"

I cut my sister a glare before glancing back at Amber. "Of course," I said. "I'll have what she's having, but make the order for here."

Amber smiled before forcing those pink lips into a line. "I've got to get home."

"Why?" I cocked a brow at her. "Working late again in an attempt to beat me?"

Tessa hissed. "You didn't get into a bet with him, did you?" she asked Amber, pity in her eyes.

Amber tipped her chin, her gaze churning with a sliver of light. Something I only now realized hadn't been present for the past five minutes.

"Where did you come from?" I asked before she could answer my sister.

She tilted her head, ignoring me. "Yes, I did," she said to Tessa. "And I'm going to kick his ass." The bite in her tone made my insides all kinds of hot, and I laughed.

Tessa grinned, reaching over the counter to give Amber a fist bump. "Nice," she said. "If there's anything I can help with to take him down, let me know." She leaned farther over, lowering her voice. "I've got tons of dirt on him."

I gaped at her. "I'll take that mocha back now."

"No take-backs." She punched in our orders.

I rolled my eyes, returning focus to Amber, who was pulling out her wallet. "Stop," I said. "I've got this."

"I told you earlier, flattery won't throw me off my game."

"No games. I just want to buy you some food. The least you can do is sit and eat with me."

She chewed on the corner of her lip, a habit I wasn't even sure she was aware of. I held my breath, wondering why whatever her answer would be was so damn important to me. I'd see her tomorrow. We'd already established that. So why was I dying for another hour?

Maybe it's that look in her eyes.

That cold, distant look that she'd had when I'd first turned around. Like she'd just come from a horror film and it had sunk beneath her skin.

I stepped even closer, watching the debate in her eyes. "Friends can share tacos, right?"

Something clicked behind those eyes when I said the

word *friends*, and I smiled softly at her. She'd told me earlier she'd sworn off guys, relationships, all of it. And I knew that had everything to do with Brandon, I just didn't know the circumstances. Brandon was an okay guy, I guess. If you liked jocks who played the jerk card too often and thought burping the alphabet was a fun pastime. Or maybe that was just the dude I knew from years of gym classes together. Either way, she'd seemed happy enough with him all last year…but now something haunted her.

And I *wanted* to know what.

Again, that undeniable sensation to break past the barrier we'd held ourselves at in the past tugged at my core, begging me to get closer.

As friends.

Yes. Absolutely. Just friends.

The sharp twist in my gut thinking the word had me wanting to take back my offer and bolt through the exit, but I told myself to not be a coward.

"Okay," she finally agreed, her voice so small I almost didn't hear it.

Tessa slid two trays piled high with four tacos, chips and salsa, and guac toward us. I grabbed them before Amber could change her mind and headed toward a free booth tucked in the back corner near the windows. Setting the trays down, I motioned for her to take a seat while I grabbed the empty cups.

I held one up. "Green tea?"

She smiled. "Yes, please."

By the time I got back from filling up our drinks, Amber was already halfway through one brisket taco, the queso fresco dropping to the paper beneath her.

She licked some stray pico off her lips as I sat down, and my breath caught for a few seconds.

This girl. I loved how she wasn't afraid to be herself and didn't give a damn what anyone else thought.

Hot.

Friends.

I stopped staring at her like she held the key to every secret I wanted to know and handed her the drink.

"Thanks," she said. "For this, too." She scooped up her half-eaten taco and finished it off. "I really needed the fuel."

"Same," I said. "It's why I stopped here."

"I figured you were just checking up on your baby sister," she said.

I glanced over my shoulder toward the counter where Tessa cleaned the surface, since there were no more customers. I turned back around and grabbed my own taco. "Don't tell *her* that," I said before chomping into the tortilla.

"Never," she said, chuckling. "I think it's cute."

I raised my brows at her mid-bite.

"I'm an only child." She scooped up her second taco. "The idea of having a sibling, someone bound by blood to have your back..." Her eyes trailed to the side, that same cold, distant gaze threatening to come back. "It'd be nice."

I swallowed my bite a little too hard.

"Where did you come from?" I asked again.

She laughed, setting down her taco to take a fast drink of tea. "You sound like a vampire."

"What?" I nearly choked on my Coke.

"*True Blood*," she said like that would explain everything. "The vamps are always asking the beautiful girl what she is. Where she came from." Her eyes widened, that blush coming back. "Not that I'm calling myself beautiful—"

Instinctively, I reached across the table, gently touching her wrist to cut off her ramble. "It's okay," I said, and she took a breath. She eyed my hand, her chest rising and falling a little too fast. I withdrew it, occupying my fingers with another taco even though I itched to feel her soft skin again. "You are," I said. "By the way." I took a massive bite, shoveling the avocado-pork gold into my mouth before I could say anything else stupid.

She glanced down at her hands like she suddenly forgot what to do with them. "Football game."

I blinked a few times, totally thrown by the response.

I tilted my head. "You want to play?"

The smile on her lips cleared the confusion and cut right through the tension. She shook her head. "No," she said. "That's where I came from."

"Oh," I said, nodding. "Why?"

"That's a damn good question." The sigh was heavy and long as she grabbed her third taco. "Went to watch Jake."

Hannah's boyfriend, right. That made sense.

The look on her face when she'd first walked in? No sense at all.

"Did we lose?" I asked, wondering if it was a game loss plus sleep deprivation combo making her look like she was drained. The normal, glittering pixie...she was *wilted*.

Maybe she really didn't want to eat with me.

Maybe she saw me standing at the counter and I ruined her idea of fun solo-tacos.

I told myself to shut the hell up and waited patiently for her to finish chewing so she could answer me.

"No," she said. "They won."

"Huh," I said.

"What?"

I shrugged, shaking my head. I knew we weren't the kind of friends who directly asked *what's wrong, tell me your problems and let me help...please.*

"What?" she asked again, wiping her hands and mouth

with her napkin.

"Nothing," I said.

She arched a brow at me.

"You seem…" *Hurt. Scared. Confused.*

"Tired?" She groaned. "You already told me I looked like crap earlier today. No need to rub it in hours later."

"I did not," I said. "And I also told you that you were beautiful seconds ago." I didn't lose her gaze and was happy that fire was back in her eyes. "I was going to say, you look distracted. Like something is eating at you." I took the last bite of my fourth taco, occupying myself like I didn't have a care in the world if she told me what it was or not. If I'd learned anything from Tessa, it was that more often than not, a lot of girls wanted the space and patience and choice to talk. The more you tried to force it out of them, the harder they dug in.

"Oh," she said, slurping down the green tea like it was oxygen. I understood the need—we all had our go-to fuels that would help push us across a late-night goal. Her eyes went distant again, and I wanted to slide around the table and sit *right* next to her. Get in her space so much I could crack whatever plagued her mind. "Ran into someone at the game. Didn't want to."

A burst of hope exploded inside my chest at her confession. At something real. Something she could've easily been vague about or blown me off altogether.

Maybe she was starting to trust me.

Who wouldn't she want to see?

Oh.

Fuck.

"Brandon?" The name blurted from my mouth, half growl, half question.

She flinched like it physically hurt her.

Damn it, what did he do to you?

"Sorry," I said. "It's none of my business."

"No." The word blasted all that hope right out of me. "It's okay," she said, and those two words amended it in an instant. "I'm just tired," she said and laughed a little. "I wasn't at 100 percent to handle his douchery tonight."

"Fuck him," I said, loving the shock in her eyes at my declaration.

"Do you even know him?" She swirled a tortilla chip in guac. "It's not like you run in the same circles."

I snorted. "That's for damn sure." I leaned a little closer over the table. "You and I both know people like us have our own circles."

"Yeah," she said, almost a whisper.

"And they normally only include a few people. Sometimes less."

"Only the ones you can trust," she added.

"Exactly."

"But," she said, blinking a few times as I leaned back in my seat. "Everyone likes you."

I shrugged. "I'm friendly with a lot of people. That doesn't mean they're in my circle. Doesn't mean I'd call them if I was in deep shit."

"I get that." She pushed a stray piece of pink-streaked hair away from her eyes. "It can bite you anyway. Letting people in."

"Not always," I assured her.

She nodded, fiddling with a strap bracelet on her left wrist. It was black with thin green lines in a random rectangular-like pattern. I rarely saw her without it.

"Are we friends?" she asked, never looking up from her bracelet.

My chest puffed at the question. At the hope in her tone.

"Think that depends on you, Pixie."

She snapped her eyes to mine. "Why?"

I gazed at her, my eyes drawing from hers to her hair to the line of her jaw, the racing pulse at her neck, and back to her eyes. "Because," I said. "I already trust you."

"How?" she asked. "This is the first time we've hung out beyond school...ever."

"Easy," I said. "*DC*."

"Our alert code?" She chuckled. "That's all it takes to earn your trust? Me giving you a heads-up when someone is about to catch you hacking instead of doing actual schoolwork?"

"It's not the only factor, but it's a big one."

"What are the others?"

I wetted my lips, grinning when the motion caught her gaze. "Too many to list."

She raised her brows. "Well," she said, her mouth opening and closing like she couldn't figure out what to say.

"It's okay, Pixie," I said, stopping her before she could speak. "I know it'll take a hell of a lot more for me to earn your trust. To earn a spot in your circle. And I'm fine with that. I'm just asking for a chance."

She swallowed hard. "As friends."

The knife in my heart was sharp, but a good reminder that was all I needed, too.

"Friends."

A soft smile shaped her pink lips, and she gathered both our empty trays, standing to take them to the trash before I could argue.

My cell buzzed with notifications, enough that I gave the screen a quick swipe.

Sabrina, resident Queen of Wilmont, had blasted a new blog across the social media feeds. I hadn't realized she was linked with mine.

"*Ask Me Anything*," I read aloud, my brow furrowing as I scanned the main page. A sex advice blog? From a Wilmont student. Person had balls, I'd give them that, and I idly wondered if whoever had pulled the prank at the assembly was the same one behind this.

"So I—" Amber's words died in her throat, her eyes flashing wide when she caught sight of my screen.

"You see this, too?" I asked, pocketing my phone. She hadn't moved to sit back down. I shifted in the booth, looking up at her, my arm easily stretched to one side on the booth railing, practically begging her to slide in next to me. The way she trailed her gaze over me, the way that sweet blush crept in her cheeks, it almost seemed like she could read my mind.

"Thanks for the tacos," she said, ignoring my question and grabbing her bag from the other side of the booth. She threw it over her shoulder. "Friend." She spun around, a flurry of black and pink and light as she left in a hurry.

I sat motionless and smiling at her back.

"Guess we know who the other member of Code Club is now," Tessa said, sinking into the seat where Amber had just been.

I straightened, switching my goofy grin to something much sharper. "Your point being?" I asked. I'd already told Sean; there wasn't really any mystery anymore.

"You're in so much trouble."

I furrowed my brow. "What are you talking about?"

She motioned to me with an opened palm. "If you could see yourself right now, you'd understand. It's the same way you were the other day after the club."

"No idea what you're talking about."

But I did. I could feel it. Sense it in the way my heart raced. The way I wanted to keep smiling but choked down the action.

"The brother who swears up and down that relationships are nothing but an unnecessary distraction. The brother who gives me shit constantly for having a boyfriend. Just had a date."

"I did not," I said. "We're friends."

Tessa just looked at me, unbelieving.

"We are." I shrugged. "She's cool. I can be happy about that without wanting to marry her."

Tessa laughed. "I never said anything about marrying the girl." She laughed. "But it's great to know where your head is at."

I smacked my palms on the table, shoving out of the booth. "Good talk, sis."

She followed me all the way to the exit, still wearing that grin.

I paused with my hand on the door. "Colt picking you up or do you want a ride?" It didn't matter how much she was currently annoying me, I would always ask if she needed me.

"Colt," she said. "He texted a few minutes ago. Already on his way."

I debated waiting until he showed up, but Tessa was already shoving me out the door.

"I've got to do closing duties in a few anyway," she said. "Go home. Sleep. Dream about taking a hacker girl to prom."

I flipped her off as I walked out the door, not sure if I was angrier at her being totally off-point or voicing thoughts I didn't dare acknowledge.

CHAPTER NINE

AMBER

After a quick check-in with Mom and Dad, I raced up the stairs and cracked open my laptop.

Newly fueled with tacos and green tea, I was ready to see if I'd gotten any questions on the site that Sabrina had plastered all over social media.

I tried not to let myself hope, but even if I had *one* question, it would be a success.

One deep breath and a few clicks later, and I nearly fell out of my computer chair.

"A thousand views?" I spoke aloud, cracking the silence in my room.

And...

212 comments?

I leaned back in my chair, gaping at the screen.

Excitement rushed through my veins so fast my fingertips shook. I quickly read the first comment, and then the next and the next.

Most of them were people cheering me on or giving me a big *hell yes* to the site. Some were more vulgar—like *RedSoxFanForLife3897* who'd left fourteen comments about how he'd like to find out just how much I really knew about sex, emphasizing that he could teach me more than I'd ever dreamed. I rolled my eyes at most, but some were downright stomach turning.

And really...I hadn't come up with a solid plan on *how*

to answer the questions. Honestly, I hadn't expected this response. Hadn't expected this many people to write in.

I swallowed hard, forcing myself to keep reading, assuring myself that when *the* question came, I'd know what to do.

A good portion of comments were people asking my real name, promising me they'd never tell anyone.

I was on my third green tea by the time I reached comment #183, still searching for *the* question I thought would need immediate attention.

There were a few I'd starred to come back to and contemplate, but there hadn't been one that gave me that *aha!* feeling. And with the traffic growing by the second—up to three thousand views in the span of the three hours I'd been reading—I needed my first actual blog to be noteworthy.

Sharp. Funny and smart and helpful.

If I blew the first one, no one would ever come back to ask more questions, and then not only would I not help anyone, but I would also lose the challenge between Dean and me.

Another hour and I swore my eyeballs were going to fall out. I only had six hours before I needed to be up for school, and I finally knew I had it when I read commenter #201's question.

ASK ME ANYTHING

ABOUT   USEFUL LINKS   FAQ   CHAT WITH ME

QUESTION OF THE DAY

Whereiswill98 asks: *"Things are getting super heated between me and my boyfriend. In a good way. But I'm wanting to get on the pill before we take the next step. I don't want my parents to know. They would flip the eff out. I saw your list on the site, but where is the most discreet place to get some?"*

I'm sorry to hear that your parents would flip. That sucks in a big bad way. But it's one of the reasons I created this blog. So you could get answers without dealing with parental backlash. I hate the idea of lying/keeping secrets from your parents, but it's your body and you have the right to protect yourself.

It can get pricey if you're not going to use your parents' insurance, but you can be prescribed birth control by a physician at a number of the Planned Parenthoods around here (I'll include a link to a list below). Some walk-in clinics who don't require insurance can also hook you up.

You'll have to go through an exam (I know, bummer) but after that, you should be set to get the protection you need. While you're waiting, if you find you *can't* wait, definitely use a condom.

Staying safe is wicked important, and it's awesome that you're already thinking that far ahead. To be double on top of things, even when you start taking the pill, I'd suggest you keep using that condom, too, because the pill doesn't protect you from other problems...like all those horrid STDs we saw in the Wilmont Way presentation.

In the meantime,
Stay Sexy. Stay Healthy.

Click <u>here</u> for a complete list of places to score BC near us!

hit publish and closed my laptop.

I'd thought my "useful links" tab would've been enough to cover this topic, but there was a real fear surrounding a lot of the people writing in about being caught trying to get on birth control.

Hard for me to relate but easy for me to picture.

Not everyone had a mom like mine. One who took me to the doctor after I told her things were starting to get serious between Brandon and me. She'd talked me through all the pros and cons and let me make the choice for myself. Ultimately, I'd been so blindingly happy and excited to be with Brandon that I'd gotten on the pill with butterflies storming my stomach.

I'd planned to tell Brandon.

I'd dreamed of the perfect moment.

And then…he'd crushed those dreams before I'd gotten the chance to share them with him.

I dodged a major bullet, and yet I still felt like I was bleeding.

The wound he'd left was slowly closing, though, and as I traced my fingers over my still-warm laptop, I knew starting this blog had a ton to do with it.

And Mom.

Dad and Hannah and Jake, too.

My small yet irreplaceable tribe.

Sometimes I forgot how lucky I was.

At least I was using the info Mom had given me back then for some good now.

Or what I hoped would be good. Hoped I was helping.

One person at a time. That's all I needed.

And the rest of me would eventually fall into place.

CHAPTER TEN

AMBER

"See ya, Gary!" I called to my boss as he waved to me while he walked out the exit. The bell above the door chimed, and I waited a full fifteen minutes before reaching for my laptop that I kept in my designated cubby behind the coffee bar.

Comic Brew—the coffee shop/comic bookstore I worked at part time—was pretty dead for a Friday night. A group of sophomores had taken up residence at one of our largest booths, completely immersed in an intense game of Clue as they sipped their cappuccinos.

One of the sweet perks—besides the comics and stellar coffee—was the insane amount of board games we had for people to play. Gary was an awesome boss and let me have flexible hours, but the chill vibe of the place was the perfect counter to my normally high-speed, high-tech life. Board games, people actually interacting with each other in the real world, it was all balancing for me—even if I rarely played where I worked. But being in the presence of it helped me keep one foot in the real world while the rest of me was often lost in cyberspace.

Doing another scan to make sure no one would see what I worked on, I pulled up my website. It had been a week since my first blog went live.

It had over five thousand hits, and the girl who'd asked the question had already emailed me to thank me. I'd felt *unworthy* of that thanks as I read it, but when I gave the email a second pass, some small piece of my jagged heart had...healed. The gratification, the notion that in this one moment I was doing the right thing—despite the fact that I'd be expelled and could kiss my hopeful acceptance letter to MIT goodbye if I was ever caught—filled me with this awesome sense of purpose I couldn't properly explain. It was enough that I was devising a plan to post every day. To try to help as much and as often as I could—and if the blog got so big it counteracted every Dark-Aged piece of propaganda Tanner's site posted, then win-win.

As I scrolled through the never-ending inbox of comments, I wondered what Dean was working on. Wondered what his challenge entailed and if it was as scandalous as mine. Knowing him, it would be more discreet. He'd already seen mine—that night at the taco shop—though he didn't have a clue I was behind the blog, and I hadn't given him a chance to offer his thoughts on it.

My stomach fluttered, even though I told it to calm down. We'd had Code Club two nights ago, and one tonight that I'd had to cut short because of my shift.

We'd worked at the same table but facing each other so neither one of us could see what the other was working on, the backs of our laptop screens almost touching. It was a comfortable yet charged silence, one I found myself looking forward to all week.

It wasn't like we chatted the whole time. Or at all in some cases, when we got fully into the zone. It was just *him*. He was this soothing, positive energy that acted like a balm to all the sticky darkness trying to smother me from my past.

I'd learned that much when we'd had tacos together. The way he talked about wanting to be friends, and how rare true friends were. He didn't want anything from me.

Didn't demand things from me or give me flack about how I spent my time.

We were the same, and yet different.

The Clue table roared with laughter, the clinking of mugs and metal spoons drawing me back to business. Not coffee business but blog business. I scrolled through a few more comments, my eyes glazing at the fourth dude to ask me if I preferred thongs to bikinis to bare.

Bells chimed, and I called my usual, "Welcome to Comic Brew," not bothering to look up. Usually people were comic-bound more than coffee, and I didn't want to hound them as they searched the endless selection.

"Whatcha working on?" Dean asked, his voice jolting every single sense I possessed.

I bolted upright from my leaned position over my laptop, slamming the screen closed.

"Nothing!"

He cocked a brow at me, his gaze widening. "We legit were just working together an hour ago." He glanced at my closed laptop, my palm still lying protectively over it. "You're already up to something that merits *that* kind of reaction?" He *tsk*ed me teasingly, wagging his finger.

I chuckled, calming my nerves. "What are you doing here?"

He leaned against the counter, his blue eyes scanning the shop. "I finished updating the school's website with the list Tanner had emailed me, and it got boring in Code Club all by myself," he said, returning that gaze to me. "Figured I'd finally come see where you worked."

He came here to see me?

The breath caught in my throat, my heart filling my lungs, my stomach melting.

Relax! Friends, remember?

"You were lonely?" I teased, hating that my voice hitched at the thought of him missing the time we spent together.

"Maybe," he said, flashing me that damn smile.

"Coffee?" I asked.

"Ah," he said. "So you missed me, too."

"What?" I furrowed my brow. "How'd you make that leap?"

"You just invited me to stay."

My lips parted, then popped closed. I shook my head, storing my laptop in my cubby. "I work here. I ask everyone if they want coffee."

"Just admit it," he said, laughter in his tone. "You like having me around."

I gaped at him. "You're so full of yourself."

"Full of *truth*. I see everything."

I froze, the words sinking beneath my skin.

Could he see me so easily? Sense that there was something dark sucking at me from the inside and that only recently I'd started to gather and toss tiny pieces of it away?

He must be able to, because the longer I stood motionless, the more the laughter left his eyes, serious concern taking its place.

"Americano?" I finally managed to ask.

"Sounds perfect." He cleared his throat, pushing off the counter to stand straight.

Damn, he could *sense* it. My fear over the fact had killed his playful mood. Something twisted inside my stomach, desperate for it to come back. I turned away from him, happy to not have his penetrating gaze on me as I pressed the espresso into the machine and waited on it to brew.

"So, what *were* you working on?" he asked as I slid the mug toward him.

Heat pulsed in my cheeks as my mind circled back to the

last comment I'd read—a girl asking if I'd ever fantasized about being with another girl. It was a solid question, one I was sure both sexes pondered, but I wasn't sure if it was *the* question for the next blog. I wouldn't know until I'd made it through the latest batch of comments. I made a mental note to file it under my starred section so that if the blog continued to be successful, I could address it later. I'd need as many valid and vital questions as I could to post daily.

"Damn," he said before I answered, and I snapped out of my thoughts. "Were you looking at shirtless photos of Ryan Gosling or something?"

A laugh ripped from my chest. "No. Why?"

He took a fast sip of his Americano before nodding toward my face. "You're blushing."

"I am not." I covered my cheeks. "It's warm in here."

"That's the only excuse you ever have," he teased, referring to our chat from two weeks ago.

"I wasn't."

He pressed his lips together, mischief in his blue-gray eyes. "Ryan Reynolds?"

I shook my head.

"Chris Hemsworth?"

"No." I laughed.

"Evans?"

"Nope."

"Pine?"

I chuckled.

"Pratt?"

"No."

He sighed, setting his mug down. "Scarlett Johansson?"

"This is a fun game." I smiled but shook my head.

"It's not as fun as I thought it'd be."

"Why?" I asked, leaning over the counter. "Because

you're losing?"

"Because you're cheating."

I scoffed. "I am not!"

"There is *no* way you're not attracted to *one* of those people."

"I never said that." I smirked. "They're all insanely gorgeous and I love them in their characters for different reasons."

"But," he said, wrinkling his nose like he was trying to figure me out. "They aren't enough to make you blush."

I shrugged.

"Give me a hint."

"Why does it matter?"

"Because," he said. "I was bored and now I'm not. Plus, I'm not good at giving up on things. You may as well just tell me."

I pressed my lips into a line, having too much fun with him guessing my all-time-favorite fangirl-crush.

"I'll figure it out." The determination in his voice made me straighten.

"*You* can't cheat!"

He feigned innocence. "How would I cheat? It's not like I can hack your brain."

Why did that sound like he wanted to? "But you *could* hack my secret Pinterest boards."

"Oh," he said, smirking. "Thanks for the tip."

"Ugh," I groaned. "You're impossible."

"One of those boy band singers?"

"Ew, gross, no." Not that I had anything against boy bands, but I wasn't fantasizing about them. I gave that up after the age of twelve.

"*Ew*," he repeated. "Good to know." He sipped his Americano, looking thoughtful.

"This is ridiculous," I finally said. "Why is it so important to you to know who would make me blush?"

"Well, I already know *I* can make you blush," he said, his smile soft, careful. "Now I want to know who and what else does."

"Why?" I asked again.

"Because it's adorable."

I glared at him.

"*And*," he added, "I like to hear you laugh."

I dropped my glare, now just looking at him. Seeing him. This friendship we'd started—the game we'd been playing—it was deepening. I was thirsty for these conversations, needed them in a way I hadn't realized. Hannah and Jake were amazing, but sometimes I needed to hang around someone who understood me. And Dean was on his way to uncovering everything about me without even trying.

What was it that made him such an incredible friend in such a short amount of time? Was it because we shared the same dreams? Kept the same hours? Laughed at the same things?

"I bet I can guess yours," I said, ready to put the spotlight back on him.

He raised his brows, his fingers on his chest. "Oh really? You think you can guess *my* celebrity?"

I nodded, studying him in the same way he had me, enjoying the way he wetted his lips—a nervous tic I'd witnessed several times this week. "Scarlett Johansson."

He burst out laughing.

"What?"

"You can't just steal guesses I've already given."

I shrugged. "There are no rules to this game."

"She's hot," he said. "But not my number one."

I pursed my lips, thinking. I didn't have much to go on—

his lack of previous relationships totally unhelpful. He was gorgeous and smart and hilarious. He literally could have any girl he wanted in a snap.

"Megan Fox?"

He shook his head. "Wrong again, Pixie."

I breathed a sigh of relief.

A thought crept into my mind, something clicking with the way he curled his tongue around my alias.

Pixie.

I shivered, a warm chill racing down my spine, then snapped my fingers. "I've got it."

"I doubt it."

"Natalie Portman." She was stunning, smart, and favored pixie cuts on occasion. I was either on the money or totally off base.

His mouth dropped, and he glared at me. "Cheater."

I clapped my hands together. "Yes! I love winning."

He growled, a low rumble that resonated deep in my chest. "How in the hell did you guess that?"

"I'm a genius," I said. "You'll learn this."

He grinned, but defeat was clear in his eyes.

"She's in a movie with mine." I dropped the hint he'd been asking for and he perked up.

"I already said Chris Hemsworth."

"Do you think I *only* watch superhero movies?"

"Is it bad to say that I like you more because I know you do?"

I chuckled. Sure, I favored the Marvel and DC universes, but I liked other movies, too. I was sure of it.

"Ugh," he said. "Not that French guy from the swan movie."

"No." I sighed. "Maybe you should give up."

"Never." The finality in the word shot sparks across my

skin. Or maybe it was the way he gazed at me, his attention fully on me in a way I'd never seen before. Brandon had rarely been this tuned in, unless he…

Flashes of his lips on mine, his tongue in my mouth, the kisses I'd given him willingly, twisted like sharp bits of metal in my mind.

"Pixie," Dean said, his fingers over my hand. "Where'd you go?"

I opened my mouth, ready to tell him, I was *that* lost in my head.

Luckily, I stopped the admission on my tongue. The confession of what robbed me so many times of my train of thought I couldn't keep up.

"Nowhere," I said, glancing down at his hand on mine. A friendly gesture—comforting and warm and enough to stop the ice that had formed in my veins.

"Someday," he said, drawing his hand back, "I hope you'll tell me."

"Tell you what?" I asked, my voice coming out as a whisper.

He leaned down on the counter so that he was eye level with me. So close I could smell him over the espresso scent that filled the shop. My mouth watered.

"What's eating at you."

I shrugged off his too-perceptiveness.

He sighed, standing straight again, so tall I had to look up to meet his eyes. "It's not our challenge, is it?"

"No, of course not."

"Good," he said. "I'd never want to cause you that kind of strain."

I swallowed hard. Damn him, he really could see through me. How did he get so perceptive? Was it from growing up with a sister? Did Tessa give him insight into the female mind or was he just good at seeing...*me*?

"Dean," I said. "You really don't have to...to worry about me."

He flashed me a soft smile. "Too late for that."

"Why?"

"We're friends, right? Isn't that what friends do? Worry about each other. Talk to each other. Vent?"

I smirked. "You want to be like Hannah?"

Another low growl. "I am so much better looking than Hannah."

"She's pretty gorgeous."

He tipped his chin. "Is Natalie Portman yours, too?" He waggled his eyebrows, the look successfully launching me into giggles I couldn't control.

"And if it was?"

"Add it to the list of other things we have in common."

"You have a list?" I teased.

"I'll never admit it." The smile on his lips was tempting, warm, and completely at ease. These little moments he'd continued to give me, they made me feel...*normal.*

The realization only made me understand just how long it'd been since I'd felt normal—months—and my shoulders sank. I hated that I'd let Brandon rob me of that ease.

I grinned at him, my sides aching from the way he made me laugh.

"What is it?" he asked.

"I'm just really glad we're friends."

He raised his brows. "Am I in your circle now?"

"Wouldn't go that far," I said. "It took Hannah two years to get in. Jake twice as long."

"Well, you know how much I love a challenge."

Heat rippled through me. I siphoned it, curled around it in an attempt to hold on to that feeling a little longer.

"Never thought your celebrity crush would be such a hard thing to pin," he said, backing away from the counter. "I'll think on it and let you get back to...whoever it is you were staring at."

I chuckled, taking his empty mug and placing it in the sink. *If you only knew what I'd been looking at before you walked in.*

I wondered what he would think. I hadn't given him a chance to voice an opinion at the taco shop—it was too fresh in my mind. Too new.

Would he forfeit, knowing it was a win? Or would he tell me to burn it before it burned me? Or would he be offended? Would he think I was insane for believing I could possibly help people when I had no real clue what I was doing?

If he brought it up again, I'd let him talk.

Turning back around, I watched him walk to the door, the muscles in his back rippling underneath his black T-shirt.

Damn, I have the hottest..."friend."

That was okay, wasn't it? I knew Hannah was gorgeous. I could think he was hot without crossing a line that would inevitably lead to heartbreak.

Totally.

"Locker," I called as he reached the door.

He glanced over his shoulder. "Yeah?"

"Portman and mine have a scene together. One where she tries to break his grasp."

He cocked that damn eyebrow at me, and I swore I felt myself melt.

"Good to know," he said. "Night, Pixie."

"Night," I said as he let the door swing shut behind him.

I had to fan myself from the heat racing over my skin. The way my *friend* kept looking at me, kept making me laugh, kept making me *feel*...he was rapidly competing for my number one *anything* spot.

And the scariest thing?

The walls I'd so carefully constructed after Brandon? They felt wobbly with each hour I spent with Dean.

If he had the power to bring them down...

Then maybe I'll be happy again?

No.

He'd have the power to crush me.

QUESTION OF THE DAY

Sk8er4Life2416 asks: *"My girlfriend and I have been together more than nine months. We're smoking hot together and have hit every base but one. I'm ready to round home, but I don't know if she is. How will I know? Is there some secret signal you chicks use?"*

Well, Sk8er4Life2416, I'm going to let you in on a total "chick code" secret. While we may have many unbreakable rules like joining your BFF on any bathroom break or watching drinks while the other dances, we don't have a secret universal symbol that spells out "we're ready for you to stick it to us."

Picture me rolling my eyes on that one.

Now picture me smiling at you, maybe even saying "aw." Because I will commend you on actually thinking about what your girlfriend wants and when she'll be ready even though you've already hit that marker. Good for you, dude. Please let all your bros know about this. It's a big deal. Waiting to make sure your partner is ready and respecting their time frame goes a hell of a long way in making a "smoking hot" relationship work.

This chick applauds you.

As for knowing when she's ready, the best piece of advice I can give you?

Ask her.

And in a way that doesn't make her feel cornered or pressured. Speaking as one of the girls, there is already a ton of pressure on her. I don't even know her, and I know that much. Be supportive, and if she says she's not there yet, it's not because of something *you've* done. It's simply that she hasn't hit that mind frame yet. And that's okay. Sex is a massive step in a relationship, but with the right—consenting—partners, it can be off-the-charts amazing.

So, keep being the good guy. Talk to her about it. And be willing to wait.

It's worth it.

In the meantime,
Stay Sexy. Stay Healthy.

CHAPTER ELEVEN

DEAN

Monday morning and at school an hour before it started. Kill me now.

The past month had been a blissful blur of chat boxes, coding, and the club that shall not be named. The image of Amber, a crease in her brow from concentrating so hard on trying to beat me at CTF, made me goofy-grin. Every. Single. Time.

Even now. When it shouldn't. Since I was headed to the principal's office.

Principal Tanner had emailed me early Saturday morning to "request" my presence here today. We both knew it wasn't a request—if I didn't show, there would be repercussions to deal with. He still blamed me for not catching the video soon enough, and I didn't need him forgetting to recommend me when MIT admissions emailed him about my grades and performance. I didn't have time for that. I barely had time for the punishment he placed upon me, although, to be fair, Code Club had turned out more incredible than I could've ever imagined. Sure, maintaining the school's website was something I could do in my sleep, but the club? It had become something I looked forward to.

Because of Amber.

I'd spent every weekend since it started resisting the urge to text her. Visiting her work a few Fridays ago had been pure instinct, and I hadn't been lying when I said I'd gotten bored without her. She was too much fun—whether I was teasing her to rile her up or talking hacks or movie preferences. Nothing seemed boring when she was around.

Maybe this weekend I'd text her.

But I knew she was still warming up to letting me fully in as her friend, and I didn't want to push my luck. Overextend myself.

My bag bumped heavily on my hip as I approached the principal's office. The halls were so quiet this early in the morning, something I might have relished if not for the reason I was here.

"Mr. Winters," Tanner's secretary—Mrs. Stone—greeted me as I walked inside. "He's expecting you." She motioned toward the second door that led to his personal office.

"Thanks," I said, not bothering to knock on the closed door.

Principal Tanner stood behind his desk, his palms placed on the smooth wooden surface as he leaned over his Mac. He glared at it, the muscles in his shoulders taut.

I cleared my throat, and Tanner snapped his eyes to me then the large clock on his wall.

I was ten minutes early. Figured that was safer than being a second late.

"I'm glad you're here," he said, and the ease in his tone as he stood to a normal position raised my hackles. "I need your *advice*."

Pinching myself seemed like the smartest move—surely, I'd fallen into some *Twilight Zone* dream—but I was too shocked to move.

He indicated his Mac then gestured to his laptop resting on the shelf behind him. "Is there a way to tell if you've been hacked?"

I blew out a breath, happy to have something to work

with that was familiar. "Are you experiencing any issues with your software?" I asked, setting my bag in the empty chair in front of his desk.

"No," he said.

"Okay." I rubbed my palms together. "Is the computer moving slower than usual?"

"No."

I dropped my hands. "What makes you think your equipment has been compromised?"

"I didn't say I thought I had been. I was asking *you* if you could tell."

I narrowed my gaze. "Theoretically, yes," I said. "If I dug deep enough, sure."

Tanner raised his brows, his eyes casting a calculating look. "Interesting."

"I wouldn't suggest hiring someone without reason, though," I added.

"Why is that?"

"Because if you have no symptoms, you'd be paying the tech hourly to look for something that may not be there."

A small, tight grin as he slid his hands in his pockets. "Well, I wouldn't hire someone. I have you."

I swallowed hard. Sean had mentioned Tanner constantly used him for tech support when he'd been at Wilmont, but Tanner's tone was what made my gut twist. Like he knew he could call on me for whatever he wanted because he understood perfectly well how much sway he had with admissions boards.

"It would be difficult to hack your system anyway," I said finally, glancing at his Mac.

Tanner straightened. "Are you speaking from experience?"

I blurted out a laugh, but Tanner wasn't amused.

"No, sir," I said, shaking my head. "I wouldn't be that

stupid. Plus, I don't have a need."

Not 100 percent lie.

I hadn't hacked him.

Yet.

I had only recently settled on an idea for the challenge with Amber—a desktop switch for every computer in Wilmont. It would take days to untangle, and even longer for me to pull off.

"I mean that Sean hooked up your security so well…" I ran my fingers through my hair, shrugging. "It would take someone incredibly skilled to crack it."

Tanner looked down at me like he was trying to unlock some sort of puzzle.

I stared back at him, totally blank. Why had he called me in here if his tech was showing no signs of tampering with?

The prank.

"Is this about the video, sir?"

He stalked around his desk, stopping in front of me. "Do you have any leads on that?"

I furrowed my brow. "No."

"I thought that perhaps those who joined your little Code Club might be prime candidates, but you've only had one person interested."

That's the main reason he forced me to run the club? To monitor who had the skills to take his system down?

That makes sense.

At least I had sound reasoning now. I thought he'd been doing it to rob me of personal time outside of school and to make sure the school's website was as pristine as his starched shirts.

"It wasn't Amber," I said, suddenly realizing what he had implied.

"You seem very sure of that."

"I know it, sir. She's too smart for something so…"

He arched a brow at me.

"Childish," I said, hoping that would appeal to his rational side.

He finally nodded. "Indeed it was."

"And," I added, wanting all spotlights off Amber and myself, "your computer wasn't hacked."

"How do you know?"

"Because it wasn't necessary. Anyone could've swapped your videos when you were out of your office." Acid climbed up my throat as I realized in my attempt to throw his gaze off us, I'd inadvertently thrown it onto someone else. Sure, the person who messed with his presentation had made their own choice, but I didn't want them to go down for it.

Something clicked behind his eyes, and my stomach dropped.

Fuck, was it graduation yet?

I wanted to be done with this shit. Wanted to win the TOC, get accepted to MIT, graduate, and earn my way into as many boot camps as I could before starting college.

"I'd like you to take another look at my laptop," he said, retrieving it and setting it before me on his desk. "Just to be certain."

"Sure," I said, and tried not to groan.

There wouldn't be anything here. I'd already checked the day of the prank.

"Sit," he said, motioning to his personal leather chair behind the oak desk.

I moved toward it, timid, like it might be a trap. Slowly, I sank into it and opened his laptop.

"Good," he said. "I'll leave you to it." He walked through his door, the lock catching before it could close entirely.

"Cynthia," I heard him say through the door. "Status

update, please."

I scanned his office, my eyes trailing over the countless awards he had decorating his walls, before focusing on his screen. I typed a few commands, going through the motions of checking his security...again.

"Fourteen total this month," his secretary said, her quiet tone pausing my movement on his keyboard.

"Fourteen?" he grumbled. "That won't do."

"Should I schedule meetings with the students and their parents?"

A deep sigh.

I strained my ears, totally forgetting about my pointless task.

"The board is giving me no options. My birthright is to be the head of this school. They'll take it from me if academics slip even a fraction this year. Plus, if I want to win Educator of the Year again and have the state award us another sizeable grant for...whatever I deem the students worthy of...then yes, Cynthia. Make the necessary arrangements."

"Should we wait?" she asked. "Give the students a chance to adjust their grades. It's only the second month of the school year. There is time to—"

"Make the calls," he cut her off, no room for argument in his tone.

Grades? Fourteen?

His job was on the line? People were failing classes? And he wouldn't even give them a chance to get them up before he called in the big guns?

Damn. No wonder he was wound tighter than ever.

His *birthright*. Awards. Grants. That's all the man cared about.

It sure as shit wasn't giving his students the chance to redeem themselves before he brought in the parents.

I always knew he was an asshole.

Why was he so concerned with maintaining his long line of principal tradition when he was so clearly annoyed by us? Or maybe he did it on purpose because he loved the drama that came with his position.

Fuck that.

It wouldn't be me.

I'd worked my ass off every year to make sure I'd never be stuck in a job I didn't love. The boot camps, the tournaments, the certifications…it was all leading to, hopefully, an acceptance letter from MIT in March.

Five and a half months.

That's all I had to get through before I heard from MIT. My dream school. I wouldn't feel at home anywhere else.

Then I'd say goodbye to this place and Tanner's drama, forever.

"Yes, sir," Mrs. Stone finally said.

"I will not be forced to retire. I will not be beaten," he said. "I will win. And Wilmont will continue to be the academy all others strive to be."

I stopped my eye roll mid-motion because he bounded back through his door.

"Anything?"

"Nothing," I said, clicking away, my eyes sharp on his screen as if I'd been searching the whole time.

"So, it's as you said, then." He sighed, glaring down at the laptop.

"Possible," I said, shutting the screen and scooting out of the chair.

"Thank you for checking, Winters." He held his arm out toward the door. "You're doing an excellent job on the academy's website. Keep up the good work. And I do hope more people join your club."

The club you forced me to host?

I didn't.

Not that I would mind teaching a few people how to do some simple coding tricks, but I liked the solo time with Amber. Even though she only wanted friendship. Plus, I'd used the time to prep for the TOC, too. Running through practice sessions and simulations after I'd completed the website work. As long as Amber and I weren't playing CTF, that was.

"Thanks," I said, but it almost sounded like a question. My head was spinning from the whiplash in his mood. A compliment? That was rare. I waved him off and booked it out of the room like I was late to class, not a half hour early.

Five and a half months to college acceptance. Seven and a half to graduation.

Then no one would call me in early, force me to check things I had no business checking. I highly doubted college professors were as strict and demanding of students' free time as Tanner.

Wandering through the halls, I contemplated killing the extra time in the coding room, but for once, I wasn't in the mood. The negative vibe in his office had axed any hope of having a good Monday morning.

Though, grabbing an Americano and an unsweetened venti iced green tea could turn things around. Plus, it would give me the perfect excuse to see Amber first thing in the morning.

Keys in hand, I bounded through the exit doors with a much better attitude than when I entered. I rounded the corner of the exterior building, heading toward my car, but skidded to a stop when I spotted Tessa.

She sat on one of the tables in the quad right next to the school's entrance, one leg hooked over Colt's hip, their mouths hardly breaking for air.

"Ah, fucking hell," I snapped, clenching my eyes shut like I could *unsee* my baby sister in heavy-make-out-central with her boyfriend.

"Dean?" Tessa yelled. "What the hell?" She scooted only an inch away from Colt, who kept his hand on her knee.

"Hey, Dean," he said.

I tried not to growl at him.

It was the same *every* time I caught them, which was more often than I'd like. Tragedy of living in the same house, but normally they kept it contained to there or elsewhere. Never school.

I stopped in front of them. "What the hell?" I mimicked her. "*You* what the hell?"

"We're just having breakfast," she said, motioning to the breakfast burritos on the table behind her. She likely grabbed them from work before coming here, and I almost asked why *I* wasn't chomping down on one right this second, but that was beside the point.

"Yeah, didn't look like it." I cringed. Tessa had dated Colt practically forever, but it didn't mean I wanted to *see* them like that together. "Just, ugh." I rolled my eyes. "I'll see you later." I headed toward my car, trying to blow off the whole thing. I needed that coffee more now than before.

Maybe the caffeine would help burn the image of my baby sister being groped out of my head. Though I doubted there was any fire strong enough.

CHAPTER TWELVE

"You're wanted in the principal's office, Ms. Henderson," Mrs. Angelo said as she stopped me mid-type on my lit paper.

My heart dropped into my stomach, splashing acid up my throat. I swallowed the garbage down, nodding silently and gathering my things.

I glanced over my shoulder at Dean, who I somehow *knew* was watching.

You okay? he mouthed, and the fact that he was worried about me warmed the cold fear clutching my spine. That, and his sweet gesture this morning when he'd been waiting by my locker with an iced green tea.

I'd have to return the favor sometime. If I wasn't about to be expelled for running an anonymous blog that contradicted everything Principal Tanner and the Wilmont Academy website stood for. Like telling students where to get birth control without their parents knowing or advising a boy on how to talk to his partner about having sex. There was also the one about role playing, the commenter worried about her partner thinking she was a freak for suggesting it. Or the one about sexual dreams with teacher appearances and other off-limits people. A month's worth of blog posts... I pushed down the thoughts and flashed Dean a soft smile before turning out of the room.

Tanner figured out I'm Ask Me Anything.

The fear amplified with each step closer to his office.

No way. I'm too careful.

It had been a month since I'd started the blog, and with the traffic increasing each day, I'd triple-checked the codes in Tor.

The traffic and buzz over the blog kept growing, along with my dual sense of anxiety and accomplishment. More content than worry—I'd gotten to posting nearly every day now and I actually felt like I was helping people. Though, if I was being fair, I supposed I should give some credit to Mom…and even Dad in some cases. They both were hand-feeding me answers to random questions without even blinking an eye. I probably should've told them about the site, but I didn't want anyone else to be held responsible if I was ever caught.

But that was super unlikely.

Why else would Tanner haul you in here midday?

Two more steps and I'd have my answer.

I halted in front of his secretary's desk for a moment before stepping toward Tanner's closed door.

"Ah, Ms. Henderson," Mrs. Stone said. "He's at a meeting with the board for the next few days."

I furrowed my brow.

She pointed to the door on the opposite side of the room. "Vice Principal Howard is who called for you."

"Oh." I adjusted my position, the short-lived relief evaporating. VP Howard was by far more agreeable and enjoyable than Tanner, but I still didn't have a clue why she'd want to speak with me.

"You can go on in," Mrs. Stone said after I'd stood in front of the closed door a few breaths too long.

I gripped the knob and entered, ordering my heart to stop racing. Tried to tell myself this had nothing to do with the blog.

Don't you want it to be about the blog?

The conflict clashed in my chest—yes, the goal was to rile up Tanner, but I'd never planned on getting caught. Why else would I venture to the dark web? Risk being expelled and kiss a potential acceptance letter from MIT goodbye? I just wanted...

What?

To help.

To do whatever little part I could to comfort someone when they were feeling alone.

To be someone who listened to classmates who had been ignored far too often at Wilmont.

To fill a role that was missing from this academy.

And this past month... I couldn't explain it. I felt stronger, less empty, and more fulfilled than I had since Brandon. I knew it had everything to do with the blog, with the comfort and soothing satisfaction through sharing stories, experiences, and advice with people who needed it. The idea that I might be making a difference.

"Hey there," Ms. Howard said as I walked in. "Have a seat, please." She indicated the lush chair in front of her slightly chaotic desk.

I sank into it, keeping my voice in check. "What's up?"

She worked her fingers across her keyboard for a moment before focusing on me, her long red hair pulled up in an elegant topknot. "I wanted to see how you were feeling about your senior year."

The breath left my lungs so fast I nearly fainted.

Ms. Howard registered the relief and tilted her head. "What did you *think* I wanted?"

I shook my head, shrugging. "I'm not sure, but originally I thought Tanner wanted to see me."

Howard sucked her teeth, a slight hissing sound escaping as she did. "Sorry about that," she said. "I know that likely caused you some stress." She scribbled something down on a pink Post-it before looking back at me. "I'll do better to emphasize who is calling you here next time."

"Will there be a next time?" We'd only spoken a handful of times throughout last school year, she only having worked at Wilmont for the past two years.

She smiled. "I truly hope so, Amber." Her green eyes were inviting, open, and actually looked like she cared. It was a wonderful contrast to Tanner's normal suspicious looks. "Anyway," she continued. "While our principal is away, working so hard to keep ties with the district board…" She ran over the last words a little sarcastically, but I totally could've imagined it. "I wanted to take the chance to speak to as many of the seniors as possible."

I raised my eyebrows. "Okay."

She sighed. "I know things at Wilmont are difficult at times. That the relationships between students and teachers or the principal aren't as nurturing as they could be."

My lips parted in shock then closed into a smile. She really meant it; I could read it in her eyes, in the hope etched in the features on her face.

"That's true," I said. "We're usually discouraged from challenging certain people's way of thinking." I wouldn't come out and say Tanner's name. Not to his VP, no matter how cool she appeared to be.

She nodded. "I'd like to try to be a buffer to that. I want you to know that you're free to come talk to me about whatever you want." She waved her hands across her desk. "Strictly confidential."

I chuckled. "Shouldn't that be the counselor's job?"

"Mrs. Kellermen is wonderful at her job," she said. "But

I would understand if students wanted someone..." She cringed like she couldn't bring herself to say the word.

"Younger?" I filled in for her. Kellermen had been here since before the dawn of time, and her methods of "counseling" were about that old, too.

"Yes," she agreed. And she was much younger, maybe only ten or fifteen years older than me. "So, here I am."

"That's..." I sighed. "Nice." It *was* refreshing, but I highly doubted Tanner would let it fly if he found out. I hated that she was in this position at all. That she felt like she had to wait to call these meetings until he was off campus.

"Great." She raised her perfectly trimmed eyebrows, waiting patiently. "Anything you want to talk about? School? Work? Boys?"

I created a sex-advice blog.

I'm crushing on a hacker friend even though I've sworn off boys.

I'm haunted by the past.

"No," I said. "I'm good." Her shoulders dropped a little. "But," I said, hurrying, "I really do appreciate the sentiment. And I know several people who will take advantage of it. I'm one of the lucky ones. My parents and I get along and can talk about everything. Not everyone has that. We've needed someone like you around here for a long time now."

"Well," she said, "I'm glad you think so. And you know I'll be here if you ever want to talk to a non-parent, non-peer person."

"Thanks," I said, and I meant it. I stood, realizing she was giving me the go-ahead to get out of here. "See you around," I said, and she smiled before I closed the door behind me.

Once I made it out of the secretary's office and into the hallway, I breathed. The relief was so sudden I felt dizzy. It had been paranoid fear causing me to think that either of them knew about the website, but it hadn't stopped me from feeling it.

The comments had tripled since I started posting almost every other day.

It wasn't a stretch for me to fear that sometime soon, it would get so big I wouldn't be able to hide behind it anymore.

But this response had to be because it was new. Exciting. A touch dangerous with some of the topics I'd already featured.

It would settle. Or I'd simply find the balance to ensure it was a steady, manageable stream. Something I could handle once I found my footing.

I repeated this to myself until I sank into my seat in Spanish class, drawing up my online workbook that the rest of the class had been working on for ten minutes now.

NightLocker: Tanner interrogate you, Pixie?
PixieBurn: No
PixieBurn: He's at a board retreat or something
PixieBurn: It was VP Howard

I discreetly glanced over my shoulder, my eyes catching on the relief that sagged Dean's shoulders. Quickly, I faced my computer again, not wanting him to see my grin.

NightLocker: Good
NightLocker: She's cool
PixieBurn: Totally
PixieBurn: She should run this place
NightLocker: Agreed

I clicked off the screen, shifting focus to the Spanish

workbook. I'd nearly reached the end when another chat box filled my screen.

NightLocker: What are you doing later?
PixieBurn: ...
PixieBurn: Like every Friday
NightLocker: We've been grinding it pretty hard
NightLocker: I think we should take a break

Something heavy sank in my stomach. Regardless of how mortifying the idea of Code Club was, it had become something I looked forward to each week since it started. Guess it wasn't the same for Dean. The notion shouldn't bother me—we were just friends—but the idea of not spending those extra hours with him had me wilting.

I reached toward the keys, prepared to type out my agreement. I wasn't about to show my borderline desperation to be around him, but he beat me to it.

NightLocker: Can I take you out?

A soft gasp popped from my lips as I read the message three times. My heart skipped and I had to swallow the thrill storming me.

Damn.

I was actually excited at the idea of him asking me out on a date. Even though I was certain I never wanted to be in another relationship until at least well into college.

When did that happen?

Somewhere between him listening, smiling, teasing his way into my heart.

NightLocker: Don't shut me down

NightLocker: I'm talking as friends, Pixie.
NightLocker: I haven't forgotten you've sworn
off guys...
NightLocker: Even hot geniuses like me

He sent the flurry of messages before I could respond. Somehow, I was both completely melting and disappointed at the same time. He was respecting my choices without pushing for the reasoning behind them. I should be over the moon at that kind of respect, but for just a moment I'd felt...wanted again.

Like I was worthy of asking out.

Like I wasn't damaged goods.

Not that he knew anything about my past, but still. The blog had eaten so much of my time recently—I hadn't even seen Hannah as much as usual because of it. The idea of taking a night off from the site, the comments, my gear, was beyond tempting.

PixieBurn: Sure
PixieBurn: I could use a break
PixieBurn: Where we going?

I resisted the urge to turn my head and look at him, worried he'd see the blush on my cheeks or the hope in my eyes.

NightLocker: It's a secret
NightLocker: I'll pick you up at 6

He closed the chat like he was afraid I'd argue or take back my answer. I hurried to catch up on my workbook, having a wicked difficult time conjugating verbs while thinking about what Dean had up his sleeve for tonight.

Honestly, he could take me to the coding room, my work, the taco shop, any of the places we'd already hung out before and it would be a good time. Something I'd slowly realized about Dean—we had fun no matter what we did. He made me laugh, made me smile, and challenged me.

Another gasp shook my chest as I closed out my workbook.

Dean was one of the best friends I'd ever had, and I didn't know it until now. Until Tanner had forced him to run a club that allowed us to have one-on-one time.

Time that had actively helped me create a site that was rapidly growing—and helping students.

Helped me see Dean as not just competition on the hacker circuit, but as an ally.

"Can't wait for tonight," he said, stopping at my desk after the bell rang.

I smiled, gathering my stuff and standing next to him. "You really won't tell me where we're going?"

A smirk shaped those impossibly perfect lips. "Nope," he said. "Too much fun to watch you try to figure it out."

I huffed. "How am I supposed to know what to wear?"

He laughed, turning toward the door. "You always look amazing, Pixie. Come as you want." He winked, disappearing into the steady flow of students in the hallway, heading toward their next class.

Come as you want.

Damn him. Damn this boy for being so perfect.

He didn't care if I was in the school's atrocious uniform or in my ripped-up jeans. It didn't matter, as long as I was there. As long as I was *me*.

He should be running his own blog—teach people around here how to properly treat their partners or romantic interests. How to really earn someone's trust.

The walls around my heart shifted, wobbling with each time Dean's kindness shook me to my core. I forced them to steady, re-laying the bricks I'd carefully constructed months ago.

He was a great friend.

And that was all I needed.

ASK ME ANYTHING

ABOUT   USEFUL LINKS   FAQ   CHAT WITH ME

QUESTION OF THE DAY

FashionIsLife229 says: *"I recently went down on my boyfriend for the first time. Now he's asking for it all the time. Do I have to do it again? I liked it, but it's not like I want to do it every single time I see him. Am I a bad boyfriend if I don't want to? Am I worse if I want him to return the favor sometimes? Is there anything I can do to make it more...fun for me, too?"*

You might be surprised how many similar questions I have like this in my inbox. So many people worry if they say *no* or that they *aren't in the mood*, they won't be upholding their partner duties. I'm not sure when or where this rumor got started, but being a good partner doesn't equate to doing whatever the other person wants regardless of if you want to.

For instance, if you wanted to watch *your favorite show (one he doesn't particularly enjoy)* every single time your boyfriend was over, I doubt he'd be up for it. Would you be angry with him for saying no? Unlikely.

Example too G-rated? Okay. Fair enough.

How about this. Say you enjoyed doing a keg stand

at a party last week. Does that mean you have to do one every time you go to a party? Would your friends or boyfriend be upset with you if you didn't? Probably not.

Need to turn the tables? All right. What if your boyfriend bought your dinner on your first date but not the second? Would you break up with him over that? Be upset with him? I doubt it.

You never *have* to do anything. Especially when you're not in the mood or don't feel comfortable doing it.

As for making it more of a fun act for you, I'd suggest slowing it down—and no, I'm not suggesting going abstinent like our school would like you to. What I mean is, take the pressure off the act. Know that what you're doing is a super-intimate thing between the two of you and that is huge for a relationship. Maybe going to completion is what throws you off—if that's the case, only take it as far as you're enjoying it and then switch it up to something else. And make sure he's giving you the attention you deserve, too.

Either way, talking to your boyfriend about it is the best course of action. If he's a good guy, he'll understand, and the two of you can figure out other ways to enjoy each other's company.

On the off chance he gives you hell over it? You might want to consider cutting him loose. A selfish partner is not worth your time or energy, and they'll likely only hurt you in the end anyway.

I'll be crossing my fingers in the hope he's awesome about the situation and that you two find a great common ground to walk together on.

In the meantime,
Stay Sexy. Stay Healthy.

CHAPTER THIRTEEN

"I can't believe you're going on a date!" Hannah practically burst my eardrum she squealed so loud. I jerked the cell away from my ear, shaking my rattled brain as I stood in front of my bed.

I'd hit publish on my latest post an hour ago, and I was behind on the non-date prep.

"It's not a date," I said once I felt safe enough to draw the cell back. "We're friends. He's totally on board with my whole *no guys for at least a few years* mission statement."

"Dude," she said. "That only makes him that much more adorable."

I laughed. "Dean isn't adorable. He's—"

"Sexy af," she cut me off.

"Hey!" I heard Jake chide in the background. "You're sitting in *my* lap."

Hannah shushed him before there was a good long smacking of lips from her end of the line. I rolled my eyes as I stared down the two outfits I had laid out.

"You're sexier," she said once the wet smacking sounds were finished. "Anyway," she said, returning her focus to me. "Amber. This is *huge.*"

"It's really not," I said, trying to convince us both.

"It is. You haven't even wanted to speak to another male since Douchenozzle...outside of Jake anyway. Friends or more or whatever in between. This. Is. Awesome."

The butterflies swarmed my stomach, swirling and spinning until my heart raced.

"Thanks for the added pressure." I groaned.

Is this as big of a deal as Hannah says?

She wasn't wrong about me shying away from every single boy at Wilmont after Brandon...but then again, I'd never stopped talking to Dean. It was simply different between us now.

"Sorry not sorry," she said over the line. "Look. Forget everything. Please. I know it's hard, but let go of all the bad ish from the past and have fun tonight. For me?"

"Yes, Mother," I teased despite the hollow feeling in my chest. I loved Hannah like a sister, but Jake was one of the good guys. She had no clue how hard it was to *let go* of things.

"Someone say *mother*?" Mom asked, rapping her knuckles on my opened door.

"Got to go," I said to Hannah.

"Text me all the details! Before, after, and during!" she yelled.

I chuckled. "Yeah, yeah." I ended the call, spinning on my bare feet toward my mom.

"Help," I said, and she strode into the room, her eyes already on the outfits on my bed.

"What's the occasion?"

"Kept from me."

She grinned. "A surprise? Who's the guy pulling out the stops?"

"Dean."

"Oh, the *second best* hacker at Wilmont?"

"My love for you knows no bounds," I said. "Now, which one?"

She eyed me then the clothes. "Is it a date?"

I groaned. "No. Friends."

"Does he know that?"

"Yes, and he's the one who reiterated this is a friend thing."

"I like him."

"Me, too." The words were out of my mouth before I could stop them, and that familiar icy fear did everything to rob me of the warmth thoughts of Dean created.

Mom rubbed my spine, her eyes on mine, catching every emotion as they soared across my face.

"They're not all assholes," she said. "But you can *not* date as long as you want." She sighed. "Just don't let one jerk ruin something special for you." She pulled me into a side hug. "He doesn't deserve the energy you use to keep those walls up, Amber."

I know.

But that didn't stop me from reinforcing them for fear of it ever happening again.

Her words sank deep into my mind. *Am I letting Brandon rob me of something with Dean? Does Dean even think of me like that?*

He'd said before that he didn't have time for a relationship, either, but the way he teased me, almost flirted with me…

"This one." Mom pointed to the lavender V-neck T-shirt and skinny jeans. "It'll go great with the light purple Converse in your closet."

"Nice point," I said. "Thanks, Mom."

"That's what I'm here for." She smiled, heading toward my door. "Amber," she added.

"Yeah?"

"Think about what I said, okay? Have fun tonight, and do what *you* want to do. Don't let anything else hold you back."

I forced out a laugh. "It's just a friend thing. So, I'm sure

I'll have fun."

Without the pressure of it being a date, how could I not?

"He picking you up?"

I nodded.

"Didn't you meet Dean online?"

I tilted my head.

"You skipped across his game or something?"

I chuckled. "I stumbled across his server the first week freshman year, yes."

"Quite the meet-cute," she said, waggling her brows. "Oh my God, what if he shows up with a bouquet of flash drives or external hard drives or something other than flowers?"

I rolled my eyes. "Mom, this isn't one of those rom-coms you love."

She held her side from laughing, finally taking a breath.

"Okay, okay," she said, tapping my door. "You know the code word. Text me if you need me to call you with an excuse to leave."

Banana Brunch. Mom had drilled that into me since I'd been old enough to sleep over at Hannah's house. If I texted that, or said it over a call, she'd come get me, no questions asked. Or, if I had driven, she'd call me with an excuse to come home immediately. Mom and Dad both taught me that they'd love me no matter what and would have my back just the same.

Luckily, I'd never had to use it before.

Hannah and Jake had been with me the night of...

I clamped down on the memory.

"Got it," I said. "But Dean is different." I couldn't help the smile shaping my lips. "I...*trust* him. As a friend," I hurried to add when Mom's grin got a little too wide.

"I'm glad, honey."

A knock at our front door jolted me. "Gah! I'm not

even dressed."

"Hurry up," Mom said, waving me on. "I'll stall him." She was gone before I could stop her.

CHAPTER FOURTEEN

DEAN

"You must be Dean," Amber's mom said after she'd opened the front door. Her smile was genuine, but her eyes were sharp as they checked me head to toe.

Suddenly I felt my jeans and tee—the one I'd picked specifically for Amber—weren't clean enough.

"Hi, Mrs. Henderson," I said, extending my hand toward her. "It's nice to finally meet you."

She took my hand, shook it, and dragged me inside. "Alice," she said. "And it's nice to meet you, too. I've heard you're almost as good a hacker as my daughter."

"Almost," I said, holding up my thumb and forefinger close together.

"Why is there a boy in my house?" A man's voice sounded from behind Amber's mom, and I stiffened as he came to stand next to her. He was one foot taller than her, with dark hair and sharper eyes. Fit. Intimidating.

"Hello, sir. Dean Winters." I reached out to shake his hand, and the scowl instantly shifted off his face to one of humor.

He took my hand. "Nice to meet you, Sir Dean Winters. Where were you knighted?"

I laughed, dropping his hand. "Manchester," I said, stating the only other city in the UK I knew of besides London.

He raised his eyebrows, glancing at Amber's mom.

"Quick. I like this one much better."

I kept my smile in place but felt my gut twist at the mention of *this one*. Thoughts of Brandon triggered my angrier self, so I took a steadying breath to calm down. It's not like I hadn't dated anyone before, or that Amber and I were even dating—but he'd somehow wrecked her, and I hated him for it.

From the look on Amber's mom's face—the way she was sizing me up, threatening me, and inviting me into her home all at the same time—she hated him, too.

"Where are you kids heading tonight?" she asked.

I rubbed my palms together, scanning the area for Amber. "She's upstairs."

"TimeWarp," I said, my voice lowered. "It's this retro arcade place that's set up next to Food Truck Lane."

Amber's dad furrowed his brow. "Amber will *hate* that."

My stomach dropped.

Amber's mom smacked his chest. He burst out laughing.

"She'll love that," she assured me, and I breathed normally again. "Forgive him," she continued. "Amber is his only child, only girl, only everything."

"That's right," he said, pointing a finger at me. "And I would kill for her."

I swallowed hard.

"Like total *Texas Chainsaw* on *Friday the 13th* in your worst Freddy Krueger nightmares kill for her."

My gaze widened as I darted focus between the two of them.

Humor seems like the key to winning them over.

"I pegged you for a Michael Myers on a *Night of the Living Dead* kind of killer," I said.

Stone silence.

Maybe I only thought I was funny.

Laughter rumbled from them both a few breaths later. Damn, they'd keep me on my toes.

Her dad pulled her mom in close, kissing her on the forehead. "I like him."

"Me, too," Amber's mom said. "Amber!" she shouted, causing Amber's dad to jump.

"Coming!" Amber yelled right back from somewhere upstairs. A few seconds later she was bounding down them, her long legs sheathed in tight light denim, tucked into a pair of purple Converse, and a shirt to match. The deep *V* of the shirt showed off the smooth skin of her chest, and I immediately snapped my eyes up to hers.

Friends.

Friends can think their friends are sexy.

Right?

I silenced the battle in myself, fastening what I hoped was a natural grin as she skidded to a stop before me.

"Where we going?" she asked by way of greeting.

I looked down at her, shaking my head. "Told you it's a surprise."

She rolled her eyes, but I could see the spark behind them. She was pumped for tonight. For spending time with *me* and not even a computer in sight.

Win.

She headed toward the front door, waving to her parents over her shoulder.

"Have her back by two a.m.," her dad said, and I did a double take.

"Have fun," Amber's mom said.

I nodded and turned to catch up with Amber. Opening the passenger side door of my car for her, I arched a brow. "Is your curfew really two a.m.?"

She laughed. "No. It's midnight."

"Noted."

With her hand on the car to step inside, she paused, her eyes widening at my shirt.

"Do you like it?" I asked, glancing down. It was solid black except for some dark green writing situated on the lower right-hand corner. I'd ordered the thing a week ago after I was sure I'd figured out who her celebrity crush was. Now was the true test.

"*I am burdened with* glorious *purpose*," she read the line, emphasizing the word *glorious* just the way Loki did in what I guessed was her favorite movie—her Loki-Emblem headphones were a big enough hint. A spark crackled in her eyes as she drew them up to mine. "You're a Loki fan?"

I grinned. "*You* are."

"Yes, that's true." She eyed me.

I pointed to the words. "*This* is your guy."

Her pink lips popped open before she laughed. "You bought a Loki shirt just to prove that you'd finally figured out who my celeb was?"

I shrugged. "Figured it couldn't hurt."

"What?"

"Now every time you look at me tonight, you'll think of me—hot genius—and *then* Loki."

"Placing you above him," she said, biting down on another laugh.

"Exactly." I snapped my fingers before motioning to the car.

She sank inside, the perfect smile still shaping those lips. I shut the door and rounded the car, sitting behind the wheel. "You ready for this?"

She smacked her palms on her thighs. "I don't even know what we're doing. How could I possibly know if I'm ready?"

I grinned at the light behind her smile, the excitement that had been too rare on her face lately.

"You'll see soon enough," I teased, and pulled out of her driveway.

"So what is it about the villain that hooks you?" I asked, trying to take my mind off the nervous energy rushing in my blood.

"He's…" I spared her a glance as she paused, trying not to laugh at the swoony look that glazed her eyes. I wouldn't… couldn't be jealous of a fictional character. "The God of Mischief."

"That's it?"

"No," she said, shifting in her seat to face me while I continued to navigate the roads. "He's got this incredible backstory. Heart wrenching and complex and he can't help but crave justice for the wrongs of his past." She sighed. "Plus, the mischief? The chaos? The way he can't help but love it? That is something I can totally relate to."

"I'll give you that," I said, turning down another street. "Sometimes I'm calmest when in the middle of a chaotic hack. When I know I'm on the brink of cracking a lock or on the verge of being caught."

"Exactly!" She snapped her fingers. "God, you say that to most people and they look at you like you're from another planet."

"Well," I said, sparing her a quick glance. "We're all prone to a little madness." I reached across the car and fingered the green and black bracelet she was never without. "Is that why you always wear this?" I asked, drawing my hand back to the wheel. "Reminds you of Loki?"

"That," she said. "And the fact that it says *Prove Them Wrong*." She flipped the bracelet to the reverse side so I could see the writing. "Loki is constantly proving people wrong. People who assume too quickly or judge too harshly. So, that's why I love him," she said, settling back into her seat. "That, and his stunning blue eyes don't hurt."

I chuckled, wondering if she'd noticed the color of mine was eerily similar.

"No way!" Amber squealed a few minutes later.

I parked in a free space in TimeWarp's lot, not bothering to appreciate the eighties-style neon sign that shot across the top of the building or the floor-to-ceiling glass windows that showed off the hundreds of classic arcade games inside. I was too busy memorizing her open-mouth smile as *she* took it in. The pink in her cheeks, the rise and fall of her chest.

"I've always wanted to come here!"

"Why haven't you?" I asked, killing the ignition and racing around to open her door.

She took my offered hand, the warmth of her fingers sliding over mine like silk. "Brandon never wanted to go," she said, then blinked a few times, cringing like she hadn't meant to say that. She took a deep breath, smiling again. "He said only ten-year-olds would like it."

"How dare he," I snapped. "I'm *eleven*." I winked at her before leading us through the doors.

Instantly, we were transported to a time before cell phones and laptops and endless access to gaming. Eighties music pumped through large speakers hung in every corner of the building—background noise to the chirps, whirs, and tinkles of the rows and rows of arcade games lining the walls and aisles. The smell of fried food, sugary drinks, and metal filled the air—change machines trilling out coins even if all you had was a card to buy them with.

Amber's gasp was like a pleasant electric shock to my chest. Her hand—still in mine—squeezed slightly as she bounced on her heels. "How do we choose where to start?" She looked up at me, her eyes wide like the choice was as overwhelming as a college application.

Fuck, that was adorable.

I scanned the massive room, the place packed with people ranging in age from the aforementioned ten to some dudes with beards that would rival Dumbledore's. I spotted a clear path to a Pac-Man machine in the far left corner. "Let's start there," I said. "Then make our way around?"

"Perfect!" She dropped my hand, heading straight to a change machine. She reached for her back pocket, but I stopped her before she could pull out her wallet. She glared at me as I put my own card in the machine, getting us enough change to play all damn night if we wanted to.

"Dean," she chided. "I can pay for my own."

I furrowed my brow, shoving the quarters into my pockets. "I know," I said, giving her a handful. "But this is my treat."

"I thought this wasn't a date." She popped her hip, the determined and confident pose drawing a smirk across my lips.

"I thought that wasn't even on the table." I stepped closer to her, unable to resist the blush on her cheeks.

"It's not." Her voice came out a whisper as she looked up at me.

"Then it's not," I said, despite the fact that it sure as hell felt like she wanted it to be one.

You're in charge, Amber. You lead me and I'll fall in line.

I'd learned enough from spending my life helping take care of Tessa—my baby sister had been the one to teach me about patience, perception, and understanding when it came to girls before I'd turned twelve. Though I really wished she would've taught me about reading a girl's mind, because I would've *loved* to know what Amber was thinking right this moment.

Something softened in Amber's gaze. "Okay then," she said. "You ready to lose?"

"Ha!" I laughed. "Which game do you think you could

possibly beat me at?"

She glanced around the area. "All of them."

"You're on." I retook her hand, trying like hell to ignore how great it felt, or how she didn't take it back until we reached the first game.

Three hours, countless games, and a shit-ton of quarters later, we'd lost count of who was in the lead.

"I'm totally winning," she said as I guided her out of the arcade and into the cool night air.

"What?" I gaped at her. "No way. I was up by five wins the last time we took a tally."

"Please," she said, rolling her eyes. There was no annoyance in her tone. In fact, I hadn't heard or seen her this happy in months. Even when she was locked in—which was normally her bliss—this...tonight...she was different.

Freer. Wild. Close to the girl I'd first met all those years ago.

"Omigod it smells so good out here." She moaned the closer we got to where all the food trucks were lined up, and I both loved and hated how much that sound drove me crazy.

Careful, I warned myself. The way my entire being was tuned in to her...fuck, it was like I was in—

No. I couldn't be.

Friends. In the past month we'd taken our friendship from cordial to matching bracelet territory. This was a totally normal reaction to a friendship this awesome.

Amber grabbed my hand as we funneled into the crowd of people storming all the trucks. She weaved us in and out until she set her sights on a French-themed truck that served crepes.

"Nutella-stuffed crepes?" I asked after she ordered one for herself.

"If you tell me you don't like Nutella, Dean, we're no

longer friends." She stepped to the side so I could order.

"Make that two, please," I said to the cashier, smirking at Amber.

"Oh thank God," she said, true relief shaping her face. "I was worried."

I took the paper cone-wrapped concoctions and ushered us to a table in the center of the market-like place and sat. "Wow," I said, smiling as I handed her the food. "You were really worried about losing my friendship."

Her eyes widened. "I was not."

"Oh, you can't deny it. I saw it all over your face."

She laughed. "You can't read me that well."

I nodded enthusiastically. "Can," I said before taking a massive bite of the crepe.

She mimicked me, her eyes rolling back in her head as she chewed. "Best. Night. Ever," she said after swallowing.

The center of my chest pulsed and puffed and warmed at the happiness in her eyes.

I did that. I put that there.

I mentally high-fived myself as we continued to eat in a more-than-comfortable silence. For the briefest of moments, I had been worried that without our gear and our challenges and our hacks that we wouldn't know what to talk about. With the way we'd been chatting nonstop tonight, it was stupid of me to worry. Amber and I were connected beyond our passion for computers, and I felt ridiculous for how relieved that fact made me.

"Thank you," she said after we'd tossed our empty wrappers in the garbage, electing to take a short walk around the place. "I didn't realize how much I needed this until you gave it to me." She stopped short, halting her steps near the corner of the arcade building. "God, that sounded so pathetic."

"No, it didn't," I said, turning to face where she'd taken up a lean against the brick building, the pink strands of hair illuminated by the neon sign far above her. The way she seemed content to stay there was like she didn't want the night to end.

I don't, either.

"It's just…" She sighed, tucking her hands behind her back. "It's been a long time since I've had fun like this."

I eyed her. "You mean with a guy."

She parted her lips to deny it but stopped herself. "You really do see more than anyone else, huh?"

"I'm good at unlocking what people are trying to hide." I smiled at her, stepping closer than the *friend* boundary probably permitted, but I couldn't help it. She was the sun and I was helplessly sucked into her orbit.

"Nightlocker," she said, my hacker name rolling off her tongue and rippling all the way down my spine. "Makes sense."

"It's easier with you," I said, shifting so one arm leaned over her shoulder, the position in front of her blocking the neon sign from glaring in her eyes.

"How so?" She gazed up at me, never once retreating from my nearness, almost like she craved it as much as I did.

I shrugged. "There is something about you that… resonates in me?" I chuckled. "Now I sound pathetic."

"No, you don't."

"I mean it, though," I said. "I've never had a friend like you before. We… It's like we're…"

"The same?" she finished for me.

"Exactly. It makes it easier to understand you."

"I get that," she said. "But you have an unfair advantage."

"What is that?"

"You don't have anything to hide." She sighed. "No walls

that need breaking down."

I stared into her eyes, the smile dropping off my face.

What did he do to you?

The words were there, but I couldn't choke them out. She would tell me if she wanted me to know. The last thing I wanted to do was push her away, to break the bond we'd formed by stepping where I wasn't wanted.

"You don't have to hide from me, you know," I finally managed to say.

Something swirled in her eyes, a churning sort of hope and want and…trust?

"I want to be the one you talk to," I said. "Not just about coding or hacks or tech. I want us to be close. I crave this…" I motioned to the small space between us, noting how her chest rose and fell like it had when we'd first entered the arcade, but now for a totally different reason.

Being this close to her was the sweetest torture, so much it was intoxicating. Whirling in my brain like I'd had a few drinks.

"I do, too," she whispered, her tongue darting out to wet her lips. "And it scares the hell out of me."

"Don't let it," I said, reaching my free hand to smooth it over her cheek, down her neck. Chills erupted where my fingers trailed, but she never lost my gaze. Never pushed me away or drew me closer. Slowly, I lowered my head, inching closer to her lips, knowing the night wasn't supposed to go this way but unable to stop it. The draw she had on me, the heat in my heart calling for more of her smiles, more of her sweet scent, more of her voice…it urged me forward.

She closed her eyes, sighing as she tilted her head upward. A clear invitation.

A feather-light brush of my lips over hers, and she tensed under my touch, jerking her head to the side.

Ice-cold water doused my insides, my chest caving in on itself.

She's told you all along she doesn't want this.

That hadn't made me immune to what I thought was a mutual current between us.

"I'm sorry," I said, quickly straightening to give her some room.

But then I *looked* at her—really looked at her. My stomach plummeted.

"Amber?" I said, gripping her shoulders. "You're trembling." I eyed her up and down, taking note of the way her fists were clenched, her fingers shaking. Slow tears rolled down the cheeks that were warm with my breath seconds ago. "What is it?" I asked, her eyes closed, blocking me from getting through to her. "Fuck, Amber, I'm so sorry," I said, panic building in me. "I didn't mean to cross a line. I swear." I'd honestly thought she was on the same page, wanting the kiss, inviting it. I never believed I could read her so wrong, that I could cause this reaction.

She sucked in a stuttered breath, finally opening her eyes.

Apologetic. Hurt. Scared.

She flung her arms around my middle, almost barreling into me despite the small amount of space between us. I instantly enveloped her, stroking her back, silently begging her shaking to stop as she sobbed into my chest.

CHAPTER FIFTEEN

AMBER

"I'm so embarrassed," I said through my tears. Unable to stop them. Unable to stop the flood of memories that had crushed the cloud-nine level of happiness I'd been on seconds before Dean had leaned in to kiss me.

I'd shut my eyes, ready and thirsting for him.

And then *boom*.

Hello darkness, my old friend.

My past slashed through all the good feelings and tossed me right back into the pit I'd promised myself I wouldn't visit tonight.

Never tonight.

Not when Dean had gone so above and beyond. More than anyone ever had. Hell, he'd brought out the big Loki guns.

"Tonight was so perfect," I said, inhaling Dean's scent, using it to calm the mortification squeezing my lungs. "The most fun I've had in so long." Having gained some form of control, I tipped my chin up enough to meet his eyes. "I'm sorry, Dean."

He smoothed his thumbs over my wet cheeks, shaking his head. "You have nothing to be sorry about, Pixie." He gave me a closed-mouth smile, his blue-gray eyes searching mine, trying like hell to break the locks I'd snapped over everything rolling inside me. "I told you," he said. "I want to *know* you. You never have to hide from me or be someone you're not. Not with me."

"I want to—" I stopped myself, sighing as I took a step backward. It was so hard to think straight standing inside his embrace. "I'm not…"

"Hey," he said, brushing the back of my hand with his. "Don't worry about it," he said, and motioned to the parking lot. "Let's get you home, okay?"

My shoulders dropped as I followed him to his car—in relief or disappointment I wasn't sure. I wondered just how much I would've told him if he would've let me stand there long enough. The way I felt around him—I was a blink away from spilling *all* my secrets. The ones eating away at my insides. The ones barely anyone knew about.

He pulled out of the lot, the colorful neon lights of the arcade filling up the back window for a moment before it disappeared. The darkness was both comforting and suffocating. I wanted to go back a couple hours and relive the night—end it differently.

At the very least I should've had my breakdown at my front door. Then I could've simply spun around and hid forever. Now I had to deal with the more-than-awkward car ride home. Not because Dean was being awkward, or because he'd been a jerk about the situation—the opposite. He'd become a better friend than I knew what to do with. And the things he was doing to the heart I was sure had been frozen solid? I was powerless against it.

Every time I spared a glance across the seat, my heart flipped. He drove with one hand on the wheel, his shoulder relaxed, his long legs bent to fit in the car. The damn Loki shirt fitting him perfectly. This boy…it was like I'd made him in a computer. A perfect combination of strong and understanding, smart and humble, funny and mature.

Damn.

And you just blew it because you can't get Brandon out of your head.

Dean glanced at me, and I snapped my eyes back out my window, hating that I got caught staring. He chuckled softly.

"How about some Nero?" he asked, reaching toward his cell hooked on the dash once we hit a red light.

"Yes," I said almost too eagerly. Music to cover up my blunder. The tears that were still drying on my cheeks.

God, what is he thinking?

I couldn't imagine—a girl crying against his chest after he tried to kiss her. I'm sure that had never happened to him before.

At least I have that going for me.

I rolled my eyes at myself as Dean pushed play on a mix called "Dean's #1" before the light turned green. He drove and cranked the volume before the song started playing.

A high-pitched, rhythmic beat blared from his speakers, followed quickly by Taylor Swift's sweet voice singing "Blank Space."

The laugh that ripped from my chest was full and snort-worthy and all the things I usually tried to tone down in public, but there was no possible way. Not with the look on Dean's face—his eyes wide, a slight color to his cheeks as he swallowed hard. Then, a low growl, this rumble in his chest that stopped my laugh in its tracks, all kinds of other tingles rippling over my skin.

"Fucking Sean," he grumbled under his breath.

I grinned. "I haven't heard this *Nero* song before," I teased.

He tilted his head, sparing me a glance before focusing on the road again. "No?" he asked. "This is totally my jam," he said, his tone mocking of what I assumed was closer to what his little sister sounded like. He bobbed his head to the beat, rolling his shoulders.

Two seconds. That's all it took Dean to recover. He was so quick.

Another chuckle and I was dancing in unison with him. "I can see why," I said over the music, grinning ridiculously when he started dramatically mouthing the words.

By the end of the song my sides hurt from laughing so hard. Watching this incredibly hot guy belt out Taylor Swift—clearly a prank from his older brother—was the perfect medicine for my earlier misstep. It was almost enough to make me forget what had happened.

Almost.

But once he pulled into my driveway and turned the volume down on another Taylor song, I was plunged right back into the embarrassing moment like no time had passed. I parted my lips, shifting in the seat to face him.

"Thank you again," I said instead of apologizing like I wanted to.

"This was fun, right?" he asked like he needed the reassurance as much as I did.

"The best. Seriously." I tried to convey with my eyes how sorry I was to have ruined it at the end.

The car, filled with his scent, seemed to shrink around me as we simply looked at each other, trying to communicate without speaking. Though it was hard to know what he tried to tell me when his eyes were so *gray* in this muted light.

"Well," I finally said, reaching for the door. "See you," I finished, cringing as I turned to open the door. *Super-clever sign-off.*

"Amber?" The use of my real name over my alias froze my movements.

My stomach hit the floor—he was going to say he *wouldn't* see me on Monday. That I shouldn't bother coming to Code Club anymore. That after tonight, he realized I was too damaged, not worth the effort to even be my friend, let alone more.

"Yeah?" I asked, barely finding the courage to turn back around and face him.

He pressed his lips together, a battle raging in his eyes. Reaching across the seat, he gently touched my shoulder, the caress firing up nerves I didn't even know I possessed.

"It's none of my business," he said. "And I don't know what happened between you and...*him*. I understand you're not ready to tell me about it, and you may never. That's fine. I just want you to know that I'm here." He dropped his hand back in his lap. "In whatever way you need me."

I swallowed the thick lump in my throat, trying like hell not to cry for an entirely different reason this time. His frame glittered at the edges, but I held it together.

Kiss him.

Thank him.

"Why?" was the only word I managed to speak.

He furrowed his brow like he'd never expected me to ask that question.

"DC." He spoke the letters of our code word, and I chuckled softly.

"What?"

He shrugged. "It's more than an alert to teachers approaching. It's...*ours.*" He gestured between us. "You and me. A small pact. *We* are in this together. *We* will always be there for the other."

"That's how you've thought of it all this time?" The question came out a whisper, but in the quiet car, it was enough that he caught every word.

He nodded as he shifted in his seat. "Too much?"

I shook my head quickly. "Perfect."

"Good." He opened his door, rushing around the side to

open mine. I took his offered hand as he walked me to my front porch. "So," he continued once we reached the door to my home, "whenever you're ready to tell me what's *really* going on up here — " He smoothed his index finger over my forehead. "Then...DC."

I leaned into his touch, craving the warm comfort and the explosive shocks. He smiled down at me, and as I looked up at him, all I wanted to do was kiss him. To redo the moment from earlier. To prove to him and myself that I could let go of my past and trust someone again.

I'd already been healing...slowly...ever since the blog and open communication between me and the people who wrote in with their own troubles. There was something cleansing about reaching out to others and helping them, and through that, somehow, helping myself. But I didn't know if I should or *could* act on that wobbly strength I'd slowly gathered.

"Night, Pixie," he said, taking a few steps back, the motions almost looking like a struggle. Like he didn't want to leave, either.

I sighed, grateful for his strength. For his words. For everything. "Night, Dean," I said, and opened the door before I could chase him across my yard and tackle him. The boy was turning me inside out with emotions — thoughts and wants I was certain wouldn't happen again for years.

Shutting the door behind me, I leaned against it for a second, eyeing my parents who sat at the kitchen island a little too conspicuously, eating out of a carton of rocky road.

"How'd it go?" Dad asked around a spoonful of ice cream.

A thrill raced up my spine at thoughts of tonight. It was quickly blasted down by the embarrassment I knew I didn't need to feel but did anyway. "Great," I said and bolted up the stairs to my room.

Digging in my drawers for my pajamas, I was swallowed by the sea of emotions storming my mind. Memories of that night…flooded me until I was right back *there*.

"*This is* so *the party that never ends,*" *I whispered in Hannah's ear. She giggled from where she sat on Jake's lap.*

"*Where's Brandon?*" *she asked, glancing around the football player's house. One of Jake's buddies was throwing the party. A massive celebration before summer conditioning for the team started.*

"*I don't know,*" *I said, slightly grumbling. "Probably getting another drink.*"

Hannah flashed me a sympathetic look. Brandon wasn't like Jake—attentive and careful with the alcohol—but I was hoping he might morph into something closer to who he'd been when we'd first gotten together almost a year ago. Fun and flirty and less enamored with the keg stands.

Still, I was ready to leave. I'd left my gear at home—at the frustrated huffs from Brandon when I went to grab it—and I had a string of code pricking my brain.

"*Amber! Babe!*" *Brandon hollered from down the hall.*

"*Speak of the devil,*" *I said, laughing as I pushed off the couch.*

"*Come here,*" *he called again. I rounded the corner, spotting him half out of the bathroom. "I need your help.*" *His words were slightly slurred.*

I sighed, walking toward him. He was probably sick and didn't want anyone to know.

"*You all right?*" *I asked as I reached the door. He yanked me inside and shut it behind me before answering.*

"*I'm perfect now,*" *he said, his breath coated in the metallic tang of cheap beer. He pressed his body into mine, my spine tight against the closed door. His tongue darted over my lips, greedier than usual.*

"Whoa, there," I said, gently shoving him backward an inch. He'd nearly choked me with how sloppy the kiss had been.

"Whoa, there, yourself." His eyes trailed the length of my body, pausing on my legs peeking out of my short purple skirt and the dark silk V-neck shirt that hugged my curves. "Do you know how fucking sexy you look?" He reached down, sliding his hand over my leg, up and over my hip, until he gripped my breast.

"Brandon," I said, shifting so his hand wound around my back. "You're drunk."

It wasn't like he hadn't touched my breasts before—we'd graduated to some pretty heavy make-out sessions the last few months. Enough for me to talk to Mom and get on the pill. And while he continuously asked to go further, it had never felt like the right time. Regardless, I wasn't into the drunk-and-grab contest he was having with himself right now.

"I'm not drunk," he snapped before easing the sharp tone with a smile. He leaned in again, kissing me with lazy lips and a generous tongue. "You make me this way." He groaned against my neck, biting and lapping and sucking a little too hard.

I cringed, my stomach twisting the harder he pushed me against the door. "Brandon, seriously, knock it off." I shoved him, harder this time, but he only retreated a couple feet.

"God, yes," he said, rushing back to me before I could move. "I love it when you play hard to get."

I brought my elbows up between us, the backs of my forearms pushing at his massive chest as he used his whole body to pin me to the door.

"Brandon," I said, panic creeping into my tone. "Seriously, stop."

It was like he had plugs in his ears. He kept me locked in place, his huge frame too much for me to push away. Suffocating.

I yelped when he shoved his hand up my skirt and between my legs.

"Ouch!" There was nothing gentle about the way he smashed his fingers against the boy-shorts I had underneath the skirt. "Brandon," I yelled, shoving harder. "You're hurting me."

"Shhh," he cooed into my ear, his fingers greedy. Grasping. Searching. "If you relax it won't hurt. It'll feel good."

"Brandon. No!" I shouted, my entire body trembling with adrenaline that wasn't enough to stop him.

His fingers finally found the seam of the shorts, and he plunged underneath them. The motion so rough I yelped, the sting from his force sharp and snaking up my center.

"Relax," he demanded as he forced his fingers inside me again. Jabbing and pinching. His other hand roamed up my shirt, fisting my breast so hard tears pricked my eyes. His body pinned me to the door.

Suffocating.

I struggled against him, the air in my lungs tight. Aching.

He released my breast, his other hand still jabbing between my legs. He kicked at my booted feet, trying like hell to spread my legs wider as he reached for his zipper.

Sheer panic bolted through my veins like lightning when I heard *the sound of it dropping. Some primal, terrified instinct inside me took over.*

I jerked my knee up as hard as I could, hitting him straight in his junk.

"What the fuck?" he yelled, finally stumbling backward.

Tears streamed down my cheeks. I couldn't get my hands to stop shaking. I couldn't catch my breath. "Asshole."

"What?" he snapped, his hands firmly between his legs. "You hurt me*!"*

"You—! You—!" I couldn't articulate any other words.

Prickles of aches and stings resonated as I stood there shaking. My fingers fumbling at the hem of my skirt that was crumpled and hiked way too high. My head whirling because the room spun.

"Me?" He gaped at me. "Whatever. Look at you, Amber!" He pointed to my skirt and silk shirt set. "Look at the way you're dressed tonight! You were begging me for it!"

I gasped, shaking my head. "I wasn't. I wasn't."

"You were!" he snapped. "And, goddamn, Amber. We've been dating a year. This is what girlfriends do. *And more."*

I'd fallen into some other dimension where I *was the one to blame for not simply letting him do what he wanted with me. Like my body was a privilege for him, not something I controlled.*

"Then I guess it's a good thing I'm not your girlfriend anymore." I spun around, flinging the door open.

"What?" he called after me. "You're seriously breaking up with me over that? You're a fucking tease, Amber!" he shouted out the door as I stomped down the hallway. The entire party heard.

Jake and Hannah met me at the end of the hallway.

One look at Jake's murderous gaze over my shoulder and I flung my arm out to stop him.

"Jake!" I tried to snap him out of it but could barely yell his name over my sobs. "Please," I said, sniffing. "Please take me home."

Hannah wrapped her arms around me, flipping Brandon off regardless of not knowing everything that happened, and ushered me through the door. Jake followed, keys in hand. Hannah sat in the back seat with me as I cried into her chest the entire drive home.

. . .

'd barely gotten changed into my favorite *Guardians of the Galaxy* sweats before Mom knocked on the door.

"Come in," I said, thankful to be pulled out of the memory as I sank onto my bed.

"Hey, there." She sat down beside me. "Did you like the arcade?"

"Of course he told you before he told me." I grinned, shaking my head. Dean was so good. In all sorts of ways. "And I loved it."

Mom narrowed her gaze. "If that's the case, then what is this?" She pointed to the creases in my forehead, the stiff line of my jaw.

I smoothed my features. "No, Mom, I seriously loved it. It was perfect up until the end."

Mom folded her legs beneath her, giving me her full attention. Waiting silently while I tried to work out the battle in my head.

"He tried to kiss me—"

Mom's excited gasp cut me off.

"But I started crying."

She jolted, then her face softened. Her arms were around me in an instant, and I willingly leaned against her. "I'm sorry, honey."

"I can't believe I was so emotional!" I snapped. "Dean... The night he planned. The way we get along... And we *laugh*, Mom. Like, I've never laughed so much in my life."

"I know," she said. "I can see it."

"But then I ruined it. I couldn't control it. At all. The memories—" I sucked in a sharp breath, demanding my mind not to fall into the past again. "They crashed my brain."

Mom shifted a bit so she could look me in the eye. "You didn't ruin it. And that isn't stupid. That's a natural reaction after something so…" The same angry gaze coated her eyes—the one from that night—for a moment before she blinked it away. It had taken everything for me to stop her and Dad from pressing charges against Brandon. From contacting his parents, who were away when he'd thrown the party. I hadn't wanted the word to spread…didn't want to acknowledge the situation by tagging charges onto it. I'd just wanted it to disappear. To never have happened.

"You did nothing wrong," she continued. "You'll kiss Dean, or have another relationship, whenever you're good and ready. Not a second before. And if Dean doesn't understand that, then he isn't the right boy for you."

"He *does* get it, though," I said, rubbing my palms over my face. "That's what's so insane. He gets my friend rule. He wants to know *why* I have it, not change it."

Mom narrowed her gaze. "But he tried to kiss you."

A flush raced over my skin. "I wasn't exactly throwing up all my barriers," I said, remembering how badly I'd wanted him to kiss me in that moment. The charge in the air, the excitement from the night, the closeness I felt to him. "Mom." I glanced up at her. "Am I awful? For wanting to kiss him? After—"

"No," she hurried to say. "Not at all. Don't you ever think that."

It was hard *not* to think it. After what had happened, I thought I wouldn't want to kiss anyone for a long time. Never want to let someone get that close again until there were years between what happened. Then *Dean* happened, and now I wasn't sure if it was even *right* for me to be having these…desires.

"It feels different with him."

"How so?"

I sighed, my body tingling with thoughts of him. "With... *you know who*, it was never like *this*. I didn't even know it could feel like this, and Dean and I aren't even dating." I chewed on my lip. "He's perceptive and kind and funny. And when he holds my hand or when I hug him, it's like being underneath my favorite blanket and skydiving at the same time." I cringed. "That sounded so corny."

Mom chuckled. "No, baby, it doesn't. It sounds like it should be."

"I didn't understand. Before. With *Brandon*. He was nice in the beginning, and hell, he still acts indifferent toward me. Like nothing happened. But there was never this sense of urgency with him. Not like I have with Dean. Like..." *Like I can't breathe until I see or talk to him again. Like I want him to keep trying despite how much time I need to adjust.*

"I see it," she said, not needing me to say it all out loud.

"But I'm scared." Something I would never admit to anyone other than my mom. Hannah knew what had happened, but she saw me as the strong girl who was swearing off boys because of it. Not the terrified girl who never wanted to get blindsided again.

"I know," she said, running her fingers through my hair. "I wish I could tell you that feeling will go away soon, but I can't. I'm afraid you'll always have that worry in the back of your mind. That voice that warns you to be careful around people. But..." She sighed. "You can't let what happened define you. You *can* let it define the time you need to let someone in again." She smiled softly. "I'm so damn proud of you, honey."

The night it happened, I'd sobbed in her arms and asked her if *I'd* done something wrong. If I was broken because I couldn't simply let him do what he wanted.

"You are such an amazing, smart girl," she continued.

"And you don't have to do a damn thing you don't want to do."

"I know," I said. "But what if I *do*? Want to."

Mom pressed her lips together, nodding. "Then you listen to your heart and your gut. Just like you did before. It felt wrong. It was wrong."

I recoiled.

That night. He said *I* was wrong.

He still felt that *I* was the one who had betrayed him.

"You listen to those instincts and they'll let you know." She eyed me. "And if they scream yes, then…" She shifted on the bed, her eyebrows raised. "You better be *safe*. You're still taking the—"

"Mom," I groaned. "Yes." I was still taking the pill she'd helped me get on all those months ago because I didn't want to deal with the side effects if I got off it, but I knew for certain there was no need for it. "I literally cried when he tried to kiss me today. I'm not even to that level yet."

She waved her hands in the air. "It can happen fast. Especially when you're already friends with the person. Trust me, I would know."

I tilted my head.

"Your dad and I were friends for *years* before he made a move. And when he did?" She whistled, rolling her eyes back in her head. "Game over. I barely waited two seconds before giving it up to him."

"Ugh, gross, Mom!" I play-shoved at her. "You have to leave now," I said as she rolled off the bed, laughing. "Write another book so you can afford the therapy I need for that comment!"

"You think your father would charge me?" She laughed.

"I'd *never* let Dad treat me! Talk about a conflict of interest!" I rolled my eyes, biting back my own laugh.

"Love you, honey." She held the doorknob.

"Love you," I said, still cringing as she shut the door.

It took me a good twenty minutes to shake off the heebie-jeebies that Mom's story had left, but I happily distracted myself with the website. It was easy enough to forget the entire night when buried in comment after comment after comment.

What color of underwear do you wear?

Do you like to use toys? Is that weird if you do?

Where is the best place to do it if you don't want to get caught?

I was overwhelmed with the questions, more than half of them totally over my head. I was a virgin. The only experience I had with intimacy was jagged as broken glass. Was I really being helpful? Or was I simply a soundboard for questions like this?

No, I could *feel* the solidarity in the posts I'd done. I had to believe I was helping or all this was for nothing.

And I did have *two* amazing sources.

Not that talking sex with Mom was enjoyable—clearly—but she was willing to do it. She never shied from a question.

And if I ever got any questions that were beyond sex and more emotional…I'd go to Dad. It was what he did on a daily basis.

My fingers itched. The whirl of emotions begging me to focus on someone else's needs for a few hours. It was definitely time for another blog post.

All I had to do was pick one out of the hundreds of questions stuffing my inbox.

No big deal.

The hard part?

Maintaining the balance—the question that would be the most helpful as well as being a big middle finger to

Principal Tanner and all the other authority figures out there who had ignored this need for years. That is, if it ever fell on his radar. And if it didn't?

Dean would look amazing in the deadmau5 T-shirt.

ASK ME ANYTHING

QUESTION OF THE DAY

TWcrashandburn asks: *"I'm on the pill. We use condoms, too. I've been with my boyfriend for so long and want to try it without one. Is the pill enough? Am I crazy to not want the barrier between us?"*

I would never think you're crazy. It's awesome that you and your boyfriend have been in a relationship long enough to reach this point of trust. That is something to be valued.

The pill, if taken according to the instructions, is 99.9% effective. The numbers say yes, you'll be fine trying it sans condom. But there is always the chance for complications, so the choice is really up to you and your boyfriend. Talk about the risks vs. rewards, and come to a decision you both can agree on.

Nothing is 100%, and while I'm sure there are plenty of couples who use only one form of birth control, doubling up is always a safer play. The choice is ultimately yours to make, but the numbers are here for you to see.

Whichever you choose, I hope you and your boyfriend take the step together and on the same page.

In the meantime,
Stay Sexy. Stay Healthy.

• • •

I sat on my bed, sipping my iced green tea for several minutes after the blog had been published. I couldn't get the concept out of my head—having sex regularly to the point where you wanted *nothing* between you and your partner.

I mean, holy intense.

But...Dean and I...the feelings I had for him were growing.

Strong.

And that was terrifying enough, but now I couldn't help but picture Dean and myself in similar situations to whatever my question of the day posed.

I'd fallen into a rhythm and had been posting every day for almost two months now. It was exhausting but so rewarding, and it was almost second nature. I was certain both my parents thought I was contemplating going into their chosen professions from all the questions I asked each of them—either an erotica novelist or a teen psychologist. Funny, I never would've thought the two knowledge bases would overlap so much.

But I was beyond grateful they did.

Because some of the answers I could dig up on my own, but the tougher stuff? They'd been a massive help. The key to everything.

A twist in my gut squashed the once-warm fluttering butterflies.

What if there came a time they pushed me on all the questions?

What if they knew what I was doing?

I swallowed down the acid bubbling in my throat.

Despite the cold fear icing my spine, I knew I wouldn't stop.

Couldn't stop.

Not when my inbox was overflowing, and there were countless people seeking help or solidarity or simply a safe place to talk.

As long as that was the case, I couldn't turn my back on them.

CHAPTER SIXTEEN

DEAN

"Tessa Rae Winters," I chided as I spotted my sister making a beeline for the front door. She stopped short at the sound of her full name.

"Ugh!" She shook out her arms. "*Don't.* You sound like Dad."

I chuckled, folding my arms over my chest as I reached her. "Where do you think you're going?"

She blinked up at me, baffled. "Colt's."

I shook my head. "You didn't forget, did you?"

Where is her head at lately?

"What?" She furrowed her brow, a flash of panic in her eyes.

My shoulders dropped.

"You want to have another heart-to-heart brownie session?" she asked, a slight teasing in her tone.

"Ha, ha." I remembered the brownie session from months ago—time was flying by, most of it consumed by TOC prep, website maintenance, and Amber. The brownies had been my attempt to reconnect with my baby sister. Tessa and I *had* talked that day, sure, but I could tell she was hiding something—she'd been more distracted and absent than me lately. But, when she'd claimed it was nothing—just girl stuff—I had backed off, hoping the gesture was enough for her to know I would always have her back. "It's Mom and Dad's anniversary," I said, and her jaw dropped.

"No, that's on Friday." She tilted her head.

I rubbed my palms over my face. "Tessa, it *is* Friday."

Did she skip class today? How else would she forget it's the beginning of the weekend?

"Oh," she said, her eyes spacing for a minute before she came back around. "*Oh!*" A bright smile lit up her face for the first time in weeks, and I breathed a sigh.

"There she is," I said, wrapping an arm around her shoulder.

"Did they already leave?" she asked, not bothering to look at me while she typed out a fast text.

"Yup," I said, leading her into the entertainment room. "An hour ago. Mom texted to say they'd checked in safe and sound. Also ordered us not to stay up all night or burn down the house."

Tessa chuckled and bounced on her toes when she spotted the coffee table in front of our couch. I'd loaded it with all the goods—two thin-crust pepperoni pizzas, three bowls of popcorn, and enough candy and soda to last us all night.

"Yes!" She clapped and then pointed at me. "I've got to get back in my PJs," she said, determined. "Colt knows I'm staying in tonight! Is Sean coming?"

"Already here, sister!" Sean called from the kitchen.

"What?" She disappeared in a blink, no doubt tackle-hugging him.

Relief swirled through my blood—she'd been ghosting us both, but clearly our annual tradition meant more to her than whatever was going on. Maybe I was making a bigger deal about it than it was. Maybe it really was just girl stuff. Stuff I'd never understand.

Amber might.

The memory of our almost-kiss last week rippled

through me. I couldn't lie to myself anymore, I had it bad. But it was way beyond the physical desire churning in my gut. I wanted every piece of her…she just wasn't ready to give them to me yet.

"Is Amber coming?" Sean asked, rounding the corner while I heard Tessa race back upstairs to change clothes.

I blinked out of my thoughts.

"Nah," I said, waving him off. "This is *family* tradition."

Not that I wouldn't love to have her here. To be a part of something so important between my siblings and me.

"Wow," Sean said, sinking onto the couch and cracking open a can of soda. "I hadn't realized we meant that much to you."

I rolled my eyes, taking my seat at the opposite end of the couch. "Sure," I said. "And you're missing college-level parties on a Friday night to watch a movie with your kid siblings because you don't care."

He set the can on the coffee table, grinning. "It's not just *any* movie. It's *the* movie." His brow furrowed and he rolled his eyes toward the ceiling like he'd forgotten something.

"What?" I asked.

"Come here," he said, whispering while he stared at the ceiling.

Is Tessa talking to someone up there?

I leaned in closer, straining my ears to hear.

A hard, solid punch stung my shoulder, and I flinched back, instantly rubbing the sore spot. "What the fuck, dude?"

"Just keeping you on your toes," he said before arching his head back. "Tessa!" he screamed.

"I'm coming!" she yelled back.

"Damn," Sean said. "How long can it take to put on PJs?"

I laughed. "Dude, you've been away too long. She takes two hours to get ready in the morning."

"No shit?"

"It's so annoying. I have to steal Mom's bathroom to get ready."

Sean snorted. "And all her products she's obsessed with are everywhere."

"For real," I said. "I walk out of there smelling like a chick every time."

We laughed until our sides hurt. Until Tessa finally came downstairs.

"Why are you two always laughing when I walk into the room?" she asked, plopping down between us.

"Because we're talking about you," Sean said.

"Naturally," I agreed.

She rolled her eyes, folding her legs beneath her before she reached for the remote. "First up?" Tessa clicked the remote's source button, pulling up the Blu-ray I'd put in earlier. "Yes!" She fist-bumped the air and hit play.

"This movie is such a classic," Sean said.

"Seriously," Tessa agreed.

"A time when it was all new and not corrupted," I added.

"Shh," Tessa chided me as the *Hackers* opening flashed across the screen. She grabbed a slice out of the pizza box and handed it to me. Then Sean, then herself. "Cheers," she whispered, tapping her pizza against ours.

"Cheers," Sean and I said at the same time.

Every year since we were big enough to be left under Sean's supervision, we held a movie marathon on Mom and Dad's anniversary. Even after he went to college, he always came back to carry on the tradition.

Somehow, this year seemed much more important. I wasn't sure if it was the fact that I'd be graduating soon or if it was the recent distance between me and Tessa, or everything that had shifted within me because of Amber.

A lump formed in my throat, so large it was hard to swallow around it.

Everything was changing, but *this*—sitting with my brother and sister, watching our favorite movie of all time—*this* would stay the same. It would be our constant. No matter what. The notion was more comforting than I'd ever realized.

An hour into the movie, I contemplated the odds that Amber had chosen her hacker handle as a slight homage to the great AcidBurn, and was reminding myself to ask her when my cell buzzed loudly on the table.

"Boo!" Sean and Tessa hollered as I hopped up to answer it, thinking it might be Amber.

I was instantly deflated when I didn't recognize the number on the screen. "Sorry!" I said, snapping at Tessa and miming her to pause it. She rolled her eyes but did as I stepped away to answer the call.

"Mr. Winters." Tanner's voice echoed on the other end of the line.

"Principal Tanner?" I asked, baffled at why I was merited a call on my cell from him.

I raised my free arm at Sean and Tessa's curious gazes. "What's up?" I asked.

"I need you to do something for me. It's imperative."

"Okay," I said, wondering why this couldn't wait until Monday.

"I'm assuming you've read or at least heard about the rebellious blog *Ask Me Anything*, am I right?"

"I've heard about it," I said, pacing back and forth as I held the cell to my ear.

"Recent posts and protests from parents across the district have made it clear I need to take action."

"Okay."

"I need you to uncover the source behind the blog. The creator's claims to be a Wilmont student have placed the academy under scrutiny."

"What?" I asked. "I can't do that." I hadn't read the blog religiously, but I knew it was anonymous.

"You must."

"It would be a major privacy violation, not to mention unethical," I explained. Not that all my hacks were completely pure, but I never did anything that would hurt someone—unless you counted messing with Sean, which I didn't, because he started it.

"Winters," he said, his tone sharp. "The person behind this blog is harming students' lives. The content is damaging to their minds."

I scoffed. *And you cracking the whip to students to ensure your precious position and awards and grants and raises isn't?* The accusation was hot on my tongue, but I bit it. "Where is the proof?" I asked. I'd heard some parents were in an uproar, but students from all different high schools were rallying behind the site. Tessa had told me that much over the last time I'd brought brownies—something I tried to do at least monthly, if only to keep up with what was going on in her life. She'd said it was a safe space to ask questions without being judged.

"I don't need proof," he snapped. "The creator claims Wilmont. That means one of mine is causing this distasteful disturbance within our academic community. The content alone is enough for disciplinary action."

"I can't do it," I said again. "Get someone else." I knew he couldn't. Not for something so obviously *wrong*. Exposing someone because you didn't agree with their ideals—regardless of the harm it would do to them upon discovery—was beyond unethical. He called me because he didn't want anyone to know what he was doing.

"I was afraid you'd say that," he said. "I was hoping to avoid this next piece of the conversation, but you've left me no choice." He cleared his throat. "You know that little stunt someone pulled during my presentation? The one you failed to prevent?"

"Mm-hmm," I mumbled, adrenaline coursing through my veins. This guy. His threats. They wouldn't work on me. I'd been on call for him ever since I failed to get the video down soon enough, but this…this task was too messed up to care about that anymore. And if he threatened to not recommend me when MIT called, then I would go straight to VP Howard.

"I discovered who the culprit is. The student *did* steal my personal laptop. Overnight. Returned it before the sun came up the next day."

"How'd you figure that out?" And what the hell did it have to do with me?

"I've known for quite some time, actually," he said. "I have cameras in my office."

I gaped at the phone. "That's…" *Creepy. Invasion of privacy when students are called in there unaware. Creepier.* "I'm not following." There was no way he could hold the theft over me. I hadn't been the one to lift his shit.

"You will uncover the source behind that horrendous website," he said. "Or I'll hand the footage over to the authorities."

My hand shook as I saw red. I lowered my cell for a second, hitting a few buttons before speaking. "Say again?"

He grumbled. "Find out who is behind the site and bring the information to me, or I'll hand over the culprit to the authorities."

"You're threatening me?" I whisper-hissed, not wanting

Sean or Tessa to be involved in this twisted conversation.

"Educating you, son. *Educating.* That's what I do."

"And blackmailing students is a modern-day teaching tool?" The words were out of my mouth before I could stop them.

He had the audacity to laugh. "Wilmont Academy is number one in the district and number five in the nation. The *nation,* Mr. Winters. I have to do whatever it takes to keep it that way."

You mean keep your job.

"And reputations, familial relationships, friendships, emotional stability—those fallouts from your *education.* Do they matter to you?"

"No," he said flatly. "Blips. A few tears. A new group of friends. None of that matters at your stage of life. It will disappear, but the Wilmont legacy will be remembered for decades to come."

"That's all that matters to you—your legacy."

"That," he said. "And justice. Those who rebel against me must be made an example of. And this little *Ask Me Anything*? The person responsible must be punished."

"For helping students?"

"Harming."

"According to *you.* According to *your* ideals," I snapped. Everything about Tanner had built up and his empty threats had brought everything to the surface. "Isn't it your job as a principal to remove your own bias and cultivate programs that help students excel regardless of their sexually active status?"

He laughed again. "You have no idea what it is like to be responsible for the young minds of the future. I do what I have to—whatever I have to—to ensure their success. What seems harsh to you is what will make this world a better place in the years to come."

Wow. God Complex much?

"Whatever," I said, wearing a path in my carpet. "This has nothing to do with me. I'm not an errand boy or your personal tech guy."

"Oh, Mr. Winters," he said. "You wouldn't want Tessa to have a black mark on her record before she's even reached her senior year, would you? I imagine something like jail time or a court date would harm her chances of following you and your brother to MIT someday."

I halted in my tracks, my eyes falling on Tessa sitting on the couch, laughing at something Sean had said.

Ice froze the fire in my veins.

Tessa.

She'd been hiding something from me.

Something had been eating at her.

Fucking hell.

She'd gone after Tanner. His presentation. She'd…

I rubbed my palms over my face.

"Are you listening now, Mr. Winters?"

"Yes," I said, the bite gone from my voice.

He had me right where he wanted me. It didn't matter that I would graduate in mere months. Tessa would be at Wilmont another two *years*. Sure, she could transfer to another school in the district, but Wilmont was the *best*. It had more academic programs and extracurriculars than any other. Plus, graduating from Wilmont increased odds of being accepted to an Ivy League.

I would do anything to protect her. To protect that future.

Bastard.

"*Sir*," he said.

"What?"

"*Yes, sir.*"

I clenched my jaw. "Yes, sir."

"I expect a report on your progress on Monday. Bright and early."

"Fine."

"And, Mr. Winters?"

"Yes."

"Don't take too long to find this person," he said. "For Tessa's sake."

"Understood." I ended the call, the cell trembling in my hands. I stared at Tessa while I caught my breath, anger and sadness and confusion storming me.

I had no choice.

I would never throw Tessa to the wolves—aka our principal.

It didn't matter how messed up outing this person would be. For Tessa…I'd break every law.

After a few deep breaths, I walked back into the living room.

"Took you long enough," Sean said, reaching for the remote.

"Seriously, bro," Tessa said, her voice so much lighter than I'd heard it in weeks. "How is Amber?"

I flashed her a soft grin.

"Whoa," she said, straightening as I sank on the couch, leaning my head back like it was too heavy to hold up. "Everything okay?"

I rolled my head to the side, locking eyes with her.

No. I wish you would've talked to me. Told me.

"Fine," I said. "Everything is fine."

ASK ME ANYTHING

ABOUT   USEFUL LINKS   FAQ   CHAT WITH ME

PrincessQueenB7634 asks: *"I think I'm allergic to latex because, reasons. I'm terrified to ask a doc and I know for sure I can't ask my parents. I'm too scared to go looking, but my boyfriend isn't. Is there anything else I can tell him to buy so I'm not in so much pain?"*

I'm sorry to hear that you're in pain. That has to be incredibly frustrating. I understand the fear of talking about it, too. That's why I'm here. Even though I know certain school officials and parents wish I wasn't.

Luckily, there are several non-latex condoms sold by recognizable brands like Trojan, Durex, and Skyn.

Also lucky, they are in almost every store you'd buy regular condoms at, so your boyfriend should be able to easily find them. Tell him to double-check the ingredients on the back and make sure it says "latex free." Common material for non-latex are super-intense words like Polyisoprene or Polyurethane, but don't let that freak you out. If you feel up to Googling it—which I totes understand if you don't—there are plenty of numbers and commenters who have used them and enjoyed them safely.

But, if the issue of whether you are or aren't allergic to latex is still bothering you, you could always present the question to your doctor or parents in a different way. For instance, saying you had to wear latex gloves for a volunteer lunch-serving sesh and had a reaction. I'm not condoning direct lying, but when it comes to matters of health, you should always do whatever it takes to keep yourself safe.

I'll be here crossing my fingers that one of these solutions works for you and that you feel so much better!

In the meantime,

Stay Sexy. Stay Healthy.

CHAPTER SEVENTEEN

AMBER

"You haven't ever been, have you?" Hannah asked, her voice a whisper as we stood outside the coding room. She held up her phone, the "useful links" tab pulled up on the *Ask Me Anything* site, focused on the list of places to score birth control.

"No," I said, swallowing hard. She'd brought up the blog a few times, and each time guilt ate at my insides when I had to act surprised by the content. "Sorry. Mom always picks the pills up for me."

She rolled her eyes, face-palming herself. "Right," she said, laughing. "I wish my mom was as chill as yours."

"Me, too," I said and wrapped an arm around her shoulder when she pocketed her phone. "Have you tried talking to her about it?"

"OMG no!" she said. "She'd lose her mind. I'd be grounded forever, plus they'd probably pull all my allowance, too." She sighed.

"But didn't you say she's one of the people on the board trying to push out Tanner's ancient way of thinking? Maybe she'd be more open to it than you think?"

Maybe Hannah was letting her fear overexaggerate her mother's response?

"Just because she wants progression in the academy doesn't mean she wants it for her daughter. It's fine. Is what it is. Let's talk about something else. Like the fact that it took you two full days to tell me about your date with—"

I clamped my hand over her mouth, glancing behind me and into the room. Dean and Mr. Griffin were in some kind of intense discussion. Once Hannah stopped mumbling against my palm, I dropped it.

"He could've heard you!" I hissed.

"So?" she whispered. "He nailed the first date to a *T*."

"Yeah, and I totally rewarded him by botching it."

"Please." She waved me off. "That's ridiculous."

I shrugged. "Back to you."

"Right," she said, sighing. "The place I normally go to now has this boutique spa thing right next to it."

"So?"

"So," she continued. "My mother now frequents said spa."

"Shit."

"Double shit," she agreed.

"Okay," I said. "Are you going to go to the one on Ninth?"

She tilted her head. "How did you know about the one on Ninth?"

I jolted internally, realizing my massive slip. Ms. *Ask Me Anything* knew about a variety of places to get birth control sans a parent's consent. The virgin Amber whose mom picks up her pills for her shouldn't have a clue. "You legit just had it up on your phone," I said, trying to sound nonchalant about it even though I couldn't have possibly read the entire post in the brief time she had it up.

"Duh." She narrowed her gaze. "And whoever *Ask Me Anything* is, she's been on point so far, right?"

"I don't know. I don't follow her religiously."

"You should!" Hannah waggled her eyebrows. "She's legit amazing." She glanced around the hallway, the place thin with students since school had ended. "I keep wondering who she is."

My skin tightened, like the jolt to my senses could somehow shrink me so much she wouldn't be able to see what I was hiding.

"You know Regent Academy ran a piece about the blog in their paper?"

"What?" I snapped.

"Yeah," she said, adjusting her bag on her shoulder. "Jake and I saw it when we went to Carla's party Friday night."

The same night I was having the best non-date of my life, Hannah was reading about my blog from *another* school's paper.

"The girl who wrote the piece was showing it off on her iPad. Said her principal lost her shit over it. Tried to get the journalism professor to take it down, but he refused. Said it was an insightful piece about the ways the peer-led blog is helping students or something."

A warm petal of pride bloomed in my chest, a small smile shaping my lips. "That's awesome," I said, then quickly added, "that a teacher was willing to back his student."

"Right?" She nodded. "That's what I said to Jake. There are a lot of cool teachers here, but most of them are terrified of Tanner." She glanced around like he might pop up at any moment. "Rightfully so. Am I awful when I say I wouldn't be sad if the board finally pushed him out?"

"No, I completely agree," I said. "But Ms. Howard is legit."

"Totally." Hannah waved enthusiastically as she spied something over my shoulder, and I didn't need to check to know Jake was headed our way. The sappy look in her eyes said it all. The same one I'm sure happened to me whenever Dean opened his mouth to say…words.

"Hi, Jake," I said before he'd rounded me to get to Hannah.

"Amber," he said, scooping Hannah in a hug that lifted her off her feet. "Gorgeous," he said to her, rubbing his nose along her jaw like he wanted to bathe in her scent.

Maybe if it was something like cedar, Red Bull, and soap. *Dean's* scent.

A warm shiver raced up my spine, some true physical heat lapping up my back.

"Hey, Pixie." Dean's voice filled my ears, and I bit back my grin as I turned toward him.

"Hey," I said, my voice cracking as I looked up at him. He was so tall and his eyes were so open and more blue than gray today. Probably because he wore a bright blue T-shirt that made his eyes—and his lithe muscles—pop.

"Hi, Dean!" Hannah said, with enough innuendo to curl my stomach inward. "Excited for Code Club?"

Dean and I cringed at the same time, but he smiled at her. "Always," he said, glancing down at me. "Are you recruiting them?"

I burst out laughing. "These two?" I motioned to them. "No way. Leave them to their own devices in a dark, secluded room?" I huffed air through my lips. "They'd never get anything done."

Dean laughed.

Jake shrugged. "Come on," he said, wrapping his arms around Hannah from behind. "You wouldn't, either, if you were dating someone as brilliant as this girl."

Hannah blushed, rolling her eyes. "Stop," she teased him. "We were just talking about *Ask Me Anything*," she said, eyeing Dean. "Do you read it?"

Dean straightened and tilted his head back and forth. "Sometimes," he said before glancing at me. "Whoever it is…the girl sure knows how to code. Any ideas on who it might be?"

A rock lodged itself in my throat, and I was certain I'd burst into flames right then and there. Why did Hannah have to bring it up? Why did he have to be curious?

I shrugged. "There are six girls in Griffin's class," I said. "Holly, Kristy, Sara, Quinn, Monroe, and me. Could be any one of them."

There. I'd included myself. Not a direct lie.

I *wanted* to tell him.

But I didn't want him involved if shit hit the fan and I was somehow uncovered.

Plus, it was the challenge rules to keep it a secret.

Didn't matter, guilt still ate at my insides. I hoped my answer would satisfy his random curiosity and he'd soon forget he even wondered about it.

"Oh," Hannah said. "I bet it's Monroe."

"Why?" Dean asked instantly.

"She's quiet, keeps to herself. Don't all the good hackers tend to do that?"

I rolled my eyes. "You always group us. Truth is, no two act the same."

"Truth," Dean agreed.

"Anyway," I said, trying like hell to steer the subject somewhere else. "Speaking of coding…shouldn't we be going?"

"Yeah," Dean said, but something churned behind his eyes. Gears constantly turning.

Jake unwound himself from Hannah, stepping closer to Dean. "You're being good to Amber, right?"

My jaw practically came unhinged. What the hell was with today?

"Jake!" Hannah and I snapped at the same time.

"What?" Jake asked innocently, crossing his arms over his chest while he sized Dean up. "I meant in this club."

He *so* didn't. Anyone could tell that. And if it wasn't so damn embarrassing, I might've appreciated his protectiveness. As it was, I'd already mortified myself enough in front of Dean. I didn't need Jake adding to it.

"It's okay," Dean said, his voice calm. He looked Jake in the eye, never losing his gaze. "Of course I am," he said. "I'm not like…" He narrowed his eyes. "Like assholes not to be named. I actually give a damn about her."

Jake tipped his chin, scanning Dean's face for a few moments before he nodded. "Good. Because she's important to me. And I already let one jerk hurt her." He spared me a glance full of regret. "I'll never let that happen again."

Dean shook his head. "I'd never hurt her. And I'm glad she has friends like you."

I gaped at them both before stomping my foot. "*Her* is standing right exactly here! And she's doing just fine taking care of *herself*." I rolled my eyes, waving off Hannah as I bolted into the coding room, leaving them to as much of their macho-protective-whatever talk they wanted.

My skin still blazed by the time Dean scooted into his seat across from me. He opened his gear with a smirk on his face, like earning Jake's approval had meant something to him.

I dutifully ignored him, electing instead to draw up a practice run of CTF, since Mr. Griffin had decided to work later than normal. Usually he left us to our devices on Code Club days, but some kind of performance reports kept him in the room with us today—which meant I couldn't possibly work on the website. Normally, I'd use this time to reassure the firewalls around the site and read more comments to get an idea for the next blog post.

The idea of Mr. Griffin catching me was enough to stop that urge dead in its tracks.

After an hour, I'd successfully completed a crypto CTF challenge—this one more math based than I liked, making it ten times harder to crack.

"You two make me look bad," Griffin said, and both Dean and I had to blink a few times to register his presence. "Work harder than I do," he continued, his bag over his shoulder.

"Code Club is no joking matter, Mr. Griffin," Dean said, barely holding back a laugh. "I've had to change the font on the school's website for the third time this month. Tanner thinks Times is outdated."

"Totally," I said. "And Code Club takes long hours and dedication and…" I never made it any further, submitting to the fit of giggles as Mr. Griffin nodded his head back and forth.

"Ha, ha," he said. "I get it. You're forced to be here." He glanced at me. "Well, Dean is, not you. And yet here you are."

"You know your class is my favorite," I said.

"Yeah, yeah," he said. "Regardless of the reasons this club was formed, you two push each other. It's good. The friendly competition. Makes you stronger." He nodded. "Be good. Don't stay too late and all the usual," he said, heading toward the door.

"Will do," I replied.

"See you, Mr. Griffin," Dean called as Griffin left the room, leaving the door wide open behind him. Dean turned his focus back on me. "What were you doing?"

"CTF. You?"

"Besides slaying font changes?" He chuckled. "Practice penetration. Password cracking. Among other things…" His eyes drifted to his screen, a flash of anger that made me tilt my head. A blink and it was gone.

"Better than me," I said, wondering if I had imagined the look in the first place. Maybe I *was* working too hard.

"Different." He grinned. "I have to take the time I can to get ready for the TOC."

I ran my fingers over the edges of my opened laptop. "Is our challenge getting in the way of that?"

He furrowed his brow. "No."

I tilted my head.

"It's not. I've got this whole balance thing happening." He stretched his arms over his head, the motion hiking his shirt up enough for me to see his chiseled abs.

Sweet Loki's helmet, when does the boy have time to work out?

I knew his brother loved to live at the gym when he wasn't hacking, but was it the same for Dean?

Sure looked like it. I swallowed hard, trying to remember how to breathe.

"Are you worried?" he asked, and I blinked out of my red-hot haze.

"Huh?"

"About me and the TOC?"

I straightened in my seat, having somehow melted partially in the last five seconds. "No. I know you'll slay it. We'll both get our acceptance letters, too. I just want to make sure I'm not getting in the way. We can call it off, if that's the case."

Dean scooted out of his chair and came around to lean against my table. "Are you wanting to call it off?"

The thought had crossed my mind. As the questions continued to pile up and my daily posts became a daily reminder that I wasn't exactly qualified to handle each problem presented.

"No," I finally said.

"You took a while to get that one out."

I shrugged. "Big hack. Big thoughts."

"Touché."

He stared down at me, easy, patient, but with something behind his eyes. A question.

I looked right back at him, thinking about our non-date, about how much I wished I could redo the end of the night.

"Do you think you might want to help me find—"

"You don't have a choice," Principal Tanner's voice from the hallway cut off whatever Dean almost asked me.

We glanced at each other, confused by the hushed but harsh tone in Tanner's voice. Then, in some silent agreement, we stood up and moved closer toward the door. A stealthy peek revealed a student in Tessa's class, a redheaded girl I couldn't remember the name of, as she stood at her open locker.

"I didn't copy anything, Principal Tanner. I swear," she said, staring up at him where he stood with his hands in his pockets.

"The matching papers say otherwise."

"Have you talked to Todd?" she asked. "Because maybe we used the same sources? Mr. Coldwell gave us all a list of preferred sites he wanted us to use for research."

Tanner shook his head, sharp like a razor. "No. What you and Mr. Langwater did was unacceptable. I have grounds to expel you."

Tears filled her eyes, and I glanced at Dean.

Should we say something? Should we leave?

Dean shook his head, returning focus to the scene happening just outside.

Did Tanner forget we had the club today? Or did he assume we were locked in?

The girl shook her head. "Please," she said. "My parents would kill me. And I swear I didn't copy."

"Then perhaps Mr. Langwater did."

The girl sagged in relief.

"However," Tanner continued, and she tensed again. "You are as culpable as he is."

"What do you want me to do?" she asked. "I'll rewrite the paper. On a different topic this time—"

"That won't be necessary," he said. "You focus on your current schoolwork. Don't let your grades dip a fraction." She nodded enthusiastically. "And," he said, placing his hands behind his back. "If I need you to tutor some struggling students, you will. It would also be beneficial if you mentioned to your father how I'm letting you off easy... dare say, *scot-free*, after such an infraction."

The girl froze, confusion transforming her face.

That made three of us by the look Dean and I shared.

"You want me to tell my dad about this?" she asked.

"He's on our academic board, is he not?"

"Yes, but—"

"Then if you want to keep this incident a secret, you could perhaps simply mention how you have an understanding principal. One who cares about what happens in your future. One who doesn't immediately punish despite there being grounds to do so."

Her lips parted, to argue or merely respond, I wasn't sure, but she clamped them shut.

"I wouldn't want to see your record marred for the sake of formalities." He straightened his tie. "Do we understand each other?"

"Yes, sir." She lowered her head, completely defeated.

Anger roared in my gut. Without thinking, I took a step toward the hallway, ready to flip him off and give the girl a fucking hug.

Dean's long arm shot out to stop me, ushering me backward into the coding room. He quietly shut the door.

"What are you thinking?" he asked, his tone sharp. "Do you want Tanner to know you saw that? Do you know what he could do to you?"

"Are you?" I snapped, pointing toward the closed door. I'd never seen Dean upset before...but he was *clearly* more upset about me being willing to go help the girl despite the risks than over what we just witnessed. "You heard and saw the same thing I did!"

He raised his hands in an attempt to get me to lower my voice. "I did."

"Then how can you stop me from going to talk to her?"

He stopped before me. "Because I *did* see what you saw. He blackmailed her."

"Right!" I flung my arms up. "So why are we standing here doing a whole lot of nothing?"

"Because," he said. "We have to be smarter than that. If he knew *we* knew what just went down..." He raked his fingers through his hair, and a calculative look flashed behind his eyes. He was somewhere else, working on multiple problems at once.

My shoulders dropped. "I can't do nothing."

"I know," he said. "I know. But I can't have you in trouble t—" He sighed, cutting off his words. "I can't, either. Just give me a minute to *think*."

He paced the small space before me, the intensity far more than I would've guessed for the situation. Was he hiding something? No, he was more open than anyone I'd ever met. I took a deep breath. Watching his mind work was like a shot of clarity and calm to my own brain. Tanner was pushing things too far—the board threatening his job had to be the culprit, but it didn't excuse this intense personal vendetta he seemed to have.

"I know what to do," I said, brushing past him. I stopped

with my hand on the knob. "You can stay here, if you want. Not be an accomplice or whatever you want to call it."

He stalked toward me, his hand covering mine on the knob. "DC, remember?"

Something warm and strong pulsed in the center of my chest.

"What's the plan?" he asked.

I motioned for him to follow me then led him into the now-empty hallway. I made the twists and turns, carefully opening the doors to the principal's office. Tanner's door was closed; either he'd left or he was in there and wanting privacy. He wasn't my objective.

The door to his left was.

Ms. Howard was behind her desk, working late, totally absorbed in her computer screen as she clicked away. Dean followed me inside and shut the door, the soft click causing Ms. Howard to jump.

"Holy sh—" She cleared her throat, laying her palms flat on her desk. "You two scared me."

"Sorry," we said at the same time.

"I need to talk to you," I said, leaning against her desk, too much adrenaline to sit in the chairs before it.

"Okay," she said, eyeing Dean and then back to me.

I took a deep breath, the image of her immediately running and telling Tanner what we saw, how we were ratting him out, icy clear and terrifying in my mind. The anger for that girl outweighed my fear, and I opened my mouth.

Ms. Howard listened to me recount exactly what we'd heard and seen only minutes ago. Nodding and pinching the bridge of her nose as the story ended. My chest rose and fell when I finished as if I'd run a 5k.

She parted her lips, but a knock on her door jolted each of us.

"I'm heading home," Principal Tanner said, opening the door without an invitation. "Do you need me to walk you to your car—" He spotted us standing there. Dean gave a little wave, whereas I stood frozen solid. "Oh," he said. "I didn't realize you had students here."

Ms. Howard smiled. "I asked them here," she said, and Tanner tilted his head.

"After hours?"

"After Code Club," she said, and I was immediately shocked. She deserved so many props for covering for us. "I wanted an update on their progress. See if they needed any help recruiting new members. It's a great idea you've had," she said, grinning at Tanner. He actually smiled slightly. "They've both taught each other things I think they didn't even know they needed to learn. And the academy's website has never looked or worked better." She glanced at us and we both nodded.

"For sure," Dean said.

"Absolutely," I added.

"Wonderful," Tanner said. "You'll be working a little later, then?"

"Yes," she said, motioning to her desk. "I've got some things to wrap up here. I'll be all right on my own, though. Thank you for the offer."

He nodded, then eyed Dean and me. "Keep up the good work."

I smiled, and Dean nodded. Then we all took one damn deep breath when Tanner closed the door behind him.

Too close.

What had I been thinking?

That Tanner was using his power for evil.

Oh right, that. Okay, so maybe not totally evil, but *clearly* he was immersed in his personal vendetta.

Anger returned. I refocused on Ms. Howard, who had stepped around her desk, her ear pressed to the door. After a few moments of silence, she sighed.

"I hate that you two were put in this position," she said, her green eyes sincere. "But I'm also honored that you trusted me enough to come to me with it." She held her hands over her chest, her pink sweater complementing her lavender nails. "Unfortunately," she continued, "this isn't the first time I've heard something like this happening this year."

"You're not serious," I said, glaring at the door like I could mentally punch Tanner in his throat. I glanced at Dean, my eyes narrowing at his complete lack of shock.

"Wait," Dean said finally. "Why hasn't something been done?"

Ms. Howard swallowed hard, her voice almost a whisper. "I took the firsthand account to the board myself. The student, naturally, was too afraid to speak for himself. With the way Wilmont students are awarded scholarships and grants..." She sighed. "There is so much at stake if they make the wrong move here." She shook her head. "The board said I didn't have enough evidence to merit disciplinary action toward their highest-ranking school official."

"That's bullshit," Dean snapped, then raised his hands. "Sorry."

She waved him off. "It certainly is."

"I thought the board was pushing for change? Pushing for Tanner's removal."

Her eyes widened. "I'm not sure how you know that, Amber, but..." She straightened. "There are pieces moving. It's not as easy as snapping our fingers. We have to have a collective vote, and the state board gets involved, too." She glanced between us both. "Trust me, I'm trying...several of us are trying to create a change. If I had more proof of the recent transgressions," she said, "something that his word wouldn't crush? I would use it." She shrugged. "But I don't."

I huffed, crossing my arms. "So he just gets to keep doing this to students? All in the name of keeping his job?"

Ms. Howard tensed, as if contemplating if she should say anything or not. "Wilmont is one of the top private schools in the nation. A majority of its students go on to get full-ride scholarships to top-five colleges. The better Wilmont's students perform, the more grants, funds, awards, and *raises* its principal receives." She eyed us, the point clearly, terribly sinking in. "That, plus his family's lineage with Wilmont… It gives him a very big platform from which to dictate his own personal views."

I ground my jaw. "Selfish bastard." I glanced at her. "Sorry not sorry."

She tugged at the bottom of her pink sweater. "I've been trying my best to counteract this behavior. Being here for students to talk to without judgment is a start, but I've also tried to go out of my way to be there for the students he…collects."

"Collects?" Dean asked.

She tilted her head back and forth. "The ones he takes a particular interest in. Ones who have something to offer him. Or those he wants to keep an eye on." She motioned to Dean. "An incredibly skilled hacker whose brother assisted him years ago. A student whose mother makes generous donations to the school but has a profession Tanner deems unacceptable."

I ground my teeth, and Dean crossed his arms over his chest but didn't say a word.

"I'm sorry." She really meant that, too, from the look on her face.

I took a few deep breaths, allowing my anger to simmer.

This wasn't her fault, not even close. She was one of the good ones. Someone who actually cared about what happened to students now *and* when they left Wilmont.

"She was a sophomore," I said, looking to Dean. "Do you know her name?"

"Jesse, something," he said. "I think she's in Tessa's art class. Not sure."

"Red hair, father is on the academic board," I added, giving Ms. Howard every detail I could.

"Wonderful," she said, but sounded far from happy. "I know her. I'll seek her out." She opened the door for us. "I'm sorry I can't do more," she said. "But," she continued, her voice a whisper, "I promise you both this. If I ever do get solid, irrefutable proof?" She pressed her lips together. "I'd put my own job on the line to make sure it was heard."

Dean and I nodded, and I gave her an encouraging smile. "Thank you," I said. "For being there." I meant it. The woman deserved a freaking gold medal for working with this on her shoulders. Knowing the wrongness of a situation without being able to do anything about it.

Dean walked shoulder to shoulder with me back to the coding room, and we packed up our gear, going through the motions, though both clearly in our own heads.

"Never a dull moment," he finally said as we headed to the parking lot, but I could tell his heart wasn't really in the joke.

"Insane." I shook my head, dropping my gear in my car. "I knew he was a…" I stopped myself from saying *dick*. "But I never suspected *this*."

Dean leaned against his opened driver's side door. "Kind of makes what we're doing have even more purpose, huh?"

I grinned. Hell yeah it did. My constant battles over whether the growing blog was too much for me to handle, too risky, too much of a middle finger in Tanner's face, evaporated. I needed to push the boundaries even more. Push it so much it would hit him over the head enough to rattle his routine. Maybe if he saw it, really saw it, and the good it was doing, the help it was giving…maybe he would have a wake-up call about his methods. Let his personal views take a back seat and allow the good of the many to overcome his own beliefs.

"Exactly," I said. "Late night coming up?" I asked, wondering if his motivations had been as invigorated as much as mine had.

"Likely. Why?"

"I'll bring the coffee tomorrow," I said, and winked at him before sinking behind the wheel.

As I drove home, I was beyond happy that Dean had been with me tonight. That we were in this twisted game together.

DC.

With a partner like him, I felt damn near unstoppable.

And now that I knew who I was truly facing?

That's exactly what I needed.

A couple of hours later, still slightly fuming from the scene with Tanner, I found a perfect question for tomorrow's post. I'd wanted to push the boundaries, see how far I could take things while also still selecting questions that I thought would benefit more people than just the one asking—but this one…

If a post on sex toys wasn't enough of a jab at Tanner, I didn't know what was.

My fingers flew over the keys as I typed up my response and then finally scheduled it to go live tomorrow morning. Powering down for the night, I crawled under the covers of my bed. The act was like taking off my mask and slipping into my real role.

Something about being *Ask Me Anything* made me feel powerful and overwhelmed at the same time. I had this huge responsibility to my followers and yet, lying in bed, sighing against my Marvel sheets, I felt...small. Like the weight of what I was doing might swallow me whole.

In front of the computer? Or witnessing a near blackmail attempt? It was easy to play the Avenger.

Alone, in the dark, in my room—I wondered how it was possible I'd gotten here. I wondered if it was okay that I had taken strength from this process, valued the help I was giving and using that pride and hope to heal my own cracked heart.

I forced my eyes to close, begging my constantly churning mind to switch to sleep mode for at least a few hours.

Sex toys.

God, I was virtually shouting about vibrators in direct opposition to Wilmont's Dark Ages approach to sex.

I chuckled in the silence.

Well, at least—I hoped—the person who'd written in would take comfort in my response. Would feel reassured and find relief in the answer.

And in the end? That's all I could ever hope for.

ASK ME ANYTHING

ABOUT   USEFUL LINKS   FAQ   CHAT WITH ME

QUESTION OF THE DAY

Volleyballstar6543 asks: *"My boyfriend recently went to college, and while we're making the long-distance thing work, I'm missing not only him but his...physical contact. We have phone sex, but I feel like I need more than just me to get me there. It's slightly embarrassing, but I want to buy a vibrator, or* something, *but I have no clue where to start. Help!"*

I'm super glad to hear that you're making long-distance work! That is such a wonderful thing and shows you two really care about each other. And you have no need to be embarrassed. It's completely natural to crave that intimacy even if your partner is hundreds of miles away.

And, lucky for us, we live in a digital age where almost anything can be ordered online. This saves you the hassle of finding a specialty shop and browsing the overwhelming selection of items out there—seriously, there is a *ton*.

My top recommendation would have to be the Smile Maker or another product from the same company. They are top-rated for their quality and execution and have over five thousand five-star reviews by customers worldwide. If none of those pique your interest, I would recommend researching what will best fit your needs and then triple check the reviews. Customer satisfaction is the number one clue on if a product is worth it or not, no matter what that product's use may be for.

If shipping to your house is a problem, there are some major retail stores that allow you to purchase online but pick up in store. Or you could always ask your boyfriend to purchase it and then ship it to you in a personal package from him to not draw suspicion. If it's not an issue, then more power to you!

I hope this helps keep things fresh and continues to fan the flames in your relationship!

In the meantime,
Stay Sexy. Stay Healthy.

CHAPTER EIGHTEEN

DEAN

Four weeks later and what had happened after Code Club with Mr. Tanner was still eating at my mind. That and his incessant demands on my progress to uncover the person behind *Ask Me Anything*. The whole situation was twisting my nerves. I had a few ideas of who might be behind it—thanks to the person declaring herself a female Wilmont student and for being skilled enough to run the site to be virtually untraceable. I hadn't begun to dig hard enough yet, instead hoping I could find a way out of this that involved clearing Tessa and not ratting out whoever was behind the blog.

After my casual questions four weeks ago before Code Club, Amber had turned my gaze away from her. I hated to even *think* it could be her, but there were—like she'd said—six girls in Griffin's class. Any of them would probably be able, if they studied hard enough, to run a site like *Ask Me Anything*. Amber could do it in her sleep, but when I'd asked her if she had any ideas on who might be behind it, she'd done the same thing I'd done and started with the girls in Griffin's class. It was a relief to know it wasn't Amber because I wouldn't want that kind of heat hanging over her head.

Even having the list of girls, though, I was still trying to work the problem—to find a solution that *wouldn't* result in me being an unethical jerk and outing someone who demanded privacy—that, and a way to free Tessa from Tanner's grasp. She didn't even know—but now I understood her distance. After our *Hackers* movie night, I'd seen her even less. I wasn't pushing her on the issue because now I fully understood why she needed space, her guilt over pulling the prank at the beginning of the year likely driving her away from me.

It was good, in a way—the constant distraction. Because my brain had already presented me with the perfect solution to get even with Tanner. One that threw my current white hat plan in the garbage.

You can't.

I forced the voice of reason out of my head.

Sure, this new idea was more gray than white...practically on its way to black, but Tanner's heart was blacker. The way he threatened me and Tessa, the way he treated his students, using them as pawns to gain favors and awards and grants and raises. Pathetic. People deserved to know the truth.

The truth wasn't black hat.

Hurting someone's reputation is.

Not my fault he behaved this way. I had the capabilities to bring to light all his wrongs. Wasn't I obligated to do so because of that power? But not before I cleared Tessa completely.

The battle went on for so long, it split my head.

I reached to shut my laptop screen but paused when a chat box appeared.

PixieBurn: You're up

My headache instantly eased at the sight of Amber's avatar. I loved that she rocked late hours like I did.

NightLocker: So are you

I shifted the laptop, scooting deeper into the four pillows on my bed. We'd spent more and more time together over the weeks, falling into this easy rhythm of back and forth that I'd come to count on.

PixieBurn: What are you doing Saturday?
NightLocker: Probably coding, why?
PixieBurn: Want to take the day off?
PixieBurn: The entire night, too?
PixieBurn: Annnd part of the next morning?

I reread each of her words a few times, raking my fingers through my hair as they sunk in.

NightLocker: Um...
NightLocker: Is this some elaborate scheme to kill me?
PixieBurn: Only if you get out of line

I laughed out loud at that, shaking my head at the screen. What was she up to?

NightLocker: I'd never?
PixieBurn: Then you're safe
NightLocker: What's up?
PixieBurn: I want to make it up to you
NightLocker: Make what up to me?
PixieBurn: The non-date I botched
NightLocker: You didn't. I told you that.
PixieBurn: Regardless
PixieBurn: Are you in?

I sighed, wishing like hell she didn't think she had anything to make up for. I'd told her as much. Maybe I should've tried a little harder these past weeks to make it perfectly clear that she had done nothing wrong. We'd gone on more non-dates each weekend—sometimes to her work to code, sometimes to a movie, others just to grab food and chill at her house. Easy. Fun. Refreshing.

I'd almost asked her a few times to help me uncover who *Ask Me Anything* was, but in the end, I'd always swallowed the urge. I wouldn't rope her into this mess. Exactly the reason I'd kept her in the coding room when she'd been hell-bent on giving Tanner a piece of her mind after we'd witnessed the blackmail on Jesse. Anything I could do to keep my two favorite girls—Tessa and Amber—off Tanner's radar was worth it.

My fingers hovered over the keys, wondering where this newfound sense of adventure had come from. Was it me? Was it all the time we spent together? A little bit of warm pride shot through my blood—the thought that I had anything to do with bringing Amber out of her recent darkness...but no, she didn't need me to do that. She was strong and standing all on her own. The girl didn't *need* anyone, but those who were in her circle were lucky as hell to be there.

NightLocker: Definitely
NightLocker: Where are we headed?
PixieBurn: You'll need to pack an overnight bag

She typed her response faster than I could blink. And the words she'd typed? Knocked the breath right out of my lungs.

A whole night with Amber?

A slew of images rushed through my head—all of them hotter than the next.

Lock it up.

I shook off the images and focused on the one thing that mattered.

This was her way of saying she trusted me.

I couldn't ignore the way my heart filled at the thought.

I caught my breath and set my fingers on the keys.

NightLocker: Is that so?
PixieBurn: Don't get too excited
NightLocker: Too late
PixieBurn: Don't make me regret inviting you
NightLocker: I don't even know where we're going
PixieBurn: It's a surprise
NightLocker: Now you're just copying
PixieBurn: Nope
PixieBurn: Mine is SO much better

I grinned. All earlier frustrations forgotten and replaced by beautifully torturous new ones.

This girl.

She was coming back to herself. To the playful, feisty banter I knew her for before. Though she'd never been this flirty before.

Thanks to *him*.

And I wasn't at all sad about it now. But I couldn't let her get away with it that easy.

NightLocker: Hard to top arcade and food trucks
PixieBurn: I will top it

NightLocker: I'll be the judge of that
PixieBurn: Thought it didn't matter anyway
NightLocker: What?
PixieBurn: Who was on top

The pads of my fingers froze on the keys, and my eyebrows climbed right up my head.

Amber twisting my words.

Flirting.

Bickering.

Fucking heaven. I could do this all night and never get tired of it.

Circling back to her last sentence, I blew out a breath. The temperature of my dark room had risen a few degrees.

NightLocker: It wouldn't
NightLocker: It doesn't
NightLocker: You'll realize that someday. If we're together it's fun. No question
PixieBurn: Maybe I already have

The girl was sending jolts of electricity throughout my system.

What was she saying?

That she finally realized we were great together? That *us* might be worth the time and risk?

Or, was it just that she could finally trust me as a friend, fully let me in? Talk to me about anything and everything?

Does it matter either way?

No. It didn't.

With Amber, I'd take whatever she was willing to give me.

I cared about her *that* much.

Didn't stop the images of tasting her kiss from rolling through my head.

PixieBurn: Will your parents be cool with the overnight trip?

That did.

Talk about an ice-cold bucket of water. Bringing up my parents.

Low blow, Pixie.

I could picture her laughing her cute butt off in her room, her laptop shaking from her giggles.

NightLocker: I'm 18
PixieBurn: So
PixieBurn: So am I
NightLocker: They'll be fine
NightLocker: Be easier if I knew where we were going
PixieBurn: You wouldn't tell me
PixieBurn: I won't tell. It'd ruin it
NightLocker: Stubborn Pixie
PixieBurn: Annoying?

I scoffed at the screen.

That asshole. He made her second-guess herself far too much.

Even though I knew she didn't need me to, I wanted to remedy every wrong action he'd taken. Help her realize how incredible she was until she never questioned her actions again. I wanted to show her there were people in the world who valued her—show her something maybe she was blind to when she looked in the mirror.

NightLocker: Not even close
PixieBurn: Cause I could tone it down
NightLocker: Don't you dare
NightLocker: I like you just the way you are

I knew the words were cheesy as hell the second I hit send, but I couldn't help it. She needed to know. To understand that not all guys were afraid of her spark.

PixieBurn: You could be a little less perfect
PixieBurn: If we're on the subject
NightLocker: I try so hard
NightLocker: But it just never works
NightLocker: I'm the perfect guy
PixieBurn: LOL
PixieBurn: Alright
PixieBurn: Be ready at 8 on Saturday
NightLocker: AM?

Oh damn. Not a.m. Where the hell was she taking me?

Thoughts of my earlier suspicion of her trying to kill me returned. Surely a wake-up call that early on a non-school day would be enough to end me.

PixieBurn: Yes
NightLocker: Groan
PixieBurn: If you're not up for it, I can ask Hannah
NightLocker: You better bring coffee
PixieBurn: Only if you're a good boy until then
NightLocker: You never know
PixieBurn: LOL
PixieBurn: We should sleep

NightLocker: Are you saying you're in bed right
now?

There went those flames again, licking my skin and
heating my blood. I tried not to think about what kind of
PJs Amber wore...but failed.

Shorts and a T?

Sweats and a tank?

Silk boxers and matching spaghetti strap?

The images flipped through my mind like fast reels of
old-school tape. Honestly, it didn't matter how I pictured
her or what I pictured her in. It was the hacker-pixie that
drove me wild. Had me thinking things I shouldn't—like
dates, and lazy Saturdays, and partnered hacking tourneys.

PixieBurn: Yes

PixieBurn: Aren't you?

NightLocker: I am

PixieBurn: So

PixieBurn: Let's go to sleep

NightLocker: Alright, Pixie

NightLocker: Sweet dreams

PixieBurn: Night, Locker

NightLocker: Ha. Ha.

She clicked offline before I could type out another
response to her totally corny pun. I shut my laptop screen,
setting it on the nightstand next to my bed. Rolling to my
back, I sighed.

My headache was gone, the internal battle I'd raged
put to bed.

Replaced by thoughts of what Amber had in store for
me.

Whatever it was. Wherever she took me. I knew it'd be incredible.

Because that was what Amber did. Made any kind of situation better.

• • •

"We're getting on a train?" I cocked an eyebrow at Amber as she ushered us through the too-crowded station early Saturday morning. As promised, I'd been a good boy all week, and she'd rewarded me with a double Americano. I clutched the warm paper cup in my hand, siphoning the life it offered.

"No," she said, rolling her eyes as she handed the clerk two tickets. "This is it. *Surprise!*" She waved her free hand in the air like she was in jazz club. "We're going to watch the trains come and go all day and pretend like we're passengers for each one. We'll make up stories for what we'll do on our travels. Whoever comes up with the best story wins."

I gaped at her before scanning the station as she led the way to the main lobby. There were eight tracks, all of them concealed by a floor-to-ceiling glass wall, doors carved out with turnstiles for each track.

She stopped near an empty bench, eyeing me.

I shrugged. "Well, I'm going to win," I declared, dropping my backpack filled with an extra pair of clothes, sleep-shorts, and a toothbrush on the bench.

Her lips popped into the shape of an *O*.

"What?" I asked. "I'm good at making up stories."

She burst out laughing. She shook her head as she scooped up my bag and shoved it against my chest. "I was joking," she said, motioning to the third door on the left. "We're on track three."

My backpack felt way too light without my gear in it as I slung it over my shoulder and followed her to the line outside track three. Glancing up, my eyes popped when I read where the train was headed. "New York?"

"Yep."

"You're taking me to New York?" I asked again as the line moved forward.

"Yes." She handed the ticket-taker her phone, and he scanned two barcodes on her screen before waving us onward.

Dumbfounded, I hurried behind her as she scanned the train cars, reading the letters aloud.

"B!" she squealed after we'd all but sprinted to the front of the train. She climbed the small set of stairs, turned right, and then plopped down into a double row of seats. Patting the seat next to her, she grinned up at me. "Or do you want the window?" she asked when I hadn't moved.

I shook my head, sinking beside her.

She leaned back against her chair, stretching out her long legs. "Wait till you see what we're doing when we get there."

"Wait," I said, shifting to face her, our knees brushing. "We're not just *seeing* New York City? We're actually doing something specific when we get there?"

She chuckled. "Of course."

"Damn." I leaned my head against the seat, never taking my eyes off her as the conductor came over the speakers, talking about the stops and lunch and drink options.

"What?" she asked.

"I'm not used to losing."

"You don't even know what we're doing yet."

I raised my arms to indicate the train that now pulled out of the station. "This is enough to put my silly arcade night to shame."

She reached over and placed her hand over my forearm. "That wasn't silly." She glanced down, her tongue darting over her lips. "It was amazing. This," she said, looking out the window before returning her eyes to me, "is my way of saying thank you for all the nights after that one. And," she continued before I could argue with her, "it's also something I've had planned for *months*. I wasn't sure I would go through with it until I realized how amazing going with you would be."

I smiled at her, adjusting so that I interlaced her fingers in mine. "Thanks," I said.

"For what?"

"For all of this. For trusting me enough to let me tag along."

She shrugged, but her cheeks flushed. "DC. Right?"

I nodded. "DC."

• • •

Three and a half hours later, we were both glancing out the window as New York came into view. Amber clapped her hands together. "We'll have just enough time to check into the hotel, eat, and then get changed!" Her voice was laced with the kind of excitement I reserved for when I won hacking tournaments. It was totally contagious and absolutely adorable. The fact that Amber had called my mother to give her all the details—including the hotel room—and clear everything with her was insanely cute. I'd tried and failed to *not* think about the two beds that awaited us in *one* room. I mean, sure, two beds, but…Amber would be sleeping not ten feet away from me. My blood rose a few degrees just thinking about it.

"You going to tell me where we're headed yet?"

"Sure," she said, and my eyes widened with anticipation. "The Sheraton Hotel," she said, a smirk on her lips.

"Ugh," I groaned. "Not cool."

She lightly smacked my chest. "I'm *so* cool! I took you on a train to NYC!"

I captured her hand, holding it in place against me. "Truth."

Her breath caught, but she didn't try to pull away.

I held her there until the train stopped.

And she let me.

· · ·

"Why do you keep checking your cell?" Amber asked, a smile on her face as we took the elevator up to our room.

I pocketed my phone, shrugging. "Honestly, I keep expecting a text from your dad, complete with death threats or an admission that they're staying one room over."

She laughed, tapping the key against the door, and held it open for me.

"You *sure* they're cool with this one-room situation?" I asked, tossing my bag on the bed closest to the window.

A flush dusted Amber's cheeks as she set her bag down and nodded. "Yes. You know my parents," she said, and it was comforting to know that I *did*. The last four weeks we'd spent plenty of time at her place, with her parents always around, and it was never a downer. They were cool, laid back, and yet...parent-y.

"I do," I said. "But I'm still thinking this is kind of a dream."

"They trust me. And you, apparently. Also, like you

mentioned before, eighteen." She tilted her head. "Your idea of a dream is sleeping in the same room with me?" She snorted. "We're in the coding room for hours together. What's the difference?"

I slowly rose from the bed, crossing the distance between us to gaze down at her. "There is a *huge* difference, Pixie. You know it."

She swallowed hard, staring up at me, her eyes churning.

"You don't snore in the coding room," I said, and she blew out a breath.

"I don't snore."

I shrugged. "We'll see about that."

. . .

Three hours and a couple room-service burgers later, Amber was stepping out of the bathroom, fully ready for our night.

She wore a black plaid skirt that stopped above her knees, a gray sweater, and some kick-ass black combat boots. Her hair was in its usual feathered style, the pops of pink complementing the smoky stuff she'd slid over her eyes.

"Whoa," I said, my eyes drinking her in. "You look amazing."

"So do you," she said.

All I'd done was shower and slide into some dark jeans and a navy-blue Henley. Still, the way she eyed me up and down like she wanted to take a bite out of me? Worth it.

I mentally thanked Tessa for conning me into taking her shopping and then forcing me to buy this shirt—which at the time I thought was too tight. She'd assured me it was perfect, said it brought out the blue in my eyes or some shit.

"You ready for this?" Amber asked, heading toward

the door.

I opened it for her. In reality, I wasn't sure. Something was building between us—had been building for months now—and I couldn't stop it, couldn't calm it, and I wasn't sure I wanted to. But I certainly didn't want to overstep a line, especially if Amber still had it firmly drawn. So, was I ready to keep things strictly friendly?

"Absolutely," I said.

Because I knew despite how strong the current sparked between us, I wanted her in my life. Any way I could have her.

She smiled like she held the biggest secret in the world.

I was more than ready to uncover it.

. . .

"Holy. Shit." I gaped at Amber as we were allowed inside the massive venue packed with all manner of people. People with mohawks. People with neon hair. People with brightly colored bracelets and glow-in-the-dark necklaces. All cramming onto one wide-open space of a dance floor laid beneath the biggest stage I'd ever seen.

"deadmau5?" I asked. "You've had tickets this entire time and didn't tell me?"

She giggled, bouncing on her feet as we claimed a spot near the front. "You like?"

"Love," I said, pulling her close so she could hear me. "I can't believe you wanted to give me your extra ticket."

The laughter left her eyes, her shoulders dropping. She shook her head, forcing a smile. "I think it was meant for you all along," she said. "I just hadn't known it yet."

I wrapped an arm around her shoulders, tucking her into my chest. "You win. Forever," I said as the lights dimmed.

"There is no way I'm ever topping this."

She tugged on my head, bringing my ear to her lips to be heard over the cheering crowd. "I'd like to watch you try," she teased. "If you feel like it."

"Oh, I will *try.*"

Before she could respond, red lights pulsed over the stage in beat with the music. Amber and I joined the crowd, screaming our excitement when the massive projector screen lit up with *deadmau5*. From where we stood, we could see him behind his epic DJ table, the massive silver mouse head—its big round eyes lit up with *X*'s—as he bounced and pressed all the magic buttons to create the perfect sounds.

The beats were epic—smooth and slow, and rapid and sharp. That was the best thing about him, he had his hand in everything and it pulsed like a living, breathing song inside you. The perfect hacking music, too, allowing you to lose yourself in the rhythm and fall completely off the grid.

But we weren't hacking tonight.

No.

This—with Amber in front of me, swaying to the beat of the music—it was better.

I never thought I'd say that in my life. But it was true.

Song after song, I held on to Amber's hips, dancing with her, watching her lose herself to the music. Watching her smile and cheer and perfectly bounce against me. She was beyond beautiful, the freedom in her eyes, the spark that fired behind them when she'd turn to glance up at me despite *feeling* that I was there.

There were at least a thousand other people surrounding us, and even more than that behind us—but it felt like we were alone.

Her body soft against the hard planes of mine.

The way she rolled her hips, and the way I gripped them,

following her with my own moves.

Perfection.

There was no other way to describe it. She made me feel awake—like she was this living flame lighting up a world I hadn't realized was dark before she came into it.

And I couldn't believe I'd gotten lucky enough to be the one holding on to her fire.

We danced the night away, and when the last song quieted throughout the loud venue, I leaned down and tucked my head over her shoulder and breathed her in. She smelled like lavender and vanilla and the smoke that coated the concert hall.

She wrapped an arm around me from behind, turning her head so our noses touched.

My heart raced like a gun had gone off.

Her eyes were excited, open, and just a tad bit afraid.

I didn't move. I wouldn't. Not again. And if this was all she wanted—dancing and comfort and fun—then I would give it to her a hundred times over and never ask for more.

A few breaths and she inched her lips closer, brushing them with a feather-light touch over mine.

I sighed hungrily but didn't dare push it. Moving back slightly, I gauged her reaction.

Bright, beautiful eyes. On fire.

In a blink, she turned in my embrace, facing me, our chests flush. Fingers on my neck, she jerked my head down, this time crushing her lips on mine. I folded my arms around her hips, hefting her to my level, holding her against me as I let her take what she wanted, and gave everything back.

CHAPTER NINETEEN

Fireworks.

White-hot heat and smooth-as-honey comfort.

The boy's lips were a crazy electric battle of hard and soft, hungry and selfless.

His kiss tasted unique to him—warmth and spearmint and energy and everything that had me craving *more*.

Whenever Brandon had kissed me, I wasn't this active of a participant, wasn't this…*starved*. I hated that my mind went there, that it compared the two, but it did. And there was no denying this was different.

Epic.

Intoxicating.

Fun.

Safe.

The stark realization jolted me out of the kiss. My feet hung off the floor as Dean held me pinned to him—his grip strong but gentle—and in that moment, I *knew* this was right. He had me trapped in his embrace, so much stronger than me, and yet, I felt no need to break his grasp. No fear of *not* being let go if I asked.

All the nerves and anticipation I'd had leading up to this trip…it vanished. Evaporated in the swell of heat that swept beneath my skin.

"Pixie," Dean said, his breath sweet on my lips. He trailed the tip of his nose over mine, pressing his forehead to mine as he slowly lowered me back to the floor.

I grinned up at him, staying tucked underneath his arm, basking in the levity of trust, respect, and excitement.

Funny, I would've never known how important those things were if not for…

I tensed, the memories hitting me hard and fast. Dean sensed the shift, the crease between his brows deep as he glanced down at me. He motioned toward the back of the audience, where I knew the exit was.

I nodded, more than happy to beat the crowd before the concert ended.

"You okay?" he asked me in the cab, our fingers laced together.

"Yeah," I said, lost in my thoughts as we rode back to the hotel.

I wanted *more* from Dean. Could feel it churning in my core.

That was huge.

But how could I truly be with him if he didn't know the truth?

Would he think less of me if he knew? Would he put distance between us? Regret the kiss we just shared?

What if he takes Brandon's side?

I shook my head, trying to force the thoughts from my brain as we rode the elevator up to our room.

Our room.

Sure, there were two beds.

Yes, I'd assured Mom we'd each be sleeping in one. But after everything…after that kiss? I sure as hell didn't want to.

"Amber," Dean said, a plea in his tone after I came out of the bathroom, totally transformed from concert-chic to comic-book-pj-fantastic. "Talk to me."

I wrung my hands, pacing the space in front of him

where he sat on the edge of the bed.

"Was it the kiss?" he asked.

"No," I said quickly. "Well, yes and no."

"I didn't mean to ruin things again," he said. "If I did."

I froze for a moment. "You didn't. I swear. I just…" I started pacing again. "I liked it. Loved it. Dean…I like you. More than I thought possible."

A wide, easy smile shaped his lips as he stared up at me. It fell in a few breaths. "Why do I feel a *but* coming?"

"I just," I said, my stomach dipping. What would I tell a person on the blog? What advice would I give?

I'd urge them to be truthful and strong and love who they were. To not be afraid of rejection, no matter how hard it was.

God, it was so much easier to give advice than take it.

"I can't be more with you until you know the truth," I said. "The reason behind my tears the first time we kissed." Heat flushed my entire body. I couldn't believe I was about to tell him, but I had to know how he'd react.

And he had a right to know. To decide for himself if he thought I was…damaged.

"Pixie," he said, standing up to cup my cheek. "DC, remember? You can tell me anything. I'm not going anywhere."

With those words, I closed my eyes. The story from that night spilled from my lips.

I sucked in a sharp breath as I finished laying the dark pieces of my soul bare. Shocked retelling the tale hadn't brought tears to my eyes. I took comfort from that strength, but it did little to ease my tangled nerves.

"We made Jake sleep at my house that night," I said, sighing. "He was in such a rage. And I didn't want him getting expelled over that jerk." I wrapped my arms around myself, the cold from revisiting the night having crept into my bones. "I had to talk Mom out of pressing charges," I said, shaking my head. "Maybe I should've let her. Maybe not. I was so confused and in shock I think…" My words died in my throat, telling the story aloud both cathartic and exhausting.

Dean was frozen on the edge of the bed, his fists clenched against the white comforter.

Oh God, he thinks I asked for it, too.

He thinks I brought it on myself dating a guy like Brandon.

I clenched my eyes shut.

I was so sick of the past. *So* sick of it ruining every good thing about my present.

Warm, almost timid, arms enveloped me.

Dean tipped my chin to meet his eyes, a combination of hate, hurt, and hope swirling in those blue-grays.

"I'm sorry," I said, sucking in a breath.

He furrowed his brow. "What the hell for?"

I shrugged. "For what happened. For — "

"Stop," he cut me off. "You didn't do a damn thing wrong. That asshole did. And the fact that he got in your head and made *you* feel like you begged for it, like you made it happen…" His gaze went dark as he glanced to the side — he was somewhere far away, doing something very, very bad. The steady rise and fall of his chest brought his attention back to me. He smoothed his fingers over my cheeks. "I didn't know," he said. "I didn't have a clue it was that bad."

"How could you?" I asked.

"I wish… Damn it. *I'm sorry.*"

"What?"

"For pushing you. Kissing you." The words seemed painful coming from his lips. He took a giant step back. "I shouldn't have… If I would've known…"

"Please don't, Dean," I said, following him as he retreated. "Don't treat me like I'm damaged. Breakable. That's the last thing I want." I cringed. "Unless that's the only way you can see me now?"

A low growl rumbled from his chest, his hands locked in place at his sides as I stopped within an inch of his body. "You know that's not true."

"I don't know anything," I said, shaking my head. "Except for the way I feel when I'm with you."

"And," he said, "what do you feel?"

"Safe."

A sigh flew from his lips as he reached for me again, his hand soft and strong as it slid from my cheek to my neck. "Pixie," he said, and my entire body reacted to the way his tongue curled around my alias. "All I want to do is erase every bad mark he left on your soul." He inched his forehead down, leaning it against mine. "But I know you don't need me to. I know you, Pixie, and you're strong enough to heal yourself. I'll never push you. Never ask you for more than you want to give. But, please, let me be here for you. In any way I can."

A bubbly laugh flew from my lips as I smiled up at him. "I'm not strong right now," I said, my cheeks flushing. "Because I can't stop thinking about how good your lips feel on mine."

Another low growl, this a test of willpower as I popped up on my tiptoes to brush my lips over his.

"Is that…wrong of me?" I asked, sinking back down when he held so still I wasn't sure he was breathing. I chewed on my lip. "Should I not want this with you? Because it hasn't even been a year yet?"

"It's not wrong," he said. "Unless it feels that way."

I shook my head. "Everything I do with you…it feels beyond right."

A small smile shaped his lips.

"Dean?" I asked, my voice soft as I smoothed my hand over his chest.

"Pixie?"

"Kiss me?" My heart filled my throat, damn near blocked the words, but within two blinks, Dean had stolen the little breath I'd managed.

His lips on mine. A sweet, long, and gentle kiss. Hot enough to make my eyes flutter shut and my body arch into his.

"I want this, Amber. I want you," he said against my lips, barely breaking our kiss. "I just don't want to cross any lines. I don't want you regretting a thing with me."

"Not possible," I said, gasping for breath as he kissed it from me. I jumped—knowing he'd catch me—and hooked my legs around his hips. He groaned, sinking onto the bed, my knees on either side of him while our lips never broke.

Warm, electric tingles buzzed underneath my skin, humming everywhere he touched. His hands were gentle as they slid up my back, in my hair, and down again, holding me to him like he couldn't get close enough.

Everything in my heart screamed *more.*

Everything in my gut told me it was *right.*

Months of connecting with others through the blog, of taking action with communication, and laying myself bare just now…I'd somehow managed to let go of my past.

I'd become the girl I'd always loved being again.

And now I was confidently, hopelessly lost in Dean's kiss.

Dean—my confidant, my challenger, my friend.

He made me feel like *his* while still being solely *me.*

That was enough to shatter the walls I'd built around

my heart, and in the span of a few beats, it belonged to him.

Slowly, I pulled my lips from his and reached across the bed to turn off the lamp on the side table. Heart hammering against my chest, I returned to the bed, lying on my side to face him. I traced the line of his jaw with my fingers, trailing them over his neck and down his chest, until I found the hem. Trembling slightly, I explored the taut skin underneath, sparks of heat traveling in my blood as he gripped my hip and pulled me closer. I hitched my leg over his hip, our bodies aligned as I found his lips again.

God, he tasted good. Felt good. The warmth from him enveloping me…his scent, the way he kissed me like my mouth was something to be savored.

"Dean," I said, sighing against his lips.

He pulled back an inch, his hand stilling on my hip, his other occupied with propping his head up to look down at me. "Too far?" he asked, genuine concern in his eyes.

"Not even close," I said, hating that I could be as vocal as I wanted on the blog but was nervous to tell him what I wanted.

I licked my lips, loving that they tasted of *him*, and grabbed his hand on my hip. I lightly kissed his fingers before moving them over my breasts, and lower, until I settled him beneath the hem of my pajama pants.

"Amber," he half said, half growled, his eyes never leaving mine. Somehow, that intense look, the connection between us was more intimate than where our hands currently rested.

"I want to know what it's like," I said.

"What *what* is like?" he whispered.

"To be touched when it's wanted. By someone who really…" I couldn't find the right words, my head swimming with desire and excitement and nerves. "Please," I continued. "I trust you. And I'm yours. If you'll have me."

"Pixie," he said before crushing his lips on mine. "You're all I've ever wanted."

A whimper escaped the back of my throat at his declaration, at the current buzzing between us. I trusted him more than I'd ever trusted anyone in my life.

I drew my hand away from his, my body arching on its own against his gentle touch as he traced the seam of my underwear. I moaned from the contradicting contact—the passion of his kiss and the sweet, almost tease of his fingers.

The sound must have unleashed something inside him, because he groaned against my lips before dipping his hand beneath the piece of fabric separating us.

I gasped at the contact, at the feel of his callused fingers against the warmth of my skin. Tiny bolts of electricity tickled their way up my spine as he explored me, and the heat was so much I was sure I would explode. His touch was gentle and searing at the same time, his kiss consuming. I moved against him, with him, until everything inside me was detached and tangled. Until my body was a coiled spring.

And just when I thought I couldn't handle a second more without combusting, Dean broke our kiss for long enough to pin me with his gaze before his eyes trailed to where he touched me, where he held me, and back up again. Holding me on the edge of a cliff when I was dying to fly.

"You're beautiful," he said, and pressed his lips against mine.

The hunger in his kiss, in his touch, unleashed that spring inside me, and I gasped as my body trembled, tumbled, and sparked, until I could do nothing but fall apart in his arms.

CHAPTER TWENTY

AMBER

Mom: I hope you had an awesome night!
Mom: Have you seen this? Interesting morning read.
Mom: www.brtv.com/protests

I leaned against the hotel bed's headboard, reading the texts Mom sent earlier this morning, my stomach dropping at the link she'd shared with me.

I glanced at Dean, who slept peacefully to my right, his hands curled under the pillow. Sometime in the night—after he'd taken me somewhere I'd never been before—I'd wound up tangled in his arms. It was the best sleep I'd had in months.

Content with his light snores, I clicked the link on my cell.

PARENTS ARE PROTESTING PEER-LED SEX ADVICE BLOG ON DARK WEB: *ASK ME ANYTHING*

Acid frothed in the back of my jaw as I read the headline. I swallowed hard before scrolling down to read the article that a local news station had picked up due to a parent's complaints.

PARENTS ARE PROTESTING PEER-LED SEX ADVICE BLOG ON DARK WEB: *ASK ME ANYTHING*

Susan Mercury reached out to BRTV yesterday in a drastic effort to bring awareness to parents who may not know about the teen-led sex advice blog that is rapidly growing in popularity among students in surrounding high schools.

"It's a blatant disregard for authority," Mercury is quoted. "Whoever is writing this blog has no respect for what parents are teaching their children at home. Or for the professionals in the schools. They work tirelessly to construct the perfect and approved curriculum. School officials left off sex advice for obvious reasons."

Mercury discovered the blog when she caught her teenage daughter reading a post about oral sex on her phone.

"If I wanted my daughter to be on birth control, she would be," Mercury says. "And if she has questions regarding when sex is appropriate, she should come to me. Not some faceless blog. Who knows who is truly behind it. What if it's a predator? We have to protect the children."

Mercury's call to action has spread throughout her community, despite her daughter not attending the blogger's claimed high school origin—Wilmont Academy. She's started her own online forum where parents can talk about their concerns. "I'm planning several protests," Mercury says, "until the person responsible is held accountable for their actions."

Mercury stated she has already contacted the principal of Wilmont Academy, as well as the principals of the other six schools in the district. All declined to comment until more information was gathered.

Mercury gave us the code to find the site on the dark web, where a variety of articles spanning all forms of sex advice and beyond are listed.

Are you a parent with a child who has been affected by *Ask Me Anything*? Do you have a comment to make? We urge you to write us at <u>brtv@brtv.com</u>.

I had to read the article twice to believe it, and even then it was a struggle.

I'm not hurting students! I'm helping them!

My heart plummeted into my stomach, my skin tightening over the length of my body. The traffic had increased every day, as well as the comments and replies. It was a positive force, not the negative agenda the news painted it to be.

My previous posts flashed through my mind, and I mentally sifted through every word I'd written. I wasn't telling people that they could have sex without consequences. I was simply answering questions plaguing those who already had or were about to. Regardless of whatever I wrote, if they were going to have sex...they would do it. With or without the blog.

Right?

Chewing on my bottom lip, I wondered. Surely I didn't have that much power?

No. No way in hell.

And I sure as hell hadn't given a play-by-play on how to give a blow job. I wouldn't even know. Not that I didn't *want* to learn...especially after last night, after what Dean and I had shared.

God, the news had blown it way out of proportion.

I'd agonized over every comment, every question, and hand-selected the ones I knew our school officials would never address and ones Google wouldn't be helpful with. The questions that got to the heart of concerns in new relationships and spoke to fears people were too afraid to voice aloud.

And with each question, I'd discreetly spoken to my best sources of information, my mom or dad. They unknowingly helped me construct responses that offered the same care and understanding that they handled me with.

If Mom sent me this link…she had to have seen the blog. And she *knew* me. She could likely tell it was me. But she hadn't said anything? And…

Tanner has seen it, too.

I gasped, quickly glancing at Dean and sighing when I realized I hadn't woken him. Sliding out of the bed, I retreated to the bathroom, dousing my face in cold water.

Mission accomplished.

Ask Me Anything had reached Principal Tanner's radar.

Something sharp twisted in my gut. I never thought it would be protesting parents that would bring it to his attention. I thought it would be a happened-upon thing. A spare glance at the right time when a student was reading it.

I never for one second thought parents would think I was a…

Predator.

Fuck.

I hated that was even a thought that crossed their minds. That I could be some evil person luring people to divulge their most intimate questions and thoughts.

An icy-cold shudder racked my body and I stretched my arms out over the sink, leaning with my head hanging between my shoulders.

I'd proven myself enough to the mass of students writing in. They would never send in comments and questions if they hadn't *believed* I was a Wilmont student.

Right. Exactly.

I repeated this to myself several times before drying my face with one of the hotel's super-fluffy towels.

This is fine.

This is what I wanted.

Okay, well, not exactly. I never wanted to rile the parents

up so much they protested. But I wanted Tanner to see what was missing in his students' lives because of his neglect to adapt to the times. Because he held his own personal beliefs over the school like it was law. Obviously there was a need for redefining the way sex and sensitive topics were approached in school—I would've had zero response if there wasn't.

Maybe he would listen now.

Maybe the news article was blowing the parents' anger out of proportion as well as the content on my site.

Maybe I'm more in over my head than I even knew.

Maybe I should torch the site and be done with it.

My spine straightened against the thought.

No. I wouldn't run away and hide just because someone had gotten offended. At the heart of my challenge with Dean—this was white hat. I wasn't hurting anyone. I was helping people find answers when all other resources failed them.

I would, however, up the security on the site the second we made it home.

Fingers flying fast, I typed out a text to Mom.

Me: Last night was amazing
Me: Tell you later. See you soon.

Laying my cell on the counter, I spun toward the shower, needing the scalding water to rid me of the ick that parent had slathered all over me.

Predator. Un-fucking-believable. It's not like they said that I was giving a how-to guide on the proper way to give a blow job. Or how unprotected sex was all the rage, or something else like that.

I rolled my eyes and scrubbed my hair a little harder than necessary.

I may as well be if they're already this pissed.

The rebellious, rage-induced thought sprinted through my head, but I dismissed it just as quickly.

Inhaling the steam from the shower, I calmed myself by focusing on last night. On the incredible weight that had lifted from my chest by telling Dean about my past. But sharing that—it helped. Just as I hoped the people who wrote in to me found some comfort in sharing their stories and questions and fears.

What would Dean think if he knew I was behind the blog?

Would he hold it against me? Advise me to shut it down? Question where I gathered my answers?

No. I could tell him anything. He'd said that last night. *Last night.*

The kisses, the way he'd touched me, the connection that crackled between us. It was intense and fantastic and made my heart race just thinking about it.

It had been hard to slow it down. To tamper off the heat sizzling between our touches, and not take it a step further. I'd wanted to give all of myself to him last night. I was ready. But we'd agreed to wait. Dean hadn't brought a condom, and despite being on the pill, I certainly knew how important safe sex was.

Slow.

We'd agreed to go so slow.

But the most shocking element to me—more so even than the protesting parents—was that I didn't *want* to go slow with Dean. Every inch of my body begged for his in a way I'd never experienced. He was like a craving that wouldn't be slaked until I'd devoured him.

I chuckled out loud at that, shutting off the water and wrapping myself in a towel.

If I wasn't careful, I'd end up enlisting Dean as an expert source for all the things I had no clue about for *Ask Me Anything*.

And with how hot kissing was between us? If I dared to write about anything *more*?

The flames would be large enough to send the whole damn town into a frenzy.

Then they'd *really* call for blood.

They already are.

The reality of that thought had me dressing in a hurry.

We needed to get home. Get to my gear. Change the code on the site so no one could find me unless I wanted them to.

. . .

"You sure everything is cool?" Dean asked me for the second time as the train pulled into the station four hours later.

I'd spent the entire ride half distracted—in part by the stunning boy who sat next to me, softly grazing his fingers over my palm or kissing me until my mind went blank. The other part was working on the site despite being sans computer. The article nagged in the back of my mind like an alarm I couldn't silence.

Everything would be okay once I triple-checked the site's security.

I could deal with the rest of it later.

"Yes," I said again. "Everything is perfect." Well, not a total lie. Things were perfect between us. And while I'd debated coming clean about my end of the challenge and asking for his help, I'd decided against it.

No one else knew about the site, so no one else could

get in trouble if worst-case scenario happened. I had no intentions of letting it happen, but I'd rather keep him safe. He was waiting on his acceptance letter from MIT just like me, and if Tanner found out I was behind the site, I'd be expelled for sure. Causing this much trouble...he'd have more than grounds to do it.

I reached up on my tiptoes to plant a kiss on his lips, reveling in the way warm shivers danced over my skin at the contact.

He grinned at me before grabbing our bags, and we walked through the station to where I'd parked in the pay-to-park lot. After I'd started the car, he reached over the gearshift to take my hand.

"Amber," he said, his tone soft and pleading. "I can tell you're chewing on something."

I immediately stopped biting my lower lip, knowing that's not what he meant.

"If it's me," he continued, "if it's what happened, if it's too much—"

"It's not," I cut him off but kept my eyes focused on the road. "I promise, Dean. Last night—" A glow warmed my cheeks as I grinned like a girl at Comic-Con. "I'm so happy."

I started the drive toward his house, but I could feel his gaze on me. He had me pinned, seeing right through the mask I'd tried to keep in place since reading the article.

"But," I said, relenting, "I am working something out in my head. Nothing to do with us. Well, sort of. It's about our challenge. My side of it. I've run into a snag. And I've been mentally trying to connect with my gear since this morning."

He chuckled, the sigh of relief not lost on me. "Wait," he said. "You hit a snag this *morning*?"

"Mm-hmm."

"You don't have your laptop. And there wasn't a

computer in the room," he said, the gears in his head turning. "So, it was something you had to see on your cell."

I spared him a warning glance. "Don't," I said. "It's not fair you trying to puzzle it out."

"Fine, fine," he said. "You know, if you wanted to drop this little bet of ours…in light of what's happened…"

"What's happened?"

"Um," he said, clearing his throat. "You being my girlfriend?"

A thrill shot up my spine. Girlfriend? I supposed I was, but the word seemed small somehow.

I had been Brandon's girlfriend.

With Dean? I simply felt like…*his*.

I laughed. "That just makes me want to beat you more."

"Really?" he teased. "Well, then. Keep on bringing it. Maybe you should come inside when you drop me off."

"Reasoning?"

"Like you need it?" he faux-scoffed. "I could distract you. Keep you from fixing this snag for a few more hours."

The thought swirled heat in my core. Being in Dean's room, in his arms, on his bed…

"No," I said a little too quickly. "It's important."

"How important?" he asked, and when I glanced at him, his eyes were wary.

Damn. He was sniffing a little too close. Because why would it be so important I couldn't spend a few more hours with him? Unless it was big. *Too* big.

"So important that I'm turning down time with you."

"That worries me," he said. "Can I help you?"

My heart warmed at his instant offer, but I shook my head.

"No," I said. "I've totally got this. I just have to get back." I pulled into his driveway, throwing the car in park and shifting to face him. "Thank you, though. For everything."

He shrugged. "You're the one who took me to see deadmau5. And then…"

I raised my eyebrows, waiting.

"Let me in." He leaned over and brushed his lips against mine. My eyes fluttered closed, a soft sigh releasing when he pulled away far too soon. "Sure you don't want to hang for a bit?"

My heart said yes.

My body said *hell yes*.

My mind?

"I'm sure," I said. "I *would* if I didn't have this thing."

"No worries," he said, flashing me a smile that shook my knees. "I'll catch you later." He winked and then stepped out of the car.

I watched him walk through his front door, trying to calm my breath. The spark between us was so new and fresh and demanding to be fed. The sensation deliciously coursed through my blood.

Too bad it was short lived. Because as I pulled out of his driveway and started the drive toward my house, I had the sudden, irrational fear that a slew of parents would be outside my home with handmade signs, screaming their hate for my site. For me.

ASK ME ANYTHING

ABOUT   USEFUL LINKS   FAQ   CHAT WITH ME

Before I get to the question of the day, I'd like to say something.

Over the weekend, I found out some parents had wandered onto this site—this little corner of the web that was meant solely for you.

Now, I'm not upset that they found it. I'm sad that some of them think I'm...something I'm not. I am one of you. I assumed I'd proven that. I can't reveal my identity for obvious reasons, but I will say this: to any parents who have found the new code and are reading this...I am no predator.

I'm a student. A teenage girl. One who is tired of hearing about how her friends can't find answers to questions they need. Tired of being ridiculed at school because we don't conform to the mold they think we should be in. This is our space. A place to find help. And I'm not going to stop as long as there are questions that need to be answered. I had intended this blog to be solely focused on questions regarding sexual health—the answers they couldn't find from school or elsewhere—but now...it's grown into something more. The questions I'm receiving go beyond sex, and I'm here, grateful to be a part of this journey. No one is going to take that from me, not when so many are reaching out for help.

So, without further preaching...

QUESTION OF THE DAY

QueenButterflyFae20 asks: *"I think I'm in love with my BFF. She knows I'm a lesbian but doesn't have a clue I'm into her. And while she's bisexual, I'm afraid if I tell her, I'll lose her friendship forever, but I don't know how much longer I can bury my feelings. Thoughts?"*

Wow, I can't imagine the tough situation you're in. Such a difficult choice to make—keep what's really on your mind hidden or tell her and risk losing her.

For me, it would come down to this: What does your heart say?

Is it telling you to hang on to her as a friend and treasure that time together while you find yourself interested in other girls?

Or is it telling you that you can't sleep until she knows how much you care about her? That you'd rather her know the truth than go another day with her being in the dark?

If you think you'll find yourself interested in another girl soon, then it might be wise not to cross that friendship line.

If your heart is set on her, then talk to her. Tell her the truth. Tell her how much her friendship means to you, but that you couldn't continue keeping this secret. As your best friend, she'll be the best source to ease your worries anyway. And a true friend won't run because of you telling the truth. She'll likely respect you for it. And you'll be able to rest easy knowing you're no longer holding on to these feelings alone.

I'm sending you all the good vibes and hoping you find your happily ever after—whichever path you choose to take. Please keep me posted!

In the meantime,
Stay Sexy. Stay Healthy.

CHAPTER TWENTY-ONE

DEAN

NightLocker: Hey Pixie
NightLocker: You busy?
PixieBurn: Not at the moment
PixieBurn: You miss me already?
NightLocker: Always

I grinned at the screen, congratulating myself on the restraint I'd demonstrated. I had waited an entire night before sending her a chat box this morning.

PixieBurn: Was thinking about you too
NightLocker: :)
NightLocker: You finish your secret important thing?
PixieBurn: For the moment
PixieBurn: Why?
NightLocker: I need your help

Something itched the back of my brain at her *for the moment* response. Whatever she had put into motion for the sake of our challenge seemed to have a bigger responsibility than she initially thought. I could tell that much by the way she'd dodged my questions yesterday. Which made me wonder if she could as easily tell that I was hiding something—that I'd been keeping her in the dark about just how far Tanner's pull over me went. I rubbed my palms against my face, forcing those thoughts out of my head.

> PixieBurn: I have a shift in a couple hours
> PixieBurn: Want to meet me there early?
> NightLocker: That works
> NightLocker: Bring your gear
> PixieBurn: Always ;)

She logged off, and I followed suit, shutting my screen. Packing up my gear only took a few minutes, and I had to remind myself not to speed to Amber's work.

It wasn't just the prospect of the team hack I had planned; it was *her*. I'd spent the entire day and night with her the day before yesterday, but I buzzed with excitement as the bell rang when I pushed through the coffee-comic-shop's door.

Immediately, as if I couldn't help it, my eyes were drawn to Amber, who occupied a table in the far back corner. Two white mugs steamed in front of her, but her eyes were glued to her laptop.

"Were you already here?" I asked, setting my bag down.

She hopped up from the table, throwing her arms around my neck. I breathed in her sweet scent, holding her light frame against my chest.

She missed me, too.

Win.

"Yes," she said when she stepped out of our embrace and reclaimed her seat. "I had some work to do before my actual work." She chuckled, motioning to the mug on my side of the table. "Americano," she said.

"Thanks." I sat and took a fast sip, glancing around the

shop. It was dead this time of evening, everyone likely rushing home after work.

"So," she said, lowering her voice, "what are we doing?"

I smirked, scooting around the table and lining my chair up with hers. I slid my laptop out of my bag and set it up. "You remember the Taylor Swift incident?"

She smiled after sipping her green tea. "How could I forget your sweet dance moves?"

I cringed a little. "Well, that was my brother."

"Sean," she said, arching a brow. "I'm helping you get revenge in a brotherly feud?"

"Too much?" I asked.

"Never. DC, right?" She clapped her hands together and rolled her neck. "What do you have planned?"

I lowered my voice to a whisper, as if Sean had cameras and devices listening in everywhere, and told her the plan. "Thoughts?"

"Brilliant." She took another sip of tea. "But I've never done anything like this before. I don't want to drag you down."

So whatever she'd done for our challenge didn't involve penetration. Good to know. I waved her off. "You could never drag me down," I said. "You're incredible. Why do you think I asked for your help?"

She'd likely be able to uncover the source of *Ask Me Anything* in one sitting. Last night, I had actually tried to track the person down—not that I would hand them over to Tanner, but for my own sanity. I hadn't been able to get through their security. But...as much as I wanted her help, I had to keep her safe.

"Because you wanted a free Americano?" she teased, bringing me back to the task at hand.

"Well, yes, there is that." I winked at her, drawing up

the back door I'd always used to get into Sean's computer.

"Here," I said, sending it to her computer. "This is what I'm working off of."

She clicked it open, her eyes reading the lines of code fast, the comprehension clicking near-instantaneously.

Damn, that's hot.

I rested my hand on her jean-covered knee then immediately drew it back.

Focus.

Maybe roping her into this prank was a bad idea. She was one hell of a distraction.

"You okay?" she asked, shifting in her seat so her leg rested against mine.

"Perfect," I said. "Just trying to learn how to hack while sitting this close to you."

She leaned over and kissed me then, a fast, hard press of her lips that heated my blood.

"Wicked Pixie," I said when she sat back in her seat.

"What's the task?" she asked, a devilish grin on her beautiful lips.

"How about you change all his commands—"

"So anytime he tries to use one it responds with 'No'?"

"Hell. Yes." I nodded, amazed she was already one step ahead of me. "And I'll do a screen shot overlay with removed icons."

She *laughed*. Damn this girl was perfection.

"On it," she said, her fingers flying over the keys as she slipped in the back door. It was no easy task—a process way above and beyond anything Griffin would ever teach us—but she was in as quickly as if I'd shown her how to do it step by step. I didn't even have to tell her to patch the back door once she was inside—she did it automatically, knowing how to exploit the vulnerability but seal it behind her so no one else could do the same.

Brilliant.

With both of us working simultaneously, we might just get in, change the commands, and get out before Sean ever detected us. That's why I'd needed her help to pull off a hack this big—the two of us cut the time in half.

And Sean more than deserved it.

An hour later, we'd managed to own his system. In addition to switching the commands and icon removal, we'd scrambled the functions, too. Pressing one would cause a different result than the original. He'd either have to learn the new pattern, or he'd have to destroy our code.

I knew he could do the latter in his sleep.

But it would still be funny as hell in the first few moments where he wouldn't have a clue what was going on.

"Are you sure he won't murder you for this?" Amber asked, packing away her laptop. "I would hate to lose my…" She stopped herself short.

"Your what?" I teased, tucking my gear away.

She shrugged, glancing at her mug. It was empty save for the few tea leaves that clung to the bottom.

I leaned in close to her, teasing her neck with the tip of my nose. "He won't," I said, loving that chills rose on her skin at my light touch. "He'll be pissed at first. Then he'll laugh. Then he'll plot the next attack." I sat back, eyeing her. "It's what we've done for years."

She smirked. "Ah, but you've stepped up your game. Recruiting help."

I chuckled. "I have to. He's way above my level."

"You're closer than you think, I bet."

"Thanks," I said. "But I'm not being humble. He's skyrocketed his skill set in the last two years. Ever since Inkheart hired him. He's getting paid for the kind of experience some people would kill for. They're teaching him more than MIT."

"Badass."

"Yeah," I said. "That's one of the reasons why I'm going to own the TOC and rock a boot camp this summer. I want the experience to shine on my resume. And as long as MIT accepts me…"

"They will," she said. "And here I am solely focused on getting that acceptance letter and not even thinking about getting hired by a company. I'm practically a slacker."

I rolled my eyes. "That's the last thing you are," I said. "You'll get your letter. I have no doubt."

"Still. You have your whole future mapped out. I haven't thought past March."

I laughed, smoothing my hand over her back. "You don't need to have a plan. You're already going to slay Security Systems this summer."

She tilted her head from side to side. "I *am* stoked I got into that one. I honestly didn't think I would, with the selection process they go through. Mom about lost her mind when I told her the cost." She shrugged. "I had more than half of it saved up." She glanced at the counter. "And in about thirty minutes I'll be clocking in to earn my way out of the loan she fronted for the rest."

"You work harder than I do. I honestly didn't think it was possible," I teased. I was so lucky my parents hadn't forced me to get a job. Between hacking and actual schoolwork, I rarely had time for anything else. Especially not a girlfriend… but here I was. Completely awestruck by Amber and beyond happy she was *mine.*

Both our cells buzzed on the table. I glanced at mine while Amber ignored hers.

"Another one?" I asked, half grumbling. "Where does this

person find the time to post so much?" I spared a glance at her cell. "Have you been following the blog still?"

Amber narrowed her eyes on my cell. "Oh," she said, slightly jolted. "Here and there."

I swallowed hard, hating that I couldn't tell her the truth…the reasons why I was following it. "Tessa told me about it the last time I bribed her with a brownie session. It's not like I've ever written in or commented or anything."

I swiped to the left, my screen instantly filling with the person who Snapped about the blog—Sabrina—and saw her commentary and all the comments below hers. "Whoa," I said, pausing in my quest to leave the group. "Tessa?" I squinted, recognizing her Snap handle.

"What?" Amber sat up straighter in her chair. "What's she saying?"

I furrowed my brow, speed-reading. "Sabrina said something about the latest blog?" I glanced at her in question before continuing to read. "Said that the creator was a hack and that she'd been interested in it at first, but after hearing all the parents' concerns, she thinks the person could be some creeper?"

"Bitch."

I raised my brows at her response.

"What's Tessa saying?" she asked again, much softer.

I read and reread all of Tessa's comments. "She's defending the blog. Said it's helped her in more ways than one. Made her feel like she had a safe place to go to talk about stuff she couldn't with other people. That Sabrina is…" *Fuck me.* "An attention whore."

Amber chuckled but quickly stopped when she saw my face. "I'm sorry," she said.

"The last thing Tessa needs is to be on Sabrina's radar." She was already on Tanner's shit list and she didn't even know it. I was doing everything I could to keep it that way, too. I rubbed my palms over my face. What was going on with her lately? Ghosting Sean's and my texts was one thing—I already knew that was because of the prank—but she'd barely even been around the house lately. And now she was defending the sex blog I was tasked with unmasking?

Fuck. My. Life.

"Sabrina probably doesn't take the time to read through all the comments," Amber said, scooting back from her chair to stand. "It would take someone *hours* every day to go through that amount. She doesn't have the patience or the care to."

"I hope you're right," I said, slinging my bag over my shoulder. "Do you like the blog?"

"Yeah," she said, her voice cracking a bit. Was she embarrassed about checking it out? "It's…" She shrugged. "I don't know." She hooked her thumb toward the counter. "I've got to get ready for my shift." She backed away as if I'd suddenly admitted I wanted to become a famous hacker who pulled stunts for the limelight.

"Okay," I said, following to plant her with a goodbye kiss. She kissed me back, but I could feel the tension in her body, so I cut it super short. "Thanks for your help."

"Always," she said. "It was fun."

"Sneaking into a system and changing commands, fun?" I grinned, covering my chest. "You're a girl after my own heart."

Heat rushed her cheeks as she headed toward the swinging door that led to the kitchen. "Isn't it already mine?"

My lips popped open, the breath stalling in my lungs.

Hell yeah it is.

I nodded, dropping my hands. "You know it is."

"Good," she said, biting down on her smile. She spun

around, hurrying behind the counter, then slipped a few brownies into a paper bag and handed them to me. "Go see Tessa," she said. "Sounds like she could use her brother and another brownie session."

"You always have the best ideas."

"It's a curse," she said, and I did a double take at the worry cracking her flirty gaze.

"See you tomorrow, Pixie," I said as she disappeared through the kitchen door.

I left in as big a hurry as I'd come. Suddenly wondering if I'd been so wrapped up in protecting Tessa that I'd neglected her when she needed me. Concentrating my time on Amber, the TOC, and doing every little thing Tanner commanded wasn't helping me be present, either.

Balance.

I needed to find it, and fast. Because things were already slipping through the cracks.

But being with Amber?

She was worth every single amount of effort it took to rearrange my life, because it just didn't make sense without her at the heart of it.

CHAPTER TWENTY-TWO

"Mom?" I called from my room, shutting my laptop.

"What's up, Buttercup?" She pranced into my room, a basket of laundry on her hip.

I took the basket, sat it on my bed, and started folding.

She arched a brow at me. "What'd you do?"

"Nothing!" I laughed, folding a T-shirt. "Can't a girl fold laundry with her mom?"

"Of course she can, but my sweet, wonderful, genius teenage daughter doesn't do it often."

"Okay, fine," I said, reaching for some Marvel leggings and rolling them up. "I was wondering…"

"Yes?" She kept her eyes on her stack of clothes, patient as always.

"What are your thoughts on…cheating? Like, if one person is in love with the other but they're married. But the married person is way older and still sees the other person?"

Mom paused her folding, her eyes finally finding mine. "You writing a story?"

"Not exactly…" I hated—absolutely hated—lying to Mom. I couldn't tell her, but she was my best source of knowledge for the blog. I wished I had all the answers myself, but there was no one I trusted more with information so important. Which gave me the confidence to try to help others who weren't as fortunate as me to have the best mom ever.

"Well," she said, sighing, "I'm not a fan of cheating. I never write it, as you know. It's a super-difficult topic. Sometimes a trigger topic for certain people who had a trauma with it. There are always circumstances where perhaps cheating was necessary in the beginning—abusive partners and such—but in the end, for it to be a healthy relationship…something has to change."

I nodded, mentally soaking up the words to apply to the next blog.

"And as for the age difference thing," she continued, "that's tricky, too. If someone is thirty and the partner is forty, there isn't much of a maturity difference, is there? But if someone is, say, *eighteen* and the partner is *twenty-eight*, then there's a major gap in emotional development." She eyed me, and I couldn't help but laugh.

"You sound like Dad." No doubt his decades of psychology had rubbed off on her over the years. Hell, it had rubbed off on me with this intense desire to help people.

"Don't tell him that." She swatted me with the pair of socks she'd rolled. "Anyway, does that answer your question?"

"Yes," I said.

More or less. I was able to draw as much from my own feelings on the topic, but I'd wanted a trusted source to confirm it. The commenter I'd selected for today's post was in a wicked emotional state, and I'd have to handle it as delicately as Mom implied.

Mom gathered the folded clothes that were hers or Dad's and placed them neatly in the basket, leaving mine on the bed. "If you're writing a book," she said, stopping in my opened doorway, "I may be able to help you, you know?"

I smiled at her. "You'd be the first person I'd tell if I was attempting to pen a novel, Mom."

"Just checking," she said, flashing me a wink and headed down the hall.

I waited a few minutes before opening my laptop again. Now prepped for my next post, I needed to publish it before I had to get ready for tonight's date. Swallowing hard, I placed my fingers on the keys.

QUESTION OF THE DAY:

Fortnite4food asks: *"I'm in love. Think about her all day and night, can't eat, can't sleep, all-consuming kind of love. There is only one problem.*

Okay two.

She's married.

She's six years older than me.

We were friendly at first. Then things happened. Amazing things. She loves me, too. I know it.

But she hasn't left her husband yet, and it's torture seeing her every day and not being able to show anyone I love her. I can't hate the husband, either, because I've met him and he's a good dude. I feel like an asshole, but she's it for me.

What can I do to get her to fess up to him?"

It sounds like your feelings are wicked intense for this woman, and I can't imagine how hard it is not being able to talk to anyone about it. I commend you on not forcing her hand and telling the husband yourself, and respecting her time frame as you both deal with this extremely difficult situation.

I understand you love her, and try not to hate me here, but have you looked at this from another angle? Is she open with you about her reasoning for *not* telling him? Or does she put it off and change the subject whenever you bring it up?

These are tough questions, but they need to be answered in order for you to know what to do next. If she ignores the questions and denies you the details, and constantly makes you feel bad for asking, then you need to search deep within your heart and ask yourself why you're staying with someone who is willing to cheat on their partner. I know every situation is different, and no one can know unless they're in the relationship, but I don't want you to be taken advantage of.

If she is open with you about the details, and this is real...then I feel you owe it to yourself to put things on hold until she has managed to tell her partner and file for a divorce. It's not fair to you to be the person in hiding.

I hope everyone in this triangle finds closure and happiness.

Keep me posted.

In the meantime,
Stay Sexy. Stay Healthy.

CHAPTER TWENTY-THREE

AMBER

"I'm almost starting to worry about you two," Mr. Griffin said, suddenly appearing in front of the table in the back of the room Dean and I had claimed on the first day of Code Club.

When did he move from his desk?

I'd been totally engrossed—not at all seeing the code on my screen, but mentally sketching my next blog post. Dean sat next to me, close enough to touch, not that I would with Mr. Griffin present.

It had been two months since the concert, since Dean and I had officially become *more* to each other, and I still wasn't used to the glow he caused to shine through me.

"You're saying you don't code the minute you're home?" I asked, smiling as I stretched my arms over my head. I'd accidentally let myself slip to the common-laptop-hunched position who knew how many hours ago.

Mr. Griffin pursed his lips in the universal *touché* face.

"Regardless," he said, tucking his hands in his pockets. "There are fun things to do outside this classroom."

I feigned a gasp. "There are?"

Dean chuckled. "What are these fun things you speak of?" he asked, diving right in with me.

Griffin rolled his eyes. "You two are lucky you're my favorite students. I might have to kick you out and force you to go do normal things. Like eat and sleep and all that stuff."

I waved him off. "Sleep is for the weak."

Dean nodded, his arms folded over his chest. "I could always eat, though," he teased.

"All right," Griffin said, heading toward the door. "I'm throwing in the towel. You two are younger and that's an unfair advantage."

I rolled my eyes. He was likely only five years older than us, one of the youngest teachers at Wilmont.

"Have a great night being old," I teased, and he laughed.

"Oh, I will," he said, halfway out the door. "Nice dinner. Netflix. Sleep. It's all the rage, you know." He waved before disappearing out the door and down the hallway.

Two seconds passed before Dean turned, his knee brushing mine as he faced me from his chair. He leaned over and his lips pressed against mine in the sweetest kiss. I sighed between his lips, the deep craving finally attended to.

"I thought he'd never leave," Dean said against my mouth.

I fisted his black T-shirt, tugging him closer. "Yes," I agreed, swiping my tongue over his.

The contact set my nerves on fire, a delicious heat that consumed my senses and burned our surroundings to ash.

Dean's hands rubbed up and down my spine as he paid great attention to my mouth, nibbling my bottom lip before soothing it with his tongue. I trembled, all at once my lungs so full and yet unable to draw enough breath at the same time.

"Pixie," Dean growled my name, the vibrations tickling my chest. "I've been thinking about that *all* day." He pressed his forehead to mine, breaking our kiss as he slowed us down.

I closed my eyes, my heart racing as I caught my breath. "Me, too," I admitted.

"Do you have any idea how hard it is to see you at school

all day and *not* kiss you?" His hands settled on my knee, an electric current tingling all the way up my spine.

"No," I said, giggling. "I don't. I've never kissed myself before."

"Well you should," he said, smirking. "It's the best."

"Really?" I brushed my lips over his lightly, so much so it was hardly even a fair tease.

Another low rumble from his chest, and he claimed my mouth again.

In the back of my mind, I waited for the panic to steal my current bliss. Panic over being swept away in his kiss, his scent, so lost in the swirl of emotions that we forgot we were at school.

But it didn't come.

Nothing but warm energy and an ache for *more*.

This was a kind of trust I'd never experienced before. A connection that spoke volumes from deep within me telling me everything was good, everything was right.

Dean, my friend, my competition. The boy who pushed me to be better—who sparked a challenge that had helped me heal myself these past months. Heal wounds I thought would taint me for the rest of my life. The dark marks that I was certain would ward off anyone else from ever truly loving me.

Dean gently pulled away again, a deep breath shuddering from his lips, and it looked like an effort to stay in his chair. "I need to finish one more page addition on the school's site," he practically growled.

"Fun break over," I said, smiling, my lips still tingling from his kiss.

"To be continued," he assured me before turning back to his gear.

The song "Friends" by Flight of the Conchords blared

from the cell on the table at my back, effectively stopping me from returning to the blog work. I swiped the cell to answer Hannah's call.

"Hannah," I said, drawing out her name so she knew she was in trouble. She'd known I was in Code Club tonight and usually waited until I texted her to call me for the recap. She was two hours early.

"Amber."

I instantly stood up, the sob in her voice putting me on high alert.

"Hannah? What's wrong? Are you hurt? Where are you?" The questions spewed from my mouth, my eyes widening as if that would help me hear better through her cries.

"Home. I'm f-fine." The stuttered hiccup in her voice combated that statement, but I breathed easier knowing she wasn't in a wreck on the side of the road somewhere—the same phantom road Mom was always hounding me about.

"Why are you crying? Do I need to come get you?"

Dean began packing up our gear, his eyes darting to me every few seconds. I loved that he was prepared to leave in a hurry if I gave the word.

"No," she whined. "It's my mom. She totally just went off on me. Kicked Jake out of the house."

"Omigod," I said. "What happened?" Flashes of them getting caught by either one of her parents doused me with ice water. Her parents weren't insanely strict, but they definitely didn't believe in sex before marriage, and they certainly wouldn't stand for it in their house.

"She found out I'm on birth control."

"How?"

Hannah was the definition of careful. She always did her research and switched up the places she got her pills from if there was even an inkling her mom would discover her.

It wasn't that she wanted to keep things from her parents; she just knew their stance on it. But she *had* to be safe. She and Jake wanted a family someday, but not now.

"I was attempting to write in to *Ask Me Anything*," Hannah said, her sobs finally ebbing. I gasped as she continued. "Was going to ask how to finally tell my mom I was on the pill and how I'm about to turn eighteen and I just didn't want to hide it anymore." She sniffed. "But I didn't hear her walk in or when she read over my shoulder. Honestly, she flipped out about the blog for longer than the birth control."

"Oh no." My voice was a whisper.

Me. My blog. That was the cause of my best friend's pain.

"Right? I tried to talk to her, but she was livid…" Her voice trailed off as she succumbed to a fit of sniffles. "She acts all progressive, but then she totally flipped," she finally continued. "So, I'm grounded. For life. She'll prob take my phone soon." She sighed. "Can you call Jake for me? Tell him I'm sorry. Tell him—"

"I will," I said. "But he doesn't blame you. You know he doesn't."

"I know. I'm just mortified. I can't believe she was so mad at me. You think she'd be happy I was being safe." She groaned. "Sorry to put all this on you."

"It's what I'm here for." Guilt churned in my gut. "It'll be okay, Hannah. It will. Graduation isn't that far off and then everything will change. She'll calm down. Just hang in there." I had to pray that she would come around. See that Hannah and Jake were being so smart. Still, it didn't stop the acid in my stomach from whirling, from sucking at the bottom of my heart, screaming that this was all my fault.

"Right." She sniffed again. "See you at school tomorrow. Unless I'm grounded from that, too."

"Love you," I said, and I hoped she knew I meant it. Even if she didn't know that I was behind the blog that led to this, I wanted her to feel how sorry I was.

"Love." She hung up, and I stared at my cell for a few seconds before glancing at Dean, who stood next to me, both our bags over his shoulder.

"Are we going to her house?" he asked.

I shook my head, recounting the conversation to him.

"Damn," he said. "That blog is everywhere. Sucks that she got caught writing in to it."

"Yeah." I sighed. "And her mom's reaction over it?" I bit my lip. "Like…the blog is there to help people, not hurt them. Not turn them toward doing bad things. It's so people don't feel alone."

Dean cocked a brow at me, setting our bags down on the table, seeing I wasn't ready to leave. "But it doesn't mean it's not dangerous," he said, and I snapped my eyes to his.

"What?"

"I checked it out after…after I saw Tessa's comments. It's on the dark web, which we both know means the person is trying to hide. And even if the topics it discusses are helping people, the owner would be naive to think people wouldn't get hurt in the crossfire."

I gaped at him, guilt and anger twisting my stomach. "Crossfire?"

He tilted his head, his eyes searching mine. "The parents who are protesting it, the people who are writing in. Tanner being up in arms about it. The stuff the blog is posting about. It's *awesome*, but it's dangerous. Things like that are begging for conflict. One person's beliefs will always offend another. It's just the way the world works."

I narrowed my gaze, trying like hell to calm the fire inside me.

"The way the world works," I said coolly. "You know, you're right." I shook my head, adrenaline coursing through my veins. "It *is* the way the world works. People get offended. By legit everything. And maybe it is risky for someone to want to help on a social media level and leave their self so open to attack and criticism, but at least that person is *trying* to create change." I huffed.

The parents' outrage, Hannah's situation, Tanner's personal vendetta against the school.

I was over it.

Over so many things.

Thousands of people wrote in to *Ask Me Anything*.

Thousands of people searching for comfort in a world full of judgment.

And I would not shy away from that. Not because of backlash or fear or any of it.

I trashed the post I'd mentally sketched earlier.

New words and ideas took shape, forged in anger and hurt for my friend. She was a great person. Her grades stellar, her aspirations for the future even better, and she had a boyfriend who loved her. Like the kind of true love you read about in books.

"I get that," Dean said, drawing me back to the present. "I'm just saying I hope the person behind it has a thick skin and is ready to deal with the hits that will inevitably come." His eyes churned with worry and…regret?

I nodded, trying to calm down. Several months ago, I might've torched the blog because something like this had happened.

Hannah didn't deserve this.

But I had gained strength and had healed through the posts, through connecting with the people who *needed* it. So, I'd have a thick skin, sure, and I'd keep on going. Keep on doing what little I could to change...something. Anything.

One post at a time.

And in the meantime, I'd just have to find a way to make it up to Hannah.

"How's your TOC prep coming? The challenge, too?" I finally asked Dean after I'd cooled down a bit as we walked to the parking lot.

When we stopped between our two cars, he admitted, "Slow. I had a change of direction." He smirked, mischief flashing in his eyes. "I'll be ready for you by the deadline."

I smiled. Good. Maybe his would be more direct and effective against Tanner's vendetta than mine. Our simple challenge of riling up Tanner had taken an entirely new turn in light of what I'd learned from the people writing in to my site. The meaning and worth went so much deeper than this now. Bigger than a challenge to get back at another male in power pushing his beliefs on the masses. There were *so* many like him in the world—people who downplayed victims' experiences, male or female, or were so set in their ways they believed all who didn't live the way they did were *wrong*.

Dean brushed his fingers over my forehead, shifting a piece of hair that had fallen out of place. "I'm slightly terrified of the look in your eyes right now."

I laughed, the tension easing in my shoulders. "I'm just pissed."

"I know."

"It's unnecessary," I said. "I hate that Tanner is even in a position to push his ideals in our faces. But he's one in a sea of powerful people trying to claim they know what's best for all of us."

Dean arched a brow.

"Like his stance against birth control and sex and all of it. He rallies against something that should be a *choice* for each individual. He's not the only one, and it even goes beyond the sex stuff."

"Like what?"

I sighed. "Like the fact that I'm just as good a hacker as you, but *you*—a boy—are the one who's been deemed the best and resident hacker genius of the school."

Dean's soft smile fell.

"I'm not blaming you," I hurried to add, furrowing my brow as I tried to rein in my rant.

"If you want the title, you can have it," he said, waving his arm toward the darkened school. "Then Tanner would have you at his beck and call because he'd blame you for the video prank and task you with—" He hissed, raking his fingers through his hair. "All his bullshit. Maybe you would've gotten the video down sooner."

"That's not what I'm saying—"

"What *are* you saying?"

"That there are problems here. That there are serious differences between the way boys and girls are treated in this school—hell, likely everywhere—and it's total BS. And that, on top of every other agenda Tanner or people like him pushes, is why blogs like *Ask Me Anything* pop up."

"Back to that now?" His tone was sharper than I'd ever heard it. "I'm sorry about Hannah. I really am. But... that blog is a direct act of rebellion. I'm not saying I don't freaking love the idea, but everyone who decides to write in should know that there is always a risk of getting caught, or catching backlash for it."

I smacked my hand on my thigh. "If people would just *talk* to each other and actually listen, not just plan a counter-argument—so much bullshit could be avoided. Being there for each other. Having some damn compassion over judgment for once. That's what the blog is about."

"I didn't realize you read it religiously," he said. "And people should know what they're getting into up front. And Tessa is one of those people writing in. Luckily our parents are cool, but with the shitstorm surrounding it, I'd rather her not be anywhere near it. There should be a disclaimer upon entry of the site. Something that warns anyone who writes in what they're really getting into—that there is a growing protest against it, that parents aren't on board and neither are school officials. That writing in could have consequences, like tonight with Hannah."

He could've thrown an ice-cold bucket of water over me and I'd be less shocked. Though I could see his side, it was hard through my internal raging.

"Hey," he said as I struggled to find words. "I get the bullshit in this school, okay? I get that all over the place there are tons of people who get flack for being different— girls or boys or anyone in between. I grew up with a baby sister and I've seen firsthand how she catches shit for things Sean and I wouldn't. I've watched Dad *teach* her things he never taught us. How to keep an eye on her drinks and how to get out of a hold if some creep sneaks up behind her." He sucked in a breath. "I get it. And you're right, the blog… whoever is behind it probably has the best intentions. And I'm sure it's awesome to have someone who understands, too. Not everyone does." His eyes were genuine as he reached for my hand. "I'm all for strong girls," he said. "That's why I like you so much."

His words, his deep understanding, melted the rage flaming in my chest.

My heart swelled and ached, and I had so many conflicting emotions storming my body I felt too tight in my own skin.

"You've always been a good listener," I said. My thoughts

flashed way back to when we first met physically—instead of online. I'd spotted him on his laptop, told him he needed more stickers as a joke, and our friendly rivalry had started. But even then, he'd always been there. Listening, helping, never hesitating when I sent him a chat box and a question. "DC," I finally said.

"What can I say?" He smirked. "I love…" His eyes widened before he forced out a laugh. "Love to hear your voice."

The air in my lungs tightened, my heart picking up its earlier speed.

"Says the boy who spent the first two years of high school only speaking to me through chat boxes," I teased, my breath catching.

"Hey," he said, stepping closer. "It's our thing."

I reached up and brushed my lips over his. "I like our things."

He walked us until my back was against my car, kissing me long and hard and sweet. I tensed for a breath, waiting for the cold to seep into my bones from being pinned against the car. From being trapped. Locked in his embrace and his kiss.

But again, it didn't come.

There was only Dean and how safe I felt in his arms. How much power I felt thrumming through my veins, knowing I was in control. Knowing he'd stop if I so much as blinked the wrong way.

But I didn't want him to stop.

The taste of him—Red Bull and spearmint—swirled and churned and wound me up so much it was almost enough to erase every thought in my head.

Almost.

"Mmm," I mumbled against his lips, loving the way his

body was flush with mine. "I told Hannah I'd call Jake for her."

He growled, his eyes on fire as he gazed at me. "Never," he said, a laugh in his tone, "say another dude's name when my mouth is on yours."

A warm shiver rippled down my spine. "Or what?" I challenged.

He kissed me again, hungrier, faster, until my entire body trembled under his. Too quickly, he ended it, stepping so far away from me, the cold air raised chills on my skin.

The grin on his lips was more enticing than Loki's when he was in the middle of chaos.

"Night, Pixie," he said, walking around his car and sinking behind the wheel.

I smirked, shaking my head.

The boy was good.

Great.

And he was all *mine*.

ASK ME ANYTHING

ABOUT   USEFUL LINKS   FAQ   CHAT WITH ME

QUESTION OF THE DAY

CrossFitandUnicornsForLife asks: *"I'm not from Wilmont. Our school doesn't have a dress code like yours does, so I know I shouldn't be complaining. But try not to hate me and hear me out. I was sent home early today because I refused to change my top during weight conditioning. This is an elective class but one I chose to take because I like to stay in shape for sports. Anyway, I had on a tank top. Not a spaghetti strap, not a cami, but a razorback tank top. The teacher told me to go put on a T-shirt because the amount of skin I showed was distracting the boys. The same BOYS who were shirtless! Like...I was stunned. I said as much and then I got written up and sent home for talking back. My parents totally understand and aren't mad at me, but we're all pissed at the situation.*

Again, I know you have a dress code at Wilmont, so this is probably super annoying. I'm grateful to have the freedom to—mostly—wear what I want to class, but this...I don't know what to do. I thought about going straight to the principal, but being that he's a guy, I wasn't sure he'd understand. So I just went home.

But I'm still fuming.

I need to do something! The guys are allowed to wear nothing but shorts and yet my SHOULDERS were distracting? How can I stop this from happening to another girl? I know the clear answer is to not wear tank tops to conditioning, but the guys get to go on not wearing shirts? How is that fair?"

I don't hate you.

I may envy your non-dress-code school, but never hate. ;)

I do, however, hate that this happened to you. Hate that it's just so typical. You'd be surprised how many similar stories and questions I have in my inbox! Or maybe you wouldn't. Either way, it's totally unfair.

It's the hypocrisy in situations like these that helped fuel my fire when creating this blog. The fact that girls are constantly reminded we are distracting to boys and we're the ones who need to change instead of going to the source of the problem— teaching the guys to chill if they see a shoulder.

And, in reality, are they even distracted? Is there a team of boys out there reporting each and every girl shoulder they see? Or each legging-covered leg? Each bare knee when a girl wears a skirt or shorts? Is distraction a legitimate excuse or is it one the patriarchy has continuously fallen back on for who knows how long? Because, honestly, I'm distracted by a hell of a lot, and it has nothing to do with what people are wearing.

I completely agree with you and am angry on your behalf.

In my opinion, if you want this to change, if you want to help spare the next girl, then speak out. Take a picture of the outfit you had on and show it to your principal, the vice principal, the school counselor. Take it all the way up to the superintendent of the district if you have to. If you have social media, use it as a way to spread the word that you were subject to a massive case of hypocrisy and you're not standing for it. The best way to create change and help others be spared from instances like this is making these instances known far and wide.

Ignorance is so often the reason for lack of forward momentum in the world, and we're lucky enough to be born in the age of technology. We have platforms—like my little corner of the web—to speak out or vent or inspire. It's up to us how we choose to use them. And it's refreshing to see girls speaking out for change, outnumbering the amount of filtered Snaps.

We're all we've got to create change for the future. The people in authority now? They'll be long gone and we'll be stuck with problems we helped create if we don't speak out.

So that's my advice to you.

Make the injustice known.

And perhaps, your voice will be enough to stop the hypocrisy in its tracks!

Keep me posted.

In the meantime,
Stay Sexy. Stay Healthy.

A little of the rage from earlier snaked out of my blood as I hit publish.

I'd selected the question specifically because of Dean and my conversation after Code Club. It had been in my starred file for a week, and it was time I addressed it. Especially when everything had hit me so hard tonight.

Dean's words about the blog—calling it dangerous.

Hannah's punishment for being caught on the site.

It was all gnawing at me, but the people I'd already helped…that was what soothed those hurts. I wouldn't leave them in the dark.

But I had thought long and hard about what Dean had said and was considering putting a disclaimer on the site. Explaining about the heat coming down on the blog, and how it could also transfer to those who dared to write in. Full disclosure—I'd always told them I'd never lie to them. Save for my true identity. And the fact that I was a virgin issuing sex advice and beyond.

I pinched the bridge of my nose, trying to ease the pressure building behind my eyes.

I'd started this blog with the intention of flipping off Tanner's personal vendetta.

It had transformed into something so much bigger now. Something that not even my BFF getting in trouble over could stop me from continuing.

That notion was terrifying enough, but I held strong to my hope.

Hope was all I had.

ASK ME ANYTHING

ABOUT   USEFUL LINKS   FAQ   CHAT WITH ME

QUESTION OF THE DAY

SevenDegreesofFantastic2356 asks: *"I'm not who my parents think I am. They think I'm their son. I'm not. I'm their daughter. I want to tell them. Ok, it's more of a need than a want. I mean, I do want to, but the need to be honest with myself and them is overpowering everything right now. I feel like if I don't tell them, or those around me, I may waste away. I'm scared of their reaction. I plan to transition fully in the years ahead and I'm worried they won't understand. They aren't bigots or anything—they were super understanding when I came out to them and as I continue to support, talk about, and rally for LGBTQIA+ rights and issues. But...this is more than that. This is me telling them I've been living a lie and my identity isn't what they thought. What do I do?"*

This is honestly one of the most touching and most intense questions I've received since starting this blog.

First, I want to tell you that you are not alone in this. That your feelings of "wasting away" are completely justified, but know that there are communities in place to help support you. And, though I may not be

able to directly personally relate to your situation, I am here. That is why I started this blog, so people like you, like all of us with tough situations we feel alone in, can stand together and lean on each other for support.

Second, I'm totally proud and happy that your parents have supported you when you came out and when you rally behind LGBTQIA+ rights! That is a wonderful sign. It shows that they love you no matter what and are open-minded.

I'm also so beyond happy you mentioned your plans to transition over the years. It means you've done your research and know this isn't a race to surgery, that there are a slew of steps you'll need to go through before you get to the complete change at the end. I commend you on this! Because of the amount of time and effort and medical assistance that goes into transitioning, it's more important than ever that you have the support of your loved ones. So I totally understand the desperate need to tell them. But I also understand the fear.

It's never easy telling those we love something about our identity that they likely have no clue about. I'm sure if you were living on your own and not in financial need of their support, you might even torture yourself by avoiding telling them until you were close to the end of your transition. But I'm so glad you're not willing to go down this road alone. You don't deserve to. Their support will only help with your success in transitioning. And it will be good for them to start seeing you now as your true self, which I'm sure will help a ton with your overall health.

I know it's scary, but everything you've told me indicates they'll support you. They may have questions regarding the process (I know I did!). I couldn't sit at my keyboard and presume to know your situation, so I took your question (anonymously) to a well-trusted psychologist and he helped me come up with what we feel is the best plan of action for you. You by no means have to follow this advice—honestly you have to listen to your heart and your instincts more than anything. But, since you came here, I'm going to give you everything I have.

First, if you haven't already found the local transgender support groups in the area, I've complied a list of them <u>HERE</u>. It is so important to talk to people who have undergone this process or are going through it currently. They will understand you and your needs in a way no one else can.

Like I said, from what you've told me, I doubt any of this applies to your parents, but you need to think about the tough questions and rule them out. Do you think they'll respond violently? If so, you need to have a plan in place to protect yourself against such measures (a public venue and a trusted friend's place to stay at until the situation calms down). Do you think they'll deny all financial support? If that's the case, you'll want to construct a plan to pay for the medical (both mental and physical) care that will go into your transition.

Now, if you've ruled out the above, then most likely your supportive parents will have questions. Before you tell them, I suggest you create a list of questions you may think they'll ask and write down the best possible answers. That way you'll have a concrete list to go to, something that will guide you through the important process of gaining their full support and attention on the matter.

I'm betting—and hoping—that they will respect the truth about your body, mind, and soul, and support you as you go through this incredibly difficult process.

secreturl.ama/staysexylatest

The road is hard, but nothing worth it is ever easy.

Sending you all the good vibes!

Please keep me posted.

In the meantime,
Stay Sexy. Stay Healthy.

hit publish and raked my fingers through my hair. I was both exhausted and totally satisfied. The question had proven my toughest yet. I'd spent hours online, scouring through tons of articles and blogs and forums from the transgender community for advice. And after that, I'd gone to Dad. More often than not, the people who commented on my blog were questions I'd go to Mom with, but I knew I couldn't possibly ignore my dad's profession when it came to this one. He'd been more than eager to talk about things in a hypothetical sort of way and helped me feel much more apt to respond to the person's question.

Because when I'd first read it?

I'd felt completely and totally unworthy.

The commenter was trusting me with such a serious and life-altering question...who was I to respond?

But my dad was a successful teen psychologist, and his advice paired with the countless research I'd done in the online transgender community had made me come alive with excitement. With knowledge. With a newfound respect and admiration for all those struggling with similar situations and having no way to know how to proceed.

And now, as I closed my eyes on a long day and finally settled myself into bed, I felt...content. Hopeful. Strong. Drawing that strength from the bravery of the person who wrote in. Who was honest with who they wanted to be in life—true to their heart. Whoever had asked the question, I hoped that perhaps they'd read the response and not feel so alone.

CHAPTER TWENTY-FOUR

DEAN

"Mr. Winters," Mrs. Francesca said, glancing away from her computer. "You're wanted in Principal Tanner's office."

Damn. Shit. Fuck.

My stomach twisted into knots as I gathered my gear, knowing I wouldn't be back to class. Not since I had yet to produce the person behind *Ask Me Anything*.

Amber flashed me a confused glance, and I made a point to walk down her row when headed toward the door. I discreetly trailed my fingers along the back of her neck as I passed her seat, the momentary contact almost enough to kill the anger and guilt eating my insides.

I hated keeping this secret from her, but I knew it was for the best. I wouldn't directly lie to her. If she asked me why Tanner was demanding my time, I would have to be honest with her. I just hoped she wouldn't push the issue. We both had enough on our plates: me prepping for the TOC, which was now only two weeks away, and her working tirelessly on her end of our little challenge. I knew she would win. Because the idea I'd had planned? Well, it no longer worked with Tanner holding my baby sister's school records over my head.

I'd also been contemplating ripping Tessa a new one— but I always decided against that, too. She'd ditched our second brownie night early—and her stomachache saved me from blurting out a lecture. Somehow, I'd find a way to talk to her, but it would have to be after the anger settled.

Mrs. Francesca waved me off as I gently shut the door behind me, dragging my feet like I wore lead shoes. I contemplated not showing up at all, but then who knows who he'd target next in order to control me. Probably Amber, since she was the other most important girl in my life who happened to be a Wilmont student. That couldn't happen. We were too close to putting this place in our rearview.

Mere weeks until acceptance letters were mailed.

Ms. Howard flashed me an encouraging look as I walked toward Tanner's closed door. A few knocks and he'd ushered me inside. Another shut door. Another secret session.

Can't wait till graduation.

A few weeks and I could stop worrying about his role in my acceptance to MIT. Hopefully I'd have cleared Tessa by then, too. But I had to tread lightly. And succeed here.

One step at a time.

"Have you discovered the source?" Tanner asked, unbuttoning his suit jacket as he took a seat behind his desk.

I had tried and failed miserably.

I furrowed my brow, clutching the bag on my shoulder. "No. It's complicated. Whoever is behind this knows what they're doing."

His eyebrows rose at my tone. "Sit down."

I sighed, sinking into the chair he indicated.

"I thought you were the most talented, promising computer science-bound student in the district, let alone Wilmont Academy."

I cocked a brow at him. "I am," I said.

"Then who is behind this blog?"

"I don't know." I smacked my hand on the armrest of the chair.

He shifted in his seat. "I don't have to remind you of

what is at stake here, do I?"

I sat, frozen, trying like hell not to lose it on him.

"Perhaps I do," he said, reaching for the mouse on his desk. A few clicks and he turned his desktop screen toward me.

A small vid-box popped up, the black-and-white images grainy but unmistakable.

Tessa.

Slipping Tanner's laptop under her sweater and leaving with it in a hurry.

I cut my eyes up to the top right-hand corner of Tanner's custom-built bookshelves that lined the wall behind him. The same angle in which Tessa's prank-gone-horribly-wrong had been captured. A small, barely noticeable red light blinked from behind a mess of green leaves—a potted plant he had on the highest shelf.

"Are you allowed to have that thing recording while you have students in your office?" I asked, my eyes returning to him.

He ignored me, clicked on the vid-box, fast-forwarding a few hours to when Tessa returned the laptop to its original place on the shelf behind him.

A few hours. That's it.

I wondered how bad the "crime" actually was. Hell, when Sean had been a senior, a bunch of them had stolen Tanner's car and put it on the football field. No one went to jail over that, so why should Tessa over this?

He didn't press charges.

Not like he would now. Because he *needed* something from me.

"Please feel free to set up your work station here," he said, motioning to the wide-open space on the opposite side of his desk.

"What?"

"You've been excused from classes for the remainder of the day," he said, exiting out of the vid-box and inadvertently revealing where he kept it stored.

Perfect. I'll get that later.

He leaned back in his seat as I rolled my eyes, reluctantly slipping my laptop out of its bag. "You know that's illegal, right?" I spared a glance at the camera hidden in the plant before cracking open my screen.

Tanner grumbled. "The person behind this blog is harming people."

"Is it, though?"

He raked his hands over his slick hair. "The parents are calling for action. Protests have been held, and there is talk of pulling students from school and enrolling them elsewhere next year—"

"Ahh," I cut him off. I didn't bother to look up from my screen as I talked. "So that's it. Forget about the content and how it bugs you, it's actually about you getting docked points from your precious ranking. Which," I said, finally meeting his gaze, "no doubt will lose you any bonuses or grants or awards. Perhaps even your job?"

"My first concern is this school and the students' education within it," he said through clenched teeth.

I scanned his walls, noting the various awards he'd had custom-framed. The pictures of his father and grandfather before him, plaques with their names and their tenure years at Wilmont engraved upon them. "Right," I said. "It doesn't make what you're asking me to do any less illegal."

"And how is that different than any other time you're doing...whatever it is you hackers do?"

I choked out a dark laugh. He was right about there being plenty of rules we bent, vulnerabilities we exploited— but I always patched those vulnerabilities behind me. I never allowed anyone to follow my tracks and I was responsible enough to never use it for black hat stuff. I had a code and I abided by it, but each word out of Tanner's mouth made me want to take my code and set it on fire. Show him just how many things I *could* do.

"Code Club is officially canceled," he said after the silence between us filled the room. "You've done well with the school's site and will be excused from that maintenance as well."

I kept my face even, but a small part of me mourned the loss. It had never been a Code Club. It was Amber's and mine. A space of our own. A chunk of time dedicated solely to our passions.

"Fine," I said, shrugging like it didn't bother me. In reality, it didn't. Amber and I were together now; I could see her whenever I wanted. That was a bright ray of hope out of all this twisted darkness.

He stood up, slowly rounding his desk, his eyes on my screen. The one I'd filled with a code box completely irrelevant to his demands. Not that he could read the program language. He pressed the tips of his fingers next to my gear as he leaned down, his face too close to mine.

"Find the source, Mr. Winters. Or I'll be sure to use the footage I have to press full charges against your sister."

I narrowed my gaze, never flinching from his too-close presence. "I'll find it," I said. "But as I've told you for weeks, this kind of hack takes time." And I sure as hell had dragged it out, waiting until I found the perfect moment to put an end to his downright tyranny.

Tanner stood, re-buttoning his suit jacket and slipping on the agreeable mask he donned on the reg. "Understandable," he said. "If it takes you longer than normal hours today, I'll be happy to stay late. And excuse you from future classes."

I gaped at him. "And the work I have to hand in in order to graduate?"

"You'll have to make it up."

The blood in my veins turned to ice.

Now he wasn't only threatening my sister but my freedom.

You're fucking with the wrong guy.

I swallowed the words I wanted to say, instead nodding like the good little student he wanted me to be.

He bought it, a self-satisfied smile on his face. "You see?" he asked. "Once you understand that *my* interests are *your* best interests, it makes everything so much simpler, doesn't it?"

Another nod.

He sighed. "That's all I ever want. Ever think about," he said, almost like he was speaking to himself now. "For Wilmont students to understand how the real world works. I push you all so hard in order to prepare you for what is to come. My students, past, present, future, they all have one thing in common."

"What is that?" I asked, trying to keep the bite from my tone.

He blinked a few times, glancing down at me. "They're winners, Mr. Winters. They learn to succeed. No matter what the cost."

Or how you push them there.

Because that's how he operated. He was talking about *himself*. He did whatever it took to succeed—to earn his top rankings, his bonuses, his awards, and raises, and all the things that blinded him to what should be most important... his students. Their mental and physical education. Their emotional nourishment, and everything Ms. Howard strived to be.

Not him.

Never Tanner.

I stared up at him, wondering for the first time ever if he'd always been this bitter, solely-focused-on-himself person, or if he had once dreamed of being a principal. Of being in charge of so many young minds throughout the decades. Had the power corrupted him? Or had he been corrupted and sought the power himself?

"I'll check on you in a few hours," he said, turning toward his door. "And don't worry," he continued. "I'll personally let Ms. Henderson know that Code Club is done."

I ground my teeth as he shut the door behind him.

It didn't matter—if he'd ever been good or not.

He wasn't now, and his abuse of power had gone on for far too long.

QUESTION OF THE DAY

ManofSteel4419 asks: *"Last year, one of my older brother's friends took things too far at a party. We were both drunk and she advanced. I was shocked, tried to tell her I was... Fuck me, this is hard. Tried to tell her I was a virgin and had a girlfriend (she was away on a family trip the night of the party). She forced herself on me. I tried to stop it, I did...but the alcohol didn't help and she overpowered me.*

The next morning, she acted as if I asked for it. Wanted it. That she'd done me a favor by "making me a man."'

Anyway, that's not the point. My girlfriend and I... things are going great. But I still haven't told her. And she's brought up the idea of taking things further in our relationship. I'm worried if I tell her about what happened, she'll either think I wanted to be with the college chick and I cheated on her, or that she'll see me as weak because I couldn't stop it. Is it better to pretend it never happened?"

I know people say "I know how you feel" all the time and sometimes don't truly mean it, but I *do*. I understand the concern, better than I like to admit.

And it makes me sick to my stomach that you think the events that occurred weren't "the point."

It *is* the point.

It's a moment in your past that is directly affecting your future. And it wasn't your fault. It doesn't matter how drunk you were or if you're a boy, girl, or anything in between—no means no. I can't believe the word is such a difficult concept to understand to so many people out there. And you're not weak—I hate that there is a universal misconception that men can't be raped, because they can. And it's unfair to say otherwise when something like this occurs.

No one *asks* to be violated.

No one wants to have their trust broken.

But it happens. All too often.

You are not alone. I feel your pain and your concern over telling the truth to your partner. The real question is: What do you want?

You have absolutely no obligation to tell anyone about your past. It's your business, but it may feel better to talk to someone about it. If talking here with me is enough to lighten the burden of the past, then wonderful. If you feel the need to share it with your partner, then do so with confidence not guilt. This wasn't your fault, and it certainly doesn't mean you're weak. Anyone who would think that isn't worth your time. I know that is hard to hear, but it's true. Especially after what you experienced, you have to surround yourself with people who love and respect you—family, friends, and partners alike. There is no foolproof way to guard yourself, but one step is by knowing who respects you for you and who is a fleeting person passing through.

Whether you decide to tell her or not, I would recommend getting tested for STDs before you move forward sexually with your girlfriend or anyone else. It will protect not only your partner but help keep you aware of your body as well.

I hope you find comfort and closure as you move forward.

Whether you decide to tell her or not...

Know that you are not alone.

Know that you are not damaged.

Know that you are worthy.

I wish I could say with certainty that the events of the past will be forgotten, but I can't. I can only be here to listen with true understanding and hope for you to find your breath again.

I'm here. Anytime you need to talk.

And in the meantime,
Stay Sexy. Stay Healthy.

My hands shook as I clicked the keys to publish the post.

Not as much as they would've when I first started the blog, but the adrenaline was still there. The cold still snaking through my veins as I carefully responded to his post. I had to swallow the anger over the situation, the rage that begged me to shout in all caps and swear words and go on an attacker-burning mission.

After some calm breaths, I focused on my own healing process and hoped I could transfer some of that to the person who wrote in. Though I knew words were a flimsy excuse for a good shoulder to cry on and a person who cared about you who was *truly* listening. Not judging. Not advising. Just listening.

Like Dean had for me.

Like all these people who had written in had unknowingly helped me heal through our connection.

Still, the post left me sticky inside.

There were too many of these comments. Too many of this variety.

And I was so powerless to stop it.

One small speck on the web, begging for change, and wishing like hell instances like these weren't such a universal occurrence.

CHAPTER TWENTY-FIVE

AMBER

"You sure you're cool with it?" Hannah asked as we walked to the parking lot. Class had let out ten minutes ago, and after the oh-so-fun visit from Principal Tanner telling me that Code Club was over for the year, I was free to give Hannah a ride home.

Dean had texted that he had to stay late and would call me later.

The days were growing tenser regardless of the happiness I had with Dean. The secret of the blog—and the protests, supporters, and popularity—weighed on me more and more.

Only two more months till graduation and less than two weeks till college acceptance letters are mailed.

I reminded myself that then I'd say goodbye to this place forever. I hadn't decided what I'd do with the blog when that time came, but I was certain I'd have to tell someone about it. Dean or Hannah or, hell, even my mom. Keeping everything to myself was turning my stomach into an acid trap. But it would have to wait. Until it was safe to admit my creation. When Tanner no longer held this major power role in any of our lives.

God, that would be some kind of sweet freedom.

"Amber?" Hannah stopped me, her hand on my shoulder as I almost walked right past my car I was so in my head.

"Yeah?"

"Are you sure you're good with tonight?" she asked again.

"Oh," I said, snapping back to reality. "Yes, totally."

We climbed into my car, heading straight to her place. She'd been grounded after the birth control fiasco, which I still felt responsible for—she wouldn't have been caught if she hadn't been writing in to *my* blog.

"I'm sure she'll let you out to help me with a project," I said, flashing a smile. It had been months. Hannah deserved to go to Jake's pre-spring-break party. And after everything that had happened in the last few months? I actually felt like going, too. Felt like escaping the comments that stockpiled in the blog's inbox and the parents who wrote in to tell me how evil I was.

"I hope so," she said. "I'm one more night away from going *Shining* on everyone."

I totally understood. The tension between her and her parents had never been so intense, and I hated that for her. She didn't deserve the reaction she'd gotten, so I had no qualms whatsoever about sneaking her out of the house.

It only took twenty minutes to convince her mom to let her go with me—*and only me*—to study at my house. Which we technically did—for about two seconds while we got ready for the party. I dressed in a pair of distressed jeans and my favorite sweater, and typed out a fast text to Dean, letting him know the plan.

> **Dean:** Tanner is keeping me hostage for a project.
> **Dean:** Fill you in later.
> **Dean:** Once he lets me out I'll meet you at the party, Pixie.

"Whoa," Hannah said as I pocketed my cell.

"What's up?"

"You're in love!"

"What?" I laughed, but it was forced.

Hannah jumped up and down, throwing her arms around my neck. Then she smacked my arm. "How could you not tell me?"

I rubbed at the spot. "Omigod, Hannah! That hurt."

"Whatever. Talk."

I gaped at her for a second before shrugging. "I don't know what we are yet! I'm…"

"Scared?"

"Yes," I admitted.

"Don't be," she said. "I see it. How it is between the two of you. It's completely different than…" She stopped herself. "It's different. You're different. You're more *you* than you have been in so, so long."

She wasn't wrong. The time Dean and I had spent together, the closeness I felt to him…

We'd breezed through Christmas *and* Valentine's Day—a flurry of kisses, Code Club, and chatting until we feel asleep at our keyboards.

I had it so, so bad.

"I know," I finally said. "I found a way to heal myself… somehow." I wished I could tell her how the blog had helped me so much. My thoughts traveled to the one I'd posted before school—the boy's story about being drunk at a party, his brother's friend taking things too far, the shame he felt, the way he'd been blamed…it had hit so damn close to home. And yet, where there once was a gaping hole of hurt had sealed over with a layer of camaraderie and strength directly from connecting with people like him. People who wrote to me daily for help. "But," I continued, "he knows everything and it hasn't changed anything between us. He doesn't see me as damaged."

"You're not," Hannah said. "That jackass *is*."

I huffed. "Yeah."

Hannah clapped again. "Is Dean coming tonight?"

I nodded. "After he wraps up a project."

"Yay!" She waggled her eyebrows. "It's been months and I've never properly BFF grilled him."

I gasped. "No, no, no. You totally can't!"

She laughed, nodding dramatically. "I have to," she said. "It's my duty." Her shoulders sank. "I won't mess up again."

"Oh, Hannah, stop." I wrapped her in a hug. "It wasn't anything any of us could've prevented. Trust me. No one saw it coming." Especially me. "Brandon"—I said his name through gritted teeth—"it's all on him. And it's in the past. I'm so over it." And it was amazing how true that felt. The guilt and shame and blame he'd made me feel over the event—it was bullshit. It wasn't my fault. I hadn't asked for it. My body was mine, my choice. Who I gave it to and what I did with it. Not anyone else's.

"Okay," she said, brightening again. "I haven't gotten to see Jake outside of school this whole time." She grabbed my hand and tugged me toward the door. "Thanks for this," she said. "Now hurry the hell up!"

I laughed, rolling my eyes as I fished my keys out of my bag.

Fifteen minutes later, I was—once again—the third wheel to the Hannah/Jake lovefest, but this time around I didn't feel so alone. There were plenty of people at the party, but that wasn't it, either.

It was Dean. The way we were together. The way he made me feel. It was like this impenetrable force field surrounding me—as long as he was mine, nothing could touch me. Was this love? Was this what that felt like?

Intoxicating, more so than the booze the party offered but I'd refused to touch.

After that night, I'd never wanted to be in an out-of-control position again—not that I faulted anyone else for indulging.

I glanced at my cell again, checking to see if Dean was on his way.

He wasn't.

I scanned the area. Jake and Hannah were wrapped up in each other, understandably making up for lost time since she'd been grounded. Jake's parents were out of town prompting the whole party in the first place. Music filtered throughout the house and a variety of couples danced in the entertainment room. Others simply chatted, played beer pong or other drinking games. The same party regardless of when or where.

My skin prickled, an awareness rippling over my skin like the sting of sunburn. I must've spotted him from the corner of my eye without realizing.

Brandon.

Drunk.

His booming laugh dominated from the beer pong table, Sabrina sloppily falling all over him.

I clenched my jaw and swallowed down the acid bubbling in my throat, something that immediately happened any time he was close. I'd assumed he'd be here, but I had hoped not to see him, or at the very least, not see him until Dean was here. Not that I needed a boy to protect me or anything like that, but because Dean made me feel like the best version of myself. Stronger. Untouchable.

Sure, I'd kneed Brandon in the junk to get away, but lately...the strength I'd gained from both the blog and Dean's confidence in me? I felt like I could lay him out flat like an NFL player if he came two inches too close.

That was a milestone, something I almost wanted to

celebrate when a few months ago the mere memory of what happened had turned me into a quivering, weak girl who locked up when anyone got too close.

I tore my gaze from him and Sabrina, for a moment worrying about her. Would he do the same to her? Or had she already consensually given him everything, so there was nothing left for him to demand? To fight over? To *take* without regard.

She looked happy by his side, not scared.

I stood from the couch, and in an attempt to outrun the sound of Brandon's voice, I wandered to Jake's room. Once I sealed myself inside, I sank onto his bed and fished out my cell.

Still no news from Dean.

I scolded myself for checking so much and decided to distract myself with the site. I had over one hundred unread comments to scroll through. Getting lost in them would be better than checking my cell every five seconds for word from my boyfriend.

The word sent chills up my spine, an ache low in my belly.

Damn that boy. I'd been *so* sure I wouldn't want a relationship until I was well into my college career. *So* sure in my determination that none could be trusted.

But he'd changed that.

My cheeks flushed hot with all the thoughts of just how deep my feelings ran for him, of how we'd been living in a slow burn I was ready to turn to full blast, and I was quickly shifting my position off Jake's bed and instead sliding into his computer chair. I spun around, fanning myself as I logged into the blog from my phone.

It only took a few minutes and I was drowning in comments and questions. Some accusations from outraged parents. Some commendations from others. A whirlwind of opinion and emotion and with each one, the weight on my chest increased.

Ignoring the hate mail, I focused on the *real* students with *real* questions. The ones actually seeking the help I wanted to give. Questions like what to do if you weren't feeling that spark when you kissed your partner anymore, or what to do if sex was painful despite mentally being into it, or what to do if your partner was more experienced than you.

Some were much more graphic than others. One made my cheeks burn hotter than ever when someone asked about the taste of a certain bodily fluid—

"What are you reading?" Brandon's voice practically shook the room as he snatched my cell out of my hand.

I jolted, having been so engrossed I didn't hear him come into the room. I spun around, darting out of the chair, only to freeze when I looked behind him.

The door was closed.

And locked.

Ice-cold fear snaked through my veins, rooting me to the spot. The air thick, I choked on my words as I glared at him. His eyes were wide, his jaw nearly unhinged as he scrolled on my screen. The private questions section that only the creator of the blog would be able to see—the ones not yet chosen to make public.

"Wait," he said, the word sliding off his tongue on a slant. He glanced at me. "*You're Ask Me Anything?*" A dark, greedy laugh tumbled from his lips as he returned to reading what was meant for *my* eyes only.

Realization rocketed through me—once again his eyes and hands were where they didn't belong.

And he didn't give a shit.

"Fucking hell, Amber," he said, that sly grin shaping his

lips. He tossed the cell at me so fast I almost didn't catch it.

My fingers flew, signing out from the blog before securing my cell in my back pocket.

"If you knew all this stuff," he said, stalking toward where I still stood, my feet frozen but adrenaline shaking my muscles, "then why the hell didn't we do *more*?"

I hissed.

I literally *hissed* at him like an angry cat when he stepped entirely too close.

He towered above me, his eyes hooded as he looked down at me. "We could've practiced all these things. I could've taught you so, so much more." Reaching out, he trailed a finger down my arm. Despite having a long-sleeve on, I *felt* it like an ice cube to my skin. "We still can." He smiled. "I've missed you."

I jerked away from his touch, backing up so much I ran right into Jake's desk. I gripped the edge, the air in my lungs tight.

"Come on," he said, his head tilted to the side. "Tell me you haven't missed me."

"I haven't," I snapped, and thanked God my voice had returned.

He rolled his eyes. "You *have*. We used to have so much fun, the four of us. You and me. Jake and Hannah. We could all be a group again—"

"Not a chance in hell," I said, gaping at him.

"Aw, Amber. Don't be like that." He leaned in closer, and I immediately tried to walk around him. His massive arm on one side of the desk stopped me. "We obviously went wrong somewhere. If you know all you do...the blog...hell, why did you dump me?"

I raised my brows. "Are you fucking kidding me?"

He smirked. "I love it when you drop the F-bomb."

"Ugh, gross," I said, trying to move again. He blocked me with his other arm. A cold sweat broke out on the back of my neck, my stomach rolling. Flashes of that night burst in my head, my body screaming at me to *run* or punch him in the throat. "You need to let me leave. Now."

"Damn it, Amber. Why can't you just listen to me?" he whined. "I'm trying to talk to you. I miss you. I want to get back together." He pursed his lips in a pout. "I could help you with your site. Work out scenarios you don't know about."

I cringed, my legs wobbling, the breath shallow as I tried to suck it down in gulps. His scent was everywhere—sweat and beer and some kind of overkill body spray.

"We're done, Brandon. We've *been* done," I said, hating that my voice shook. "Now back up."

"No," he said. "Not until you tell me *why.*"

I gaped at him. "You know why."

"I really don't," he snapped. "Especially now that I know you've messed around *before* me. You have to know all that shit you post on the blog. And yet you've made me feel like an asshole all these months because, what? You just weren't in the mood that night?"

Tears burned the back of my eyes I was so angry. "No," I said. "I…I don't have to explain myself to you. *You* wouldn't listen when I said no."

"You were my girlfriend," he said, his tone sharper. "You weren't supposed to say no to me. Besides," he said, shrugging, "everyone knows girls say *no* just to play hard to get for a few minutes before that no turns into a *yes.*"

In that moment, as his words sank into my brain, I felt not only *my* fear, my pain, but the pain of so many others before me. The ones whose faces I didn't know, but whose souls I could feel. The ones who were made to believe *they* were in the wrong—wore the wrong outfit, drank a little too much, trusted the wrong friend to take them home. Boys and girls alike.

Something deep inside me grew and screamed—no, *roared.*

I clenched my hands into fists, barely moving my lips my jaw was clenched so hard. "Let me go," I said, glaring at him.

"No," he said. "You owe me this. I deserve to know why you've apparently said yes to a shit-ton of other people but said no to me."

"Like that matters?" Not that it was true, but *fuck.* "Because I have experience means I have to say yes to you whenever you feel like it? Like I'm some piece of fucking property?" I scoffed, shaking my head. "You're delusional, Brandon. And legit effed in the head." I cut my eyes to where his arms still caged me. "Move. Now."

"You're the one who's messed up," he said, sneering down at me. "You hide behind this blog. This poor excuse to validate that you're just a big slut."

I laughed darkly.

"You're damaged," he said. "No wonder no one else wanted to be with you." A devious smile shaped his lips. "And now everyone is going to know the real you. Once I tell them all who you are."

My spine stiffened, but I cocked a brow at him. "I fucking *dare* you, Brandon," I snapped, stretching myself to be bigger, taller, wishing like hell I could match his strength and shove him out of the way. "You mutter one word, one *whisper,* and the next post will be complete with all those dick pics you texted me."

He flinched. "You wouldn't. You said you deleted them."

"Did I?"

I had. Instantly. But he didn't have to know that.

Something like fear flashed over his glazed eyes.

"More than that," I continued, drawing on his one moment of weakness, "if I hear you've hurt someone else... like you did me? I'll steal every record you've ever had and mar it. I'll own your bank account and keep draining it to zero. Hell," I said. "Maybe I'll even sneak into UMass's servers and turn whatever grants they awarded you into an actual rejection for admittance."

"You can't do that," he said, but his voice was a whisper.

"You don't really believe that, do you?" I folded my arms over my chest, holding my ground.

A blink and he gripped my shoulders too tightly. I tried to move, but he held me locked. "Don't you fuck with me, Amber," he snapped. "I mean it."

"Or what?" I trembled in his grasp, struggling to free myself. The adrenaline rushing my veins was no match for his strength, but my threats were nearly as strong. "Keep touching me and see what happens. I won't stop at where I said. I'll *ruin* you, Brandon."

His grip loosened, but he didn't let go as the truth of my words caught up in his mind. He knew how good I was, even if he never acknowledged it.

If he truly knew me, then he'd know I wasn't that kind of hacker. That I wouldn't ever follow through with it. If he kept a hold of me like this, though, I might just reconsider.

"Don't," he said, almost a plea. "Please. I won't say anything. I swear."

"And you'll stay the hell away from me."

He nodded, and I eyed the hands still on my shoulders. His fingers slid down my arms too slowly, but I sighed. Finally, I'd faced him.

I'd voiced the fact that I had done nothing wrong. That even if I had had the sexual experience he'd said I had, and then said no, I was still in the right. Because it should always be my choice what I did or who I did it with. No one else's.

I'd won.

"Get the fuck away from her!" I heard Dean's voice, the rage in the words, before I saw him fly across the room.

CHAPTER TWENTY-SIX

"*Stay the hell away from me.*"

Amber's voice had sounded from inside Jake's closed door—Hannah had sent me this way saying she'd seen Amber head in there a while ago.

Hand on the knob, I'd turned it, but it was locked.

Before I could blink, before I could *think*, I'd busted the lock, my shoulder stinging something fierce.

"Get the fuck away from her!" The words had flown from my mouth the second I saw Brandon towering over her.

Red.

Everything was red as I lunged for him now.

"Dean, stop!" Amber, a flash of pink, stepped in front of me, her hand on my chest.

Every sense narrowed to her, the adrenaline in my veins cooling a fraction.

"He's not worth it," she said, eyeing where Brandon stood, fists clenched, not a foot away.

"Are you hurt?" I finally asked, taking her face in my hands.

"No," she said, but I could *feel* her trembling. She gripped my forearms, holding on to me like I was the only thing that could keep her solid as she craned her head around my shoulder. "He didn't…" She shook her head. "I handled it." Her eyes turned to slits as she glared at him. "You won't bother me again," she said. "Right?"

Brandon's jaw flexed, but he shook his head.

"Damn right you won't," I said, wanting nothing more than to stalk the distance and make my threat stick. The trembling pixie in my arms stopped me. I walked us to the door. "You step an inch within her space, and I swear to God I will make you disappear."

I didn't bother waiting for him to respond. Instead, I glanced down at Amber, her eyes wide and panicked, her body jerky while she walked. I swiped an arm underneath her legs, picking her up and cradling her to my chest as I walked down the hall. She kept a tight grip on my neck, and I mouthed *I've got her* to Hannah and Jake, who gaped at us from across the room.

I'd owe Jake for the door, but I couldn't care less.

I set Amber into the passenger seat of my car and drove. As far away from the place as I could. Like the distance would erase the situation.

Amber was silent, inside her head the entire ride to my house.

I didn't push. I *knew* better.

My pixie, impossible to catch. She had to come to me. Always.

She let me take her hand and lead her up to my room, a deep sigh flowing past her lips when I'd settled her onto my bed. I took a seat in the chair at my desk, watching her. Waiting.

The gears behind her eyes clicked and churned. She opened her mouth a few times before those beautiful lips popped closed. A frustrated groan and she shoved her palms against her eyes.

I went to her and pulled her hands from her face.

"Pixie," I whispered, brushing some tears off her cheeks.

She groaned again. "I'm sorry, Dean," she said. "This is

like the third time you've wiped away my tears. I swear I'm not doing this crap on purpose."

I furrowed my brow and shook my head. "I don't care," I said, holding her face in my hands, forcing her to look in my eyes. "As many times as it takes." I swiped my thumb under her eye. "As long as it takes." I trailed my index finger in the path of wetness. "I'll be here. Doing whatever is in my power to help you."

Her eyes glittered again, more so, if that was possible.

"You don't have to," she said. "I…" Anger sharpened her features. "I'm okay. I am. I stopped him on my own. Stood up to him. Shut him down. I just thought I was stronger than this. That my *hate* would prevent me from"—she held out her trembling fingers, gesturing to the way her entire body still *shook*—"*this* reaction."

"You can't possibly control it," I said, interlacing our fingers in her lap.

"I should be able to," she said, her eyes lilting to the side.

"Do you…?" I pressed my lips together before continuing, not wanting to push her. "Can you tell me about what went down tonight?"

Another shiver raked her body, and I pulled her into my lap, trying like hell to double my size and *envelop* her. Instead, I folded my arms around her, my chest absorbing the shock from her vibrations.

"I went into Jake's room for some space," she said without looking up at me. "I was checking the—" Her words stopped short and I could feel her face clench where she rested it. "Checked my cell to see if you'd texted. Then got distracted with some other stuff. Didn't hear him come in."

She was silent for so many breaths.

"Then," she said, shrugging, "he…it was like he wanted closure. Or to get back together. Acted like I *owed* him both those things. That I was the one who had ruined us. Led him on." She rubbed her palms over her face. "And the more he blamed me, the more he spoke like what he'd done was normal, and that *I* was the broken one…the angrier I got. And then—" She choked on a sob, the desperate sound kicking up the adrenaline still lingering in my veins. I wanted to kill him in that moment for whatever it was he'd done to her…again.

"I threatened him," she said, shocking the rage right out of me. "I threatened him with the worst possible things, Dean." She hid her face. "Told him I would do all kinds of black hat stuff if he came near me again, or if I found out he'd done something to another girl."

I smiled at her, pride storming through my chest. I pulled her hands away, shifting her in my lap so I could catch her gaze. "That's a good thing, Amber," I said, my tone soft. "Why are you crying?"

"Because," she said. "I *wanted* him to feel weak and vulnerable and terrified. I *enjoyed* watching the reality sink in and know what I could do to him."

"Good," I said. "He deserves it. He doesn't deserve your tears. And you sure as hell don't need to feel guilty over it."

"But it makes me *no* better than him!"

"You *are* better than him. You are a million times better than trash like him." I sighed. "Amber, you needed to use whatever weapons you had to get him to back off. It was smart. I'm proud of you."

She raked her fingers through her hair, the tears finally ebbing.

"I wish I would've gotten out sooner," I said, the anger in my gut roaring at Tanner for keeping me so damn late. All in the hopes I'd find the wraith that had become the bane of his existence—and my new hero. Anyone who could scare

Tanner this much had me in their corner.

"I shouldn't have gone," she said.

"No," I snapped. "You can't let him dictate when and where you have fun with your friends."

"Damn," she said. "I've never been so ready for graduation."

"Me, too," I agreed.

She smiled, and it turned the hot anger in my blood to soothing warmth. One I wished I could inject in her to stop her from shaking. I rubbed my hands up and down her arms. "Hey," I said, glancing over my shoulder as I tugged her from the bed. "You want to take a hot shower?"

Her eyes flew to mine, the swarm of emotions from before switching to one: full-on desire.

My mouth dropped, and I cleared my throat. "No," I said before cringing. "I mean, *yes*, but...not what I meant." The words tangled in my mouth. "I meant for you. To get warm? To take the edge off the shock."

A small smile shaped her lips as she stared up at me. "I don't really want to go home right now," she admitted.

"I don't want you to, either." I wanted her with me, where I could draw her from herself, from overanalyzing the situation and somehow letting that jerk make her feel guilty when she was so far from blame.

"Are you sure it's okay?" she asked, then glanced down. "I don't have any other clothes."

"I'll find something," I said, opening the door to the bathroom that connected to my bedroom. I locked the other door, just in case Tessa wandered this way. I leaned over the tub, twisting the handle in the secret-code way in order to get it to not scald her. "Don't touch that," I said, grinning. "Any movement and you'll either get burned or iced."

"Noted," she said, folding her arms around herself.

"Okay," I said, grabbing a clean towel from the cabinet, thankful Mom had stocked it before she and Dad had left for a weekend business trip. "I'll just…be out here." I spun on my heels, hating how damn heavy they felt. Split in two: wanting to stay and knowing I needed to go.

"Dean?" she said as I stepped out the door.

"Yeah?"

"Thank you," she said. "For being there. Here."

I glanced over my shoulder. "DC, remember?"

"Always."

I nodded and shut the door behind me before that hot, churning want inside me convinced me to stay.

After riffling through my drawers, I found an old pair of sweats and a smaller black T-shirt for Amber, which I set safely on the sink when I was certain she was in the shower and hidden by the curtain. Booking it out of there, I opened my laptop, trying like hell to distract myself.

Don't think about her in the shower.

Don't think about her naked in the shower.

Don't think about her naked.

Damn. You.

It was impossible.

The girl of my dreams, my Pixie, was taking a shower not twenty feet away.

I shifted in my seat, unable to read the line of code on the screen. Another five minutes and I gave up, shutting it.

I could've used the time to continue my search for the source of *Ask Me Anything*, but my brain was one-tracked. The entire time at Tanner's office I'd researched the site, filing through every blog and published comment the blogger allowed.

It wasn't anywhere near close to the evil Tanner had spouted. Honestly, it seemed no worse than the magazines

Tessa kept stocked in her room. The content was fun and exciting and helpful—a killer combo. But, with the content being about sex or more sensitive topics, I could see why the parents were in an uproar about it. I just wished Tanner didn't have what he did to force me to find the source—but now that I knew where he had the footage hidden...

Maybe, if everything went like I *wanted* it to, I wouldn't have to reveal the source in the end. That is, if I ever found out who it was in the first place.

I racked my brain, shuffling through all the information I'd gathered recently. There was something familiar about the voice of the blogs that I couldn't put my finger on—a nagging that itched the back of my mind. Maybe I'd heard the person speak before in class? Like in those presentations Griffin had us do bi-weekly or something—

Amber cleared her throat, snapping me from my thoughts. I spun around in my chair, my heart leaping into my throat at the sight of her. The sweats hung low on her hips—she'd rolled the band twice to get them to stay—and the black shirt was wide around her shoulders. Her normally feathered hair was now wet and slicked back, her face fresh and free from makeup.

"Beautiful," I said, unable to stop the whisper from my tongue.

She chuckled, fingering the ends of the oversize shirt. "It's a new look."

"I love it." I swallowed hard. "Better?"

She nodded, moving to sit on my bed.

Heat churned in my core—the sight of her in *my* clothes on *my* bed...

"No more shaking," she said, holding up her hand proudly. "See?"

I moved, unable to stay away. I took her hand in mine,

planting a kiss on her steady palm. "Good," I said, finally breathing now that I knew the internal cold had faded from within her.

"Are your parents going to be upset that I'm here so late?" she asked.

I shook my head. "They're out of town."

Her eyes widened for a moment, the truth of that realization settling in behind them.

"But I can take you home whenever you feel like it," I said, not wanting her to feel obligated to stay just because she *could.*

She wetted her lips, glancing down at our hands. "Mom thinks I'm staying at Hannah's tonight."

"Or I can take you there, too. Whatever you want."

"And if I want to stay here?" Her eyes found mine, and the breath stalled in my lungs.

"Of course," I said, finally finding the air in the room.

Her shoulders relaxed, and she flashed me a soft smile. "Good," she said. "Because I feel safe here. Not that I have a reason to *not* feel safe but—"

I cut off her ramble with my lips against hers. Kissing away the blame and guilt she kept pointing at herself. The way she continued to brush off her past like it hadn't haunted her continuously. Like there wasn't a part of her that would always be afraid after what had happened. I knew it didn't matter how fast or how far it had gone—it was an act of betrayal, something she'd never seen coming and could never forget.

Her fingers were in my hair, tugging me closer. She kissed me harder, longer, her breaths full and deep between my lips as if she was siphoning the energy from within me. I snaked my arms around her waist, hefting her onto my lap and locking her above me. Letting her be in control, letting her take whatever she wanted...needed to *feel*.

I wanted to kiss her and breathe into her until she found herself again. Wanted to claim her mouth until there was no doubt in her mind that I loved her. That I needed her on a level I couldn't comprehend. Wanted to show her what my heart screamed but my tongue was too afraid to say out loud.

"Dean," she said, sighing as she broke our kiss, her forehead against mine, a leg on either side of my hips. I held her warm body over mine, terrified to move.

"Pixie." I breathed slowly to ease the race in my heart. The demand for more in my core.

She didn't release the soft grip on my hair as she moved away enough to lock eyes with me. "I love you." Her breath was warm on my lips as she said the words. "I know that's fast," she hurried on. "That it's only been five months and probably way too soon after everything that happened. But—"

"Pixie," I said, smiling as I cupped her cheek. "Always trying to top me."

"What?" she whispered.

"You had to say it first." I smiled. "I love you. So damn much. Couldn't help it. Despite what we kept saying, that neither of us wanted *this*." I kissed her quickly. "Guess it's what we *needed*."

She kissed me again, soft and sweet. When she pulled back, she laughed. "This is kind of intense, huh?"

"Yeah," I said, gazing up at her. "I can put on some T-Swift if it'll lighten the mood?"

Her full, rich laugh shook us both until we were falling sideways on my bed. She shifted next to me, tucking an arm underneath the pillow to face me. "I'm actually kind of tired," she said, biting her lower lip.

I stretched before rolling out of bed. "Rain check on the T-Swift," I said, snapping my fingers. "I can turn the light

off and let you rest. I'll go crash on the couch downstairs."
I headed toward my door.

"Or you could stay," she said.

I glanced back at her, arching a brow.

"We have slept in the same bed before," she said, a
wicked smile shaping her lips.

"I remember the night with stunning clarity," I said,
swallowing hard.

Color flooded her cheeks. "I haven't stopped thinking
about it...about *you* for one second since," she said, her
voice slightly breathless.

I flicked off the light, my heart hammering in my chest
each step I took back to the bed in the darkness. Sure, we'd
slept in the same bed the night of the deadmau5 concert,
and we'd shared something more intimate than I'd ever
experienced before, but we'd slowed it down.

Now she knew I loved her.

And I knew she loved me.

And my heart knew just how much more I wanted to
give her. Share with her.

Everything.

But I wouldn't move an inch without her say-so. I'd be
content to hold her all night, and happy as hell to wake up
to her in my arms, too. I'd wait forever for my Pixie.

Lifting the blankets, we both settled under them, and
Amber scooted into my open arms until the tip of her nose
brushed my chin.

I rubbed smooth circles low on her back with one hand
and rested my other against her hip, a deep sigh slipping
past my lips with her slight weight against me.

Slowly, she shifted, hooking one leg over my hip, drawing
her body flush with mine as she tilted her head up. I glanced
down, locking eyes with her before she pressed a kiss to

my lips.

There was something different about this kiss—maybe it was the way she arched against me, maybe it was because she was in my clothes, in my bed, but there was a primal need behind the way her tongue parted my lips, a hunger neither of us could stop.

And I didn't want to.

I held her against me, locking both arms around her until there wasn't an inch of space between us. I flicked my tongue along the roof of her mouth, and she whimpered, sending all my nerves flying. I rubbed my hand up and down her back, my fingers grazing the bare skin of her hip where the shirt had ridden up.

Amber sighed between my lips, arching into me once again, only this time...

She gasped, breaking our kiss enough to look at me.

She could *feel* me.

Feel my desire.

And as she surveyed me, her eyes churning with want and love and need, I held absolutely still.

"Dean," she whispered, her lips inching toward mine. "I want you."

I wetted my lips, the breath in my lungs tightening. "Are you sure?" I asked, reaching up to cup her cheek.

She nodded. "I love you. I'm already yours and you're already mine. DC, right?"

"DC," I said, my voice shaking as I gently rolled her to her back. I planted a quick kiss on her lips, the buzzing current between us like an unbreakable chain.

My fingers shook slightly as I reached for the hem of the shirt she wore, but she smiled at me as I hiked it up and up until it was over her head on the floor behind me. She hadn't bothered to put her bra on after the shower, and the sight of her…

"You're stunning," I whispered, leaning over her, trailing a soft line of kisses over her skin. My lips grazed over the small globes of her breasts, and farther down. I reached the sweats she wore and flashed a look up at her. "Amber?"

"Yes," she said, her breaths coming fast as she arched off the bed, making it easier to hook my fingers in the band of the pants.

I slid them down slowly, my fingers lingering on the soft skin of her legs. Soon, the pants joined the shirt on the floor, and not long after, so did her underwear.

A groan slipped out of me at the sight of her, and she rose up, grabbing the end of my shirt and pulling it over my head. She kissed my chest, my abdomen, as I kneeled there, and I'd never been more grateful for my morning workouts in my life. Especially when she trailed her tongue along the seam of my pants, before flashing those eyes up to mine.

I read the intent in them easily enough. She was done with slow, and so was I.

I quickly hopped off the bed, ridding myself of my pants and boxer-briefs, and quickly riffled through my nightstand drawer, retrieving the foil packet from the box I'd picked up after we'd returned from the concert. I would never pressure her, but I was never going to be unprepared again.

Tearing it open, I looked at her again, lying on the bed, watching my every move. "Are you—"

"Yours, Dean," she cut me off. "I'm sure. I want this. Want you."

The words, the confirmation that we were in this uncharted territory together, soothed the nerves as I rolled on the condom. How could I be nervous when the girl of my dreams was ready to give me every piece of herself and me the same for her?

I climbed back into the bed and gently settled myself between her knees. I took my time, kissing the line of her jaw, the seam of her neck, before working my way back up to her lips. She moved underneath me, her body seeking mine like it was an instinct. I ran my fingers through her hair with my free hand, my other arm holding me up enough to look down at her. And I never lost that wild gaze as I slowly, gently slid inside her.

Her brow furrowed for a moment before she sighed.

And this time when she moved, she moved *on* me.

With me.

Rolling her hips while I slid in and out, our bodies flush, the heat of her skin soft and slick against mine.

I kissed her despite our gasping breaths.

I drank in the taste of her, swallowed those delicious sounds she made.

The connection between us tightened, strengthening as our bodies crashed against each other. As she arched and met me move for move, like we were made for this. Like we'd been doing this all along.

When her legs locked around my back, when her nails dug into my shoulders, when she let out the sweetest damn sigh I'd ever heard, I lost myself in her. Watched her as she flew apart in my arms.

And I held on.

Held on so tight I wasn't sure I'd ever be able to let her go.

CHAPTER TWENTY-SEVEN

AMBER

I couldn't stop smiling.

My cheeks hurt from smiling so much.

Dean glanced my way from behind the wheel, and I tried and failed miserably to act like I hadn't been staring at him, cheesing like I'd just met Tom Hiddleston at Comic-Con.

"You know," he said, turning down the street that would lead us to Jake's house—where we'd left my car last night. "You're dangerous when you look at me like that."

I feigned shock. "What do you mean?" Everything inside me was giddy and overwhelmed with happiness.

"You could get anything you want from me with that smile."

"Oh," I said, rubbing my palms together. "What a useful weapon. I wonder what I should request first?" I tapped on my chin. "Maybe your vintage Super Nintendo?" I laughed when he gaped at me. "Or perhaps your ticket to the TOC?"

He kept one hand on the wheel while the other flew to the center of his chest. "Wicked, Pixie."

I chuckled, shaking my head. "Never," I said as he parked behind my car lining Jake's street.

He hopped out, opening the door for me before I could get a chance.

"You could be that wicked," he said. "And I'd still love you."

A warm shudder rippled through me. I fisted his shirt,

yanking him down to my level, my lips a millimeter from his.

"It sounds like I've managed to ensnare the *second*-best hacker in the school," I whispered against his lips. "I believe I'm drunk on the power of it."

He smiled, maintaining the game, never once breaking and kissing me already.

We could joke all we wanted, but we both knew he had me totally wrapped.

Dean trailed the tip of his nose over mine, before grazing the line of my jaw. My toes curled in my sneakers, the pleasant soreness between my thighs solidifying that last night was real. That *he* was real. And the way we loved each other...that was more real than anything I'd ever felt before.

Strong.

Consuming.

Brilliant.

The kind of simmering chaos I lived for during hacks, manifested in a boy who was beyond perfect for me.

"Do you have to go?" he asked, kissing the corner of my mouth enough to shoot sparks across my skin.

"I don't want to," I admitted. "But I have things I need to do." I wanted to tell him I had another blog post to schedule. Wanted to tell him he could keep the deadmau5 shirt and simply ask for his help.

But I couldn't.

Because I would never put him in a position to lose everything. Like I was.

At least I had him. Despite everything else going on...I had Dean.

"Busy, busy," he said, an easy smile on his lips. "I get it. I have...obligations, too."

I furrowed my brow, noting the suddenly plagued look in his blue-gray eyes.

"You okay?" I asked. "Need help with anything?"

A muscle in his jaw ticked before he schooled his features. "No thanks," he said. "I'm good." He smoothed his knuckles over my cheek. "I'll call you tonight?"

I nodded, heading toward my car. "Dean?"

He stopped outside his open driver's side door. "Yeah?"

"Thanks…for everything." It was a pathetic use of the word, but I didn't know how to convey how much he'd helped me. How much him loving me for me meant to me.

"DC, Pixie."

"DC."

I sank behind the wheel, not bothering to spare a second glance at the cars still parked in Jake's driveway. Last night may have started off bad, but it had ended better than I could've ever imagined.

ASK ME ANYTHING

ABOUT　　　USEFUL LINKS　　　FAQ　　　CHAT WITH ME

QUESTION OF THE DAY

Anonymous457 asks: *"I don't go to your school, but I got the code from a friend. Hope I can still post here, and if not, well, I guess just getting it out will be good enough.*

This past weekend, something happened. Something that...shifted things inside me. Perspectives and prejudices and bias and all that stuff.

As I'm typing, I'm realizing I don't know what race you are...I guess it doesn't matter. Maybe that is why this whole anonymous thing works. If you're a woman of color like myself, then you'll get it, and if not...well, that's what I'm getting to.

This white girl and I have fought almost my entire high school career. I don't know what started it, really, but it's been a constant. And I've always felt race was the source of our frigidness. We don't go out of our way to be vicious, but we constantly butt heads in class, in the quad, etc. We've never had any love for each other.

This weekend, while at a senior party, I thought

I was opening the door to the bathroom. I was alone—my BFF was busy on the dance floor. Anyway, I opened the wrong door. Walked in on... damn, it's turning my stomach right now.

I walked in on a guy—one of the few college dudes at the party—forcing himself on the white girl. It was clear it was forced because...God, her eyes were wide and panicked and she was trying to push him off but she couldn't.

I didn't think.

I just launched at him.

I wasn't stronger than him.

Wasn't stronger than her.

But together, we managed to shake him up enough to get her free.

I clutched her hand and yanked her ass down the hallway.

Locked us in the bathroom I had intended to find in the first place.

I held her.

We were both trembling, speechless.

But I held her.

In that moment, we weren't enemies.

We weren't two races.

We were women.

Just two girls who understood how it felt to be powerless.

We were the same.

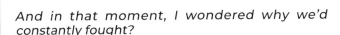
And in that moment, I wondered why we'd constantly fought?

Was it because I thought she had privileges I didn't?

Was it because she was afraid of or judged me because of her own bias?

Was it the social stereotypes of the world we've grown up in that fueled our fights in the first place?

I couldn't stop my head from spinning as my soul shifted in those moments I held her while she cried.

As I felt her fear as real as if it were my own.

Because it was my own.

I had a similar situation happen last year.

I was lucky, though—my brother was with me at the party.

But still...we were the same.

Women.

Fearful of reporting the assault because who knew if anyone would believe us.

Fighting for the right to be viewed as human and not a prize for those around us.

Desperate for anyone older than us, or in authority, to stop trying to control or have entitlement to our own damn bodies.

And it has never occurred to me that we may be more powerful if we stopped fighting each other, and started working together. Not as different races or different ages or different income backgrounds or education levels.

But as girls.

Women.

Us.

I know that was a long story to get to my question, but I didn't know how to ask it without the context. You can edit it out.

My question is—now that my perspective has shifted—what can I do to fight the bigger battle? The girl and I have already made peace. I'm shocked at how long we talked after the assault...how much we had always wanted to say to each other and never did because we were scared of each other.

I want to help other girls figure this out.

I want to inspire girls to stand up for each other and lift each other up as opposed to tearing them down.

It's a hurdle, I know. A fucking big one.

But we have to change.

We have to.

Or else our future will be exactly the same as the women who came before us.

So, any ideas on how I can do this? How I can help create change? You already took your stand, but I'm not a blogger. What can I do?"

I can't tell you how long it took me to get my fingers on this keyboard after reading your story. I've finally wiped the tears off my face and I'm ready to connect with you. How could I *not* post your story in its entirety? I would never dare to edit your words, and maybe that is a huge problem in our society—too much editing. With filters or sugarcoated words or authority figures sweeping tragedies under the rug...it all ends with us getting hurt. Because there aren't enough stories like yours told.

I've also experienced something similar.

I hate to think of how many people can say the same thing, and yet, it's one of the reasons I started this blog. Because I was tired of the patriarchy telling us how to feel about what happens to us, to our bodies. Telling us how to dress, to smile more, to go into certain career fields and not others. It's completely unfair and I'm so damn tired of it.

You are, too.

Not only that, you've dug in to the real deep and gritty darkness of the relationships between girls and between women. Despite race, we, as women, have a tendency to claw each other down when we should be building each other ladders.

I'm in total agreement and awe of you. Your honest and raw story has brought light to my eyes. There are girls here at my own school who I clash with for numerous reasons...and now I'm left wondering *why*?

You're right. As girls, we have it hard enough without adding competition and hatred and judgment to it. Why do we do that? How far back does this go?

I want change, too.

And, on this massive, monumental topic, I know I don't have all the answers.

I can say that your story inspired me, and I hope it is inspiring every single reader out there who is with us now. Not just the girls but the boys, too. I want you to let these words sink in. Be better than the attacker. Inspire your friends to be better. If you see a frightened girl, help her, don't look the other way.

As for you, I hope you speak in a public forum

sometime. I would listen to you all day. And I would spread your words to anyone who would listen. I like your mission and I want to support it.

It's hard to say exactly how to fight this battle on the bigger front, but I think a good start would be researching our politicians and their policies and find out who has the best one to support the change we want to see in our future. We're about to be able to vote—if not already. Electing the right people is the first step in being heard on a major level.

As girls.

As women.

And on the smaller front, you've already inspired change. Because of your story and your honesty, you've posed a question that has desperately needed answering for too many decades too long. Why is it easier for us to tear each other down than it is to build each other up?

It starts with one woman—like yourself—and has now spread to me. I will make an effort to listen to those who I may have written off before.

Because you're right. We're females, and only we know what it's like in today's world.

It's time to band together.

Thank you.

I hope you continue to be a force for change.

Please stay in touch.

In the meantime,
Stay Sexy. Stay Healthy.

• • •

The question of the day had nearly slayed me when I'd gotten home. The story had hit me right in the chest and there was no way I couldn't post it.

Not when she'd been so brave.

So honest.

And beyond that, it was enlightening. Inspiring.

The hope and inspiration still warmed my chest as I shifted to continue digging through the site's inbox.

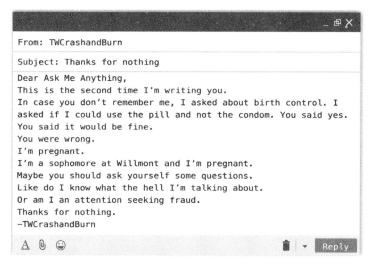

From: TWCrashandBurn

Subject: Thanks for nothing

Dear Ask Me Anything,
This is the second time I'm writing you.
In case you don't remember me, I asked about birth control. I
asked if I could use the pill and not the condom. You said yes.
You said it would be fine.
You were wrong.
I'm pregnant.
I'm a sophomore at Willmont and I'm pregnant.
Maybe you should ask yourself some questions.
Like do I know what the hell I'm talking about.
Or am I an attention seeking fraud.
Thanks for nothing.
-TWCrashandBurn

I read the email three times in a row, certain it was some kind of sick joke. An angry parent with a fake email and a goal to hurt me — scare me into taking down the blog.

But I remembered *TWCrashandBurn* from a few months ago. Not only was her handle a cool homage to the cult-classic *Hackers* — one of my favorite movies — I'd also thought the question presented was relatable and an opportunity to help people who were wondering the same thing. I'd spoken to

Mom about it—hypothetically posing the questions about birth control and if "doubling up" was really necessary.

I never said it was impossible to get pregnant while on the pill.

I'd given statistics on the accuracy of the pill when used by itself, but I also went on to say that nothing is foolproof.

You got a girl pregnant.

Pregnant.

I snapped my eyes open, the email like walking on thin ice and falling straight through.

All the blissfulness I'd felt this morning vanished.

Acid bubbled in my stomach, rolling and crashing worse than waves in a hurricane. The first six emails I'd read for the blog this morning had been hate mail from protesting parents.

Now this.

Another wave, and my skin tightened and the backs of my jaws tingled.

I leaped out of my chair so fast it tipped over. I barely made it to the bathroom before I lost my breakfast.

Pregnant. My fault.

What else had I done?

Who else had I harmed?

I rinsed my mouth out with ice-cold water before brushing my teeth twice.

I'm so careful.

Talking to Mom or Dad, doing more research than I ever had before, and combining both to create an answer I thought was perfect.

Maybe I really didn't know anything. And that fact was ruining people's lives.

After splashing cold water on my face a few times, and sure my stomach had nothing left to throw up, I righted my computer chair and sat in front of my opened laptop.

The email stared me down, accusing me of the worst.
How could I possibly make this right?

My fingers hovered over the keys, ready to reply, but I *couldn't*. What could I say? There was no combination of words that would make this right for a girl who'd trusted me — trusted *Ask Me Anything*. No magic response that would alleviate the guilt nibbling at my insides — eating me slowly. No more than I deserved.

The room spun around me, swirling with the wide popularity of the blog, the protesting parents, the girl who'd gotten pregnant. All of it a massive tornado of emotions — hate and hope and regret — whirling with the sheer intent to swallow me whole.

What have I done?

A cold sweat broke along the back of my neck, and I hated myself in that moment. Hated that I'd thought I was smart enough to *help* students where Tanner had hindered them.

Tanner.

All I'd wanted was to make him *see.* Rile him enough to open his eyes. Force a change for the better.

What did I know about *better*? Obviously, everything I had done — despite the growing numbers of hits and comments and questions — was wrong. I'd led a girl down the wrong path and now she'd suffer that consequence for the rest of her life.

My stomach twisted where I sat.

Torch it.

The solution whispered from the back of my racing mind.

Torch it.

It said it again.

Hit the delete button and pretend none of it ever happened.

I stared at the email, my knee bouncing uncontrollably

under my desk, my hands interlocked in front of me.

No one would ever know.

No.

I couldn't. Wouldn't.

There was no running away from what I'd done, the beast I'd created. I'd have to figure out a way to help. To make amends with the girl, and then do one final post. A goodbye post with an apology.

Running is easier.

It would be, but I couldn't do that.

What if they catch you before you end it?

The traitorous paranoid voice in my head had me chewing on my lip, visions of Tanner pressing charges on me for emotional damage to his students.

Shit.

I'd been careless in more ways than one, apparently. I had no contingency plan in place—nothing to save me from whatever Tanner would do if he found out the truth.

Maybe I deserved whatever I had coming to me.

Maybe I didn't.

I needed to talk to someone about it. Sort my chaotic mind out before I did anything drastic.

Dean.

He would help me work this out. Help me understand what to do. He'd already done so much for me, and he never judged.

DC.

I exited out of the email, knowing I'd have to think on what to say before replying, and pulled up a chat box.

PixieBurn: I need a favor

I only had to wait a few seconds before Dean responded.

NightLocker: I'm good at favors
NightLocker: What's up?

Hope bloomed in my heart with his immediate support. The sourness in my stomach was almost enough to kill the good vibes connecting with Dean gave me. I hurried before I could lose my nerve.

PixieBurn: If the need came about...
PixieBurn: would you be willing to torch some things for me
NightLocker: ...
NightLocker: talking contingency plans here?
PixieBurn: Yes
NightLocker: Who are we hiding from?
NightLocker: Parents?
PixieBurn: No

I sucked in a deep breath, the decision to tell him everything the only solid thing I could hold on to. I contemplated typing it all out but knew in person would be better. Safer.

PixieBurn: Can we meet tonight?
NightLocker: Of course
PixieBurn: I'll explain everything then
PixieBurn: I promise
NightLocker: Ok
PixieBurn: I'll send you everything you need to bury my stuff
PixieBurn: Just...promise you won't look until we talk tonight?

Every nerve ending buzzed, begging me not to send him what he needed to torch the site. To put an end to it just in case. I knew he wouldn't look before I had a chance to explain, but the worry was still there in the back of my mind.

What if I told him and he saw me as Brandon had? A liar. A fake.

NightLocker: You know I won't
NightLocker: You can trust me, Pixie
PixieBurn: I know
PixieBurn: Sorry for the cryptic
PixieBurn: Tonight.
NightLocker: I'll be waiting

His words reassured me as I closed the chat box, but they weren't enough to ease the guilt threatening to suffocate me. The email sat in my dock, glaring at me, begging for attention. Even after talking to Dean, I didn't have a clue what to say.

Maybe tonight, after I told him everything, he'd help me figure it out. He had this calm about him that quieted my mind enough to think clearly.

Yes. Tonight. Dean would never think like Brandon. He was different. He was special.

And he loves you.

That truth helped give me the courage I needed to send him the darkest secret I'd ever kept, and the means to destroy it.

CHAPTER TWENTY-EIGHT

A*ding* indicated Amber had uploaded the goods I'd need to help her with her contingency plan, but I didn't dare check it. The temptation was there, but I resisted. She said we'd talk tonight and I believed her.

After five minutes I closed my laptop, ensuring she'd logged off and didn't need me anymore.

What is she hiding?

I stretched my arms behind my head, rolling my neck. I'd already been coding for an hour before she popped up, but now my mind was working *her* riddle.

What could possibly be so bad she'd need to bring me in? And to torch the stuff.

Something itched the back of my mind—the wraith I'd been chasing. *Ask Me Anything.* The blog was under serious fire…enough that the person behind it might contemplate torching it…

No.

Amber couldn't be behind it.

I'd asked her about it more than a month ago. She'd said…

My heart raced for a few beats, considering.

No. The person behind the blog *knew* stuff. More stuff than Amber did. Last night…that had been her first time, *my* first time. She couldn't be behind it. This secret of hers had to be something else.

I sighed, wishing like hell the girls in my life weren't dealing with such heavy issues, but surely Amber's thing wasn't as deep as Tessa's.

Fuck me, if it is.

Hard enough dodging Tanner's incessant requests for updates on my progress, now this?

Relax. I don't even know what it is.

I took a deep breath. Amber was smart; she wouldn't be in over her head. She probably was just being extra careful, folding me into her plans. Nothing major.

A loud, retching sound jolted me from my thoughts.

I raced to my bathroom door—the one I shared with Tessa.

"Tessa?" I asked, knocking.

"Go. Away." Her words were garbled with the sounds of too much spit. Another gagging sound, and a splat.

I cringed, totally thinking about vacating the house. But it was my baby sister, so I knocked again.

"Let me in," I said.

"No." She growled the word.

I jiggled the handle, finding it unlocked, and stepped through.

"Damn it, Dean," she said, glaring up at me from where she kneeled over the toilet.

I rolled my eyes and gathered her hair off her neck and away from her face, securing it with one of those damn ties she left all over the counter. "Did you go to a party last night without me knowing?"

It was absolutely possible. She could've *thrown* her own party, inviting the entire school over, and I likely wouldn't have noticed. Not when I'd been wrapped up in Amber.

The memory scorched my insides, and I wetted my lips. I could still taste her kiss. Could still smell her on my skin.

Puke splattered the water in the toilet, and I snapped the eff out of it. I leaned over, rubbing my sister's back, cringing as she lost her guts over and over again.

"How much did you drink last night?" I asked, trying like hell not to let disappointment leak into my tone. It wasn't that she drank; it was that she'd obviously had way too much.

"I didn't," she said.

Grabbing a washcloth, I soaked it with cold water, wrung it, and handed it to her. "You don't have to lie to me, Tessa," I said. "I'm not Mom and Dad."

She wiped her face, resting her forehead on the arms crossed over the toilet she'd just flushed. "I'm not."

I folded my arms over my chest, leaning against the wall near the tub.

"Go away, Dean. Please." She closed her eyes, tears leaking from the corners.

"Not until you talk to me."

She groaned, clutching at her stomach with one arm. "No."

I ground my teeth, sucking in a long breath through my nose. "Please, Tessa," I said once I knew my voice would be even. "You've been ghosting me. Sean. For way longer than normal. It's time you tell me what's going on." I now knew the reasoning—her prank on Tanner was likely eating away at her—but it didn't explain her distance from us. Was she so sure we'd lecture her over it?

"I have not—"

Another wave cut her off, and I hissed. "You sure you didn't drink?"

"No," she said, wiping her mouth after flushing again. "I swear. I haven't drunk since…" She closed her eyes again, more tears that rolled into a full-on sob.

I kneeled next to her, my hand on her back. "It's okay, Tessa. I know."

"What?" she snapped, glancing at me through glittering eyes. "How?"

"Tanner," I said. "He has footage. I'm doing everything I can to get it from him. But there are complications." I sighed. "You could've told me. Come to me. I would've helped you."

She gaped at me like I had glitter shooting out my nose.

I furrowed my brow. "The stunt you pulled before the assembly?"

Realization clicked in her eyes before she rolled them. "Oh," she said. "The stupid video? I don't care about that."

"What?" Anger rippled up my spine. "How can you *not* care? He's using it against me! The footage of you *stealing* his personal laptop out of his office, Tessa. You could go to jail for that if he decides to press charges. At minimum, he could expel you. Ruin your perfect record."

"Asshole," she said, scrubbing the wet cloth over her face but not moving from her spot over the toilet. "I didn't know he had a camera. Or that he'd use it against you." She sniffled. "Just a dumb prank. Something to show you and Sean I could keep up with you." She rolled her eyes. "Was going to rub it in your faces before—"

"Wait," I cut her off. "What did you *think* I knew?"

"What?"

I grumbled. "You didn't know I was talking about the video. You thought I was talking about something else. What did you think I knew?"

She dropped her head again. "Just go away, Dean."

"No. Forget that. My ass is on the line because of *you*. Because I will always do whatever it takes to protect you—"

"No one asked you to protect me!"

"I'm your brother!" I stood and paced the small space of the bathroom, not wanting to yell in her face while she was sick. "Look," I said, calming down, "you need to care about this. If I don't get that footage or do what he's asking me to do, there will be real consequences."

She laughed, a dark, cold laugh.

It raised chills on my skin, a deep pit opening in my stomach.

"Doesn't matter," she said.

"It does! I don't know what the hell has gotten into you, but it matters—"

"I'm pregnant!" she blurted, stopping me from speaking, from thinking, from *feeling* anything besides a massive punch in the gut.

I stumbled backward, the backs of my knees hitting the edge of the tub so hard I sank down on it. "What?" My voice was a whisper.

"I'm pregnant," she said, sighing like it was a relief to say the words out loud. She waved her hand over the toilet. "Eleven weeks."

A wad of tears clogged the back of my throat as I stared at my sister—my *baby* sister. My eyes trailed to where one arm clutched her stomach. Or was it a protective hold?

Adrenaline coursed hot and wild through my veins as I bolted off the tub. "I'm going to murder him." I stomped toward the door, prepared to get in my car and beat the living hell out of Colt.

Tessa's clammy hand grabbed my own before I could reach the knob. "Stop," she pleaded. "It's not Colt's fault."

"Like hell it isn't."

She rolled her eyes, not releasing my hand. "It takes two."

I cringed, clenching my eyes shut like it could block the mental picture. I shook out my limbs. "Ugh, scoot over," I said. "Now I think I'm going to puke."

"Get your own bathroom."

"This *is* my bathroom."

A small, barely audible chuckle tumbled from her lips. It was sad enough to stop me from leaving. Instead, I sank to the floor beside her.

"Tessa," I said, my hand on her back. "Fucking hell."

"I know," she said. "I *know*. I should've...ugh..." She groaned again. "It was that damn blog. I asked something and I thought I read it right and then...boom. Pregnant."

"What?"

"*Ask Me Anything*," she said. "I trusted it." She set her forehead on her arm again. "I shouldn't have."

Another wave of anger rippled over my skin. "You did something it told you to and this happened?"

"Sort of," she said, not bothering to look up at me.

Fucking jerk. Whoever it was—now I *did* want to find them. Forget Tanner's reasoning. I would do this for me. For Tessa. Someone had to pay for this. For the fact that my baby sister now had to become an adult. Had to deal with things that *I* couldn't even comprehend.

"It's going to be okay," I said, rubbing her back.

"How?"

"I don't know," I admitted. "But I'm here. Sean will be here for you, too, whenever you want to tell him. And Mom and Dad—"

"You can't tell them," she cut me off. "Promise me."

"I won't," I said. "But you're going to have to."

"Obviously." She finally looked up at me, her eyes wet and red and her face pale.

"Does he know?" I asked through ground teeth. I knew on some level it wasn't his fault, but I wanted to blast blame everywhere, I was so fucking mad. Hurt, for my sister, for the baby, for everyone.

Could've happened to you.

Part of me knew that. Knew it last night while wrapped

up in Amber, in how much I loved her…but we'd been safe. We'd used two kinds of protection to prevent an outcome like this.

"Yes, of course he does," she said, snapping me out of it. "And?"

"And he's amazing, Dean. You'd know that, if you gave him half a chance." She sighed. "He wants to keep it. He wants to marry me when I turn eighteen. Wants to take care of me."

"He loves you."

"Yes."

"Good," I said. That was something, at least. "And you?"

"Me what?"

"What do you want?"

She swiped at the tears running down her cheeks. "I wanted to marry him, thought about our lives together beyond college. Someday, making babies and having SUVs and all that stuff."

"And now?"

"I love him. I do. But I'm scared, Dean. I'm so freaking terrified. I don't know how to be a mom," she cried. "How can I be good? How can I do this and not ruin the baby for life?"

I wrapped my arms around her and let her sob into my chest. "We'll figure it out," I said. "Together. You have people who love you, Tessa. No matter what. I promise. You won't be in this alone."

A heavy weight sank to the bottom of my lungs, cutting off my air supply.

My baby sister was going to have a baby.

Way sooner than I ever imagined, if I even imagined it at all.

A buzzing in my pocket had me fishing out my cell while Tessa still dumped buckets on my shoulder.

Tanner.

Demanding I come in today. On a Saturday. To finish what I'd started.

To find the source of *Ask Me Anything.*

I typed out a fast text and coaxed Tessa back to her bed. I placed a glass of ice water on her nightstand and tucked her in like she was seven years old and having nightmares after Sean and I made her watch *Jurassic Park* with us. Grabbing the trash can from the bathroom, I set it next to her bed.

"Thanks," she said, curling on her side.

I pushed a few strands of hair off her face and kissed her forehead. "I love you, Tessa," I said. "Somehow, this will all work out. For now, just rest." I headed to her door. "Call me if you need anything. I'll be back in a few hours."

"Okay," she said, her eyes already falling closed in exhaustion.

. . .

"You got here quick," Tanner said as I stepped into his office. "And with no resistance about it being a Saturday?" He tilted his head. "Perhaps you're finally understanding that this is best for everyone."

"Sure," I said, half mumbling as I set my gear up.

Couldn't be further from the truth.

I now wanted to find the source for *me*. Because I couldn't shake the fact that my kid sister was pregnant. That she'd been led astray by some blogger hiding behind a website. Sitting behind a computer screen, telling people what to do without a care for what happened to them after.

The person had to pay.

Somehow.

They had to be held accountable.

Fuck, I sound like Tanner.

But he didn't have a clue. Not really.

Didn't matter. This wasn't for him.

I dug and searched and scoured. For so hard and so long that Tanner left the office for a late lunch, unable to sit there and watch me for a moment longer.

Nothing.

Not a trace.

It wasn't possible. Everything left a trace. The person had simply hidden it too well.

Where would you hide content if you wanted no one to discover you?

A lightning bolt hit my brain and I face-palmed myself.

Of course.

Tor. One of the dark webs I hadn't checked yet.

A memory, buried and cloudy, begged for my attention. Who had I spoken to about the dark web? Had Amber and I talked about it? I was already too in the zone to think on it for long.

I switched servers, slipping in easily.

Once inside, it only took a few lines of code-recognition and some analytics before I'd locked on to a social media account that had been logged in while connecting to the site. A few clicks of the keys and—

"No." I froze, my fingers on the keys, as I saw the profile picture. Read the name. "Amber."

I checked and re-checked, desperate for it to be a mistake. That I'd accidentally stumbled upon something else of hers. Some other project—

The challenge.

The contingency plan.

Tessa.

Everything made sense in a sick, twisted sort of way.

Amber reaching out this morning, scared so much she was contemplating torching something vital.

Tessa blaming the blog for her pregnancy. For the next eighteen years of her life not belonging to her anymore.

How could she do this?

I wasn't sure who I was more upset with—Amber for being the source or Tessa, for listening to it.

Months ago, when I'd asked Amber who she thought could be behind the blog...

"There are six girls in Griffin's class," she said. *"Holly, Kristy, Sara, Quinn, Monroe, and me. Could be any one of them."*

Her words echoed in my head.

"Me."

Fuck.

She'd included herself.

But *I* hadn't included her.

I'd thought she would've told me then and there.

And if not in front of her friends, the second we were alone.

Something sharp sunk into my chest, jagged and hot and *hurting.*

Because the blog was the end-all-be-all on sex advice. And yet, last night, when we'd had sex...it was supposed to have been her first time. Like me. We'd been taking it slow because of her past, too. Not that it had ever bothered me. But...

Was it all bullshit?

No.

It couldn't be.

But how could I know for sure?

After everything.

Amber...who are you?

"Amber Henderson?" Tanner's voice shocked me out of my heart shattering inside my chest, and I slammed my laptop shut two seconds too late. "She's the source?" He straightened, a smug smile on his face.

"No," I said, shaking my head. "That wasn't — "

"Don't," he cut me off. "Don't lie for her. I read it over your shoulder. Saw the shock on your face." He *tsk*ed me. "She kept it from you." He sank behind his desk. "Good work, Winters," he said, turning his desktop screen so I could see it. He clicked open the vid-file of Tessa stealing his computer, before dragging it to his trash, and then emptying it. "As promised."

I swallowed hard, feeling like sharp pieces of glass tore at my throat all the way down. I knew he likely had a copy of that file. I'd find it later and trash it for good. But I couldn't focus on that right now, couldn't focus on much beyond packing my gear and nodding at him as I left his office in a numb stupor.

"Dean?" Ms. Howard's voice called before she stepped into my path in the hallway outside their offices. I wondered if she'd made a point to come in on a Saturday because Tanner did, or because she knew Tanner was going to ask me to. "Are you all right?"

No.

"Fine," I lied and kept walking. Ignored her as she asked again. Forced my feet to move until I'd sunk behind the wheel of my car.

Another buzz vibrated my pocket.

A text from Amber I read through blurry eyes.

Pixie: Can I head over in 30?
Me: Sure

I pocketed my phone and started the car, anger replacing

the break in my chest. Filling it with heat and blame and rage.

I loved Amber.

And she had broken my heart without even knowing.

I wasn't sure I'd survive it.

CHAPTER TWENTY-NINE

AMBER

I can't believe I'm going to tell him.

The words repeated over and over in my head as I drove to Dean's house. I'd spent the day crafting my final blog post—filled with apologies, intentions, and hopes for the future—and I planned to post it tomorrow.

After I talked to Dean.

Because my stomach was still in knots and my brain was trying desperately to take everything back—the blog, the girl's mistake, the misunderstanding. I hadn't eaten anything all day, the nausea killing any hope of the bliss I'd experienced the night before. The elation at being loved by Dean.

I knew talking to him about everything would help. It always did.

Didn't make me any less nervous.

For five minutes, I sat in his driveway, unable to turn off my car. The traitorous voice in the back of my mind, whispering that Dean wouldn't understand, that he'd be disappointed in me or would judge me over the secret I'd kept.

I shook off the cold fear.

Dean is different.

And he told me he *loved* me.

He would not only understand, but he'd also help me work the problem just like he had with the Brandon issues.

I nodded to myself and stepped out of the car with a fresh wave of hope washing away the sourness in my stomach.

The door opened before I could knock on it, an older, larger version of Dean smirking down at me. I remembered Sean from the two years we attended Wilmont together, but he had grown into a man since he graduated. His shoulders broad, the evidence of scruff on his strong jaw. His eyes were more blue, where Dean's had that slate gray to them that always sent shivers over my skin.

"Dean's in his room," Sean said by way of greeting.

"Thanks," I said, stepping in after him. "How are things at Inkheart?"

"Fantastic." He stopped by the stairway that led up to Dean's room. "It gets better," he said. "After high school. Know that." He winked at me before heading around the corner.

God I hope so.

I'd done such a great job at screwing up these last few months, I wasn't sure if I could ever dig myself out of the hole I'd created.

Dean's door was closed, and I shifted on my feet outside of it, not sure if I should knock or simply walk in. My hand darted from a fist to reaching for the knob and back again before I finally rapped my knuckles against the door.

It flew open in a matter of breaths, and I was fully expecting Dean to yank me inside and kiss me like we'd been apart for months.

"Shhh!" He held his finger to his lips, his brow furrowed as he turned his back on me, walking deeper into his room.

Okay. I didn't expect that.

I tiptoed into the room, quietly shutting the door behind me. "Sorry," I whispered.

"Tessa is asleep." Dean's tone was sharper than I'd ever heard it.

"Okay, sorry," I said again, not mentioning that it was near five p.m. "Is she sick?"

"Something like that." He didn't look at me as he spoke. Instead he was rifling through his dresser drawers, frantically searching for something.

The metallic tang returned to my stomach, sloshing and rolling and twisting.

"Dean?" I wasn't sure what I was asking, but I couldn't think of anything else to say with the way he was acting. Since we'd crossed that line with each other, he'd never *not* touched me or smiled at me when we were together. "Everything all right?"

A dark laugh shook his shoulders. "You tell me."

Oh. Right.

Maybe he was misunderstanding my earlier cryptic messages. Maybe he thought this was about me and him.

"Okay," I said, my fingers trembling. "I need to talk to you. About—"

He spun around and tossed something at me. I instinctively caught the black T-shirt, eyes darting between him and it.

"Unfold it," he demanded.

I shuffled the fabric around in my hands, taking in the rainbow design within the outline of deadmau5's signature oversize mouse head.

"What's this for?" My throat suddenly dry, I had to talk around the cracks.

Dean folded his arms over his chest. "You win."

I refolded the T-shirt, slowly tilting my head. "What?"

His features hardened, and my stomach dropped.

"You *win*," he said again.

"Dean, I'm confused."

The muscles in his forearms flexed as he laughed again, but there was no light in his eyes. "Let me clear it up for you, then."

A lump formed in my throat as I recoiled from his words.

"You win the challenge," he said, eyeing the shirt. "My simple desktop switch for all the computers at school would've taken them hours, maybe days to figure out and fix, but it's nothing compared to what you did."

My eyes widened.

"Yeah," he snapped. "I *know*."

"You looked at my stuff before I could…" I sighed. "I came over here tonight to tell you about it. To explain—"

"I didn't need to look at your stuff!" He cut me off. "I've been searching for you for months. And to explain what, exactly, Amber? That you lied to me?"

"What?" I shook my head. "We weren't supposed to tell each other about what we were working on. That was part of the challenge."

He huffed. "Sure, play that card."

"I'm not trying to play any card," I said. "And what do you mean you've been searching for me for months?"

He raked his hands through his hair. "Tanner," he said, shaking his head. "He likes to blackmail people, remember? I've been searching for the person behind *Ask Me Anything*—"

"You didn't tell me." Hot tears welled behind my eyes.

"I was protecting you. Or I thought I was. I had no idea *you* would be the source!"

I stepped toward him. "I came here for help. To talk to you about—"

He *flinched* away from my touch, and I dropped my hand.

"You don't need my help," he said. "You're clearly on your own level."

I retreated an inch. "What's that supposed to mean?"

"It means that you were able to navigate the dark web without an assist. Keep this site buried. And manage to *know* so many things…"

Each word stung my insides. "Why are you so upset with me?" I asked, tears building, but I held them back.

"I asked you who you thought was behind it. You kept this from me—"

"This was part of a challenge!" I cut him off. "I *had* to keep it from you. And it was my way of riling up Tanner *and* helping people who need it."

He scoffed at me. "Helping?" He rolled his eyes before focusing the sharp gaze on me. "Right," he said. "You have no idea what you're talking about. You have *no* idea."

I sucked in a stuttered breath.

"Was last night research?"

I snapped my eyes to him. "What?"

"Last night? With me. Was it just research for your next blog?"

The accusation hit me in the center of my chest. "What? No! How could you think that?"

How could he say that?

A vibration in my pocket said someone was calling me, but I didn't care.

"I don't know what to think anymore, Amber."

The way he said my name, hard and cold—so drastically different than the way he normally purred *Pixie*—broke something inside of me. I swiped at the few tears that had leaked past my defenses. My cell buzzed in my pocket again, but I ignored it.

"Last night was…" I drew a breath. "It was about me

loving you. About me wanting to willingly *give* you a piece of me I'd never given anyone before. It was about trusting you. Dean, I gave you *all* of me."

A flurry of emotion churned in those blue-gray eyes—hope, love, anger, betrayal—then they glittered for a second before he dropped a wall over them.

"Amber—"

"Damn it," I snapped, jerking out my phone that buzzed for the third time. Set to turn it off, I froze when I saw the screen. Four missed calls from Mom. Before I could blink, she was calling again. Flashes of tragedy—my dad in an accident?—had me swiping to answer. "Mom, is everything okay? I'm in the middle of something." I stared at Dean while I spoke, his statue-like stance softening as he waited.

"Dad and I are fine," she said, and I sighed so hard I slumped against Dean's closed door.

"Great," I said. "I'll call you back in a little bit. I'm—"

"Honey," she cut me off. "We need you to come home now. We've got to talk about some things." Her voice was calm but she had *the* tone—the one full of weight, of serious business. "Principal Tanner just got off the phone with your father."

I bolted upright, all my muscles locking.

"He told him some things," she continued. "We're worried. Please, just get home soon, okay?"

"Be there in a few." I ended the call, my hand shaking around the phone as I cut my eyes to Dean. "You told Tanner?"

I waited for him to deny it, but I knew it was true.

"You really were looking for me. The whole time."

My entire body shook with the betrayal. The one person I'd trusted—after *everything*—had turned me over to the enemy. And he was the one chewing me out over this.

The blood drained from his face, his arms falling loose

at his sides as he stepped toward me. "Amber, wait," he said, reaching for me. "You don't understand."

Now I was the one jerking away from him—it didn't matter that he finally sounded and looked like *my* Dean. The one I fell in love with. Like whatever rage had a hold of him had finally cleared.

"You sold me out," I said, tears blurring my eyes. "I understand enough." I reached for the knob and swung open the door. "So much for DC, huh?"

"Wait. Please," he said, and I stopped in the entryway, glancing over my shoulder.

"Why?" I sniffled. "For you to shatter my heart completely?" He flinched. "No," I said. "I think I'll go while I can still *breathe*." I slammed the door behind me and raced down the stairs, reaching my car in a matter of seconds.

I saw Dean fling open his front door as I reversed out of his driveway, and left him standing on his porch yelling after me.

• • •

Mom met me in the foyer the second I'd stepped through my front door. Her arms flung around me, holding me to her like she *knew* everything that had just gone down—but she had no idea.

She led me to the dining room table, where Dad sat, a crease between his brow as he took in my face—red and swollen from crying all the way home.

"Pumpkin," he said. "Let's talk."

I sank into the chair, Mom's hand still on my back as she sat next to me. Nodding, I rubbed my face, breathing deep.

"I'll start at the beginning," I said, my voice cracking. "For a challenge between me and..." I sniffled, unable to say his name. "I started a blog—"

"*Ask Me Anything*," Mom cut me off and Dad nodded.

"Right, yeah," I said. "Tanner told you."

"Oh honey," she said. "We knew long before he told us."

"What?" I jolted. "How? When?"

She glanced at Dad, who flashed me a small smile. Mom laid her hand over mine. "Since you asked me about what to do if you're allergic to latex."

I chuckled through my tears, shaking my head.

"I mean, it was kind of obvious," Dad said, his tone light, understanding. "It was like you were trying to write a self-help book for teens." He held up his hands. "Which we'd totally support, by the way."

I glanced between them, then crumpled with my head in my hands. "I messed up so bad."

"We're not upset with you," Mom assured me. "We just wanted to talk. After the principal called, and with the parents protesting, we knew it was escalating to a point where we couldn't *not* say anything anymore."

Warmth pulsed in the center of my broken heart, but their support wasn't enough to mend it.

"We want to help you," Dad said. "Whatever you need. We're here. We can talk to Principal Tanner as a family. Help you make a statement on your blog, whatever you need."

I bit my lip, wishing it was that easy. "Thank you," I said, wiping my face again. "But..." The breath tightened in my lungs as I tried to force the words out. My parents waited patiently, their eyes understanding and open and not at all angry. "I got a girl pregnant!" I blurted, and they both blinked at me.

Dad tilted his head, leaning farther over the table. "You know...I mean...that's not *possible*..." He glanced to Mom for help.

"You can see where we're having a hard time understanding that statement, right?" She raised her eyebrows. "But if you like girls, we're totally cool with that, too. I just thought you and Dean—"

"No," I cut her off before we could reopen that still-bleeding wound. "The girl. She wrote in. Told me after I answered her question about birth control that she took my advice and wound up pregnant." I hid my face in my hands, unable to face them. "I ruined someone's life."

"Oh, honey, no," Mom said as she folded herself over my back. "There is no way that is your fault."

"It is," I mumbled against my hands.

"I've read every single blog post," she said. "Your father, too."

I peeked through my fingers to find them both nodding. A full-body blush coated my skin, and I hid again.

"And the piece on birth control and doubling up was exceptional," Dad said.

"Yes," Mom agreed. "You stated the odds and even went on to say that it's always better to be safe than sorry."

I dropped my hands. "She blames me."

"She's a teenager who just found out her world has changed. She's looking for *anyone* to blame but herself."

"You can't take on that kind of responsibility," Dad said. "You weren't the one who didn't use protection."

"But I'm the one who thought I could *help* people. Not hurt them. It's my fault. I should've never started this blog. I just wanted to give people a taste of what we have." I looked between them. "I can ask you both anything. Always. No judgment." I shrugged, completely, utterly exhausted. "I wanted everyone to have that luxury."

"We know," Mom said.

"What do I do?"

She glanced at Dad before looking at me again. "We'll talk to Tanner with you—"

"I don't care about him," I said. "I care about the girl. My responsibility or not. How do I make that right?"

"Do you know who she is?" Dad asked.

I shook my head. "She used an alias."

"Do you think she attends Wilmont?" Mom asked.

"She said she would be a junior at Wilmont next year."

Mom nodded. "Well, if you really want to make it right, you'll need to find out who she is and speak to her in person. Offer her support. That is what she'll need most, regardless of what she decides to do."

My stomach clenched. "If I can't find her?" The question was a whisper.

Both my parents eyed me.

"You know you can find her," Dad said.

"Yeah," I said, sighing. "I know." It wouldn't take much to trace backward from the alias's email, but I was terrified. "But...what if she doesn't want to be found?"

"You aren't obligated," Dad continued. "You can make a blanket statement apology post. You could email her back."

"No," I said, rising from my seat. "I want to see her. Talk to her. Be there for her. Whoever she is." I headed toward the stairs, wanting to fall into bed for the rest of forever.

"Amber," Mom said, stopping me at the foot of the stairs. "Anything else you want to talk about?"

I parted my lips, wanting to tell her about Dean, about the knife in my heart, but I was just so damned tired. "Not right now," I said.

"Okay," she said. Hugging me again. "We're proud of you, baby."

I shook my head. "I don't deserve that."

"You do," she said, releasing me. "You'll see that someday."

I took the stairs two at a time, sealing myself inside my room. My computer stared at me from the desk, begging me to find the girl.

I didn't have the energy. Wasn't in the right frame of mind. But I sank into the chair anyway.

Dean—someone I'd given more of myself to than anyone in my life—had betrayed me. Wrecked me. He didn't even give me a chance to explain. To tell him the knowledge came from an outside source—my mother—not from personal experience.

Clicking on the girl's email address, I worked my way backward, hitting the keys on autopilot. I guess I really could do this in my sleep because that was exactly what the search felt like—like I was hacking through a thick fog.

Last night? With me. Was it just research for your next blog?

I flinched as Dean's words echoed in my mind, stinging me just as fiercely as they had before.

I never expected any of this.

The blog's popularity, the consequences, falling for Dean, and then him hurting me more than I knew possible. Brandon had tried to take what wasn't his—he scarred me with his treatment of me as a possession, and it haunted me. But Dean? I'd given him my heart willingly, despite all my efforts to protect it, and he'd taken it. Taken it and crushed it.

A few more clicks.

A gasp.

Another break in my chest.

TWCrashandBurn was connected to a Snapchat account I'd seen before.

TW.

Tessa Winters.

Dean's little sister.

The light of his life.

Fuck. My. Life.

He'd been angry over the blog. Over the secret I'd kept. Over the fact that I'd told him I was a virgin and yet somehow had this wealth of knowledge about sex. He'd lashed out because he thought he hadn't *known* me.

Did he know about Tessa? Or had she not told him yet? If he knew what I'd *really* done?

That I'd had a hand in getting his baby sister pregnant?

He would *never* speak to me again. More than that, he'd likely crash my system over and over—a reminder of the pain I'd caused his family.

I rubbed my palms over my face, backing away from my computer like the distance would help me breathe.

He accused me of using him.

He'd sold me out to Tanner.

But this…this was worse. This made everything he'd said before no more than I deserved.

Maybe he had known about her…

I sank onto my bed, my head buzzing, and the shattered pieces of my heart trying to beat normally as if it hadn't just been obliterated.

CHAPTER THIRTY

DEAN

"You look miserable," Tessa said as she walked into my room.

I leaped to my feet from where I'd been sitting on the floor of my room, my back against the bed. Somewhere in the night—while not sleeping—I'd ended up there and simply stared.

"Are you okay?" I asked, my voice raspy.

"Yes," she hissed, glancing over her shoulder. She whirled around, shutting the door behind her. "Can you *not*?" she asked, taking a seat in the chair at my desk. "Mom and Dad got back this morning."

"They did?" I blinked a few times, my eyeballs grainy.

"You'd know that if you bothered to leave your room."

I scratched my scalp with both hands, trying to force life back into my brain. It was useless. Everything in there was broken, and my heart? Fuck, it was shredded.

"Have you even slept?"

I shook my head, sinking onto my bed.

"You want to talk about the fight?"

"What?"

"With Amber?" she asked. "I slept through it, but Sean said she left here in a hurry yesterday. Crying."

The image burned my mind. I wanted to take back everything I said. I'd been *so* angry. In a rage-filled cloud brought on by sheer panic. Tessa's news had drowned me, and I was so scared for her. The blame on the blog...on Amber...I'd lost it.

I should've waited. Should've breathed. Should've *listened* to her.

And with Tanner knowing...hell, he'd probably find a way to stop an MIT acceptance letter from coming.

I'm an asshole.

"What did you do?" Tessa snapped.

"I don't know. Ruined things." I rolled my neck and stretched my arms, focusing on her. "We don't need to talk about this. There are far more important things happening right now," I said, eyeing her slightly bulging tummy. How had I not noticed it before?

God, that will change soon.

The idea of me being an uncle was both terrifying and exciting. But Tessa being a mom? It was straight alien-planet territory. "Tell me what I can do to help you, Tessa," I continued.

"You can start by fixing things with Amber."

"What?" I pointed at her. "It's not that simple, and besides, you've got way too much to handle on your own right now. Tell me. What can I do?"

She sighed, her hand rubbing back and forth over her stomach like it wasn't even a thought. "Forgive me?"

"Oh, Tess," I said, scooting along the edge of the bed until I was almost knee-to-knee with her. I took her hands in mine. "I'd never judge. You know that. This...it just happened a lot sooner than you expected."

She smiled, but her eyes were shining with unshed tears. "That's true," she said. "But I did something bad."

I arched a brow at her. "Tessa," I chided. "I know about the video prank, and the"—I lowered my voice to a whisper—"soon-to-be Winters baby. What else could you have possibly done?"

A crease formed between her brow, and my stomach dropped. "You know I was running off like *zero* sleep yesterday? I had been averaging one or two hours a night for weeks. I was so stripped and raw. It wasn't until you forced me to tell you everything that I could breathe. I slept for what felt like forever after that."

"Okay," I said, waiting for the ball to drop.

"And you know how it is when you get *so* exhausted," she said. "You lash out. Do things you shouldn't?"

"Tess."

She sighed, the tears finally falling. "I sent a super-bitchy email to *Ask Me Anything*," she said through the cries. "I blamed her for this." She pointed to her stomach. "Told her it was her fault that my life was ruined. Called her some horrible things." Her face fell in her hands, her shoulders shaking. "It's not true. None of it. Yes, I asked a question, but Colt and I had already…" She shook her head. "I was looking for validation for something I'd already done. I re-read the blog, Dean. It was solid advice." She sniffled, wiping her face as she looked up at me. "This was my fault. Mine and Colt's, but mainly mine. I messed up. I didn't take my pill at the same time every day." She shook her head. "I'm such a jerk."

"Hey," I chided. "Only I get to call you that."

She smiled weakly, and I wrapped an arm around her shoulders.

"You're not a jerk," I continued, hating that I knew exactly who she'd sent the email to. Hating it more because I *knew* Amber, and she would torture herself over this for God knows how long.

Yesterday I thought she deserved it. Yesterday I'd felt betrayed on so many levels that my warped mind had manifested so many scenarios where Amber was just using me for the blog content and hurting people without care.

That wasn't her.

That was never her.

Stomach rolling, breath catching, I cursed myself.

I had the best girl in the world, and I somehow managed to ruin that in a day.

"What should I do?" Tessa asked.

"I don't know," I said, and that was the truth. I was so lost in this tangled web.

"Should I write her back? Apologize?"

"Maybe?" I shrugged. "I highly doubt anyone would ever blame your reaction, Tess. You're kind of going through something major."

She sighed. "That's an understatement."

"I know, but I'm here. I'm going to be here every step of the way. And," I said before grinding my teeth, "I know Colt will be, too. He's a good kid."

Her mouth dropped. "Seriously?"

"What?"

"It takes me getting…" She glanced down at her tummy before looking back at me. "For you to finally admit he's a good guy?"

I shrugged. "I didn't say I liked him."

She rolled her eyes before blowing out a huge breath. "So," she said. "Amber."

Her name hit me with like a sledgehammer. Guilt gnawed at my insides.

"She'll never forgive me. Not after the things I said." Not after what I'd done—practically handed her over to Tanner. Not directly. It was an accident. Sheer bad timing when he walked in on me, but it didn't matter. She blamed me. And why shouldn't she? After the things I said to her in anger…

"That's bullshit," Tessa snapped.

"It's not."

"It is," she said, smacking me lightly on the shoulder. "You make it right."

"I can't."

"Ugh," she groaned. "The only way you know that is if you don't try. I've never seen you happier than when you're with her, and I've witnessed you win more hack-wars than I can count."

Shit. The TOC was two days away. In light of everything, I'd completely forgotten about the tournament I'd been working on for half the year.

"It's like you're this totally different person," she continued. "Like…Super Dean."

I laughed but knew she was right. Knew Amber had made me better in so many ways and yet still loved me for me.

Love. She loved me.

Then she gave me pieces of herself, and her whole heart, and I—

"Snap out of it, bro." Tessa smacked my shoulder again.

"Ow!" I growled. "I am. I mean, damn it, Tessa." I sighed, rubbing my shoulder. "I don't know how to fix everything."

"Boys." She rolled her eyes. "You be real with her. Tell her you're sorry for whatever dumb stunt you pulled." She eyed me, giving me a minute in case I wanted to divulge just how badly I'd screwed up.

I didn't. There was no world where I wanted Tessa to know I'd lost my shit because of her news. It wouldn't be fair to her, and it hadn't been fair to Amber.

Ass. Hole.

"Fine," she continued. "Keep it bottled up, but *talk* to her." She stood up. "And fast. I know you're TOC bound in two days. You need to go into that with a clear head, and that means fixing things with Amber."

I nodded, completely unsure of how to accomplish that. "Are you sure I can't do anything for you. Feed you?" I asked, tilting my head.

She laughed from my doorway. "No," she said. "Thanks but I can manage." She snapped her fingers at me. "Don't be like those guys who make a mistake and bury their heads in the sand for the rest of their lives. Be the guy girls lose their minds over."

"I don't want *girls*. I only want Amber." The words cleared the fog over my brain, my heart restarting like the first breath after an ocean dive.

Tessa eyed me knowingly. "Exactly," she said before shutting the door behind her.

Exactly.

But after what I'd done...

The trust I'd worked so hard to earn. Broken in a matter of minutes.

How could she ever find her way back to me?

A sharp realization hit me over the head—I already had the means to prove it to her, or at least, I'd already started it without even realizing.

Now, all I had to do was get to work.

And get her to listen to me.

CHAPTER THIRTY-ONE

AMBER

NightLocker: Please talk to me
NightLocker: Let me explain
NightLocker: Pixie...I'm sorry
NightLocker: There are things you don't
understand

I tucked my fingers under my arms, ignoring the tingle to respond immediately.

Damn straight I don't understand.

Betrayal stung like a paper cut while opening a package of lemonade mix.

My heart *hurt.* Like, I'd been burned before...but this? This physically turned my stomach and seared my chest.

This...

This was true heartbreak.

This was can't sleep, can't eat unless it's chocolate, can't breathe without sharp spikes rattling my lungs, *relentless* heartbreak.

NightLocker: Give me a chance
NightLocker: I can make this right
NightLocker: I want to...
NightLocker: I need you...DC remember? Doesn't
that mean anything anymore?

Tears stung my eyes as I read his pleas. His use of our secret word, a code that had become something so much more than a warning. Something as vital as breathing and as true as the ache in my heart.

Some deep part of me, the one he'd branded his name on, wanted to forgive him. Needed to.

Because who was I to judge…after what I'd done?

I *should* forgive him. I should tell him the truth about what I knew.

But what was the point? Once he uncovered it…once he learned what I'd *really* done…

He'd hate me.

I reached for the keyboard, the motion almost painful.

NightLocker: I need you…DC remember? Doesn't that mean anything anymore?
PixieBurn: everything & nothing
NightLocker: Amber
NightLocker: Please
NightLocker: What does that even mean

I paused my response, choking back a sob.

It didn't matter. He'd find out soon enough.

Might as well endure the break now.

I just wished like hell it didn't have to hurt so damn much.

PixieBurn: It means
PixieBurn: Hack my gear like this again
PixieBurn: for a chat
PixieBurn: for help
PixieBurn: for anything
PixieBurn: and I'll crash your entire system

I hated myself a fraction more with each message sent.

NightLocker: No!
NightLocker: Amber
NightLocker: Listen to me

God, did I want to. I wanted him to not be breaking into my system, showing up on my screen…I wanted him *here*. Telling me we could find our way back to common ground, or, hell, hit the reset button and start fresh. Erase every dark piece of our past.

But this was real life.

And it was heavy and hard and harsh.

PixieBurn: goodbye, Dean

I logged off and shut my gear down. He couldn't find me if I wasn't online.

Unless he shows up at my door…again.

My heart skipped at the thought—it betraying me as much as he had.

I'd barely survived his friendship, his light…

I certainly wouldn't survive his hate, his disappointment, the way he'd judge me when he knew…

It didn't matter that I'd blocked him after his first attempt to send me a chat box—he'd found his way back in.

It had only been a day since he'd wrecked me, and he was already trying to apologize. That meant something, but even if I wanted to forgive him, he'd never be able to forgive *me* once Tessa told him the truth. About the blog, *my* blog, harming her. Led her in the wrong direction.

I cringed, knowing I needed to find a way to talk to her. To make things right.

But I'd barely caught my breath since yesterday, and I had about ten minutes before my parents and I had to have a meeting with Principal Tanner.

Another shudder.

It shouldn't matter that he would likely find a way to jack with my potential MIT acceptance. Tessa's predicament was so much more important than that, but I couldn't help the sinking, hollow feeling in my chest. Whatever Tanner had planned for me…

I deserved it.

"You ready?" Mom asked from my doorway, causing me to jump.

"Yeah," I said, spinning in my chair. I left my gear in my room as I followed her out. I didn't need it. Not for this meeting.

Dad drove, and with Mom in the passenger seat, I felt like I was ten years old again, not eighteen. Silent, my arms folded over my chest like that could hold me together—it could've been the time I'd got caught sneaking out after dark to meet Hannah for a midnight pool party. They were more upset that I'd gone behind their backs than with the act itself.

Kind of like today, except they supported me.

Something I was grateful for after this blog had cost me so much.

And yet, it had helped heal me, too. How was that possible?

Ms. Howard waved at me encouragingly from behind her desk as we passed her office, the look of confusion on her face indicating Tanner hadn't told her about me yet. Once again, I wished she was Wilmont's principal. Someone who put students' well-being first. Someone who listened and understood and went the extra mile to ensure everyone was getting what they needed.

I waved back before following my parents inside Principal Tanner's office as he held the door open for us. A smug, self-satisfied smile on his face as he closed the door behind him.

Mom, Dad, and I all took a seat in front of his massive desk, the silence in the room near deafening. Tanner took his time walking around his desk, unbuttoning his suit jacket, and finally plopping down on his plush leather office chair.

"Dr. and Mrs. Henderson," he said, pressing his index fingers together and bringing them to a point under his chin. "We spoke briefly yesterday regarding why all of you are here today." He glanced at my parents, his eyes darting back and forth between the two like he was waiting for something—an apology or an outburst over my actions. *Something*.

They were silent.

I almost laughed.

The cold churning in my stomach killed that urge.

"Right," he continued. "Amber," he said, looking directly at me. "What do you have to say for yourself?"

I parted my lips but then closed them.

Tanner sighed. "I thought not," he said, dismissing me and returning focus to my parents. "Your daughter has cost this school gravely." He shook his head. "The content she hand-fed to my students, and countless other schools, is deplorable. It is no example for a Wilmont graduate or an MIT hopeful."

"You can't possibly plan to not let her graduate," Mom said. "There are barely two months left in the school year. And she deserves to go to MIT as well. You know that."

Tanner laid his hands flat on his desk. "This behavior cannot go unchecked," he said, glancing at me. "Regardless if she's only my student for two more months."

"Not graduating or putting a barrier between her and the acceptance letter that I'm sure is on its way soon," Dad said, "seems a little harsh considering the circumstances."

Tanner's eyes cut to Dad's, the glare sharp as a razor. "The circumstances?" He tilted his head and pointed at me. "Your daughter created a website that condones teenage sexual activity. Not to mention recounted stories of rape attempts, sex changes, and even more subjects not worth repeating. It was practically a promotion for it with handbooks on sexual acts provided."

"What?" I snapped, finally finding my voice.

Mom rested her hand on my knee, a warning look in her eyes. I sat back, my lips sealed.

"That is hardly true," Mom said, her tone soft, respectful. "We have read each of the blog posts several times. There was never an instance where she promoted sex. She merely offered advice for those students who had already participated in such acts."

Tanner's jaw clenched, and he motioned to his computer. "I've gotten over a hundred emails from outraged parents. Some of whom have direct connections to the district's board. All of them read the blog very differently."

"The *students* came to her," Dad said, "with questions and concerns they weren't finding answers for anywhere else."

"What are you implying, Dr. Henderson?" Tanner asked. "That I'm denying my students knowledge?" he said before Dad could answer.

"I'm saying they came to her. And her responses were carefully constructed and thought out. As a teen psychologist for over two decades, I know a thing or two about handling sensitive subjects. And with the popularity of the blog, she could've posted a slew of things merely to get attention, but she didn't. She took the time and care to *answer* them without judgment or fear of reprimand."

"When kids are left without safe places to ask the hard questions, they wind up…" Mom glanced at me, her eyes sympathetic. "They make poor choices out of sheer ignorance. Denying them the option to *ask* is like putting blinders on them."

Tanner smirked. "I'm sure a person in your line of work would run this school very differently," he said. "No topic would be off-limits, would it? I daresay there would be a class that teaches how best to get someone off—"

"That's enough," Dad cut him off, his tone lethal. "Watch what you say, Ed."

My eyes widened at Dad's use of Tanner's first name. It sounded like a slap in the face.

"You called us here," he continued, "to discuss the situation at hand. Don't make this a personal attack."

Tanner straightened, a slight nod as if to say he knew he'd gotten carried away. "An example must be made," he said again. "*I'm* willing to allow Amber to graduate and to leave her fate at MIT up to the admissions board with no marring on my end…"

My heart filled with hope as I waited for him to finish.

"If *she* is willing to appear before the entire school and district board and take responsibility for her actions."

"But—"

Tanner held up a finger, cutting Dad off. "As well as have the appearance live so the other schools affected by her actions can find closure as well."

"Closure?" Mom rolled her eyes. "That can be achieved with a final statement on the website. A written, heartfelt apology before the site is taken down."

"That's not enough," Tanner said.

"If her identity is confirmed," Dad said, leaning forward in his chair, "the protesting parents could confront her directly. Not to mention the students. It puts her at risk for emotional backlash at the very least. Physical at the worst."

Tanner flinched slightly but shook his head. "She should've considered that before she created this torrid website." He folded his hands together. "Those are my terms. If you don't like it, I'll be fine with convincing the admissions board at MIT that she's not the material they're looking for and to deny her graduation until she completes another year here at Wilmont."

"You can't do that," Dad said.

"I can," Tanner fired back. "You're free to pull her and try to complete her year elsewhere, but no one will approve her when they receive my letters explaining her…" He cut his eyes to me. "Character."

"You son of a—"

"Mom," I said before she could continue. "It's fine." I nodded at Tanner. "I'll do the assembly, or whatever it is he wants." I shifted in my seat, rising to stand. My parents following suit as they headed toward the door, this meeting clearly at its end. They waited for me in the entryway, but I stood before Tanner's desk.

"Know this," I said, glaring down at him. "I *see* you. I've *seen* you. And while I'm prepared to stand up and admit what I've done, you sit behind your desk and *pretend* to care." I sighed. "I've been your student for over a decade. And I'm willing to brave the public backlash if it means I don't have to spend another year with you. Think about that. Let it sink in."

He rose from his chair, too, and I had to crane my neck to keep our gazes locked.

Nothing.

Not a word I said hit home.

Would it ever? Would there ever be a day when he didn't value his precious lineage, awards, and grants and rankings over the students who earned it for him?

"Be here tomorrow at nine a.m." He re-buttoned his suit jacket. "I'll call a mandatory school assembly with parents in attendance," he said. "And we'll make sure it's live on the school's site as well, for those who can't make it, and for our sister schools that you've harmed."

I rolled my eyes. "Your definition of harmed and mine are drastically different." Yes, guilt bit my insides over what had happened to Tessa, but I never set out to hurt anyone. And through return commenters and emails, I knew I *had* helped some people. "There *are* sites that would make you piss your pants," I whisper-hissed. "Sites run by kids with lists and agendas and hate in their hearts." Tears pricked my eyes I was so mad. "And you're upset about this? A little information on something as natural as sex?" I shook my head.

"We're done here," he said. "I'll see you tomorrow."

"Right." I turned my back on him.

Mom wrapped an arm around me as we left the building. "You don't have to do this," she said as we got in the car.

"We can find a way to get you to graduate. And I can speak with someone in admissions at MIT," Dad said, pulling out of the school parking lot.

"No," I said. "This is something I have to do." I leaned my head against the window as we drove. I hoped my acceptance letter came next week regardless, but even if it didn't...even if I somehow didn't get into my dream school, I knew it was all worth it. Those few souls I'd helped feel not so alone? That was worth all of this...agony.

• • •

From: TWCrashandBurn

Subject: I'm sorry

Dear Ask Me Anything,
I'm sorry. I SO didn't mean to be a bitch with a capital B the
other day. I was running on fumes. And I was terrified.
It's not a fair excuse, but there it is.
It was all me.
You, a stranger, were easier to blame.
Again, sorry.
I liked your blog from the start.
So do a ton of other people.
Hope my email didn't make you think about stopping because Ask
Me Anything is SO needed.

—TWCrashandBurn

I honestly don't know what spurred me to check the site's email the morning before the assembly, but I was beyond glad I did.

The relief at Tessa's email was so fast and needed it almost hurt. The sensation storming me like a whirlwind.

It didn't change the fact that I was an hour away from going on stage at Wilmont and confessing my role in *Ask Me Anything*, but my heart...it felt full for the first time in two days.

The shards and cuts from Dean were still there, but this gave me hope. After the assembly, I would seek out Tessa. Talk to her. Let her know I'd be there for her in whatever way I could.

First, I had to survive the assembly.

And pray that no one would be outraged enough to take action against me.

I still had two months to survive here before I graduated. The thought sent shivers down my spine.

Thirty minutes later, my parents filed into the massive seminar room in Wilmont while I sat and waited in the small office attached to it. My knee bounced, the chatter of practically the entire school and their parents vibrating through the closed door.

"Amber." Ms. Howard's voice drew my attention away from the palms of my hands. She closed the door behind her and sank down to my level to meet my eyes. "What is going on?" she asked. "Tanner hasn't told me, the students, or the board anything."

"The board *is* here, then?" My voice was a whisper, my nerves killing any strength I had.

"Yes. Tanner demanded it."

I nodded, interlocking my fingers to keep them from shaking. He probably thought my admission would be enough to shock them into allowing him to continue as principal. He'd found me, after all, and was holding me accountable. Scrubbing out the dark stain in his perfect, pristine school.

"Amber," she said. "I can't help you if you don't talk to me."

"I'm beyond help," I said. "But thank you for the gesture. It means a lot."

"I refuse to believe that," she said. "Tell me what's going on, and I'll find a way to help you."

I sighed. I supposed it wouldn't hurt anything. Everyone in a fifty-mile radius was about to learn the truth, anyway. I opened my mouth, the story tumbling from my lips easier than I imagined. And when I was done, my over-firing nerves had ebbed to a low buzzing.

Ms. Howard pressed her lips together, trying to hide her smile. "You're so damn brave."

"What?"

"You are. I can't believe you're about to go out there and face this. I admire you so much."

My cheeks flushed.

"How did he find out?" she asked, her brow furrowed. "I thought you were way too good for him to catch you."

"I am," I said. I'd left Dean out of the story. Probably because it wasn't relevant, but more so because it *hurt* to think about him. About how much I missed him despite what he'd said. What he'd done.

"Then how…" A gasp cut her off, something clicking in her eyes. "That's what he was using Dean for." She ground her teeth.

"You saw him?"

She nodded. "I wanted to get him out of it, but Tanner had something over him. Dean wouldn't tell me, but whatever it was, it was huge."

I chewed on my bottom lip.

"I was sure he'd told you." She glanced over her shoulder. "Is he out there? I can go get him. Escort him back here."

"No," I said too quickly. "He's at the TOC." I'd known the date for months. And despite *everything,* I hoped he won. Hoped he slayed it and earned the recognition he'd been working for all year. Hoped his MIT letter was on its way. He deserved that regardless. "It's fine. I'm ready to get this over with."

She patted my leg, standing with me. "I will meet with the board after this is over. Talk to them. See if I can testify to your character and dispute Tanner's over-exaggerated allegations."

"Thanks, Ms. Howard," I said, eyeing the door behind her as it opened and Tanner came inside. "But don't. You have to stay here. I'll be gone in two months."

"Ms. Howard," Tanner said, holding the door open for her. "It's past time for you to take your seat. I've reserved you one next to me and the board."

She nodded, glaring at him as she passed him.

I didn't envy her position—his second-in-command. I couldn't imagine how difficult that day-to-day must be. It was amazing she hadn't quit.

Tanner folded his arms behind his back after he'd shut the door. "Five minutes. Are you prepared?" He scanned my empty hands like I should be holding a stack of note cards with a meticulously crafted speech.

I tipped my chin, not wanting him to see the fear swirling inside me. "Can I ask you a question?"

He smirked. "It's too late to talk your way out of this."

"I'm not trying to," I said. "I'm curious."

"About?"

"What did you want to be when you were a kid?"

"Excuse me?"

I raised my eyebrows, knowing he'd heard me.

"Hardly relevant—"

"It's an easy question. Was it always to be the principal of a school? Because your dad was? And your grandpa?"

"Yes. Wilmont has always been my birthright." He cleared his throat, shifting on his feet. "Though, at your age I wanted to be president," he said. "Or a senator."

I huffed, wondering how he'd lost the aspirations and knowing he'd be horrible at democracy. Not with the way he ran this school—like a tyrant.

"It's not too late," he said. "I *could* run for mayor. Governor. But Wilmont is too important to me."

"Right," I said. "The power you wield here, it means something. Out there?" I jerked my head to indicate the real world outside the school. "Wouldn't be nearly as much."

He stiffened, narrowing his gaze. "I've prepared a slew of visual evidence to go along with whatever admission of guilt you have prepared," he said. "It will be as jarring on the projector screens as—"

"As your abstinence video was?" I cut him off, no longer caring about formalities. He was going for the hurt, and I was beyond over it.

"…as on a small screen," he continued like I hadn't spoken. He yanked the door open, his arm extended for me to lead the way. "And don't you worry," he said, stopping me when I hit the entryway. "Your boyfriend already paid his little sister's debt for that stunt she pulled at the assembly."

"What?" I snapped, glancing up at him.

Tessa had planted the video? And he had proof? Enough to force Dean to…

Omigod.

That's why he'd searched for me. Found me.

For Tessa.

"In case you were feeling like I was singling you out for justice," he said, stepping out of my way.

"Oh no," I said. "I know very well how many students you've manipulated over the years. Threats for favors. All to keep you on your imagined throne." Anger swarmed my blood. "Someday, Tanner," I whisper-hissed, "I'll laugh as *your* character is brought to light."

I walked out of the office and around the corner, fully exposed to the thousands of eyes staring. Halting at the steps that would carry me up the stage, I took a breath and scanned the crowd.

Hannah and Jake sat together, next to my parents. They were behind Ms. Howard and who I assumed was the board in the front row, because Hannah's mom was seated in the middle of them. Hannah shaped her hand into the universal *I love you* symbol, and I flashed her a soft smile. She'd hugged me and cursed at me when I'd told her everything—her only anger stemming from the fact that I'd kept a secret from her—but she supported me nonetheless. Jake followed, naturally.

I was lucky.

I had been scared their reactions would be like Dean's, but it seemed only he had hated what I'd done. Well, him and who knew how many outraged parents.

He's tried to apologize.

True. But I hadn't let him. Because I wasn't sure if he knew about Tessa. And even if she let me off the hook this morning, it was still *there*. My hand in her situation. Something I'm sure he wouldn't forgive and shouldn't have to, and then the hurt would happen all over again.

So, I had a new wall around my heart, and every brick had Dean's name chiseled on it.

Another deep breath.

I took one stair, then two.

And as I reached the podium in the center of the stage, the two massive projector screens behind me, I felt as if I'd come full circle. It was in this room where my anger had festered, which led to the idea for the blog in the first place. It was here where Hannah had been desperate for answers she couldn't find or dare ask.

This room was where it started.

And now it's where it would end.

I cut my eyes to the left, trailing Tanner as he walked across the room to take his seat. Front and center. His eyes were full of satisfaction.

He should be up here. Being exposed for all the actions he'd taken against students. His secrets should be laid bare. Not mine.

I sighed, gripping the edges of the podium.

He held all the power.

And I was *done.*

Sickness churned in my stomach, threatening to rise instead of the words I knew I needed to say. To admit.

"I'm sure you're all ready to figure out why you're here," I said into the microphone, my voice echoing loudly in the quiet room. I cringed against the sound, but pushed on. "You've been called here today because I—"

Tanner snapped at Mr. Griffin who sat at the computer desk off the stage, effectively cutting me off. Griffin cringed, glancing at me apologetically before he clicked a button, and I saw my website's homepage fill the screens behind me. Sighing, I turned halfway—enough to look at the audience and *my* work at the same time.

"Like I was saying," I said, flashing Tanner an *eff-you* look. "You're here because there are things you need to know. Apologies I need to make." My eyes trailed to where a student had his cell phone out and pointed directly at me. The live feed for all the other schools. At least the kid looked like he didn't want to be there.

"First, I want to say I'm—" Something flashed on the screens, killing my words.

DC.

It blinked in the bottom right corners of the screen, on *my* site.

Flickered like a beacon of hope for a ship caught in a storm.

"I, uh…" I stammered, my eyes searching the audience, finding him like he'd been standing in the back all along. Like I *knew* he'd be there, laptop in hand, his blue-gray eyes full of regret and hope and *love.*

The TOC. He was supposed to be there, winning. Earning

his credibility so a major-company would hire him in the fall. But he was here. I assumed he'd gotten the mass email Tanner sent out yesterday for the assembly, but I didn't think for one second he'd miss the TOC to come here.

DC.

The letters blinked at me as I released the podium, the fear falling away faster than it had gathered.

DC.

Our code pulsed in rhythm with my heart, each beat pulverizing the bricks I'd laid. Healing, wanting, hoping.

But most of all *beating* with the knowledge that I was no longer alone.

And this moment was no longer about me.

"*Talk.*" Tanner mouthed the word, rolling his hand discreetly in front of him.

No one had registered the game-changer I had—the two simple letters that held me frozen in gratitude and hope.

"Sorry," I said into the mic. "Here's what you need to know—"

A small murmur echoed through the crowd, stopping me once again. The screens blinked in and out, my website disappearing, and a vid-box replacing it.

The audio filled the room, filtering from the same speakers attached to my mic. But it was no longer my voice hitting the crowd—it was Tanner's.

"*You have no idea what it is like to be responsible for the young minds of the future. I do what I have to—whatever I have to—to ensure their success. What seems harsh to you is what will make this world a better place in the years to come.*"

I glanced down to Tanner, wide-eyed. He was frozen in his seat.

"*Whatever.*" That was *Dean's* voice now echoing through the speakers. "*This has nothing to do with me. I'm not an errand boy or your personal tech guy."*

"Oh, Mr. Winters," Tanner said. *"You wouldn't want Tessa to have a black mark on her record before she's even reached her senior year, would you? I imagine something like jail time or a court date would harm her chances of following you and your brother to MIT someday.*

"Are you listening, now, Mr. Winters?"

"Yes," Dean said.

"Sir," Tanner said.

"What?"

"Yes, sir."

"Yes, sir."

"I expect a report on your progress on Monday. Bright and early."

"Fine."

"And, Mr. Winters?"

"Yes."

"Don't take too long to find this person," he said. *"For Tessa's sake."*

The chatter from the crowd grew, whispers and gasps. I locked eyes with Dean, my heart breaking for him.

Beeps and buzzes and "holy shits" rang from the crowd, nearly everyone gaping at their cell phones.

Dean motioned toward the screens.

The motionless vid-box had started to play.

I stared at it, my brow furrowed, as student after student—their faces blurred—recounted stories of their own instances of threats or borderline blackmail by Tanner.

There were so damn many.

Dean—how long had he been gathering this?

I looked to him, and it clicked.

This was *his* true portion of the challenge. He'd said it was a desktop swap, but no. This was so much more dangerous. More so than my blog. A hack he might not have pulled if not for Tanner's actions against me.

The audience fell stark silent as the video continued to roll. Tanner bolted from his seat, stomping to Griffin at the computer, who held his hands up in innocence. He couldn't kill the feed. No one but Dean could unless...

Tanner yanked every plug out of the floor sockets, and the screens and audio went dead. He stomped up to the podium, and I barely had a chance to move before he was hovering over me, the purple vein in his forehead throbbing. He held his hand over the mic like the room wasn't silent enough for them to catch every word.

"Fix this. Fix this now," he whisper-snapped. "You tell them you faked that audio. That video."

"I *didn't*," I said with all honesty. "You did this. *You.*"

He raked his hands through his hair, a growl at me as he turned to face the audience. "This girl is responsible for *Ask Me Anything*." He pointed at me. "She's the one behind it all."

His words fell on deaf ears. Everyone was glued to their cell phones—no doubt watching the rest of the video.

"The truth is out there," I said, watching as the board hovered over one person's phone. Watching. Learning.

"*Your* truth will be out there," he said. "You won't graduate. You won't get into another school. And after I call the admissions director at MIT and show them who you are, what you've done, they'll never let you in."

I gaped up at him, ready to spit fire.

"DC," Dean's voice filled the space behind me, and I spared him a glance, using his words to calm the acid eating my nerves.

Focusing back on Tanner, I narrowed my gaze.

"Prove it," I said before spinning on my heels, leaving him there to clean up the mess he'd taken years to create.

CHAPTER THIRTY-TWO

DEAN

I followed Amber off stage, taking care not to bump into the board members who walked toward Tanner. She stopped once she was out of the room and in the quiet of the hallway.

"Dean," she said, spinning to face me. "I don't know what to say."

"Don't," I said. "Just listen. Please." I was fully prepared to beg.

She popped her lips closed.

"I'm so fucking sorry," I blurted, tucking my laptop into my bag and slinging it over my shoulder. "I didn't mean a word I said. I swear. It wasn't about you. It was about Tessa."

She flinched. "You knew?"

"She'd just told me. That day. And I lost it. Temporary insanity. And I know that's not good enough. I know I don't deserve a second chance, but I swear to you I didn't sell you out to Tanner." I glared at the wall, hoping like hell Tanner felt the effects of the evidence I'd gathered. "He walked in at the wrong fucking time." I sighed, refocusing on her. "I don't care what he threatened," I continued. "I would've never given you up."

She was quiet, too quiet.

"Please, Pixie," I said. "You have to believe me."

Her eyes glittered, but she didn't let a tear fall. "You're not supposed to be here."

The air flew out of me, my shoulders dropping. I lowered

my gaze to the floor, unable to take her rejection. "I know," I said. I'd been expecting her to push me away, rightly so, after everything. "You don't want me here. Don't want anything to do with me. I get it. I do. But I needed you to know that I was sorry. That I wish like hell I could take back everything I said that day."

"No," she said, gripping my chin and forcing me to look at her. "I mean, you aren't supposed to be *here*. Today. The TOC."

Realization clicked, and hope swarmed my chest. "I meant it when I said I loved you," I said, reaching for her hand. She *let* me take it and the contact was so damn sweet. "You mean more to me than any tournament."

"But you've been working for that *all* year—"

"Doesn't matter. Nothing does, if you're not mine."

She sighed. "I made a real mess of things."

"We both did." I dared to pull her closer, my free hand falling on the small of her back. "And I should've been there for you."

"You were when it counted." She glanced toward the room behind us, the vibrations of too many voices talking at once coming through the walls.

I drew our interlocked hands up to my mouth, brushing my lips over the back of her fingers. "Can you forgive me?"

"Can you forgive *me*?" she asked.

"That had nothing to do with you," I said. "I shouldn't have put blame where it wasn't due." Tessa had been the one to knock the sense into me. "So," I said, inching closer to her face. "Can you forgive me?" I asked again, needing her answer more than anything else in the world in that moment.

"After what you did for me today?" She threw her arms around my neck, her lips crushing mine.

I captured her with my arms around her waist, lifting her

to my level, holding her against my chest as I tasted her lips.

"I'll kill him." I heard Amber's dad's voice behind us, and I immediately dropped Amber on her feet.

"Oh, stop," her mom said, as we turned to face them.

They'd just come out of the seminar room, a mass of people filing out behind her.

"You missed all the chaos!" Hannah said, bounding up to Amber. She glanced at me and before I could blink she'd punched me square in the chest.

"What the hell was that for?"

"You know why!"

"Right." I nodded. "Yeah."

Jake glared at me before looking to Amber, who waved him off. His features softened as he moved to Hannah's left.

"The board took Tanner into the office," Hannah continued. "And Ms. Howard. I bet he's getting fired."

Amber looked up to me, then back to Hannah. "I guess we'll know more tomorrow?"

Amber's mom patted her shoulder. "We'll see you at home?" she asked, her eyes darting to me. "But don't hang around here too long, okay? I don't want you here when they're done with him."

"Right," Amber said, and her parents headed down the hallway toward the exit.

"You want to ride with us?" Jake asked, never taking his eyes off me.

"No thanks," she said. "I'll be all right."

"You sure?" Hannah asked.

"Absolutely."

The certainty in her tone gave me all the hope I needed.

Hannah and Jake relented, falling into the flow of foot-traffic that passed us in waves.

Amber turned toward me, a shy, sweet smile shaping her

irresistible lips. "Where were we?"

I took her face in my hands, staring down at her as I breathed her in. "Missing you. Making it up to you. Whatever you need me to do," I said. "That's what we were up to."

She folded her hands over mine. "DC."

"DC." I pressed my forehead against hers, savoring the moment as the world faded away.

"DC sucks!" someone snapped right next us. "Marvel is way better!"

We glanced in the guy's direction, finding Brandon smacking his friend's chest, shaking his head and glancing at us while he mouthed *sorry*. They kept walking, Brandon's friend glaring at him in confusion.

We laughed until my sides hurt, the motions breaking through the sticky tension that coated everything. After we caught our breath, I tucked Amber under my arm and walked her out of the building.

When she was safely in my car, I grinned at her. "I missed you, Pixie."

"Missed you, too, NightLocker."

CHAPTER THIRTY-THREE

DEAN

"I'm sorry to say," I said, glancing at Amber from the passenger seat of her car. "But you'll likely never top the last time you surprised me."

She smirked from behind the wheel. "Want to bet?"

"How much?"

"How about a deadmau5 shirt?" she teased.

"How about a kiss?"

She rolled her eyes. "Like you need a bet to get one of those out of me."

Heat churned deep in my stomach, a craving I'd never satisfy. I could never get enough of my Pixie.

It had been two months to the day since the mandatory assembly where I turned the tables on Tanner—exposing him instead of him laying Amber out for the wolves. Her identity was still safe, and *Ask Me Anything* had been resurrected in a new corner of the dark web, Amber taking more precautions and leaning on her dad's profession more to answer the still-incoming questions.

Ms. Howard was now *Principal* Howard of Wilmont Academy and finished out the school year, helping to ensure our MIT acceptance letters came as expected.

Tanner had "resigned" for his own reasons, but everyone knew that was bull. Rumor had it he was petitioning the city council for a shot at mayor. I prayed my leaked viral video would be enough to save the city from that.

The days had passed by in a blissful haze where I spent every single moment trying to make it up to Amber, regardless of her saying I already had ten times over. She and Tessa had grown close, spending almost as much time together as we had. Hannah and Amber had folded Tessa into this protective trifecta of powerful girls, and it kind of terrified me—not that I'd ever tell them that.

My parents—after the initial shock—had rallied to support Tessa's decision to keep the baby. I'd held Tessa's hand as she'd come clean to them, and I'd never loved my parents more than in the moment they hugged Tessa. I didn't know why I'd been afraid they'd react rashly...like I had.

"I love you," I said, just because I could.

"Love you," she answered. "But still not telling you."

"Damn." She'd picked me up this morning and refused to tell me where we were going. "Do I at least get to spend the night with you in a fun hotel again?" I asked, the tease full and present in my voice. It didn't matter how many times I'd had her, I always wanted more. My pixie made each moment with her that much sweeter.

"As much as I would love being in a room with you without worrying about one of our parents hearing us," she said, "and I would really, really love that... No."

"Damn again." I groaned.

"But," she said. "I wouldn't say no if you wanted to surprise me with that." She cleared her throat. "When you get back."

"When *I* get back?"

She pulled into a packed parking lot in front of a massive glass building. I hadn't caught the sign, and I tilted my head at her when she parked. An excited giggle left her lips as she hopped out of the car and popped the trunk. I hurried to follow her.

"Pixie," I chided. "What is my duffel doing in there?" I pointed to the fully stuffed bag in her trunk. "And my gear?" I moved my finger to the laptop bag sitting next to it.

"Sean helped me," she said. "I figured he'd be a better source to pack for you than Tessa."

My eyes widened.

"Don't worry," Amber said. "I checked the bags earlier. It's all your stuff."

I sighed, thankful she'd made sure he hadn't packed me a bag full of Tessa's extra-small shirts. "Okay," I said, still not understanding. "Is this like a prison sentence or something? It looks like there are enough clothes in there for a month."

"Six weeks, actually," she corrected me.

"What?" I snapped.

She handed me an envelope before I could press further. "Open it."

I obeyed, pulling out a badge with my name and picture on it. The title underneath...

"Holy shit," I blurted, snapping my eyes to her.

Her smile stretched wide.

"No," I said, and her grin faded. "I can't take this from you. This is yours." I shoved the badge at her.

"Uh, pretty sure that's your picture." She refused to take the badge. "I transferred my ticket," she said. "It was an easy sell. I think the boot camp managers were more excited to have you than me."

"Not possible," I said. "I can't take this, Amber."

"You can. And you will," she said, stepping so close to me her chest brushed mine. "You gave up the TOC for me. I know how much that meant to you. This boot camp is my way of paying you back."

"But—"

"No buts," she cut me off. "You deserve this, Dean. I'm

not as gung-ho as you about getting a job the second we're at MIT. This will streamline your process. There will be other boot camps for me later."

"How did I get so lucky?" I asked, pocketing the badge and envelope.

She wrapped her arms around my neck. "You're a good hacker."

I gaped at her. "And if I wasn't?"

She shrugged. "Wouldn't even be on my radar," she teased.

"Oh," I said. "You will pay for that remark."

"Bring it." She nipped at my bottom lip, eliciting a growl from me. "I love a challenge."

"Nope," I said, swiping my tongue over her lip. "No more challenges for us."

"Is that so?"

"Mm-hmm," I mumbled, leaning closer to her mouth.

"What if I were to say…" She rolled her eyes up, plotting. "That if you bring home a medal we can…" She pushed up on her tiptoes and whispered the most exciting, terrifying, and wonderful thing in my ear. It sent warm shivers along my skin, firing up that deep craving in my blood.

I gasped, popping back to catch the wild gaze in her eyes.

"You better hurry," she said, closing my mouth with the tip of her finger and planting me with a kiss. "You don't want to be late on your first day."

I grabbed my bags, shaking my head as I backed away a few spaces, certain if I touched her again after that comment, I would spontaneously combust. "DC," I said, continuing to back up toward the building.

She opened her car door, that smooth, confident grin shaping the mouth I couldn't get out of my head. "DC," she said, one leg in the car. "Oh, NightLocker?" she asked before I could turn around.

"Yeah?" I asked, pausing.

"*Everyone* gets a medal." She winked at me before sinking into the car and driving away.

My heart skipped a beat and it took me a few seconds to remember I had a place to be. I walked toward the building, a wide smile on my face.

Six weeks was a long time to be away from her.

But she was worth every second.

My fierce hacker of a girl.

The one I thought I'd never be able to catch.

My pixie.

EPILOGUE

AMBER

One year later

NightLocker: What are you up to?

I straightened in my seat, blinking out of the haze I'd been in seconds ago while I waited on the professor to get his PowerPoint together. A full-body flush and about a thousand tingles tickled my skin at the sight of Dean's chat box on my screen.

PixieBurn: I'm in class
NightLocker: what class?
PixieBurn: Psychology
NightLocker: Oh
NightLocker: So that's why you snuck out of bed this morning

The flush deepened, my mind instantly jumping backward to last night. And the night before.

And the one before that.

I'd spent them all in Dean's arms.

Each night better than the next.

One year at MIT behind us—a new semester starting today—and he still had the power to melt me with a simple sentence.

I glanced away from the screen, checking to make sure the professor was still in hold-mode until his presentation came up. Once I was sure, I reached toward the keys.

PixieBurn: I didn't sneak
NightLocker: I woke up to an empty pillow and cold sheets
PixieBurn: Awh, poor baby
NightLocker: Exactly
NightLocker: I didn't think you had a class this early
PixieBurn: I didn't either. It was a last minute addition. I'm lucky they let me in.
NightLocker: Psychology
PixieBurn: Yes
PixieBurn: I'm...
PixieBurn: I've decided to minor in it
NightLocker: Makes sense
PixieBurn: It does?
NightLocker: Yes. You're good at helping people
NightLocker: Now you want to be great at it
NightLocker: Did your dad do a backflip when you told him?
PixieBurn: I haven't yet
NightLocker: Why?
PixieBurn: I decided this morning. When they let me into this class.

I bit down on my lip to stop my smile from spreading too wide.

Of course he understood—even when I hadn't had the time to explain it to him. The class, my decision, it had all happened this morning when they'd allowed my late admission.

> NightLocker: A $10 says he cries
> PixieBurn: lol
> PixieBurn: Sometimes it's scary how much you get me. Get my family.
> NightLocker: Too much?
> PixieBurn: Never
> NightLocker: Good
> NightLocker: Now get out of that class and come back to bed

Tempting. So very tempting.

> PixieBurn: Tempting
> PixieBurn: But I've got to focus. This isn't easy like all my other classes
> NightLocker: Then what are you doing talking to me? lol
> PixieBurn: The professor is struggling with his powerpoint
> NightLocker: You could help him
> PixieBurn: This super hot guy is distracting me
> NightLocker: ...
> NightLocker: Do I need to enroll in psychology?
> PixieBurn: lol why?
> NightLocker: Don't want the hot guy stealing you
> PixieBurn: I was talking about you
> NightLocker: Of course you were
> PixieBurn: Besides
> PixieBurn: No one could steal me from you

Literally no one. Loki himself could walk into this class…
Mmm. Loki.

No. I would say no to his advances because that's how much I loved Dean. How close we'd grown over the last year.

My best friend.

My boyfriend.

Love of my life.

But I could *appreciate* Loki. From a distance.

NightLocker: Good
NightLocker: I really didn't want to add another class
NightLocker: But I would
NightLocker: for you lol
PixieBurn: I'm so lucky
PixieBurn: Powerpoint is back up

I focused on the professor as he started his opening lecture. It was so hard to split my attention—I really wanted to do well in this class. Wanted to go on to minor in it and have the knowledge necessary to volunteer at an advice hotline or perhaps, maybe, qualify for a guidance counselor position. It would also be nice to stop asking my dad for advice on the questions that continued to roll in for the blog.

After *Ask Me Anything* I found a calling I never knew existed. I wanted to explore it, see how long I could keep the blog successful, helpful, streamline it and maybe someday bring in other people with different experiences and relationships and viewpoints. But first, school. Furthering my knowledge, that was most important.

NightLocker: Fine
NightLocker: Go learn stuff

PixieBurn: I have a two hour break after
NightLocker: I'll cook you lunch
PixieBurn: :)
NightLocker: DC, Pixie
PixieBurn: Love you, too

I clicked off the chat box, the same smile shaping my face.

Seven pages worth of notes later, I left the class, anticipating the next one. The feeling settled deep in my heart—the path I'd chosen was right. I would major in Computer Science and minor in Psychology. Then, perhaps by combining both, I could find a balance and really launch the blog—take it further than the surrounding area. Maybe make it a virtual refuge for young girls and boys across the country.

A real place.

Not on the dark web, but in the light.

Until then, there were only three things I wanted to focus on.

School, hacking, and...

"Dean," I said as I walked through the door to our incredibly small and overpriced apartment. "It smells amazing in here."

"Spaghetti," he said, stirring a pot on the stove.

"Your mom's recipe?" I set my bags down on the chair by our front door.

"Yup."

"Score," I said, walking into the kitchen to wrap my arms around him from behind.

He spun to face me, his hands sliding over my hips and hefting me to his level. I wrapped my legs around him, and he kissed me so long and deep my breath caught. Pulling back, he grinned at me. "Can I ask you something?"

I wetted my lips, relishing his taste lingering on my skin.

"You can always," I said, brushing a light kiss over his mouth. "Ask me anything."

ACKNOWLEDGMENTS

My first thank you always goes to you, the reader. These characters wouldn't be alive and kicking without you picking up this book and I'm beyond grateful for each and every one of you!

Dare, my partner in crime, the love of my life…thank you for your constant support as I poured my soul into this book. Through countless hours of research and formatting and creating images, you are seriously *the* man.

N0decaf, I don't have enough ways to say thank you for all your guidance on this book. All the emails, calls, and chats. All the scenarios and "what-ifs" that you met with an open mind and easy grace. Thank you. I couldn't have finished this book without you.

Thanks must be given to my family for supporting this dream of mine, even when I started dreaming about it in the second grade.

Stacy, my brilliant editor, I can't thank you enough! This book was a dream to write and you're so much fun to work with. I simply can't wait to see what we come up with next!

To Liz, Jillian, Heather, and everyone else at my Entangled home, thank you for all the work behind the scenes! I'm honored to be part of this awesome family.

Karen, you're a constant source of wisdom and advice and happiness. I'm honored to call you friend and I'm thankful for all of your notes that continuously shape me to be a better writer.

Molly, my soul-sister, thank you for being the first one

to read this. Double thanks for finding that massive typo (that I repeated eight times) before I sent it to my editor. LOL. You will always be the coolest half of #MollySquared.

Esther. I love you. You're my hero. My inspiration. The strongest woman I know. Every badass girl I write has a whole lot of you in her.

Cindi and Rebecca, thanks for plot chats and vent sessions and staying up until two a.m. at signings! I'm grateful I have the pair of you in my corner!

Amber, thanks for the support that never ends. The fire you have for this community never ceases to amaze me and I appreciate all the awesome things you do!

To the amazing bloggers who constantly work on the behalf of authors and readers alike, you are EVERYTHING. I'm grateful and honored and appreciative of every single one of you who sacrifice time in the name of love for books! I see you and the hard work you do and it means the world to me!

Mayhem Members! Thanks for making our group so positive and fun and for being understanding when life has me hiding in the writing cave for months at a time!

And finally, again, to you…most awesome reader. Thank you for choosing this book. You make all things possible.

New York Times bestselling author Rachel Harris delivers a passionate, emotional romance perfect for fans of Sarah Dessen or Huntley Fitzpatrick

eyes on me

by Rachel Harris

Look up the word "nerd" and you'll find Lily Bailey's picture. She's got one goal: first stop valedictorian, next stop Harvard. Until a stint in the hospital from too much stress lands her in the last place a klutz like her ever expected to be: salsa dance lessons.

Look up the word "popular" and you'll find Stone Torres's picture. His life seems perfect—star of the football team, small-town hero, lots of friends. But his family is struggling to make ends meet, so if pitching in at his mom's dance studio helps, he'll do it.

When Lily's dad offers Stone extra cash to volunteer as Lily's permanent dance partner, he can't refuse. But with each dip and turn, each moment her hand is in his, his side job starts to feel all too real. Lily shows Stone he's more than his impressive football stats, and he introduces her to a world outside of studying. But with the lines blurred, can their relationship survive the secret he's been hiding?

Don't miss the next book in the fast-paced, sexy
hockey series from *New York Times* bestselling
author Julie Cross

ON THIN ICE

by Julie Cross

Brooke Parker never expected to find herself in the tiny town of
Juniper Falls, Minnesota. Of course, she also never expected to
lose her dad. Or for her mom to lose herself. Brooke feels like
she's losing it…until she finds Juniper Falls hockey. Juniper Falls
girls' hockey, that is.

Jake Hammond, current prince of Juniper Falls, captain of
the hockey team, and player with the best chance of scoring it
big, is on top of the world. Until one hazing ritual gone wrong
lands him injured, sitting on the sidelines, and—shocking even
to him—finding himself enjoying his "punishment" as assistant
coach for the girls' team.

As Jake and Brooke grow closer, he finds the quiet new girl
is hiding a persona full of life, ideas, and experiences bigger and
broader than anything he's ever known. But to Jake, hockey's
never just been a game. It's his whole life. And leveraging the
game for a shot at their future might be more than he can give.

"I am the daughter of the first female POTUS, and today is about to become the longest day of my life..."

T-MINUS

by Shannon Greenland

24 hours—that's how much time I have to save my mother before terrorists assassinate her. But now my father and brother are missing, too. This goes deeper than anyone thinks. Only someone on the inside would know how to pull this off—how to make the entire First Family disappear.

I can't trust anyone, so it's up to me to uncover the conspiracy and stop these madmen. Because little do they know, they picked the wrong person to terrorize.

My name is Sophie Washington, and I will not be a victim. No one, I repeat no one, is taking me or my family down. But the clock is ticking...

entangled teen

an imprint of Entangled Publishing LLC